THE LICHING HOUR

BILL OF THE DEAD SAGA

THE TOME OF BILL - 12

RICK GUALTIERI

COPYRIGHT © 2022 RICK GUALTIERI

Cover by Damonza at damonza.com

Published by Freewill Press

Visit the author at:
www.rickgualtieri.com

Listen to Rick on the Authors & Dragons Podcast:
www.authorsanddragons.com

ACKNOWLEDGEMENTS

Thank you to my awesome crew of beta readers – Brannon, Tracy, Randal, Chris, Tom, Clifton, David, and Faith – for holding my feet to the fire on this one.

An extra special shoutout to Anthony. There's little doubt in my mind, good sir, that your odds of surviving in Bill's world are almost certainly higher than his are.

PART I

1

THOSE WHO DIED AREN'T JUSTIFIED

Dying kinda sucks. Take it from me, I've been there – three times as a matter of fact.

Mind you, the first two were worse, mostly because in both cases I'd woken to crowds looking to kick my ass. Vampire or not, that wasn't the sort of drama I needed in my life.

This time was a bit better, though. Not only had I been reasonably sure that I'd be coming back, but I'd woken up in the same spot where I'd purposely chosen to *die*.

Okay, perhaps that was being a bit melodramatic. This wasn't some death wish on my part. I'd just wanted an *upgrade*. Dying was simply part of the process.

You see, my name's Bill Ryder and I'm what some call a Freewill, a rare type of vamp both resistant to mind-control and able to temporarily boost my power by ingesting the blood of other undead.

That was all well and good, but as of late it just wasn't enough.

My friend Ed was the first of a new breed of vampires, an evolution brought about by a series of events best described as convoluted as fuck. Unlike *normal* vampirism which, if left unchecked, tended to spread faster than a cluster of horny rabbits, he was the only one capable of making these *neo-*

3

vamps. All the rest were mules, not exactly a bad thing for those of us not into spreading this shit like the plague.

Anyway, my main reason for wanting this change was simple: Ed could walk in the sunlight without bursting aflame while I, funky powers or not, crisped up like a piece of napalm-encrusted toast.

Speaking of my friend and former roommate, I had no idea where he'd wandered off to in the hours since biting me, but that could wait. For now, I sat in bed and took stock of myself, biding my time until sunrise.

There was no doubt about it. I felt different, but it was hard to quantify – more of a feeling that something had changed. Although, in all fairness, that could've simply been the trauma of dying and waking up ravenous.

Fortunately, we'd thought ahead as I found two pints of pig blood waiting on the nightstand. Good for me, but even better for the couple next door who, judging by the sounds they were making, were preoccupied with a vigorous morning blowjob.

The walls themselves were already pretty thin, but not so much that I wasn't able to give my supercharged senses a test run to make sure everything was working like it should. Sure enough, I was able to hear every lick and suck as if they were trying their damnedest to get to the center of the world's best Tootsie Pop.

Ah, the lucky fools. They had no way of knowing my breakfast in bed was the only thing keeping me from interrupting their sloppy bj with some sloppy murder instead. I'm sure neither of them would've appreciated getting offed before they could get off.

As the blood settled in my stomach, I sniffed the air – continuing to run down my personal vampire checklist. That brought with it immediate regret as the *fragrant* scents of Jersey City assaulted my nostrils. Check!

I next willed my fingernails to extend, watching them grow into two inch talons. Another check.

So far so good.

Glancing toward the window, I noticed the sky was

rapidly lightening. Soon enough it would be time for the real litmus test, but for now I got up and walked to the mirror hanging on the wall.

All right, let's see how I look in yellow.

I focused on my eyes as I stared at my reflection – thankful that some Hollywood tropes were bullshit. Just yesterday I would've found soulless pits of darkness staring back at me. Now, I watched as the irises, pupils, and whites of my eyes became a golden yellow instead.

Yes!

"You seeing this, Wanderer?" I asked aloud.

There came no answer, other than the guy next door imploring his partner to, "put them both in your mouth."

Hope her teeth aren't as sharp as mine, bro.

I next turned my focus inward, toward the spirit that resided in my head – the other-dimensional entity known as the Wanderer. He was the reason for my state of undeath, vampires being a result of two souls crammed into one body, one human and the other ... not so much.

During my first year or two as a vamp, back before magic was banished from the world, the thing sharing my body had been a hell-beast I'd called Dr. Death – a rampaging asshole who'd have liked nothing better than to paint the streets of New York red with blood.

When magic abruptly returned five years later, I found myself *revamped* if you will. So naturally I'd assumed he'd taken up residence in my noggin again.

In the moments leading up to my most recent death, however, I'd finally learned the truth. The spirit inside me this go-around was actually the same entity that had once been bonded to my late friend James.

He'd been a seven-hundred year old vamp, smart as fuck and surprisingly cool for his age. Knowing he was a part of me now had given me comfort as I'd slipped away.

Now to hope he was still there. Going into this upgrade I'd known what changes to expect on the outside, but nobody seemed quite sure what happened on the inside.

"You in there, buddy?" I asked, trying my best to focus despite the increasingly fervent fuck-fest going on next door.

It was the perfect time to test yet another aspect of the change from vampire to neo-vamp.

"Knock it the fuck off," I hissed, putting some of my will into it.

The words came out as nothing more than a harsh whisper – no psychic echo, bizarre reverberation, or anything else freaky-deaky.

That was perhaps the biggest tradeoff with the upgrade. One gained resistance to daylight but lost the power of compulsion – the ability to control younger vamps as well as humans.

Oh well, it was an evil as fuck power anyway, used in the past as a means of control. Heck, I'd even abused it myself on occasion, once cursing a dude with a case of limp dick simply for dating a girl I'd liked – not exactly my finest moment.

Speaking of girls I liked, my thoughts turned toward the real reason for wanting to undergo this change – Christy.

Just days ago, I'd survived an all-out war in upstate New York, pitting my friends and I against a small army of vampires, mages, and a jet-sized monstrosity that could best be described as Rodan covered in black jizz.

Most of us had made it out, but not everyone had been so lucky.

First there'd been my old dungeon master Dave – shredded to bloody chum as I watched. Sadly, the asshole had kinda deserved it – selling us out to Gan, a 300 year old vampire princess with a hardon for two things: world domination and me.

His death had sucked, but it was nothing compared to what had happened next.

Sally, my partner in crime for all things vamp-related, had been possessed by a godlike entity known as the Great Beast, only to end up badly wounded in the ensuing battle, perhaps fatally so. I had no way of knowing her fate, though, as she'd been scooped up by the aforementioned winged monstrosity shortly before it flew off, headed for parts unknown.

Horrific as that was, the worst had been what happened to Christy – a powerful witch who I'd only recently come to realize I was deeply in love with.

In order to save us all, she'd tapped into a mystical portal that lay buried beneath the Earth – one of the thirteen Sources of magic itself. Though the result had been explosively badass, it hadn't come without a price. The power had demanded a sacrifice in return, dragging her into its strange waters and leaving me helpless to stop it.

I'd been crushed, thinking that she'd surely died, but then a sliver of hope had been dangled before us in the form of her daughter Tina – five-years old, yet possessing unprecedented magical potential.

Tina had received a vision of her mother trapped and calling out for help. Though we couldn't be certain it wasn't just a dream, her incredible power suggested otherwise – telling us there was a chance Christy was alive out there somewhere and waiting for us to rescue her.

That was all we'd needed to start working on a plan – with heavy emphasis on the *starting* part.

I couldn't do it alone, though. I'd been way off my game since returning from Gan's, and only being able to operate at night was a limiting factor – so I'd pestered Ed until he finally agreed to bite me.

I guess deep down a part of me was hoping that being rebooted, so to speak, would help kill those two birds with one stone.

Guess I'll find out soon enough. For now, it was probably best to focus on the mystery of where Ed had meandered off to.

Fucker better not have gotten his stupid ass kidnapped again.

That seemed to be his forte, forever acting as our small circle's damsel in distress. Go figure, he had quite the knack for it.

Before jumping to conclusions, though, I perked up my

ears, trying to listen past the moans and grunts going on next door, until I finally picked up the faint sound of his voice.

Aha. It was coming from the lot of the motel we'd holed up in – ensuring I was sequestered far away from anyone in case the transformation went badly, or at least anyone I gave a shit about.

Noticing the light hitting the window was growing brighter by the minute, I figured this was as good a time as any for the final test – stepping outside and rejoining the land of those who could enjoy a day at the beach.

Heck, maybe we could even stop and grab some breakfast on the way back, taking in the sunrise over some blood-infused coffee and doughnuts.

First things first, though.

I stepped to the wall and banged on it with my fist. "Tell her to call you papi. I hear she likes that."

There came an abrupt end to the grunting, along with a confused, "What the fuck was that?" as I turned with a grin and opened the front door.

Sure enough, Ed was out in the parking lot, his ear pressed to his phone as he paced back and forth.

"I can't even begin to tell you how rough it was," he said into the receiver. "Thinking about you was the only way I managed to get through it all."

The tearful cadence from the other end told me he'd finally, after more than a fucking week, called his fiancée Kara to tell her he was a free man.

"Was that before or after your daily swim in Gan's Olympic sized pool?" I remarked.

Ed looked up, his eyes narrowing before he quickly covered the receiver. "Do you mind?" Then he uncovered it to add, "No, I wasn't talking to you, hun. Bill's here. Yes, I'll be sure to thank him for *rescuing* me."

He was no doubt adding a healthy dollop of bullshit to whatever he was telling her. His official excuse for not calling had been wanting to take some of the ever growing burden off our plate before contacting her, but I had a feeling it was more him freaking out over how she'd react to learning he was a vampire *again.*

Pussy.

Nevertheless, being party to his lies meant needing to cover my own ass as well. I was already on thin ice with Kara for the three weeks I'd spent avoiding her after Ed's initial abduction. We'd need to sync our stories on the way back, then make sure our other friend Tom was brought up to speed, mostly on account of Kara being his sister and him being a dumbass.

Oh, what a tangled web of intrigue we wove.

I grinned as Ed quickly switched gears to tell her something about his stepfather. That was fine. He could catch me up later. For now, it was time to enjoy some sweet sunlight.

And away we go...

As I stepped out from beneath the shade provided by the second floor walkway, I heard a voice stirring from inside my subconscious.

W-wait. Not yet. We don't know what it...

About time you woke up, I replied, glad for perhaps the first time in my life to have another voice inside my head. *Now chill. I've got this.*

I walked out into the morning sunlight, feeling it touch my skin for the first time in two months – since falling victim to the vampire DNA infused hand cream Dave had been hawking.

Oh yeah! I'd almost forgotten how warm it was.

Within an instant it staved off the coolness of the early fall we were experiencing after a way too hot summer.

Speaking of hot ... *damn*! Had the forecast called for an unexpected heat wave or something?

"Um, Bill?" Ed called out, raising an eyebrow my way. "You might want to..."

You need to get back inside, now!

Sadly, the Wanderer's warning came a moment too late as my exposed skin burst aflame in the parking lot.

SHIT! I let out a scream, staggering forward as fire engulfed my body.

"I gotta call you back," Ed cried. "Yeah, love you too."

So glad he took the time to add that closer as I tried to back up, hoping to reach the shade before I could fry like a fucking shrimp on a hot grill.

Thankfully, Ed's next course of action was a bit more decisive – rushing my way just as my eyeballs began to boil over.

Son of a...

In the next instant, he plowed into my burning midsection – the pain combined with the force of the blow more than enough to send me spiraling downward into merciful unconsciousness.

2

PUSSY WHIPPED TOPPING

The first sensation I felt upon regaining at least partial awareness was the incessant drip of something wet on my face.

Those fucking werewolves had better not be pissing on me again.

The second sensation was the incredible pain of my nerve endings firing a twenty-one gun salute directly into my brain.

Goddamn it!

I opened my eyes to fortunately find no hick werewolves hosing me down with their inbred Johnsons. Instead, far as I could tell, I was in the tub of the motel bathroom. The door was closed and the shower was raining down upon me – the cold water unpleasant against my skin but still far better than being on fire.

Why?!

"Everything's fine," Ed said from out in the main room. "My friend ... just got some bad news about ... his grandma."

"Whatever," another voice replied. "Just keep it down. People are trying to sleep."

Apparently not the couple next door, I noted as the incessant banging was once again in session. Guess my screams had inspired them for round two.

"No worries, man," Ed replied. "Thanks for checking on

us." There came the sound of the door shutting and the lock being reengaged. A few moments later he popped his head in to check on me. "You okay?"

I lifted my arms, the charred skin bubbling as it healed. "Do I fucking look okay?"

"Rhetorical question." He shrugged. "So, what the hell happened?"

I narrowed my eyes, reaching for my glasses which he'd helpfully left on the lip of the tub. "Depends on which part you mean. Are we talking about the fuck buddies next door, your web of lies, or the fact that I just turned into a fucking tater tot?"

Almost as if in response there came a throaty moan of, "Oh, Reg," from the adjoining room.

I turned that way. "Oh just hurry up and come already, so the rest of us can get on with our fucking lives!"

Ed let out a sigh. "Feel better now?"

"Don't make me kick your ass." I looked down at myself, seeing a mess of ruined clothing over rapidly healing skin. "What the fuck happened?"

"Pretty sure I just asked that."

I warned you to take it slow, the Wanderer said, his voice barely a whisper.

"Don't start," I growled. Then, noticing Ed's look, I explained, "The voice inside my head."

"Dr. Death?"

"No. Turned out I was wrong about that. It's actually James."

"James? You mean the guy who used to run Boston?"

"Yes and no. Somehow I ended up with the thing that was a part of him."

I must say, I resent being called a thing.

I ignored him. "Anyway, he kinda did a shitty job of letting me know."

You're the one who kept refusing to listen to reason. Now, if you'll kindly stop embellishing the truth, I need to rest. This whole process ... it's taken a bit out of me.

"Yeah, yeah. Go take a nap, or whatever." I waved Ed off

before he could say anything, pointing to my noggin again. "I'm the one who was lit up like a tiki torch, but he's complaining about being tired. Anyway, the fuck, dude? You were supposed to give me the full upgrade, not some bullshit free trial version."

I grabbed a towel and wiped my face, leaving behind copious amounts of dead skin. Oh well, that was housekeeping's problem now.

"So it didn't work?" he asked, sounding as confused as I felt.

"I wouldn't exactly say that." I blinked, causing my eyes to go all yellow.

"Okay, then what about...?"

"Everything else checks out," I snapped. "I did a few test runs before I went looking for you. Yellow eyes, no compulsion, all that shit. Everything except the part that counts!" I stood up and stormed out of the bathroom. "Like, what's going on? Does it take a while to become fire retardant or something?"

He shook his head. "Not that I've noticed. Far as I'm aware it's worked like clockwork every single time."

"So why didn't it work for me?"

Ed sat down on the edge of the bed. "I have no idea, man. Could be all that metal Gan fused to my face, or could be because you're..."

"Don't say it."

"A Freewill," he finished anyway. "Let's not pretend that hasn't complicated shit before."

I planted my ass against the cheap desk sitting in the corner, just as there came a relieved grunt next door of, "That's right, baby, take every last drop."

Dude had obviously spent way too much time watching Pornhub. "Okay, fine, let's assume for a second that being a Freewill could be the reason," I said, dragging us back on track. "If that's the case than this really fucking sucks, because so far as I can tell I gained absolutely nothing in the process."

Talk about ironic. In the distant past, Freewills had been

lauded as heroes, conquerors, monsters to be feared even by the things that went bump in the night. How *hilarious* would it be if the process of becoming a neo-vamp reversed all that – making Freewills into nothing more than slightly shittier vampires?

That would be just my luck.

"I don't know," Ed said after a few moments. "Maybe we need to test it out on someone else, see if this happens to them too."

I let out a mirthless laugh. "My misery does love company."

"As I'm well aware." He paused as if unsure whether to continue. "Unfortunately, that'll have to wait."

"For what?"

"For me to get back."

I raised an eyebrow. "From where?"

"You caught the ass end of my conversation, right?"

I nodded. "You mean all that bullshit you were shoveling? Yeah. By the way, I appreciate the credit for your rescue."

He made a non-committal gesture. "Whatever works. The problem is, she kinda thinks you guys broke me out just a few hours ago."

"More bullshit, but I guess that's to be expected."

Ed nodded. "Anyway, I'll probably need to come clean eventually, but first I really need to see where we stand. Don't get me wrong, she sounded happy enough on the phone, but..."

I walked over and clapped him on the shoulder, ignoring the impulse to smack him upside the head. "You'll be fine. Trust me, she's just glad to have you back."

"For now, but after that wears off I'm still ... well, *this*." He extended his fangs.

"I'm sure she loves you for who you are, despite your myriad shortcomings."

He flipped me the finger. "Hopefully. But I still need to make sure."

"Wait. She's not flying out here is she?"

"With us looking over our shoulders every five minutes?

No fucking way." He shook his head. "Hell, I'm still processing what went down at Gan's, but I'm pretty sure it wasn't a check in our win column."

He wasn't wrong on that end. "So what's the plan, then?"

Ed stood up and stretched. "I'm flying back to California."

"What? You do realize a pack of werewolves is still hunting your ass, right? And forgive me if I'm wrong, but weren't they bragging about being able to track you anywhere?"

"Trust me, I remember. I talked to Pop about it, though. He's got some stuff from his hunting days that supposedly helps eliminate scent. He thinks that should keep them off my tail."

I nodded. "I suppose that could work. Still..."

He held up a hand. "Don't worry. I'll only be gone long enough for us to figure things out. After that, I'm coming back."

"I appreciate that, man, but you really don't..."

"Just shut the fuck up, okay? I'm your friend, Christy's too. No fucking way am I abandoning you guys, not when you need all the help you can get. I just ... need a few days to settle shit."

I didn't trust myself to answer him, at least not without my voice cracking, so I simply nodded again. Besides, it's not like we didn't have the time. Things were moving forward on the rescue plan, but it was barely a snail's pace so far.

Fortunately, Ed wasn't one to let the mood get too heavy. "Just use Tom as a human shield until I get back."

"And have him complain that I'm staring at his ass?"

"Hey, at least it's a lot more pleasant to look at these days."

I raised an eyebrow. "I suppose."

"Anyway," he continued, quickly steering away from that bit of weirdness, "Pop's driving in to pick me up. He's gonna hose us both down with that descenting shit and then we're gonna fly out together."

"Wait. You're leaving *now*?"

"I've kinda put this off long enough, don't you think?"

"Yeah, but..."

"We both know how this works, Bill. If I put it off, something's going to come up to make me put it off even longer. So it's either now or..."

"I have to listen to you make even more excuses for being a spineless wimp. Yeah, I get it. It's just kind of abrupt."

"Well, that's what you get for insisting I call her while you were lying there dead for half the night."

"I suppose."

Ed deserved his happiness, and I wasn't so selfish as to try and talk him out of it. Even so, I couldn't help but be worried at our already dwindling group becoming yet another man short.

With all of us already stretched thin, I had to hope the next few days passed without incident – something that was beginning to feel more like wishful thinking as of late.

3

I HEAR YOU KNOCKING

I wasn't happy to part ways with Ed, having only recently gotten him back again, but at least this time it was for a positive reason – hopefully. Could be hard to tell with Tom's sister sometimes, especially since she'd adopted a decisively anti-vampire stance in the last five years, despite having been one for a time.

So, I could kind of understand his reluctance in reaching out to her. Regardless, the ball was now in his court. I hoped they were able to work things out, but ultimately that wasn't my problem. I had bigger fish waiting to be fried.

I just needed to make sure I wasn't one of them.

After waiting around to make sure Ed got picked up safely, it was time for me to vacate the premises as well. I hadn't packed for the unexpected complication of still being vulnerable to sunlight, but the motel had bed sheets ripe for stealing and I trusted my undead constitution to ward off any STDs, bedbugs, or scabies.

At least I didn't have to take mass transit back home. I'd finally managed to coerce a loaner out of my insurance company after my Camry had sustained enough werewolf-related damage to ensure it was going to be in the shop for a while. I obviously didn't tell them that, mind you, blaming a home invasion gone badly. Nevertheless, I had a feeling I shouldn't be surprised if my premiums suddenly went up substantially.

For now, I was stuck with a subcompact shitbox – small enough that a light breeze could've tipped it over. Still, it was a set of wheels.

The windows weren't tinted, which double sucked for me, but the sun was now high enough in the sky to chance the drive back without much risk of combusting on the Staten Island Expressway.

Soon enough I was back in Brooklyn, headed for Christy's apartment.

It didn't feel right squatting there. Her place was haunted by too many memories – all of them happy to remind me of my failure to protect her. However, it was the last safe haven we had left.

The werewolves, after Ed for reasons still unknown to us, knew where my building was. Hell, they'd even managed to plant a spy in the basement apartment – a guy named Mike Walden. I couldn't evict the fucker either. Werewolf informant or not, New York law was pretty strict when it came to signed leases.

Regardless, it's not like that was an option anyway as my apartment was currently serving as the temporary headquarters for the vampires of Village Coven, on account of their former lair – Sally's home – having been blown to hell by a gaggle of British witches.

Like I said, it had been a bit of a week.

With our backs to the wall and real estate not exactly cheap these days, Christy's place had become our temporary safe haven. Fortunately, thanks to the shitload of wards she'd installed all over the building, it was pretty damned safe.

I let myself in with the spare key then headed up, discarding the motel blanket in the vestibule because I was out of fucks to give by that point.

Thankfully, Christy wasn't the only witch we knew, otherwise we'd have been shit out of luck if any of her wards had decided to get squirrelly with us. Her coven sister Kelly had fortunately stepped in to help out – both in planning our rescue effort, as well as to rejigger the wards just enough to keep the rest of us from being vaporized.

Kelly wasn't as strong as Christy, but she was smart as can be. That, and she also had help in the form of Liz, a witch who'd betrayed the fuck out of us not too long ago but was now trying to make amends.

We were all still a little leery of that, but beggars couldn't be choosers.

I put the key in the lock then placed my hand against the door, feeling a tingle in my palm as the magic worked to identify me as...

UGH!

A wave of vertigo passed through me, almost driving me to my knees. One second I was fine, the next my head was swimming – as if I was coming down off a weekend long bender which, sadly, wasn't the case.

I pulled my hand away and ... that was it. It was gone. Suddenly I felt fine again.

Before I could wonder if the wards were going wonky, the doorknob glowed for the briefest of moments, letting me know it was safe to enter.

"The fuck was that about?"

It was a rhetorical question but the Wanderer was quick to answer, *I don't know, but that was quite the odd sensation.*

"Ya think?"

It's more than that, my friend. Can't you smell it?

I took a sniff, not noticing much. "What? Did they shampoo the carpet while I was out?"

The magic, he replied with a sigh. *The scent's changed. It feels much more ... distinct than it was.*

"If you say so."

The Wanderer had a shitload more experience than me in these things. Personally, I had no idea what magic was supposed to smell like. Heck, I could just barely tell humans apart from other vamps. Maybe one of these days he could give me a lesson.

That would have to wait for later, though.

For now, I wanted to get inside, change my clothes, and

maybe suck down another pint of blood to make up for my unexpected trip to Burning Man.

Everything else could wait.

It was quiet inside. No big surprise. Kelly was watching Tina for a few days, remaining coy as to exactly where but assuring Tom and me that it was safe. That sort of secrecy would've been a big red flag for anyone else, but Kelly and her husband Vincent were two of the good ones, having more than proven themselves time and again. There was absolutely no doubt in my mind that they both adored Tina – treating her as if she was their own.

As for the current silence, that meant Tom was likely out with Glen, our other roommate. They'd taken to patrolling the streets together, more so in the last few days. In Tom's case, I had a feeling it was his way of coping with things – as we were mostly stuck waiting while Kelly and Liz observed Tina, trying to get a read on whether she was truly in contact with Christy, and if so what our next steps would be.

As for Glen, the freaky little eyeball blob who'd taken a shine to us, well, I think he just liked wandering the city.

I wasn't too worried for them either way. Tom could mostly take care of himself these days, not that there'd apparently been much cause. From what he'd told me, they'd run into a couple of vamps at most this past week, all of whom had run for the hills the second he'd activated his faith aura – lighting up like a vampire-killing flamethrower.

With them out and Ed flying to the west coast, that left me alone with my thoughts – free from distractions so I could torture myself with all the various *what if* scenarios of things I could've done differently.

Problem was, much as I wanted to fool myself, I suspected none of them would have ended in a win for us. Hindsight really was a bitch when it wanted to be.

The reality was, the fight at Gan's had been a true Kobayashi Maru situation. The entire thing had been one massive ass fucking with more than enough dick to go around.

There we were – Ed grievously wounded and the rest of us exhausted after battling scores of enemies. Then, to top it all off, a creature straight out of a Toho flick had swooped down, hell bent on corrupting one of the thirteen Sources of magic – conveniently enough located directly beneath Gan's mansion.

Hell, even Matthias Falcon – a wizard powerful enough to turn his hotel room into its own pocket dimension oasis – had been done by that point, lacking even the power to stabilize Ed's wounds.

Alas, my solution to that problem hadn't won me any favors – killing a witch from his coven and feeding her blood to my friend.

Losing an ally to save a friend was a price I could live with, but it had also cost me precious moments – time I could've used to try and save Christy.

That, of course, assumed it was even possible to have freed her from the hungry grasp of the Source – a portal of near infinite power.

That was the problem right there, I considered as I grabbed some cow blood from the fridge.

Had I chosen differently, Ed almost certainly would've died. But, no matter how many times I played it out in my mind, I knew deep down there was no guarantee I could've made any difference for Christy.

That was the true kick in the balls – the uncertainty of it all.

Saving Ed had been the right choice, but was it the *only* choice or could I have done more?

I didn't know, couldn't know. That was the only real conclusion I'd come to after a week of turning this over in every conceivable way.

So, rather than continue to drive myself slowly insane with indecision, I decided to do what I normally did at times when I was down, alone, and in desperate need of some distraction – prey upon those deserving of my wrath.

"You sound old."

"Old enough to bang your mom," I replied into the headset, just barely dodging the grenade the little prick had thrown at where I'd been camped.

"Try telling that to my dad, asshole."

"I banged him too." *Come on, show yourself.*

"Like, don't you have a job, loser?"

Grinning to myself, I replied, "I don't need a job. I'm a vampire."

"Do you sparkle in the sun, too, you bitch cuck?"

"What?! Fuck you, you little..."

Sadly, whatever comeback I might've had was cut short as I got sniped in the head. *Son of a...*

"Suck it, newb!"

"Oh yeah? How about you suck on my...?"

There came a knock at the door, an incessant tapping sound that caught my attention.

What now?

My first thought was that Tom must've locked himself out, the idiot. But if so, then why not just have Glen ooze under the door to open it, like he'd done every other time?

The knock came again, a tiny sound as if coming from a rather small fist. Tina? Probably not. She and Kelly weren't due back yet, not that either of them actually needed to knock.

I considered the time of year. Had Girl Scout cookie season started? I wasn't sure, but it's not like I'd have said no to drowning my sorrows in a case of Thin Mints.

Fuck it. That was all the motivation I needed.

"Hold on, I'm coming."

I closed my laptop, instantly muting the shit talk from my opponent, then quickly downed the blood remaining in my cup. Didn't need any nosy pre-teen cookie hawkers thinking I was enjoying an early Bloody Mary. That was a good way to get blackmailed into a much larger order. Once was enough for me, thank you very much.

That done, I crossed to the door and opened it.

What in the fucking hell?

I was quick to realize, staring at the inhuman forms standing before me, that whatever my immediate future might hold, delicious cookies were almost certainly not destined to be a part of it.

4

SALE OF THE CENTURY

Let's be realistic here. This wasn't the first time I'd opened the door to find a pair of supernatural monsters waiting to kick the shit out of me.

I really needed to invest in one of those doorbell cameras. It would almost certainly save me a lot of trouble.

The taller of the two looked like he'd been sent by Thanos to inquire as to whether I had any Infinity Stones on me. He had bluish grey flesh, long pointed ears, an angular face with red eyes, and a skeevy soul patch that looked like a spider had climbed onto his chin and died there.

The other was a good foot and a half shorter, with a creepy big nose and wild hair. It was like some mad scientist had seen *Masters of the Universe* while high as balls and had decided to recreate Guildor from memory.

Both were dressed in multicolored and mismatched clothes, as if they'd just blindly robbed a Good Will box — each with a comically oversized backpack upon their shoulders, making me wonder how the shorter one walked without tipping over.

Great, supernatural vagrants. Maybe they'll ask for spare change after kicking my ass.

Whatever the case, I tried to ready myself against whatever nefarious schemes they might've...

Not so fast, Freewill! Remember the defensive wards.

The Wanderer was right. I took a step back instead. If these assholes wanted to throw down they could eat a face full of magic first.

The smaller one cocked its head before directing its attention toward the threshold as if studying it. Then, quick as a whip, he pulled something out of his pocket – a crude voodoo doll of some sorts.

Oh crap.

The creature held it up and two things happened. That strange feeling of vertigo returned just as the entire doorway flared with light. Sigils and glyphs appeared midair, glowing brightly for a few seconds before fading away to nothing.

Then the dizziness passed, leaving me standing on wobbly feet.

The hell was that? Had Ed's neo-vamp upgrade somehow given me a fucking brain aneurysm in addition to failing me on sunlight?

As I backed up a few more steps, I realized the fetish in the smaller ... um ... troll's hand had disintegrated, turning to dust in its grasp.

I didn't know what that meant, but I doubted it was anything good.

The larger one then stepped forward, crossing the threshold as if there was nothing more ominous there than a welcome mat.

"Oy, friend. Mind if we come in?"

What?

The creature had a low-pitched voice that was far different from the growl I'd expected.

The other one let out a sigh and followed, elbowing his taller buddy in the spot where his crotch should've been.

"Manners," it snapped, its voice even deeper than its friend's. It was like someone had compressed the essence of Barry White into four feet of freakish intruder.

"Sorry, Be'af," the first replied, before turning toward me and ... bowing? "My apologies, oh Great One."

What the?

"Mighty One," the shorter of the two said a few seconds later. "We sensed your awakening and have come to offer our services."

I held up my hands in a placating manner as I took another step back. Fighting seemed to be off the table, at least for the moment, but I had no idea what these two weirdos wanted with me. "Listen, guys. No offense, but I've had a long night and really don't need any trouble."

"What a coincidence," the taller one said. "That's precisely why we're here."

Guess fighting was still on the table after all.

"I mean we're here to save you some trouble, not cause it," he quickly added after getting some side eye from the other.

"What my slow-witted partner is trying to say," the smaller one interjected, "is that power follows power. When a warrior such as yourself awakens, others are certain to seek them out. We are here to prepare you for what lies ahead."

"Is that so? Because you're about five years too late."

"Pardon?"

I shook my head. "Let's back up a bit. Who are you guys and why are you here?"

"An excellent way to start," the short one replied. "I am Be'af."

The sound of his name was like a pretentious French waiter trying to pronounce beef with two syllables.

"And this is my partner, Kwe'af."

"So ... you're Beef and he's Queef?"

"Close enough," the tall one, Queef, said jovially, removing his pack and setting it on the floor before turning to his friend. "This one's a bit older than usual, no?"

"Who are we to judge?" Beef, obviously the smarter of the two, said dismissively as he closed the door and likewise started removing his pack.

"Uh huh. Anyway, so ... why the fuck are you guys here again?"

Is it too much to ask that you at least attempt some diplomacy?

I ignored the Wanderer, waiting for one of them to answer.

Looked like Beef was on deck as he spread his arms wide. "An excellent question, Mighty One. We are of a race known as the Kutbai, eternally pledged to seek out beings of power and light so that we might prepare them for their trials to come."

Trials to come? That stopped me in my tracks, forcing me to remember what Gan had said right after Christy disappeared.

"You will face a great many dangers if you choose to follow in her footsteps. I would spare you that suffering, but I also know you better than that."

At the time, I'd thought she'd been spewing her typical lovestruck bullshit. But now, with these two weirdos here giving me a similar song and dance, I had to reconsider.

"Did Gan send you?"

"Who?" Queef asked.

"Gansetseg, daughter of Ögedei Khan, and the person who tries to ass fuck me and my friends as often as humanly possible."

"I know of no such being," Beef replied, looking genuinely confused. "We simply go where the threads of fate lead us, and if they have not led us to this Gansetseg then I must conclude hers is an unremarkable existence."

I considered this. If I knew one thing about Gan it was that she rarely employed those stupid enough to call her unremarkable. No, definitely not her style.

But if that was the case, then why were these guys here? "You sure you have the right address?"

"No doubt about it," Queef said. "We felt you and came as soon as we could."

"What my partner means to say is we sensed your power blossoming, that your time had come."

Blossoming? "Wait. Are you guys here for Tina?"

"That depends," Queef replied. "Are you Tina?"

"Do I look like a Tina to you?"

He shrugged. "Honestly? You all look alike to me."

That caused Beef to elbow him again. "You must understand, Mighty One. Our sensitivity to those with great power is able to transcend space and time, and yet..."

"It doesn't give us names to go by," Queef finished.

"Oh. Well, then I'm Bill Ryder."

"Ryder?" he replied with a snort. "I barely know her!"

"Yeah, haven't heard that one before. Anyway, I'm the Freewill."

"The what-will?"

"The vampire Freewill," I repeated. "You know. The prophecy and all."

"Which prophecy?"

"Me and the Icon. I'm the guy who basically shut off magic for five years."

"That was you?!" Queef cried. "Holy grizzle-balls! Do you know how much business you cost...?"

"Calm yourself, brother," Beef interrupted, putting a hand on Queef's arm. "What interests me far more is what he said about being a vampire."

"Yeah, so?" I replied.

The two shared a look before Beef turned back toward me. "It's ... rare that we deal with vampires, that's all. They're not our *usual* clientele. But, if you are who you say, then you must be special indeed. And a special individual must have special enchantments with which to face their destiny."

Enchantments?

Queef was quick to jump back in with, "Oh, definitely. The most special of enchantments, of which we have come to provide."

"For a moderate sum," Beef added.

So these guys were actually here to sell me magic?

Call me crazy, but that might've been the one thing better than Girl Scout cookies.

Hell, if years of playing *Final Fantasy* and *Fallout* had taught me anything, it was to never bypass a merchant without checking their wares out first.

Besides which, Tom had his sword and there was no doubt it increased his badass factor – the same way it had done for Sheila before him.

In the days before magic had gone kerflooey, I'd managed okay without much else besides my friends and Freewill abilities. However, these days that didn't amount to nearly as much. Outside of Gan there were no more elder vamps around for me to steal power from, just youngsters like me. That, and I didn't seem able to turn into a hulking rage monster anymore, as I'd been when Dr. Death was lurking in my subconscious. Somehow that didn't work with the Wanderer, or so he claimed.

It's not merely a claim, he replied. *Your connection with him was different than it is with...*

Uh huh, whatever, I interrupted. *Internal monologuing here, if you don't mind.*

My point was, I couldn't exactly say I was fucked because of how things were now, but let's face facts. I kinda was.

If these guys were on the up and up, though...

"All right. Let's see what sort of shit you've got for me."

⟵————❦————⟶

"No, you can put that one away."

"Are you sure, Mighty One?" Beef asked. "This unguent will protect you from..."

"Yeah. Save the first level healing potions for some other schmuck."

"As you wish." He stuffed the vial into his pack again.

"And you can forget any of this plus one crap too." At his confused look, I explained, "Anything with a ... minor enchantment. For instance, Sting looked cool in the movies, but all it really did was glow in the dark. Fuck that noise. Sneaking around orcs is fairly useless when you're lit up like a fucking road flare."

"No glowing swords, check," Queef said, rummaging through his pack.

"Yeah. Besides, my buddy Tom already has one, and the

last thing I need is him giving me grief for being a copycat. Oh, and while we're on the subject, nothing faith-based. Doesn't really go well with the whole vampire schtick."

"Got it."

Queef started pulling out an assortment of weapons and armor, proving his pack was almost certainly bigger on the inside. Tempting as it was to ask whether their handy haversacks were up for grabs, I held off. Shit like that was cool when you were looting a dungeon, but I had a feeling it would end up being more trouble than it was worth, especially if Tom got hold of it. With my luck, the asshole would use it as a never-ending trash can, or worse a portable toilet.

No way did I want to open it up only to find it smelling like month-old shit. I'd already dealt with that back in Dave's game, when I let an orphan hide inside my bag of holding and ended up forgetting he was there.

What I needed was something more *proactive* to help me in the days ahead.

"What's this?" I asked, pointing toward a blunt metal rod.

"It extends into a mighty polearm," Beef replied. "One capable of spearing enemies…"

"Hmm. Looks too much like a butt plug."

"See, told you," Queef said, earning some stink-eye from his partner.

I went through their lineup, noting the interesting stuff. There was a steel helmet with the ability to sense invisible foes – useful but not all that subtle. They showed me a dagger that doubled as a compass – not bad, but nothing my cell phone couldn't do. I did a doubletake at a horn they said was capable of summoning spectral allies. Can't say I would've minded having my own ghost army. However, both seemed unsure on what happened once the fighting was done. Screw it. I didn't need to hear Tom bitching about the place being haunted.

"Okay, so a lot of this stuff is kinda cool," I finally said, "but most of it seems kind of specific. Don't you have anything that's both badass and all purpose?"

The two merchants exchanged a not insignificant look.

"Do you think he could be the one?" Beef asked his friend. "The one fated to possess *it*?"

It?

"You mean the one the seers spoke of?" Queef replied. "I don't know."

"Hold on," I interrupted, shades of Gan once more popping into my head. "Seers? We're not talking blind weirdos huffing cave fumes, are we?"

Queef shrugged. "Could be. What do you know about them?"

"Not much. Although I'm pretty sure they've said one or two things about me."

"Truly?" Beef asked, raising an eyebrow.

"Not to brag, but yeah."

Beef got up and paced for a few moments, looking somewhat hesitant before he finally said, "You are correct, mighty Freewill. The wares we've shown you are exceptional, yes, but only one item in our possession is truly unique – a weapon forged by the gods themselves."

"He's not ready for it, Be'af."

"Forged by the gods?" I asked, intrigued. "What kind of weapon are we talking about here?"

Beef leaned in closer, lowering his voice as if afraid he might be overheard. "You are familiar with the legend of the Monkey King, yes?"

"Are we talking Goku or Vegeta here?"

"I'll take that as a no. It is said the great god forged it from a piece of the sun itself, creating a cudgel capable of striking down any foe."

"No shit."

"No shit, indeed," Queef replied.

Whoa. "And you guys have it?"

Beef nodded solemnly. "Indeed we do. For eons untold it has passed from hand to hand, forever trying to find one worthy of its power."

"It won't accept him," Queef protested.

"We should at least let him try."

"It could strike him down like it did all the others. We can't risk that..."

"You felt his awakening same as I," Beef snapped. "Can you deny it?"

"No," Queef said, averting his eyes. "I can't. It's just, how can we be sure?"

Getting struck down didn't sound like fun, but still. It's not like my vamp healing hadn't pulled my ass out of the frying pan before. "Okay, so what are we talking about here? At least let me see it."

"I'm not sure..."

"Come on! You can't just dangle shit like that in front of a guy."

"I don't know..."

"Seriously? Do I have to say please?"

"Very well," Beef said, turning to his partner. "Do it."

"But..."

"I said do it!"

Queef nodded then reached reluctantly into his pack, rummaging for several long seconds before pulling out...

"Wait," I said, nonplussed. "Isn't that just a claw hammer?"

"So it appears, yes."

"You do realize I can get the same fucking thing at Home Depot for less than twenty bucks, right?"

"Not like this one."

"Give it to him," Beef ordered. "Let him try."

Queef shrugged. "If you say so, but it's on your head if anything happens."

He held it out to me with trembling hands, giving me pause. Taking hold of magical weapons hadn't worked out so well for me in the past. Sheila's sword for instance.

On the other hand ... nothing ventured, nothing gained.

Fuck it.

The Wanderer screamed out a warning to be careful, but I decided it was best to just rip this bandage off. So I grabbed hold of it, prepared to drop it at a moment's notice if...

Except nothing happened. It was just a stupid fucking hammer. Nothing out of the...

Holy fuck!

The hammer began to glow, flaring up until it was nearly blindingly bright.

As I closed my eyes against the glare, I felt it change in my hand – growing larger and heavier, to the point where I almost dropped it.

When I looked again, gone was the pedestrian carpentry tool and in its place was a weapon of destruction – a four-foot long war hammer with a massive glowing head.

What the shit?

"He did it!" Queef cried.

"Thundersmite has acknowledged him as its rightful master," Beef said, his eyes wide. "All glory to the Monkey King!"

"Thundersmite?" I asked, gobsmacked.

"That's what its name translates to in your language," he explained. "But that matters little. The important thing is the hammer has chosen you. Nay, *fate* has chosen you!"

Both he and Queef dropped to one knee before me as I stood there feeling the weight of the weapon and the power thrumming through it.

Perhaps it would be wise to take this cautiously, rather than...

"And perhaps it would be wise for you to shut up and let me handle this," I replied.

"Excuse me, mighty one?" Beef asked.

"Sorry. Talking to myself," I replied, taking in the gleaming weapon. "What I meant to say is I'll take it."

"Excellent. Now for the matter of our meager compensation..."

5

DUELING ARTIFACTS

Following the destruction of the original Source – banishing magic from this world and ending the war between the vampire nation and their ancient enemies the Feet – Sally had bequeathed me a small windfall, part of our former coven's vast holdings.

It wasn't exactly mega-yacht money. Nevertheless, it had allowed me to buy my apartment building outright, leaving me enough to comfortably exist with little more than some part-time consulting to keep from getting bored.

It might as well have been pocket change compared to what these fuckers were demanding.

"I think you may have me confused with the Sultan of Brunei."

"If such is the case," Beef said, "then perhaps we should take Thundersmite to him instead."

"Hold on! Didn't you just say fate chose me?"

"That we did," Queef replied, holding out his hand for the hammer, "but fate don't pay the bills."

"Oh come on. Aren't you even gonna try to haggle?"

"What for?" Beef asked, raising an eyebrow.

"Well, what else do you guys want? Maybe we can make a trade."

"What did you have in mind?" He put a hand under his chin as he started to look around.

"Like, for instance, I own an apartment building a few blocks away ... if you don't mind a mild werewolf infestation."

"We are not interested in pets. This place, however..."

"Yeah, about that. I'm just crashing here. Most of this stuff isn't mine."

"The property does not interest me so much as the magic inscribed upon it."

"The magic?"

He nodded. "This apartment, nay this building, it practically seethes with magical energy. Your doing?"

It was all I could do to keep from laughing. Instead, I merely shook my head.

He waved a hand. "It matters not. A skilled practitioner has obviously put much time and energy into this place."

"As I'm well aware. The problem is, it's not mine, so I can't really..."

"Did I mention that if you were to trade us this magic then perhaps we can lower our asking price ... a bit?"

"What exactly do you mean by *a bit*?"

It was shitty of me to barter all the work Christy had put into fortifying her apartment. However, the fact that these guys had simply waltzed in kinda implied that a Monkey King hammer was perhaps a more solid defense plan than a few wards on the doors and walls.

Mind you, their final asking price, magic included, was still going to nearly wipe out my bank account, but by then I had my heart set on owning something badass enough to let us go on the offensive.

I'd played it safe enough times to know how likely it was to screw us over. So, I decided to take the initiative on this one. Besides, Kelly and Liz were good at what they did. They could probably just reinstall the wards afterwards.

At least these two didn't ask me to set up an account at Gringotts, convert the funds to dragon eggs, or do anything weird like that. No, turned out that Beef and Queef had a PayPal account standing by for just such an occasion. Yay for modern convenience.

Following a rather heart-wrenching transfer of funds, they both opened their packs wide – positioning glowing crystals atop them as they began to chant in some incomprehensible language.

Moments later, the entire apartment lit up the same as the door had. Wards and sigils appeared on every surface, glowing like they were on fire just as...

Ugh!

And suddenly I found myself on my knees, a strange sensation inside my head like ... well, almost like my brain was glowing every bit as much as the apartment. It kinda felt like I'd stuck my tongue in a power outlet, except with my mind.

What the fuck is going on?

The weirdest part, though, was that, strange as it might've been, it wasn't necessarily a bad feeling. Crazy as it sounded, a part of me wanted more – to push my metaphorical tongue further in and taste that electric rainbow.

And then it was gone. The apartment ceased glowing and in that very same instant I felt fine again. I stood up, feeling right as rain, and looked around, noting everything seemed...

The magic. It's...

I didn't need the Wanderer to finish, though. Somehow I knew. The magic was gone. This place was once again nothing more than a normal apartment.

The hell was that all about?

Once again I had to worry about the transition from vampire to neo-vamp and whether it had somehow fucked with my brain. Because that shit was not normal.

"Something weird is going on here," I said, despite the relative normalcy of the room.

"I'll say," Queef replied.

"What my brother means," Beef quickly interjected, "is

that an awakening such as yours is ... truly rare." He paused as if thinking it through. "Rare enough that I find myself fearing for your life."

"How so?"

He let out a sigh. "Enemies, Mighty One. Surely they will seek you out, hoping to find you before you can master the power of Thundersmite."

Great. Just what I needed to hear.

"But perhaps we can help. I have another enchantment that will..."

"Seriously? You guys have already squeezed me dry."

"This one is on the house, as I believe is the saying." He turned to Queef. "The amulet. Quickly!"

"Amulet?"

"Yes. You know the one."

"Are you sure, Be'af? It's made of brighdril, and you know how much that stuff is..."

"I'm well aware. Trust me, this is worth it."

"If you say so."

Queef dug into his pack again, this time retrieving a necklace of sorts. Beef took it from his brother and held it up for me to study.

The chain was metal and hanging from it was a pair of tiny wings – like an angel's, or maybe a butterfly's. What the heck?

Hold on, Freewill. I'm not sure that's...

Before the Wanderer could finish, Beef stepped forward and pressed it to my forehead – the metal strangely warm to the touch, like it had been lying in a sweaty pocket.

Eww.

A shudder passed through me as I felt the barest of tingles and then ... nothing. All at once, I actually felt like myself again, which was probably the first time I could honestly make that claim since waking up. *Huh.*

When I looked up again, the pendant was missing from Beef's fingers. "Um, where did it go?"

"Inside you, Mighty One. It is a construct, one with powerful shielding magic."

"Which does what exactly?"

"Duh. It shields you," Queef said, slipping on his backpack.

"My brother is correct," Beef added, likewise putting his pack on too. I guess their business was done here. "It will hide your power from the prying eyes of those who seek to undermine you, until such time as you have mastered your newfound gifts."

Queef clapped me on the arm. "That means don't tell anyone about it."

"Exactly," Beef said, turning toward the door. "Keep both it and the hammer a secret until you are ready. When that is, only you will know."

"Wait. What does that even...?"

"Tell no one!" he repeated, reaching for the doorknob. "Be assured, my brother and I will return to check on your progress."

"Yep," Queef said, following his brother out. "Until then, have a nice day!"

Fucking magical gremlins and their stupid fucking riddles. Like I needed another goddamned chosen one prophecy hanging over my head.

At least they'd stopped long enough to show me how to activate Thundersmite. A quick swing and a bit of will from me and *poof*, instant doom hammer. Do it again and *bam*, you were ready to fix the drywall instead.

It wasn't quite as cool as tapping it against the ground and being hit with a bolt of lightning, but it was still pretty freaking awesome. I could only imagine how badass it was going to be when I finally got a chance to go all Thor upside someone's head with it.

Maybe that's what I needed to do. Rather than sitting around with my thumb up my ass, I could join Tom and Glen out on patrol while we waited for news from Kelly.

I spent the next half hour doing my best Star Wars Kid

impression in the living room – swinging my hammer at imaginary foes, most of whom looked like Gan – until I heard the sound of footsteps approaching.

I reengaged Thundersmite's claw hammer mode just before Tom entered, bags under his eyes and a plastic paint bucket in his grasp.

"Hey, Bill," he said, upending the bucket's contents which, unsurprisingly, turned out to be Glen.

"Long night?" I asked, eying them both.

"You could say that," Glen replied. "An alley cat took offense at my disguise. It was most unpleasant."

Tom nodded. "Yeah, I had to stop off at the hardware store to grab something to carry him home in."

"Probably for the best," I said. "That corgi suit was getting a bit ratty."

Glen released a few air bubbles in an approximation of a sigh. "I thought it was rather charming. And the ladies certainly seemed to like it."

"At some point we need to discuss the difference between squeals of delight and shrieks of terror."

He raised two tendrils of slime in a shrug. "It's not my fault human vocal cords lack the refinement for nuance."

"Uh, yeah. So ... any luck out there?"

Tom slipped off the easel bag containing his broadsword before brushing a lock of blonde hair to the side. "Some college assholes offered to show me their dicks."

"Did you take them up on it?"

"He told them he didn't want to make their mothers jealous," Glen replied.

"A fair response."

"Yeah," Tom continued. "They tried to give me shit about it, so I pulled out my sword and lit up. You should've seen them. Pretty sure at least one pissed himself."

"Subtle too."

He shrugged as if he couldn't have given a shit, which was likely the case. Then he raised an eyebrow at me. "How about you? Surprised you're not at the window waving your dick at the sun ... not that I want to see it."

"Me neither, since it would just end up on fire."

"Wait. It would?"

"So let me get this straight," Tom said, after I'd brought them up to speed. "Not only did the asshole screw it up, but then he ditched you to go fuck my sister."

"A bit of an oversimplification, but yeah."

"Damn, that sucks."

"I'm sorry to hear it, Freewill," Glen said. "I was looking forward to getting a new disguise and letting you take me for a walk in the park."

"Thanks. Just for the record, though, that was never going to happen."

"So where the fuck does that leave us?" Tom groused. "You're still useless during the day and now we're down a person."

"You would know all about being useless."

He let out a huff of breath, disturbingly similar to how Sheila used to after a stressful day at the office. Goddamn. More than two months in and it was still way too fucking weird that my best friend's soul was residing in my ex-girlfriend's body.

"You can't walk in the sun and I need another disguise," Glen remarked, slithering up onto the couch. "Quite the disappointing day so far."

"Maybe not a complete bust." I considered Beef's warning for a moment, then decided to ignore it. What fun would life be if I couldn't share a bit of awesomeness with my best buds? So I grabbed the claw hammer from the coffee table and held it up. "Check it out."

"Check what out?" Tom replied, sounding unimpressed. "Or did you finally fix that squeaky floor board in the kitchen?"

"Oh I hope so. It's really been annoying me," Glen added.

"Not quite," I said. "But maybe I can fix a few of our other problems."

I stood up and gave the hammer a swing, transforming it with a flash of power.

Judging by the look on Tom's face, you'd have thought I'd surprised him on his birthday by taking him down to Tijuana for a donkey show.

"What the fuck?"

"Allow me to introduce ... *Thundersmite*."

The cat out of the bag, I told them about the Queef brothers and how they'd shown up at our doorstep with their bottomless backpacks of holding.

"That's fucking wild," Tom replied. "Except for the part where you didn't think to buy me anything."

"Do you know how much this thing cost? You're lucky I have enough left over for a fucking Happy Meal."

"Ooh, I wish I could have seen them fawning over you, Freewill," Glen added. "It's always nice to meet other fans."

I shook my head. "I'm not sure they even knew what a Freewill is. They seemed to think that whatever Ed did to me awakened some great power."

"Yeah," Tom remarked. "Maybe if someone jams a steam generator up your ass and pushes you out into the sunlight."

"Tell me about it."

"Still," he continued, "cool as this is, don't you think it's kind of anticlimactic? Epic weapons are supposed to come from impossible quests, not traveling salesmen."

"Says the guy who got his sword by waking up in the previous owner's body."

"Yeah, but at least I had to die first. You've gotta admit that's pretty epic."

"Touché. But come on, you've played *Skyrim*. Sometimes you go out, get your ass kicked in a dungeon, then ride back to town and find the shop is selling better shit than you found."

"I know!" Glen cried. "You two should fight to see which weapon is better."

"Not a bad idea," Tom said. "Excalibur versus Mjölnir."

"I'll go get my camera."

"Hold on," I said. "We can't."

"Pussy much?" Tom replied.

"No. I just don't want to trash the place, because I sure as shit know you won't be the one cleaning up. Also, they said I should keep it a secret for now."

"Why?"

"I don't know. Something about destiny and enemies hunting me down. Hard to tell with this crap." I gave Thundersmite another swing, turning it back into a normal hammer again. "Either way, I need you guys to keep this on the downlow for now. Let's make it our little secret for the next asshole who decides they want a piece."

Tom appeared to consider this before nodding. "I guess that makes sense."

"I think so too," Glen replied. "I just hope I'm there when you finally decide to whip it out."

"You have fun with that. I, for one, have no interest in seeing Bill whip *anything* out."

I was about to comment on that when all at once the room lit up around us, as two brilliant beams of light appeared at opposite ends of the apartment.

The fuck?!

Guess the time to debut my new weapon was gonna be sooner than I thought.

6

THE ROAD TO PURGATORY

In the space of an instant, the apartment went from chill to DEFCON 2. Two forms materialized and immediately lit up with battle magic, while Glen and I were forced to dive for cover as Tom's aura ignited in response.

"Is everyone okay?"

Fortunately, the concerned tone and familiar voice quickly clued me in that this wasn't some eldritch home invasion.

"Hey, Kel," I said to the first witch, picking myself up as I realized it was a false alarm. "Um ... any particular reason you guys look ready to blast the shit out of us?"

Across the room, Liz powered down the magic around her. "I dunno. You want to maybe tell us what the hell happened here?"

"Nice to see you too, Elizabitch," Tom remarked, reining in his aura.

"I liked you better dead," she replied.

"You should try it sometime. Would work wonders on your attitude."

Kelly might've vouched for her, but I couldn't really blame anyone on our team for still disliking her, not after the shit she'd pulled.

Liz was Christy's former coven sister. She'd also been part of

43

the group Sheila had assembled to restore magic to the world. However, whereas Sheila had wanted to do it peacefully, Liz and her vampire boytoy – a paramilitary alphahole by the name of Komak – had chosen a different route. Under their watch, Sally had been nearly tortured to death while Tina and Kelly got to experience the *joy* of being held hostage at gunpoint.

So imagine our surprise when Kelly recently broke the news that she and Liz had mended their fences.

The thing was, much as I was firmly in Tom's camp on this one, I trusted Kelly. If she said Liz was trying to make good on what she'd done, then that carried a lot of weight in my book – doubly so now when we needed all the help we could get.

Of the two, Liz was older, more powerful, and clearly far more experienced. With Christy lost in another dimension, Sally's fate unknown, and Ed flying out west for some poon, we simply couldn't afford to ignore this olive branch.

"All right, everyone calm down," I said, playing peacemaker. "Let's back up to the point where you guys popped in like we owed you money."

Kelly took a look around, her expression unreadable. "That one's easy. I was getting Tina ready for school when I suddenly felt every single bit of magic around this apartment just up and disappear."

I shared a quick warning glance with Tom, hoping he took the hint to keep his mouth shut. "Wait, you felt that?"

She straightened her glasses then put one hand on her hip, looking at me as if I was a moron. "Of course. It was one of the safeguards I set up while modifying the wards to let you guys stay here."

"Why exactly?"

"Because aside from Tina, none of you knows the first thing about magic. So I added a few charms so that if anything went haywire, I'd be the first to know." After a moment, she added, "No offense."

"None taken."

"That's why I went and got Liz. With the amount of

work Christy put into this place, I figured something big must've happened."

Oh. I hadn't considered that possibility when I'd tossed the apartment's enchantments onto the bargaining table. I figured I'd just make something up after the fact ... which in retrospect wasn't a particularly great plan.

"So are you going to tell us what happened or not?" Liz asked.

Oh crap. Beef and Queef had warned me about keeping things quiet. Normally, I wouldn't care, but then they'd thrown in that amulet for free, despite not striking me as the altruistic sorts. That kind of suggested they'd been serious. Telling my roommates was one thing, but perhaps I didn't want to widen that circle of knowledge too much.

I waited a moment to see if the Wanderer was going to play devil's advocate, but there came no response from him. Fine. When in doubt, play stupid and redirect the subject.

"No idea what happened. I was kinda too busy trying not to burn up under the sun to notice much else."

"Burning up?" Kelly replied. "I thought you were..."

"So did I, but Ed's bite didn't work as advertised. It's like it went halfway or something. I can't use compulsion, but sunlight works the same as before." A thought hit me, so I decided to run with it. "I dunno, maybe whatever happened somehow screwed with the wards."

Kelly shrugged. "Maybe. But if so you're damned lucky it didn't blow you and half the building to bits."

"Tell me about it." *Holy crap, are they actually buying that load of shit?*

"Now that you mention it," Liz said, "there is something kinda off about you."

"Off? How so?"

"Your aura. It's a bit ... fuzzy."

"My aura?"

"It's a witch thing."

Interesting and disturbing as that was, it was time to steer this ship back to less contentious waters. "I see. So ... um, anyway, do you guys think you can put it back together again?"

"Are you for real?" Liz replied. "Do you have any idea the amount of work that went into the wards here?"

"Not really."

"Nor would we expect you to," Kelly said, her tone conciliatory. "But think of it like ... painting minis. You know how much effort goes into that, right?"

I nodded. "Lost a good chunk of high school to my orc horde."

"Nerd," Tom remarked.

"Like you didn't help."

"Anyway," she continued, "imagine dumping a couple dozen in acetone and then asking if you can just spray paint it back on."

That was one analogy I could understand. "Oh."

Liz nodded. "Yeah. We're looking at maybe the better part of a week to get it even close to where it was, maybe longer. And that assumes dropping everything we're working on which, in case you're curious, ain't gonna happen."

That sucked, but as the owner of a brand new god-forged hammer I wasn't particularly worried either. "Fair enough. Operation Find Christy is still top priority. We'll just be extra vigilant when it comes to opening the front door."

Glen raised a tendril. "I'll gladly volunteer my services as guard dog."

"Sure, go nuts," I said with a shrug. "At least Tina will get a kick out of that."

"No."

I raised an eyebrow at Kelly. "What do you mean no?"

She instead turned toward Tom. "I know she's your daughter and I have no real authority to say this, but you'd have to be out of your fucking mind to bring her back here. She's made a ton of progress, yes, but we're talking about a girl who's not even six. If she gets mad or loses control..."

"Or something comes looking for her here," Liz added, before quickly amending, "Yes, I know it's a sore subject coming from me, but you both need to be realistic about this."

Much as I wanted to call her a bitch for bringing up the past, she had a point. Still, this was Tom's call. Yes, he could be a complete dumbass regarding his own life, but I got the impression Christy's disappearance had sobered him up a bit when it came to Tina.

"What do you suggest?" he asked, sounding serious for once.

Liz let out a sigh. "I suppose we could recruit some help if we wanted to go down that route. I know a few Magi who owe me a favor."

"We can do better than that and you know it," Kelly replied, sharing a not insignificant glance with the other witch.

"No way. Not a good idea."

"What's not a good idea?" I asked.

Kelly ignored me, though. "It's perfect. It's safe, secure, and will keep us from having to travel back and forth all the time."

"I'm telling you..."

"Not to mention Tina loves it there and you know it."

"I'm not arguing with that," Liz countered. "I'm talking about these two. You know for a fact that inviting them will go over like a lead balloon with a lot of folks there."

"So we'll talk to them first. Everyone understands that these are strange times. Besides, they know the rules."

"Uh huh. Those rules didn't keep you from almost getting your ass killed when you first showed up."

"I know, but it's been a lot better since then."

"Which is why I don't want to see it get worse again. No offense, Kel, but you're small potatoes compared to these two. People might not be so willing to turn a blind eye when it comes to the Freewill or Icon."

"We have to at least try. Isn't that the whole point of the community?"

Liz averted her eyes and let out a huff of breath. "I

suppose, but ... I can't agree to this without running it up the flagpole first."

"Running what up the flagpole?" I finally asked.

Kelly turned toward us, her face a mask of determination. "I think it's time we told you guys about Purgatory."

"Tell me. Did either of you ever give any thought to what happened to all those people who were down at the Source with us, the ones working to bring magic back?"

"Not really," Tom replied, pretty much echoing my sentiment. "I figured most of them were just assholes."

"Which is exactly why I'm against this," Liz muttered before continuing. "I know you have trouble thinking past the end of your own non-existent dick, but I need you to try. Desperate times make people do desperate things, but that doesn't make them assholes."

"It doesn't make them *not* assholes either," I countered.

"Fine. Then what about him?" she asked, pointing toward Glen. "Is he an asshole too? Because let's not forget, he was with us when you met him."

"Of course not," Tom said. "Glen's the man."

"Technically speaking, my species is hermaphroditic," Glen replied. "Although I personally identify as awesome."

"Fuck yeah!" Tom held up a hand which the little blob slapped with a tendril. "Don't ever let anyone tell you otherwise."

"*Anyway*, as I was saying," Liz continued, "everyone who was down there had their own reasons, most of which had nothing to do with anything dark or evil. Unless that is, you two are about to tell me that simply wanting to rebuild their lives makes them dangerous."

I said nothing, but Tom of course had an opinion. "Depends on the circumstances."

"That's kind of the point of Purgatory," Kelly interjected. "It's a sanctuary for those with extenuating circumstances. A place for them to live, judgement free, until such time as they're ready to move on."

"So it's like a homeless shelter for witches?" I asked.

"It's a community for extranormal beings who are down on their luck in some way, shape, or form."

"Okay, so then what are you and Vince doing there?"

She shrugged. "We had ... some things to work out."

"And that required a magical hippy commune?" Tom replied.

Kelly appeared to think it over for a moment or two. "Actually yes. I think we needed it to move forward."

Interestingly enough, that was all I needed to hear. "Okay, I'm sold."

"Wait, you are?" Tom asked. "Don't get me wrong, I'm all for free love, but maybe let's get Christy back before you go looking to get your dick waxed by some hemp-sucking vegan vamps."

"Not that, dumbass. Think about it. Vincent was one of the Templar. He's pretty much the last person on the planet I'd probably want to bring to a place like that." I glanced Kelly's way. "No offense."

"Don't worry," Liz remarked, "that was pretty much my thought too."

"Anyway," I continued, "the fact that he hasn't tried to burn the entire place down says a lot. And they're right. If it was just us, I'd say we could run the risk of staying here, but not with Cat."

"Cheetara, asshole," he corrected, using Tina's middle name.

"Whatever. You know I'm right. Let's face facts, the city isn't particularly friendly for us right now. So why not scope this place out? If it's cool, maybe we can see if the coven wants to relocate too. That would leave us with nothing left to worry about here – other than making sure my tenants keep paying their rent on time."

Tom appeared to mull this over for a few minutes. "Just tell me there's no giant monsters to worry about."

"Not last I checked," Liz replied.

"Or Gan."

"Nope, no Gans either."

"What about werewolves? Because those guys are A-plus pricks."

Liz raised an eyebrow. "Werewolves don't exist, stupid."

"Actually, they apparently do," Kelly said. "Christy was telling me about it."

"Seriously? Goddamn, this world is more fucked than I thought."

"You ain't whistling Dixie, sister," I replied.

"Well, in that case, I can't say for certain, but I'm fairly sure there aren't any in Purgatory. Best I can do."

I locked my gaze on my two friends until they both nodded – well, okay, Glen kind of bobbed his eyes up and down a bit. Still...

"I think that settles it then. We're in."

"Oh, one other thing," Kelly added. "I didn't think I'd need to mention this after last night, but there's one other bonus. The barrier around Purgatory. It was designed to diffuse direct sunlight, meaning it's vampire safe."

I had to admit, it was a hell of a sales pitch.

I almost had second thoughts when Kelly told me Purgatory was located in upstate New York, but I tended to forget how large of an area that was. Though both of them remained mum on the exact location, they at least were able to confirm it was nowhere near Salisbury Mills and Casa De Gan.

Can't say I wasn't happy to hear that.

Unfortunately, with Tom being resistant to magic and none of us having any blood of Baal handy so as to dampen his powers, that meant we'd have to drive.

That wasn't necessarily a bad thing, though. As Kelly had already indicated, she and Liz still needed some time to ensure we'd be welcomed there.

Besides, we weren't going anywhere yet – not with the sun high in the sky. It was one thing to chance driving back from Jersey City, quite another for what was sure to be a multi-hour road trip.

"All right then," Liz said, standing up. "We'll head back and sort things out. Once we do, we'll text you the coordinates to meet us at. In the meantime, pack some clothes and whatever camping gear you have."

Tom held up his hands. "Wait, why do we need camping gear?"

"You said it yourself, cupcake. This is a magical hippy commune, not a four star hotel. So unless you like sleeping on the ground, I'd suggest you pitch a tent. Oh, I'm sorry, I meant *bring* a tent."

Tom narrowed his eyes. "We don't own a fucking tent."

"Then you'd best get your petite ass to the store and buy one."

"All I need is a pail," Glen opined.

"Not so fast," Tom said, ignoring him. "Like, what happens if we need to, y'know, take a shit while we're there?"

"And I think that's our cue to leave Grizzly Adams here to figure things out." Liz rubbed the bridge of her nose before turning to Kelly. "You coming, trash witch? Or do I need to speak to the council about these two myself?"

Kelly let out a sigh, her apologetic look saying it all. "I'd better go with her to make sure everything is cool."

"Good luck," I said.

"Thanks. I'll let you know what they decide. Until then, sit tight, figure out what you need to bring ... and maybe don't open the door for anyone you don't know."

7

CAMPINGTOWN RACES

Tom and I spent the first half of the day packing most of our shit up, which wasn't too difficult since we'd only recently moved in.

I finally got a text from Kelly around three in the afternoon. Purgatory's high council wasn't exactly thrilled to have us, but she'd managed to stuff their own charter back down their throats. After all, they were a place for magical refugees with nowhere else to go – which kinda described us to a tee.

The GPS coordinates she sent pointed to a spot in the northeastern part of the state, close to the Massachusetts border – a three or four hour drive depending on traffic.

I texted Leslie, one of the Village Coven vamps, to let her know what was going on. In Sally's absence, she'd stepped up, acting as unofficial second in command – making sure the coven was kept fed, reporting in regularly as to any goings on, and keeping her eyes open in case Mike Walden or his werewolf buddies tried anything suspicious.

I brought her up to speed, then wired her some cash for them to get by on – depleting my already stricken bank account even further.

Then it was time to go shopping.

Brooklyn wasn't exactly what you'd call a Mecca for

survivalists, but it had at least one Army Navy store and a few camping supply shops.

Once the sun had set enough to make it safe to go out – and yes I was still fucking pissed about that – Tom and I left to pick up what we needed.

I would've sent him out earlier, but I knew better. Despite him taking things a bit more seriously following Christy's *accident*, I'd have still sooner trusted Glen with our shopping list. Too bad I had a feeling the sales staff would've reacted badly to a glop of mustard yellow puke rolling in the door and asking where they kept their sleeping bags.

Finally, maybe an hour and a half later, the three of us were able to get on the road – my tiny hatchback rental loaded to the gills with luggage and gear. Call me cynical, but I had a feeling we'd been taken to the cleaners, especially after Tom had ever so *helpfully* admitted to the salesman that we had no idea what we were doing.

I mean, it wasn't a lie. The last time we'd been *camping* had been at a supernatural peace conference in deepest darkest Canada, right before war had broken out between the vampire nation and the Sasquatches running things up there. And even then we'd been able to stay in an economy-sized hut furnished with all the grubs and dead hikers we could eat.

The only upside was it didn't sound like it was going to cost much to get by at this Purgatory place. That was good, because in the space of a day I'd gone from being comfortably well off to, "Can you spare some change, sir?"

On the upside, I now had an epic artifact with a badass name.

I hadn't gotten much chance to use it yet, but that would have to wait.

For now, we had a road trip ahead of us.

"I'm telling you, Zeus had all the moves. This was a guy who got a chick to fuck him even after he turned into a swan. Like, how the hell does that even work?"

"You could always Google it," Tom said from the passenger seat.

"Want me to do that?" Glen offered from the back.

"No!" I snapped. "You should most definitely *not* search for that. Back to my point. Why would anyone even want to bang a swan? But regardless, Zeus pulled it off."

Tom shook his head. "Gotta disagree, man. Loki was the pimp daddy of the gods. The dude literally fucked anything that moved. If it had a slit, he was fucking it."

"Maybe…"

"Oof," he grumbled as the car jostled. "Watch the potholes."

"Sorry."

"Anyway, there's no maybe about it. Nobody had a wetter dick than Loki, not even Zeus. And do you know why?"

"I'm sure you're gonna tell me."

"Because he didn't have Hera trying to cockblock the shit out of him every time he found a hole to shove his cob into. That alone puts Zeus into second place."

"Fair point."

"Thor was the dude all the chicks wanted, but Loki was the one they all went home with because that fucker had game."

"I must admit, Tom Hiddleston is quite charming," Glen bubbled.

"Fuck yeah. If I swung that way, he'd be top of my list."

I considered the magical hammer stuffed deep in our luggage. "I'd probably be more of a Chris Hemsworth guy myself."

"Like he'd want your dumpy ass."

Our banter was nice and light, but I'll admit to gripping the steering wheel ever tighter as we continued on.

Eventually, GPS had us exit off the Taconic State Parkway. By then it was well past dark, which I can't say I personally minded.

With maybe forty minutes left to go, I found us taking

turn after turn onto smaller, increasingly more rural roads, the sort of places where I could easily imagine banjo music drifting out of the woods.

Finally, maybe two miles from our destination, I pulled onto what was probably better categorized as a game trail than a road, something my front wheel drive rental was none too happy about.

As we jolted up and down thanks to the uneven surface, I saw a sign warning us about oncoming traffic – telling me that some shitbrain-addled state employee had been here and decided the ditches on either side of this dirt path somehow constituted two lanes.

"Dude, speed up," Tom griped. "I need to take a piss, and the way you're driving it'll take another three hours to get there."

"Feel free to step out and make like a bear."

"No way. I don't need poison ivy in my vag."

"That is way more info than I ever needed."

"Hey, what's that up ahead?" Glen asked, sticking an eyeball-filled tendril between us from his spot in the back.

Following his gaze, I spied a pair of blinking lights a couple hundred yards away. The car they were attached to was off to the right side, partially in the ditch.

As I turned on the high beams to get a better look, both front doors opened and two svelte figures stepped out.

"Holy shit, check out the ass on that one," Tom remarked. "I think we got us some hot hitchhikers here."

"Or hot serial killers. Don't forget where we are."

"They could be headed to that hippie commune too."

"Maybe. And it's not a hippie commune."

"Whatever the fuck. Pull over. Maybe they'll offer us a rub and tug if we call them a tow truck."

I glanced at him sidelong. "You do remember that we're not out here looking for roadhead, right?"

"There's always time for road..."

"I'm sorry I asked." I did a double take as we got closer, kinda hoping the Wanderer had an opinion to offer. "You know what, screw this. Something about it doesn't feel right.

We can let Kelly know when we get there. It's not like we're far from..."

That's when the two women turned to face us, just as we were about to pass them. The driver looked to be in her mid-twenties, with pale skin and dark hair. Truth be told, she bore a slight resemblance to Christy, enough so that I found my foot moving over toward the brake.

Then I caught sight of the passenger. In profile she appeared similar to the driver, making me guess they were related. Then she finished turning around and I saw the rest of her.

Holy fucking Two-Face!

Half her face appeared to have been seared off. Parts of her jaw were visible past the scar tissue covering the side of her mouth, as if there hadn't been enough skin left to finish the job. That itself wouldn't have caused me to freak out. After all, Tom might've been dick enough to mock someone who'd been in an unfortunate accident, but I wasn't.

The problem was the eye on that side of her face. It was missing, yet there came a faint reddish glow from the hollow of the socket. No way was that normal. Then there was the grin she was wearing. Regardless of her injuries, there was something utterly unhinged about it – the sort of shit you saw on an anime villain's face right before they leveled a city block with their psychic powers.

Yeah, fuck this noise.

I fully expected the Wanderer to chide me about judging a book by its cover, but he remained silent. Guess he was still wiped from whatever fuckery Ed's bite had caused.

Either way, I sped up – a teeny bit anyway, not wanting the rental to shake apart on the shitty road. I passed them and kept going. If I was wrong about things, I could always apologize later.

"Um, Bill...," Tom said, looking back over his shoulder.

"What?"

"You might want to check the rearview."

I did, noting the bright light coming from behind us – thinking they'd turned on their high beams as a farewell fuck you. However, it was another second for me to realize it wasn't coming from their vehicle.

The girl with the burnt face was lit up like the Phoenix Force, a halo of fire rising from her body – right before she shot a bolt of flame straight toward us, sending it careening toward the back of our car like a runaway meteor.

Oh crap.

8

IN YOUR FACE

As the back of our car exploded from the force of the fire blast, I had a moment to consider what was worse: the attack itself, the car being launched into the air like a *Dukes of Hazzard* rerun, or that Tom's aura picked that moment to ignite – acting like an eldritch airbag, for him anyway.

Too bad he happened to be sitting right next to me in the cramped hatchback.

At least I didn't have much time to worry about it as the car flipped end over end, causing my head to alternately slam into the steering wheel and the roof as shards of flaming metal went flying past me in every direction.

On the upside, at least I could throw it in Tom's face that I'd been right about not stopping for hitchhikers. Small victories and all that.

As we finally skidded to a halt upside down, helped by a conveniently placed tree alongside the road, I found myself hanging by my seatbelt.

Half my body was sizzling, thanks in no small part to being in contact with Tom's aura – yet another thing Ed's so-called upgrade had failed me on.

And that wasn't even telling what condition my friends were in.

Fuck, fuck, fuckity fuck!

I wasn't going to be able to help anyone if I was nothing more than a pile of flaming ashes. So, I pulled my left arm back then let loose, shattering the already spider-webbed window with my elbow. My vampire claws did the rest, freeing me to scramble out of the vehicle before I became a pile of burnt toast.

"Guys!" I cried as I got clear, a little crispy but otherwise okay.

"Sorry about that," Tom replied, his aura having protected him from everything save his locked seatbelt. "Um, a little help here. I'm kinda stuck."

I slid around the totaled vehicle, trying to keep an eye open for any more attacks headed our way. "Turn off the light show, dumbass."

He doused his aura as I reached his side, allowing me to wrench the passenger door open and drag him out. "You okay?"

"I'll live. You?"

"Remind me to plant your ass in the backseat next time." Speaking of which... "Glen! Are you...?"

"I'm good," came the answer. "Some luggage fell on me, but it ended up blocking Tom's power."

That was good. "Can you ooze out of there?"

"Sure, not a problem."

"Okay, make your way out then lay low. I don't know what the fuck that was about, but I have a feeling..."

Before I could finish telling him we were in deep shit, a flash of green from the corner of my eye told me that much was probably obvious.

Goddamn it!

I dove out of the way as Tom's power once again flared up, no doubt preparing to tank the blast. However, the bolt of eldritch energy wasn't aimed at him.

Instead it slammed into the tree my poor rental had crashed into, blowing apart the trunk and sending a barrage of splinters in every direction. I hit the dirt, literally, trying to avoid death by a thousand toothpicks.

That's it! Soon as these two psychos were finished blowing their loads, I was scrambling around back to pull Thundersmite from the wreckage. It was time to turn this shit around and show our attackers they'd fucked with the wrong fuckers...

Or at least that *was* my plan before the rest of the tree slammed down onto the remains of the car, crushing it, and causing ... um ... yellow pus to squirt out the sides like an oversized pimple?

"Well, that was certainly unpleasant," the closest puddle of goo complained, two eyeballs blinking at me from the surface.

"Pull yourself together, man," I told him. "We'll take care of this."

Hopefully.

The car itself was pancaked. I could only imagine what my insurance company was going to say about this later. For now, though, I couldn't help but realize that both our weapons – Thundersmite and Tom's sword – were trapped inside.

Unfortunately, I doubted our assailants would be so kind as to give us time to fish them out, as my ears picked up the sound of approaching footsteps.

Tom no doubt noticed them, too, igniting his aura again as I pulled myself to my feet behind him. The faith magic radiating off him appeared strong and steady for the moment. Hopefully that would remain the case with his sword, and the action figures zip-tied to it, currently beyond his reach. I didn't want to outright say he used it as a crutch, but he definitely did.

I stepped over a few glops of Glen, oozing toward each other like a low rent T-1000, and moved to Tom's side, albeit keeping enough distance to avoid immolating.

The two women were approaching at an almost casual pace – both of them obviously witches. The slightly taller of the two, the Christy lookalike, was lit up bright green with battle magic. The other, the chick with the messed up face, pulled a butterfly knife from her back pocket and swung it open – revealing the blade was glowing red hot.

That's new.

"Ah, look at what happened, Pammy," the taller one said. "Maybe they should've stopped to help us after all."

"Just so you know," Tom replied, "we were gonna call you guys a tow truck."

"Now you can call a hearse instead," the other one, Pam I assumed, replied in an emotionless whisper. I got the sense this was a chick who'd watched one too many episodes of *Dexter*.

"Which one do you want?" the first witch asked.

"Can I have them both, Claire?"

"Don't be greedy. Remember, sharing is caring."

Pam pointed her knife my way. "Fine. That one. I want his eyes."

Oh yeah, definitely a nutball.

"Works for me," Claire said, turning her attention Tom's way. "I've heard all about you, you know. And I just want to know one thing – *why?*"

Tom glanced my way, confusion on his face. "Um, why not?"

"Do you think this is funny?!" Claire snapped, right before she let loose with her spell.

She might've been a witch, a powerful one by the look of it, but she obviously wasn't as bright as she thought she was. If she had been, she'd have known that attacking the Icon with magic was...

An effective strategy?

She'd aimed the spell at my best friend, yet not directly. Rather than hit him dead on with the attack, which would've done nothing against his shield of faith, she'd angled it downward – hitting the ground right where his aura ended and causing it to explode like a landmine.

Tom was launched off his feet by the blowback, his faith aura blazing around him. It cushioned his landing, acting like a metaphysical mattress. When he pulled himself back to his feet, though, surprise shown on his face. Worse, there was little doubt his aura was smaller than it had been.

Fuck me sideways with a leaf blower!

When Tom had taken over Sheila's body, he'd inherited her awesome abilities as well, mostly. Lost in the translation, though, had been the unshakable confidence she'd had as the Icon – the source of her power and the thing that fueled her *faith*. In a sense, he was a pretender to the throne, having taken over her kingdom but not the armies that kept it safe – a bit of a false Icon if you will.

Fortunately for him, he was already a bit of an egomaniac. However, unlike her, his self-esteem wasn't an absolute. He needed an external boost to keep going, something he could focus on. That had taken the form of his myriad *investments*, shitty collector's items he was certain would one day pay off big. Without them, it was possible to shake his self-confidence, causing his powers to fizzle and allowing him to be overwhelmed.

I needed to ensure that didn't happen.

"Anything you can say to him, you can say to me," I said, stepping forward and hopefully giving my friend a chance to get his shit together.

"Him?" Pam asked, grinning ever more broadly despite her face looking like it might crack from the effort.

Claire apparently couldn't have given a shit about any of that, though. "Ah, how cute. The Icon and the Freewill, a fairy tale romance – except for the fact that you fucked over the entire world to be together."

"Just for the record, I have never fucked Bill," Tom said from behind me. "And I don't plan on starting."

"Thanks," I replied over my shoulder. "I'm sure that helps."

"Just putting it out there, dude."

Claire wasn't having any of it, staring past me at Tom while she powered up again. "I believed you when you said you had a change of heart. My *parents* believed you!"

"Listen. He's not who you think he..."

A pillar of flame erupted from the ground at my feet, causing me to leap for cover before the soles of my sneakers melted. So much for meaningful conversation.

"She wasn't talking to you, vampire," Pam said.

"We were there at the Source," Claire continued as if she hadn't been interrupted. "We listened to your lies about helping us rebuild our lives. Even after the Freewill showed up to stop us, you said it would all work out. And then the fighting started."

"So?" Tom replied. "It was a fucked up situation. You want a medal or something?"

It was safe to say my best friend had chosen diplomacy as his dump stat.

"Our parents died down there!" Claire snapped.

Oh crap. And suddenly that explained it all. These two, sisters obviously, blamed us for the fuckery that had ensued, despite it being all Gan's fault. Hell, Tom hadn't even been in Sheila's body at the time – being a disembodied ghost for most of it.

Sadly, Claire didn't seem in the mood for rational explanations. As for her whackadoo sibling, well, I had a feeling her bus had already left on a one-way trip to Crazy Town.

"And now we find you here with the Freewill," Claire said, her voice dripping with hate. "Just like they said you'd be."

"Wait. Someone told you we'd be here?"

She shrugged, continuing to focus on Tom. "We're not the only ones who remember what happened. The fancy speeches, the promises, the grandiose plans ... all of it leading to betrayal."

"Yeah, about that. We didn't..."

"So was it all a lie?" she continued, talking over me. "Was

our parents' death just a game to get your boyfriend back, some sick thrill you both got off on? Is that it?"

"I try not to kink shame," Tom replied, his tone cocky despite his stunted faith aura, "but you two cunts are fucked in the head if you think Bill and I are together."

That's what he was most worried about?!

Goddamned idiot!

Sadly, his words had the opposite effect of whatever point he'd been trying to make.

Unless, that is, he'd been hoping for both witches to open fire on us with everything they had.

9

A SONG OF FIRE AND MORE FIRE

Claire once again aimed wide, blowing apart a set of saplings to Tom's left and causing him to divert his power in that direction.

It was impressive. She couldn't have been much older than me when I'd first gotten dragged into the world of the supernatural, yet she was showing a knack for strategy I could barely believe.

Other Magi could've learned a thing or two from this as I watched her quickly put Tom on the defensive, despite his power effectively negating hers.

Sadly, now was not the time to cheer for child prodigies as I found myself just barely dodging – *holy shit* – an actual fireball. It was almost enough to make the gamer in me cheer, had I not been busy desperately trying to survive.

One thing was clear. The craziness inside Pam's head really liked fire. Normal battle magic could be hot as fuck, trust me on this. I'd seen it burn through steel and fuse angry rock monsters into statues. But it was more like a downscaled phaser array. Pam's power was more on the level of a freaking fire bender, a fact driven home as her footprints flared with every step she took.

Any thoughts on this, man? I could really use some strategy right about now.

Sadly, if the Wanderer had any opinions on fighting a fire witch, the lazy bastard was keeping them to himself. Strange. It wasn't like him to let me charge into battle without telling me everything I was doing wrong.

Guess I'm on my own.

That shouldn't have been a problem. I mean, I'd faced off against Magi before, plenty of times as a matter of fact. Something about Pam was off, though.

Normally, mages were artillery fighters. They preferred to blast the shit out of you from afar, only closing in once they could gloat in your face without reprisal. Pam, however, was calmly closing the distance between us as if looking for a fistfight.

I wasn't at one-hundred percent, not after the crash and eating Tom's aura, but I was in more than good enough shape to take down a glorified high schooler.

No doubt about it. Pam was either stupid or bugfuck crazy.

All I needed was one good punch and it would be lights out. Then I could go help Tom.

Easy peasy.

I waited for her next volley, a ball of flame I easily dodged, then I put my all into it – launching myself into a zig zag pattern with my vampire speed, confident I could outmaneuver anything she threw at me.

Except she didn't do anything of the sort. As I raced forward, dodging and weaving, she merely stood there grinning.

Yeah, definitely batshit. It was time to send this chick on a one way trip to Hurtsville.

Or at least it should've been. However, my conscience was having second thoughts.

Angry and crazy as she might've seemed, Pam was, in essence, still a kid. None of this was necessarily her or her sister's fault. Assuming Claire was telling the truth, they'd both seen some shit. Thanks to Gan's machinations, they were every bit as much the victims here as anyone else.

In the past, I'd have decked this witch into next week and

walked away whistling, but recent events were forcing me to rethink my stance.

Maybe I was going soft in my old age, but helping raise Tina was slowly starting to make me see things from a new perspective – especially after Christy's disappearance.

Don't get me wrong. I had no intention of letting Pam fricassee my ass, but I decided to pull my punch once I was in striking distance.

Maybe then I could talk Claire down before things truly turned ugly.

"You fucking crazy bitch!" Tom cried from somewhere.

Okay, maybe things were already ugly, but I could deal with that after I was done with Fire Lord Zuko here.

Pam took a sloppy swipe at me with her glowing pocket knife, ridiculously easy to dodge for someone with vampire reflexes, allowing me to pull back my fist to deliver the finishing...

"Hey there, handsome. Wanna fuck?"

I hesitated at the words coming from her ruined lips, probably the last thing I expected her to say. "Um..."

"Made you look!"

In the next instant, her body seemingly exploded in a pyre of pure flame, so hot and bright that I was instantly blinded – literally as my glasses melted, dousing my eyes with molten polycarbonate.

FUUUUUCK!

I tried to back away, only to realize she was following – no doubt to prolong the agony for as long as possible.

My nerve endings finally overloaded, leaving me unable to see or feel a goddamned thing. However, much to my dismay, my hearing was still working just fine.

"You know what I like best about vampires, cutie? No matter how much I slice away, they keep healing. So I can keep cutting and cutting for as long as I please."

Pam was good to her word. I couldn't see for shit and my skin was pretty much toast, but the nerves deeper inside me still worked well enough to know that this nutcase was trying to turn me into a fucking pin cushion.

I was stabbed maybe half a dozen times. None of the wounds were lethal, to a vamp anyway, but all of them became pools of instant agony as they were cauterized from the inside out – making it feel like my blood had been replaced with gunpowder and someone had shoved a lit match up my ass.

So much for being chivalrous and holding back. Pam was obviously a sick fuck. The second I was able to turn the tables, I needed to knock her fucking block off and end this – assuming I was actually given the chance.

Sadly, it didn't sound like things were going much better for Tom.

"What's happening to that vaunted aura of yours, traitor?" Claire asked from somewhere off to our right. "I thought you were supposed to be a shining beacon of hope, but you're barely even a nightlight."

The injury and pain of this battle was bad enough, but the sheer embarrassment wasn't exactly helping either.

Not to toot my own horn, but I was the freaking Freewill. I'd faced Sasquatches, the Jahabich, Alexander the Great, and even Calibra – the progenitor of all vampires. Yet, here I was, getting my ass absolutely handed to me by a *kid*.

And the *legendary* Icon over there wasn't faring much better.

Hell, just a few hours ago I'd had two gremlin dudes practically sucking my dick as they told me how fate had chosen me as its champion.

It was ironic. In the past that had been my one advantage – facing off against assholes arrogant enough to believe their own hype, causing them to underestimate me until I was able to take them out. And yet here I was, making the same goddamned mistake.

Mind you, I wasn't dead yet.

Blinded and in agony, I still had one option left – something that neither Calibra nor Alex would've ever done, as their egos simply wouldn't have allowed it.

I, on the other hand, wasn't too proud to run for my life.

That didn't mean I wanted to get shot in the back doing so. No. I had to time this correctly – which meant tuning out the agony until I could...

"*AIEEEE!*"

Until I could be sliced up like a Christmas ham. Pam jabbed her knife into my shoulder then began to work her way down, sawing through my charbroiled skin like I was a slab of roast beef.

God fucking damn!

Crazy as the pain was, though, I realized it told me exactly where she was.

I twisted away from her, slicing even more of myself in the process, but it gave me a chance to swing my right arm. It was a crude, sloppy blow, but I wasn't going for precision. I just needed to connect.

Yes! I managed to make contact, hitting Pam with just enough force to shove her away from me. It wasn't going to win me this fight, but that was okay. I just needed to knock her on her ass for a second or two.

Now to hope for a bit of luck on my end.

I spun, pulling the knife from my torso and flinging it away with all my might. Then I ran, hoping there wasn't a tree directly in front of me.

"Oh my! Are you okay, Freewill?"

Glen!

Though his question was mindbogglingly stupid considering my injuries, I could've kissed the little yellow snot bubble. His voice gave me a direction to turn in as I leapt blindly, trying not to trip over any roots.

I landed in something slippery, almost losing my footing in the process – either a mound of bear shit or...

"Hey, watch the feet!"

"Sorry, m-man," I slurred, my lips little more than charcoal briquettes. "I need you to get me behind some cover, fast. The car or maybe a tree."

Fortunately, he seemed to get the hint as something slimy wrapped around my wrist and began to guide me along toward... "Oof!"

"You might want to duck."

"Thanks for the warning."

Clonking my head on a tree branch was thankfully the worst I had to deal with, as moments later my hand touched upon the crushed steel and plastic of the rental – allowing me to inch around to the other side and duck down.

Now I just need a few minutes to...

The melted remains of my lenses fell from my face as my healing finally began to compensate.

Hopefully my spare set of glasses had survived the wreck, because otherwise I wasn't going to be able to see dick once this fight was over. But first I needed to survive that long.

"This is a most exciting battle, isn't it?"

"Not quite the word I'd use," I replied. "Besides, I can't see shit right now, exciting or not."

"Oh, my bad. I sometimes forget how limiting having only two eyes can be."

"Uh huh. Spare me the sympathy card and tell me what's going on."

"You've got it, Freewill." There came the sound of slithering as Glen repositioned his tendrils for a better look. "Ooh, the witch you were fighting is back on her feet. She seems awfully cheerful about something."

"Probably a combination of handing me my ass and being fucking batshit. What else?"

"Tom just ducked down behind some bushes. I can see his aura shining from behind them."

Apparently he wasn't the only one, as Claire called out, "I see you, traitor!"

A moment later there came the sound of splintering wood.

"The good news is the other witch looks winded," Glen continued. "I don't think she has much left."

That was promising, assuming Tom could keep ducking her long enough to...

Hold on, what's that whooshing sound?

"Oh wait. The bad news is the other witch just set all the trees around him on fire."

Fuck!

"If your friend won't come out and play," Pam cried, "I'll just roast you instead."

Double fuck!

In making a run for it, I'd instead made it two against one.

I blinked, realizing I could sort of make out shapes again. Gone was the darkness, and in its place were blurry shadows and the occasional flash of light as the battle continued.

Fuck it. That would have to be good enough.

For what, though?

"I wish I could help," Glen said, "but fire really isn't my thing. Too much heat and my vacuoles turn to steam and explode. It's ... rather unpleasant."

"Tell me about it. I bet it's a real..."

"I hear you!" a crazed singsong response interrupted.

"I should inform you, Freewill, the fire witch is turning our way again."

Just then, something sizzled by over our heads, the heat hard to ignore. "Yeah, kinda gathered that."

"What should we do?"

I wish I knew. I was still mostly blind, my skin was a charred mess, and my brain was slowly filling with sand as my body ate up its energy reserves to heal me – gradually replacing rational thought with a desire to do nothing but eat.

That, and the Wanderer *still* wasn't speaking to me.

The fuck, dude?

Unfortunately, I had a feeling Pam wasn't going to be a good enough sport to let me take a bite out of her. But maybe I didn't have to. "Hey, quick question. How fast do your vacuoles ... explode?"

"Against that kind of heat?" Glen replied. "Pretty quickly."

"Will it hurt you?"

"It's not exactly fun, but if I slough off that part fast enough I should be okay."

"That's all I needed to hear. You're not going to like this next part, good buddy, but I'm gonna need a bit of help if we want to survive this."

Pam approached as I slowly backed away on my hands and knees, the car no longer a viable hiding spot. Fortunately, injured eyes or not, she wasn't very hard to pinpoint. Her body was lit up like the Fourth of July – a blazing pyre of living flame about five and a half feet tall.

It was painfully obvious she knew where I was, so there was no point in pretending anymore.

"Let my friend go," I said, popping my head up, "and you can do with me whatever you please."

"Whatever I please?" Pam replied in a disturbingly wistful tone.

"Um, yeah, sure. I'm yours for the taking."

"What if I wanted to make ... a mask outta your face?" she asked, continuing to saunter my way. "Just a little something to wear around town."

"I ... suppose you could do that." *Come on. Just a little bit further.*

"What if I wanted to make five? Would you keep on healing the more I carved?"

Jesus! "Why not? But I'll need some blood if that's what you're planning."

"Blood isn't an issue," she said, moving ever closer. "Blood is *never* an issue. Just promise me one thing."

"What?"

"That you'll scream."

Somehow I didn't think that would be an issue. On the upside, she was now close enough that I could make out her silhouette inside all that fire. "It's a deal. I'll scream all you want, but first you have to let my friend..."

"Good. Then why don't we quit with the foreplay and get started?"

"Works for me. You first!" *Please don't miss!*

I wasn't much of an athlete growing up. Hell, I'd actively avoided sports like they were the plague. Too bad it wasn't possible to avoid them altogether since there was always gym class. Those forty minutes of the school day were its own special Hell for kids like me, especially whenever it was time to play *dodgeball*.

Heck, if I closed my eyes, I could still feel the impact of those damned red rubber balls colliding with my face.

I just had to hope I remembered it well enough to turn the tables ... with maybe a little help from a friend.

"Now, Glen!"

I'd asked the little blob to compress himself as much as possible, resulting in a goopy ball of snot within my hands as I finally stood up. Go figure, he was about the size of one of those accursed dodgeballs, had one been covered in copious amounts of Vaseline.

Whatever the case. I squinted as I lifted Glen up, seeing Pam tilt her head curiously from inside the blanket of flame, probably wondering where I'd picked up the Beholder-themed beachball.

Then I reared back and threw. I'd never had much of a fastball, but vampire strength was the great equalizer in all things.

Well, maybe all things except aiming.

Even in my blurry nearsightedness, I saw my throw was off. It was going to go high. Fortunately, much like horseshoes and hand grenades, this was one game where close was good enough.

Glen stretched out midair, extending his body until he was more gloppy boomerang than ball. Then a generous piece of him snapped off, slapping into Pam's face while the rest of him went sailing past.

She cried out in surprise at receiving a facial that would've put any porn star to shame. Then, a second or two later, she screamed for real as the heat from her flames reacted with the piece of Glen, just as he'd predicted – exploding in a small cloud of superheated steam.

Disturbingly enough, her cries sounded more annoyed than pained, further driving home the point that this was one witch in desperate need of a good therapist.

Assuming she didn't need a mortician first.

"Pam!"

I once more raced forward into the fray, hoping Claire was as tired as my friend had made her out to be, because if not I was going to be in a world of even more hurt.

I couldn't worry about that, though, at least not until I'd snapped Pam's neck in at least half a dozen different...

As I closed the gap between us, however, my conscience cried out again – reminding me that Pam was just a kid. She was a psychotic, murdering nutcase of a kid, yeah, but a kid nevertheless.

Once again, I found myself thinking about Tina and how she'd been indoctrinated into the weirdness of our lives at a far younger age than any of us would've ever hoped for. What if this had been her?

Don't get me wrong. The tyke could be a bit mercenary when it came to her Disney fund, but I didn't expect to ever find her ambushing people in the woods and making masks out of their skin.

The thing was, violence wasn't exactly uncommon in our world. What if one day she faced a similar situation, in which a vamp like me had to choose between ending her life and sparing it?

I didn't exactly believe in karma but, despite all logic, I pulled my punch nevertheless – reining myself in until I hit her with a blow that was barely more than a vampire love tap.

It might've been the right thing to do, but it was the space of an instant for me to realize it sure as fuck wasn't the *smart* thing.

At the same time I connected, her powers flared up again – burning away the remnants of Glen's squishiness and revealing that the good side of her face now almost matched the rest, her skin scalded red like a lobster's.

She spat out a tooth as she stumbled back – her power having softened the impact even as it turned my hand into a baked potato.

Worse, that creepy smile had returned to her face.

"Well, aren't you sweet," she said, her voice slurred a bit. "I like the sweet ones. They taste better."

Fuck me and my sentimentality.

I saw this was one good deed that wasn't going to go unpunished.

She had me dead to rights, too – at point blank range. Even had I been at my best, I'd have been hard pressed to dodge at this distance.

I doubted Pam was anywhere close to fresh. No way could she be after expending the amount of magic she had. If she was winded, though, she was doing a damned fine job of hiding it.

"I'm gonna boil you from the inside out," she cackled as the flames around her intensified.

Son of a...

This was it. I was done for. And it wasn't even by someone like Turd, Alex, or any of the other heavies I'd gone up against in the past.

Instead, I was about to be ganked by Sabrina the teenage nutjob.

As Pam let loose with her spell, I...

Cried out as there came a sudden flash of purple in the air. Then the flames seemingly parted around me like Moses and the Red Sea.

The fuck?

As I tried to figure out who had suddenly cast a defensive spell to protect me, there came a weird pain in my head – like someone stabbing my frontal lobe with an ice pick.

Oh for Christ's sake! What now?!

"Stop playing around, Pam," Claire cried out from somewhere close by. "Finish him off!"

"I'm not the one doing this."

At least that was good to know. The last thing I wanted was to be offered a lifeline only to have this weirdo shout, "Psych!" before roasting me like a brisket.

However, that still left the question of who had come to my rescue and where they...

Thunk.

"Only warning shot you're getting, bitch."

What the hell?

The flames around Pam died down, allowing me to see what appeared to be a dagger embedded in the ground at her feet.

The fact that it wasn't stuck in my back gave me hope that the cavalry, whoever they might be, had arrived.

"Let's go," Claire cried out. "Time's up."

"Not yet. I want to play with them."

"*Now*, Pam!"

Pam might as well have been a toddler being sent to bed judging by the look which appeared on her ruined face. Murderous nutcase or not, Claire apparently held some authority over her in a demented Master Blaster sort of way.

Either way, Pam disengaged and headed toward the blurry form of her sister. A moment later, there came the telltale flash of light that told me they'd bamfed out of Dodge.

Guess Claire had saved enough in reserve to beat a hasty retreat. That told me she'd either expected us to put up a better fight, or had known company would be joining us.

But who?

That was answered as multiple figures stepped out from behind the surrounding trees.

I still couldn't see very well, but I caught the flap of ornate capes as well as the sight of drawn swords.

When it came to that combo, there was only one group that came to mind – the Templar.

However, the person approaching me at their vanguard was most certainly not Vincent.

So much for our situation improving.

10

WHEN THE SAINTS
GO MARCHING IN

As the newcomers approached, I was forced to rethink my assumptions.

For starters, the Templar typically wore red capes, not blue. Secondly, nobody was screaming about Jesus – at least not yet anyway.

Finally, the biggest tell was when the woman in the lead got near enough for me to make out the black pits of her eyes.

A vampire.

And that wasn't even counting the magic that had been cast.

No doubt about it. Definitely not the Templar, not unless they'd radically changed their membership requirements. Regardless, it would've been the height of stupidity to drop my guard after the last unpleasant surprise.

"Are you okay?" the woman asked, as a handful of others fanned out around us.

"Not really the word I'd use," I replied, trying not to scream as my body continued repairing itself.

With the rush of battle ending, I became acutely aware of how exhausted I felt. It was like my head was rapidly filling with cotton, making it hard to think. The rumble now coming from my stomach wasn't helping either.

Needless to say, it was probably a good thing the Templar weren't here because I'd have probably latched my teeth onto the nearest one.

Fortunately, their leader, whoever she was, seemed to sense my dilemma. She kept her eyes locked on me as she pulled a heavy canteen from her side and handed it over.

"You look like you need this more than I do. It's deer blood. Should be enough to..."

I didn't give her a chance to finish, snatching the canteen from her hand the moment the B-word left her lips. I fumbled with the cap, unscrewing it with shaking hands until...

Oh God!

The scent of the blood hit my nostrils, erasing silly concepts such as good manners and banal pleasantries.

An involuntary hiss escaped my lips as I stepped back and upended the contents into my mouth, chugging it down like it was the last beer at a frat party.

It wasn't quite as good as cow or pig, and most certainly didn't hold a candle to human blood, but whatever. It could've been tainted with horse shit for all I cared at that moment. What mattered was that it was blood and there was almost a gallon of it.

As I guzzled the red nectar, the fog in my head started to clear – forcing back the urge to bite through the bottom of the canteen like a fucking animal so as to get every last drop.

Finally, I felt like I could have a human conversation again. However, along with rational thought came the realization of how badly I'd just gotten my ass handed to me.

No doubt about it. I'd gotten pimp-slapped by a girl barely old enough to drive.

So, of course, Tom picked that moment to meander over and *help* the situation.

"Dude, you look like the gimp piñata at a BDSM convention."

I narrowed my eyes despite being glad that he was okay. "Says the asshole who just spent the last ten minutes running for his life."

"I wasn't running. I was trying to find a strategic location for a counterattack."

"Yeah, good job with that, Davy Crockett."

He shrugged before turning toward the vamp seemingly in charge of this rescue party. "So what's the deal, you guys larpers or something?"

Goddamn it all.

The woman, tall, broad shouldered, and with her blonde hair pulled back in a ponytail, raised an eyebrow at him. "You're welcome by the way."

Before I could try to undo whatever grief Tom had caused, one of her crew approached, another vamp judging by his scent. He locked his gaze on me as he said, "All clear, Zoe."

The unasked for eye-fucking continued for a few uncomfortable moments too long. "What? Is my fly down or something?"

Rather than have the good graces to look away, he continued to stare. "So, you're the Freewill?"

"So I've been told. Why? You want an autograph?"

That prompted the other vamp to tell him, "Go check the perimeter and make sure they're really gone."

The guy locked eyes with me one more time before turning to do what he'd been told.

Once he left, she turned to face me. "Sorry about that. Eric means well, but he can be a bit intense at times."

"Zoe was it?" I handed her the mostly empty canteen. "Thanks for the blood ... and the save."

She acknowledged me with a faint smile.

"Oh, and don't mind him," I added, hooking a thumb Tom's way. "He tends to get testy after getting his ass kicked."

"Fuck you, dude."

"Not on your best day."

The woman waited for our banter to end and then said, "I'm sorry about what happened. We didn't think Claire still had any friends on the inside. Had I known, we would've done everything we could to head them off at the pass."

"What do you mean on the inside?"

"Purgatory, of course."

Tom turned her way. "Wait. Are you telling me those fucking psychos are yours?"

Zoe shook her head, though. "*Were* ours. They and some of their friends orchestrated an ambush a few weeks back. People got hurt – Liz, your friend Kelly, and a few others. We got some of them, but the sisters managed to get away. They've been in the wind ever since."

"Seems Kelly failed to mention that little factoid during her sales pitch."

"Don't be mad at her. Purgatory's an accepting place, that's kind of the point. Hell, it's the whole reason me and my crew are here."

"But?" I prompted, waiting for the other shoe to drop.

She shrugged. "*But*, there's a lot of people living there. Some have had a rougher time of it than others. And a few apparently still carry a grudge."

"No shit," Tom remarked.

I couldn't disagree. Earlier, Liz had reminded us of our time down at the Source chamber, right before launching into a speech about broken people just wanting to get their lives back. It had served to make me forget there'd been some hard cases in that bunch, people who hadn't hesitated to kidnap or kill to get what they wanted.

Thankfully, before this could devolve into a full blown argument with our rescuers, one of them cried, "Glen? Holy shit, is that you?"

I turned to see the little blob slithering toward one of the caped do-gooders who'd been surveying the wreckage of our car. "Oh, hey, Brent. Long time no see."

"Where have you been all this time? A bunch of us looked for you ... well, *after*."

"I've been rooming with the Freewill and the Icon. It's been a most thrilling experience."

"No shit, really? I thought you were trying to get home."

Huh?

"So, anyway, what's the deal with the capes?" Tom asked,

dragging me back to our conversation with Zoe. "Were you guys out playing Robin Hood or something before realizing those assholes were fucking us up in Sherwood Forest?"

I spared a quick glance toward Glen before realizing that would have to wait. I probably needed to keep Tom from being a total dick to these people.

Not to mention, I was curious as to their attire too.

Rather than run my friend through for being a prick, Zoe lifted the edge of her cape and smirked. "These are the official colors of the Order of Saint Cyprian. Although, just for the record, I'd have been happy with a t-shirt. But that's what you get when an ex-Templar is calling the shots."

Apparently I was right in making the connection. "Wait. You don't mean Vincent, do you?"

She nodded. "One and the same."

"But the Templar were..."

"Against people like us?" She glanced around, as if making sure nobody was eavesdropping. "Trust me. I've heard all about it. I used to read about them when I was a kid, but I didn't realize until recently they'd gone from fighting in the Crusades to a secret order devoted to hunting monsters."

"Devoted is one word for it."

"Again, so I've heard. But we're not them. Vincent founded the Order as a kinder, gentler offshoot of the Templar. Same mission and devotion, but with more nuance allowed for judging people by their actions and not whether they have fangs in their mouth."

"Really?"

"It's all in our name. Cyprian was both a wizard and a priest back in the early days of the church, long before they decided to burn anyone who looked at broomsticks the wrong way."

"Wait, a wizard *and* a priest?"

"Yep, apparently they knew how to multitask back in the day."

"So then that means you're a vampire..."

"As well as a practicing Catholic? Yep." She reached into her shirt and pulled out the tiny crucifix worn around her neck.

Huh. Well if that wasn't a kick in the balls, I didn't know what was. "Then what about faith magic? I mean, obviously vamps can't use it, but those who can..."

She shrugged. "Another form of magic, like all the rest – just one that regular folks can tap into. Belief based, yes, but not necessarily having anything to do with God."

I glanced Tom's way. "I hear you there."

"Fuck you, dude. You're talking to their Blessed One here."

"Not anymore," Zoe said with a smirk. "Vincent told us all about you, and well, after having talked to you, let's just say I understand why he put heavy emphasis on the nothing to do with God part."

◆————✦————▶

It turned out Zoe and her team had been sent to the coordinates we'd been given, to escort us the rest of the way. We'd simply gotten lucky in that they'd realized something was amiss – probably thanks to Pam's over-enthusiastic attempts to burn down the forest.

Her people helped us salvage what we could from the wreckage before heading out. A good chunk of our belongings were lost in the magic fueled rampage but not all, thanks to some hard case luggage I owned from years back – as well as some of it being a bit harder to destroy than others.

Soon enough, with spare glasses on my face and clean clothes covering my freshly regrown skin, we followed Zoe and her merry men through the forest – Tom's sword strapped to his back while a certain magic hammer was tucked safely among the rest of the stuff I'd recovered.

As Glen slithered along in front of us, catching up with his buddy Brent, Tom and I fell to the back of the procession.

"What the hell was up with you back there?" he asked,

his voice low – albeit probably not low enough for any vamps listening in.

"What are you talking about?"

"The fight. You had at least two opportunities to finish off that nutcase."

"Me? You're the one who's supposed to be magicproof. What, did you forget to charge your batteries last night?"

"I couldn't get to my sword and you know it."

"You don't need your sword. Sheila used to..."

"I'm not her," he snapped before dialing it back a notch. "I'm still figuring out this shit, okay."

"Figure it out faster."

"It's not that easy, asshole."

"Why not?"

"You don't understand. Inside my head I'm still me – the old me. You know, awesome yet still killable. It's not always so easy to remember things are different now, especially when some witch is trying to cook my ass. The sword and the figures I tied to it give me something to focus on."

I got what he was saying. It was easy to talk a big game, but absolute confidence wasn't necessarily a given – especially considering our recent failures.

"I know. I'm sorry I gave you shit about it."

"It's cool," he said. "So anyway, what's your excuse?"

I was tempted to give him some bullshit, but instead opted for the truth – I'd gotten sidetracked looking at Pam through the lens of knowing Tina.

After I was done, he shook his head and sighed. "Goddamn, dude. We must be getting old. None of this pussy shit would've ever bothered us before."

I shrugged. "Feels that way sometimes."

"That says a lot coming from the guy who's going to live forever."

"Or the one who can't be hurt by anything."

He nodded. "How much you want to wager all the fuckers we took out over the years are laughing at us from whatever Hell they're in?"

"I'm not taking that bet."

He let out a chuckle. "I'll make you a deal, man. Next time something like this happens, remind me not to be such a fucking basket case."

"Can do."

"Good. And the next time a teenage girl is kicking your ass, I'll remind you of all the times you tried to punch Gan's lights out."

"Fair enough."

He had a point there. Of course, the person I'd been in those days had never had to care for a small child. Hell, the concept of kids hadn't even been on my radar back then, despite Christy being pregnant for a good chunk of it.

The old me wouldn't have thought twice about decking a witch, even one in training pants. Mind you, that probably made the old me a bit of an asshole. At the same time, he wouldn't have gotten schooled by a girl who still needed a fake ID to buy beer.

Goddamn. I swear, next thing you knew, someone was going to take one of my friends hostage, tell me to drop my weapon, and I'd actually do it – naïvely believing they'd keep their word.

At that point I'd be less a vampire and more a walking TV trope.

Shit. If that were the case I might as well wait for the sun to rise, lest I start hanging out around high schools pining for lost love.

Fortunately, my trip to the land of bad clichés was cut short as the group ahead of us abruptly stopped.

For a moment, I wondered if they'd overheard us. But then the wind shifted and I caught a change in the scents around us. It was subtle, barely perceptible against the smells of the forest, but there nevertheless. I couldn't quite put my finger on what it was, but something had changed.

"We taking a rest break?" Tom asked.

Rather than answer, Zoe drew her sword and held it out in front of her, where the tip seemingly disappeared as the air around it rippled like waves in a pond.

Magic!

Was that what I'd just smelled?

With the Wanderer still giving me the silent treatment, there was no way for me to know for certain.

I was pretty sure of one thing, though.

We'd finally made it to Purgatory.

11

THE MEDIUM PLACE

I'd never liked camping, something my family and friends could attest to, so I already suspected that Purgatory was going to be closer to a living hell, but I didn't realize how much until I stepped through the magical barrier.

My head started pounding the second I was inside, feeling like I'd woken up with a hangover. Maybe it was a reaction to the deer blood, another side effect of my failed evolution, or the Wanderer playing handball inside my skull just because he could. Either way, I suddenly had a headache that seemed to defy all vampire healing logic.

Apparently I was alone in this, too, because Zoe and her crew didn't give the slightest indication that they were experiencing any discomfort.

Just my fucking luck.

It didn't get much better as we reached the main encampment. Glen practically received a hero's welcome upon our arrival. Judging by the numerous greetings that met him, you'd have thought he was Norm returning to Cheers.

At first, people likewise seemed happy to see Tom, which I found kind of strange – at least until I realized they probably thought he was Sheila, their would-be savior having returned. It was easy to forget the vast majority of the supernatural world wasn't aware they'd done a soul swap.

However, the warm reception quickly turned frosty when they saw me. Even had I not punched out my fair share of Magi back in the day, they probably all remembered me as that guy who'd tried to stop them from getting their magic back.

My vampire hearing was quick to catch the snide whispers that followed.

"Is that the Freewill? What's he doing here?"

"Guess they'll let anyone in this place now."

"Hold on, are they together?"

"No way. She can't be shacking up with him again."

"Play it cool," I whispered to Tom, "Pretty sure most of these guys think you're Sheila. Maybe we can use that to our..."

That stopped him dead in his tracks, a look of horror on his face as he turned to the gathered crowd of onlookers.

"Wait, what are you...?"

"I don't know what you assholes are thinking," he cried out for all to hear, "but my name is Tom, and I can assure you that Bill and I are *not* fucking."

Go figure. That was precisely what I didn't want him to do.

If Zoe was hoping to find whoever had sold us out to those two psychos earlier, I had a feeling her work was cut out for her. Far as I could tell from the glares we got after Tom's proclamation, we were surrounded by nothing but potential suspects.

They'd just finished showing us to our tents when the most welcome of voices caught my attention.

"Daddy! Uncle Bill!"

We both looked to see Tina running our way, turning an otherwise shitty night just a little bit brighter.

She practically launched herself into Tom's arms as I

spied Kelly approaching in her wake, accompanied by a four-winged pixie thing that looked vaguely familiar.

They stopped to confer with Zoe, giving us a few moments to dote on the tyke.

"Did you and Uncle Bill really get all beat up?" Tina asked as her father lifted her from the ground.

Guess gossip traveled fast here.

"Nah. Daddy's fine," Tom said. "Your uncle's the only one who got his ass beat."

"Don't lie to her, dickhead."

Tina turned solemnly my way. "You said a bad word, Uncle Bill."

"Me? What about him?"

Tina shook her head, for a moment looking older than her five years. "Mommy says Daddy doesn't know any better."

"That's because your daddy is a fucking moron." I instinctively reached for my wallet before remembering it had been incinerated in the attack. "Um, I'll have to owe you."

"It's okay, Uncle Bill. Daddy taught me about IOUs."

"That's right, Cheetara," Tom said, a big grin on his face, "you take Uncle Bill for everything he's worth, which isn't much right now."

I quickly changed the subject before the idiot could spill the beans on why I was really broke. "So how are you doing, Cat? Do you like it here?"

"It's great! There's lots of other kids. We play, go hiking, and practice our magic together. It's so much fun!"

I raised an eyebrow at that last one, just as Kelly and her companion joined us.

"Holy shit," she cried. "We heard what happened. Are you okay?"

I waited to see if Tina was going to chide her on her language, but of course she didn't. "Yeah, we'll live."

"Thank goodness."

"Was a hell of a welcome wagon, though."

"I'll bet. I'm so sorry. I didn't think they'd..."

"It's okay," I replied. "We're fine. Although, speaking of

unexpected surprises, Tina just said she's been doing magic with the other kids."

"I bet she's totally blowing them out of the water," Tom remarked.

"I'm more concerned with her blowing them up." I lowered my voice. "Am I wrong here or is that about the most dangerous thing she could possibly be doing?"

"We should probably catch up," Kelly said with a sigh. "Come on, we can talk in private while Ux is giving you the tour."

"We've met, haven't we?" I asked as we were shown around Purgatory, keeping the discussion light while in earshot of any onlookers. "I mean, down below at the..."

"Indeed, Freewill," the pixie, Ux, replied. "Please allow me to once again apologize for all that transpired there."

"It's cool, man. No changing the past. We can only move forward."

"I very much agree," he replied diplomatically. "Hence why I moved to found this sanctuary. It is my way of atoning for what happened – offering succor to those who are either unable to return to their former lives or not yet ready."

I got the sense he was being sincere. That and it was obvious people looked up to him here, as many of the hostile glares from earlier subsided once they saw him showing us around.

I had to admit, headache aside, it wasn't a bad setup once you got the lay of the land. The air was clear, most of the food was grown locally in the various gardens scattered about, and the water came fresh from a nearby brook. I had a feeling the latrines were going to suck donkey balls, but it's not like Ux was trying to pass this off as a five star hotel.

From what I could tell, roughly half the denizens lived in simple tents or makeshift shelters, while others had magicked up a network of wispy looking tree houses in the branches high above. I got the sense the latter was to help keep watch over things as well as accommodate some of the more esoteric looking guests, of which there were plenty.

If anything, I was reminded of the gathering up in the Mourning Woods years back, minus the giant murder apes waiting behind every tree.

Though most of the populace appeared to be Magi, with some humans and vampires scattered about, I also caught sight of beings made of both rock and fire, creatures with three or more arms, winged thingamabobs, and even a few amorphous blobs rolling about. Some I vaguely remembered the names of – terrocks, wisps, and a few others. The rest, well, I was sure I'd find out eventually.

In short, there was no doubt this place was a magical melting pot.

"That's where I go to school," Tina cried as we passed a meadow encircled by tents and alit with glowing orbs that hung midair, as if that were the most normal thing in the world.

"Yes, you do, sweetie," Kelly said, stepping in. "Speaking of which, you have class tomorrow. I let you stay up late so you could say hi, but it's probably time for you to turn in."

"Aww!" She turned to her father, no doubt hoping he'd intervene, but the big yawn that followed immediately undermined her position.

"Go on now," Kelly continued. "I need to talk to your father and Bill for a bit. Ux, if you would."

"Of course. Come, child. I'll tuck you in."

"Okay." She took one of the pixie's delicate hands. "Can you tell me a story?"

"Indeed," he replied gently, leading her away. "Perhaps the tale of my ancestor Zirx the Glorious, and the grand adventure he had in the yawning hole of oblivion?"

"Ooh, that's a good one," she replied happily before turning to wave at us. "Night, Daddy! Night, Uncle Bill."

"Goodnight!"

"Go straight to bed," Tom called after her. "Don't stay up late listening to stories about glory holes."

"Seriously?" I replied.

"Like there was any chance of me letting that one slip by."

Once we were alone, Kelly led us down a path away from the main encampment.

"There's regular security patrols," she explained, "but we should have time to catch up in between."

"Those blue-cloaked guys?"

"The Order of Saint Cyprian," she said with a nod.

"I see Vincent's been busy."

"We all have. It's been nice seeing this new version of the Templar evolve – still fighting evil while being far less dickish about it."

"Not gonna argue on that one."

"Where is he by the way?" Tom asked.

"Ironically enough, back in the city with some of the new members. He's trying to recruit some of his old brothers." She shook her head. "Personally, I think it's a lost cause. Most of them have their crucifixes jammed too far up their own assholes. You didn't hear that from me, though."

"Too bad," he remarked. "I was hoping to get in some practice."

Just a week ago, hearing that from Tom's lips would've left me wondering if he'd been replaced by a pod person, but it just went to prove he was taking things more seriously after what happened to Christy. Mind you, not serious enough to keep from telling a glory hole joke within earshot of the guy running this place.

Oh well, Rome wasn't built in a day.

"So, anyway, about Tina and her magic," I said, changing the subject. "I can't help but notice this place isn't a smoldering crater, which is good. Even so, having her practice..."

Kelly held up a hand. "I understand your concern, but you've got it all wrong. V, Liz and Ux are the only others here who know what she's really capable of. And before you say anything, I had to tell him. I owe him that much after everything he did for..."

"V?" I asked. "Hold on, is...?"

"Yeah. Veronica's here too."

She was another of Christy's coven sisters from five years ago. Last I'd heard, she'd moved away to pursue a degree in physics. Now that magic was back, I guess she'd decided breaking the rules of nature was more fun than studying them. "Cool, what's she up to?"

"Hopefully asleep in bed. She's still recovering."

"What from?"

"She was hurt pretty bad by the mutual *friends* you met earlier. Almost didn't make it, but Ux made sure she had the best care possible."

"Oh crap. Glad she's okay."

"Me too," Kelly said, a faint smile upon her lips. "But anyway, back to the point. Most Magi come into their power in their teens, but it's not unheard of for it to happen to children. Considering who her mom is, nobody's really batting an eye at Tina being a prodigy. They just don't know to what degree."

"Hey, she takes after her dad too," Tom complained.

"Sure, whatever. Anyway, you wouldn't have been able to tell from the dress she was wearing, but she had leggings on beneath that are embroidered with binding wards. In fact, all her undergarments are."

"Warded underwear?" I asked, raising an eyebrow.

"I know how it sounds, but trust me it works. You can thank Liz for that. She's been trying to get Vince to incorporate some protection magic into the Order's cloaks. Once Tina got here, though, she offered to test out the idea with binding magic instead."

"And it worked?"

"Like a charm. You'd never suspect she was anything other than a normal witch. Mind you, I don't think they'd contain her if she put her heart into it, but so far so good."

"Glad to hear it. Is she getting along okay? Any blowback? I mean, Christy wasn't ... *isn't* exactly universally beloved among the Magi."

"None that I've seen," she said. "Everyone here loves her. And the mentors have been absolutely tickled pink at the idea of teaching magic to someone so young. Trust me, considering the rest of their pupils are all moody-ass teenagers, Tina's a breath of fresh air."

"That's my girl," Tom replied. "Kicking ass and taking names."

Kelly inclined her head. "You're not too far off. She's soaking up lessons like a sponge. The kid truly is amazing. I swear, she could become the youngest Grand Mentor in history if she wanted."

"Probably not arrogant enough," I remarked.

Either way, I was glad to hear she was fitting in. Neither Tom nor I had been overeager to let the tyke out of our sight. However, the stark reality was, though I liked to think we were capable of doing right by her as a child, neither of us was even remotely qualified to care for her needs as a witch, whereas Kelly was.

That said, hearing about her progress was awesome, but I had a feeling it was only part of the reason we'd been led out here. "So how's it going with her *otherwise?*"

Kelly took a deep breath before replying, "Promising, and that's putting it mildly."

Tom and I shared a glance, although I had a feeling neither of us wanted to get our hopes up prematurely. "How so?"

"Remember what she said earlier, when you guys first got here?"

"About Bill owing her money?"

"No. She said that her mother told her you didn't know any better."

"So?"

"Well, I don't know if you caught it or not, but she was speaking in the present tense. I'm fairly sure that's no accident."

"Go on."

"I didn't want to say anything earlier, not with the apartment compromised, but that isn't the only time. She's been talking about conversations they've had, things her mother has told her. Not to mention, just look at her. She's not acting like a child who's lost a loved one. If anything, the opposite is true. She's happy as a clam. No tears, no nightmares, none of that. And then there's Liz."

"What about her?" Tom's eyes narrowed. "Just say the word and I'll shove my sword right up her..."

"It's not like that. I'm no expert in mind magic. Neither is Liz, but she's better than I am. Anyway, she's been doing some light aura scrying around Tina's tent. Nothing too intense so as to be noticed, but she's convinced this isn't just a child's overactive imagination at work. There's some kind of psychic connection being made. She can't track it, but she's convinced it's there and I have no reason to doubt her."

I leaned in, trying not to get more excited than was warranted. "Are you saying what I think you are?"

"Yep. Tina's reaching out and making contact, which almost certainly means Christy is out there somewhere waiting for us."

I hadn't doubted it for a second, but hearing her say so out loud finally made it truly real.

12

SNACK RUN

"Fuck you, dude! Try that shit again. I dare you!"

"Come on." I grabbed Tom's arm and escorted him out of the all-night convenience store. "Let's find someplace else, since this one is obviously off the list now."

Fortunately, his aura didn't ignite on the way out, which would've made things even more awkward.

"Seriously?" I asked, slipping behind the wheel of the old Jeep. "Did you have to make a scene?"

"Hell yeah. Five bucks for a bag of Funyuns? You've gotta be fucking kidding me."

"You're not even the one paying for them."

"It's the principle of the thing, dude. The folks back in Hell will thank me."

"Purgatory."

"It's Hell for those of us who remember the joy of real toilets."

He wasn't entirely wrong, toilets or not. These supply runs were my only moments of peace. That headache I'd gotten my first night had turned out to be a chronic issue. I still wasn't sure why, but it seemed to have something to do with Purgatory itself.

Maybe it was the magic dome shielding it from outsiders, or perhaps my upgrade had made me allergic to other supernatural beings. Either way, the only relief to be had was stepping foot outside – something I wasn't keen to do for fear Claire and her crazy-ass sister might be waiting, despite Liz's assurances that security had been stepped up.

After a week of that shit, though, I'd had enough – practically leaping at the opportunity to join the supply run roster.

Tom joined, too, although in his case it was more because the other option was real work, like tending the garden or helping out during school hours. The lazy fuck had been none too pleased to find that being the Icon afforded him no special privileges in Purgatory.

The supply runs also served as a distraction while waiting for progress on the Christy front, not to mention the fact that the Wanderer was still nowhere to be found in the recesses of my mind. As much as I appreciated having the premises to myself again, it was starting to worry me.

From a practical standpoint, it had given me a chance to pick up a burner smartphone along with a prepaid data plan.

There was no cell service back in Purgatory, but it gave me something to do on our jaunts – like learning that none of my tenants had been eaten by werewolves yet, good to know since rent was due.

I also managed to briefly touch base with Ed a few times, enough to know he and the others were safe and that so far the coast was clear.

Glad to see shit was working out for at least one of us.

Best yet, having a phone again gave me an excuse to tune out Tom, who was still busy bitching about the price of snack food. So, rather than listen to him complain, I turned it on one-handed only to find five messages waiting on my voicemail.

The first two were from tenants – one asking me to fix a leaky faucet, no big deal, the second complaining about their garbage disposal being clogged. All minor shit.

The third message was too garbled to make out – probably some shitbag robocaller wondering about my car's extended warranty. I deleted it and moved on.

Next was Ed, checking in again and letting me know that all was still quiet. He made no mention of how things with Kara were going, but I suppose that was his business to deal with.

I was thinking it was all going to be a big bag of nothing, when my eyes meandered down to the last number on the list – my parents'.

That was always enough to cause a flutter in my chest, especially during these uncertain times. I'd managed to keep them in the dark about my supernatural lifestyle, but there'd been some close calls – enough to make me paranoid.

Fortunately, I needn't have worried as my dad's voice blared from the tinny speaker.

"It's your father, William. Call me when you get a chance. We need someone to watch Petunia for a while. Your mother won a free weekend down in Atlantic City from her church raffle and I figure maybe we'll stay a few extra days on top of that. Anyway, I'm heading into the city tomorrow on business, so I'll pop by your place first and drop her off."

Ugh. That could be an issue.

"Who's Petunia?" Tom asked from the passenger seat.

"Mom's new kitten."

"Dude, I don't want some cat shitting on my bed."

"Not a problem since neither of us has one."

"Touché." He shook his head and let out a sigh. "This fucking sucks. I don't know how much more of this Swiss Family Robinson bullshit I can take. Half the people there look at me with goo-goo eyes like I should be blessing their dirty asses, while the rest think I'm riding your dick in the woods every night. It's driving me nuts."

"I hear you there."

"And don't even get me started on Glen, slithering around like he owns the fucking place."

"Never knew he was so popular."

"Me neither. Anyway, next time you run into Liz check how things are going. Not to rush shit, but the sooner we save Christy, the sooner I can stop brushing pine needles out of my ass crack."

"Why not ask her yourself?"

"I would, but the last time we spoke she threatened to fill my sleeping bag with leeches."

"What did you say to her?"

"Nothing. Or at least nothing I haven't said before."

"Which is kind of the whole problem right there."

He wasn't wrong on me needing to check in. The last day or so had been too hectic, thanks to one of the resident witches going into labor, which had set the community into a tizzy of preparing for the newborn's arrival.

Therein lay the problem. Liz was helping us, but she was still very much one of Purgatory's leaders – meaning her time was split. There were only so many hours she could devote to working with Kelly.

Maybe I could do something about that, though. I had an ace up my sleeve, one I'd been holding back – at least until I was sure Liz wasn't going to stab us in the back. Watching her work with the community this last week, though, had gone a long way toward easing that worry.

I glanced down at the touchscreen in my hands.

Yeah. I didn't know dick about magic but I was pretty handy around a computer, which meant that maybe I could be of more assistance than either witch might've suspected.

Coherent thought wasn't the easiest thing with the perpetual ice cream headache I seemed to have when beneath Purgatory's dome.

Regardless, after returning from our supply run I took the time to consider my plan of attack before seeking out Kelly and Liz – finally finding them conversing together just off the main encampment.

"So ... any luck?" I asked, approaching.

"Yeah," Liz said. "The nursery is almost finished and a group at the northern end of camp thinks they can whip up an orb of Amun-Ra to keep the lights on. That should be a hell of a lot quieter than a generator."

"I meant with our *secret project*."

Liz shook her head. "I know what you meant, and I figured the answer was kind of obvious. Sorry, nobody expected Ellen's water to break for at least another three weeks."

"Fine, but now that the nursery is almost done..."

"We're working on it, Bill," Kelly interrupted. "Believe me, we are. I want to find her as much as you do."

"Not doubting that, but..."

"Let me guess, you're going stir crazy?"

"Not to put too fine of a point on it, but yes. What about Tina? Could she...?"

"It's like I told you, Tina can sense her mother from time to time, but it's vague. Not to mention, sensing her and finding her are two different things."

"It would be different if she was just lost out in the woods somewhere," Liz added. "But this is the freaking multiverse we're talking about here. It's not like there's a roadmap for what we're doing."

I turned to Kelly. "What about that time you guys brought Decker's soul back? It seemed like you found him easy enough."

"Not the same thing," she replied. "Harry's spirit was still partially tethered to his skull. All we had to do was follow it and give a tug. That's child's play compared to what we're trying to do now."

"Heretical child's play," Liz remarked, drawing a quick glare from Kelly.

"What's a little heresy when your so-called sisters have already dismissed you as a traitor?"

"Excuse me for respecting our rules."

"Because that's so much better than being loyal to your friends."

I backed up a step. "Do you two need a moment?"

Liz looked like she wanted to say something, but then shook her head. "No. Just a minor disagreement over *politics*, that's all. Anyway, back to the point, finding Christy is going to require precision work, and that's not even counting rescuing her. We can't just go knocking on metaphysical windows and asking the resident entities if they've seen a brunette witch wandering around."

"Why not?"

"Because some of those entities will eat our faces off."

Kelly nodded. "She's not wrong. There's also the amount of power it's going to take. Random shots in the dark would exhaust every witch here in short order, and that's assuming they'd all be on board to help, which I can guarantee won't be the case."

"Yeah," Liz confirmed. "People here might grudgingly respect Christy for her accomplishments as a witch, but that doesn't mean they're going to lift a finger to help her."

Kelly made a derisive sound. "Too many of them still think the White Mother's shit didn't stink and that we're the bad guys for stopping her."

"And nothing you do is going to convince them otherwise," Liz pointed out, not unkindly.

"I know." She shook her head. "But that's kind of getting off track anyway. The fact is, Christy fell through one of the thirteen Sources Gan opened."

"With a little help," I added.

"Obviously. My point is, they collectively channel all of Earth's magic. That means she could literally be anywhere in the multiverse. If we could access that Source again, maybe we could trace her, *maybe*."

"Except that it was destroyed."

Kelly nodded. "I think you're beginning to see the problem here."

She was right. Even had it not been, I doubted Gan would've given us access again, willingly or otherwise – not that I wouldn't have been willing to try.

"So that leaves the big question of how we go about finding one of the other Sources," Liz replied. "Preferably without Gansetseg's assistance, because I don't know about the rest of you but I would sooner put a bullet in that fucking bitch's face than give her the time of day."

Ah, if it were only so easy.

Liz had a point, though. Gan knew where the remaining twelve Sources were. It was possible we, and by that I meant *I*, could get her to tell me where another was. The problem was knowing what price she'd demand, and I wasn't just talking about me ending up tied to her bedpost.

No. I would scale mountains to get Christy back, but becoming Gan's personal hitman against one of my best friends – assuming Sally was even still alive – wasn't something I was ready to agree to, not yet.

That was a deal with the devil if ever there was one.

"Okay, so then how do we find one without tipping Gan off?" I asked.

"I'm not sure we do. Let's not forget the original remained hidden for something like five thousand years. Who's to say how long it'll take us?"

Kelly, however, wasn't as quick to dismiss that idea. "What about the ley lines? I mean, we know they're connected to the portals."

"Same deal," Liz said with a dismissive shake of her head. "It's a snipe hunt. You could easily devote the rest of your life to it and still come up empty. Let's not forget, each one circumnavigates the entire globe, crisscrossing with the rest. We're talking tens of thousands of miles here – and that's not even counting where they run deep and can't be easily tracked."

"So where does that leave us?" I asked.

"Up shit creek without a paddle, at least so far anyway. We'd need some way of tracking one down without getting anyone else involved. That's either going to require someone already in the know..."

"Doubtful, considering Gan's employment contracts call for death before disloyalty."

"Barring that, we'd need access to tracking magic more

precise than anything I know of, which I'm not sure even exists."

Bingo! Maybe it did and maybe it didn't, but I knew of one way to find out for certain.

Now I just needed to figure out how to share the news without getting vaporized on the spot.

13

HONOR AMONG THIEVES

"So where's this breach in the dome you found?"

"There isn't one. I lied to get you out here alone."

Kelly raised an eyebrow. "This isn't some ploy to put the moves on me, is it? Because I have to tell you, that ship has sailed. Me and Vince are good these days and, no offense, but I'm not sure he'd be into a vampire threesome."

Okay, that was a bit unexpected. "Intriguing as the idea might be, let's put that one to bed. I mean separate beds." Okay this was going nowhere fast. It was time to get to the point. "I have something you need to see but I couldn't show you in front of the others, not even Liz – at least not yet."

"Why?"

"Because Christy freaked out when I first showed her."

She raised a dubious eyebrow to that.

"No, I'm not talking about my dick."

"Sorry, just making sure."

"Anyway, I sort of get the impression that Liz is even more of a stickler for the rules – Magi rules that is."

Kelly nodded. "Okay, I'm listening."

"This way," I said, heading toward the edge of the protective dome.

"Why?"

"Because I can't get any bars in here, and it's easier to think outside."

"Huh?"

"Never mind that last part. Just follow me."

I stepped through the protective glamour, just as the pounding in my head subsided. I swear, if it weren't for Tina I'd have said fuck this shit and taken my chances back in Brooklyn.

Kelly hesitated before following. For a moment I wondered if it was me, but then I remembered what she'd told me about Pam and Claire.

Well, okay, it could've still been me. After all, here I was leading her into the woods without telling her why.

Yeah, safe to say I could have thought this strategy through a bit better.

However, as I was pondering whether I'd inadvertently stepped over the line into the creep zone, she finally followed me out.

"Okay, we're here. So what's the deal?"

"This is." I pulled out my phone and powered it on, checking the signal strength. One bar solid and a second flickering. *Good enough.*

I took a listen, making sure nobody else was in the area, then said, "I take it you're familiar with the Falcon Archives."

"I've heard of it. Supposedly it's a super-secret library of forbidden arcana." She cocked her head. "Wait. How do *you* know about it? When I say secret, I mean..."

"Top secret, trespassers will be shot on sight. Yeah, I kinda figured. But just for the record, Matt Falcon never fucking shuts up about it."

"Hold on. You mean that guy Christy said was helping you out is actually *the* Matthias Falcon? Holy shit! She even mentioned his name but I didn't make the connection. That's freaking wild. They're supposed to be one of the oldest and richest Magi families in Europe."

"No supposedly about it. I saw the guy's setup back in Manhattan ... before we accidentally destroyed it. Long story."

Oddly enough, she didn't seem all too surprised by that last part. Guess I had a bit of a reputation.

"Okay, so he told you about the Archives," she continued. "And you think we should maybe ask him for his help with our secret project?"

"Not exactly. See, we didn't exactly part on good terms last time we saw each other."

"Why not?"

"I sort of murdered a witch right in front of him."

"I can see how that might be an issue."

"Trust me, it was extenuating circumstances. Anyway, that's not the point. This is." I loaded the web browser and held up the screen for her to see.

"What am I looking at?"

"The login screen to said Archives. Apparently Mattie's minions have been busy little bees, working to digitize it these last five years."

"Wow! Are you saying he actually let you have access?"

"Let is a very strong word."

Kelly's eyes opened wide. If she was going to lose her shit like Christy it was going to be now. Instead, she let out a laugh. "Holy shit, Bill. You fucking hacked the Falcon Archives?"

"Pretty much."

"That is so badass!" She stepped back and appeared to consider this. "So did their security suck or what?"

"How'd you guess?"

"Call it a hunch. I tried to show a Mentor from Long Island how to use Gmail a while back. You'd have sworn I was speaking in tongues."

"You're not wrong. Took a few hours, but that was just running a brute force cracker, nothing more."

"Okay, so security aside, are you saying there might be something in there that can help bring Christy back?"

I nodded. "Possibly. Remember when Liz mentioned tracking magic? Well, before ... y'know ... Christy had found something to help us rescue Ed. It was a supercharged tracking spell capable of blasting through wards and other shit."

"Wait. *Christy* found it? I thought you said she freaked out."

"At first, yes, but then she had a change of heart."

"Son of a bitch. Guess our girl is a rebel after all."

"Oh yeah. She used a bunch of stuff from the Archives to save our asses up at Gan's. That's how she was able to tap into the Source's power."

"That was an Archive spell? Actually, that makes perfect sense. Back when you were telling me what happened, I thought something got lost in the translation since I couldn't for the life of me figure out how she could've tapped into that much power. It didn't add up. But now..." A big smile crossed her lips. "This is great news!"

"You think?"

"I don't just think, I know! You see, a skilled witch can reverse engineer a spell down to its components and then create something new from it. Christy could've done it and I'm pretty sure Liz can too. Hell, even if there isn't the sort of tracking spell we need, if we can find what she used to tap into the Source, then maybe we can isolate the frequencies and use that to find where she is."

"Totally losing me now."

"That's fine. All you need to know is this doesn't seem nearly as impossible anymore."

"Exactly what I was hoping to hear." I called up the keyboard and started typing in the credentials from memory.

Then I typed them in again.

And then a third time.

Motherfucker! "No good. He must've changed his password."

"Can't you just crack it again?"

"Probably, but not with this piece of shit."

"Okay, tell me what you need."

"A laptop someone isn't going to miss and an internet connection that's faster than the dialup speeds I'm getting out here."

Kelly nodded. "Let me take care of the laptop. As for the rest, I think I'll join you on tomorrow's supply run. Sounds to me like it's time for a little road trip."

Kelly was good to her word. She managed to borrow – or steal, I didn't ask which – a relatively decent laptop. After that it was a minor effort to find a coffee shop that kept late hours and had free Wi-Fi.

Sadly, that was where our streak of good luck ended.

A couple hours later found me scrambling away from the smoking and sparking computer, while trying to shield it from the bored barista's eyes.

It wasn't hard to put two and two together.

Goddamn it!

Right before her disappearance, Christy had let the cat out of the bag – heavily hinting to Falcon that she'd gained access to his precious Archives. I'd hoped nothing would come of it considering the confusion and chaos of the time, but alas hope was a fool's errand.

Not only had Falcon changed his password, but the security had been upped significantly since my last foray onto the mystical wiki. SSL, a firewall, and top notch intrusion detection had been added – and that wasn't all. Something I'd done had triggered a power surge in the borrowed laptop, frying its innards and leaving it no more useful than an oversized Frisbee.

No way was that normal.

The son of a bitch had somehow managed to ward his fucking internet gateway and I couldn't help but think it was purposely aimed at me.

I'd almost forgotten that Falcon had done his research prior to our first meeting. He'd come prepared with details on us all. It had probably been a minor effort on his part to deduce that Christy's technical skills might've been subpar at best, but mine weren't.

I doubted the smarmy motherfucker actually understood

the new security measures, but he'd at least been smart enough to throw money at the problem until it was fixed. Not only that, but his acolytes had apparently figured out a way to ensure anyone tripping the site's defenses learned a harsh lesson on how limited a warranty could actually be.

Despite us owing someone back at Purgatory a new laptop, Kelly wasn't to be deterred.

"If you had better equipment, do you think you could try again?" she asked from behind the wheel as we drove back.

"Oh, I could definitely *try* again. I'm just worried about what will happen. I'm not sure how up on technology you are, but firewalls that shoot back actual fire aren't exactly common."

"Maybe I can come up with a counter spell, something to insulate whatever you're working on."

"Do you think that'll work?" I asked, glancing down at my phone and noticing another voicemail had come in at some point.

"I'm willing to try if you are."

I gave her my best withering glare. "This is Christy we're talking about. I'll keep trying even if I have to wear fucking oven mitts."

"Good. Then tell me what you need."

"The desktop back at my apartment would probably be a good place to start."

"Oh?" she asked, glancing at me from the corner of her eye.

"Relax. I'm not Mathew Broderick hacking WOPR, but I've done some security work for a few clients. Part of the job is playing digital velociraptor and testing their perimeter fence. I have a whole hard drive full of tools to get the job done. And, not to toot my own horn, but if I can't beat a wizard with more money than sense at the tech game, then it might be time for me to consider a new career."

"Sounds like a plan to me."

"It does ... except that maybe we don't need to," I said,

holding the phone to my ear as it connected to the voicemail server.

"What do you mean?"

"Well, maybe we can just ask Falcon for his help."

"I thought you said he..."

"Isn't happy with me? Yeah, pretty sure that's the case. But this is Christy we're talking about. Maybe I can convince him to help us out for her sake."

"Do you think he will?"

I shrugged. "No idea. But I think we need to consider it. Asking him is going to suck. I'm gonna need to kiss a lot of ass to make it work, and even then he might tell me to eat shit and die in a fire. The flipside is, we could try to break in again, but there's the risk, not just of blowing up another computer but of being caught."

"I take it that would be bad."

"A vampire caught hacking the Magi's biggest chamber of secrets? You tell me."

"Yeah. That would be bad."

"Uh huh. I have enough people who hate me as it is without having an entire continent of Magi deciding I need to be nuked from..."

I trailed off as the voicemail played in my ear, my eyes opening wide.

Oh my God.

"What is it?" Kelly asked when I didn't continue.

"I need to go back regardless," I told her, switching my phone to speaker and rewinding the message for her to hear.

"*Bill, it's Sally. I don't know why nobody's answering their goddamned phone, but I figured I'd try leaving another message. Hopefully the signal doesn't crap out again. Anyway, I managed to hitch a ride back to civilization. I don't know what kind of shit-kicker airports they have out here in Oklahoma, but I think I have just enough cash on me for a ticket home. If you get this, don't bother calling back. I'm on a borrowed phone. I'll try to find you once I'm there. Hope everyone is all right.*" Her voice trailed off for a second before resuming. *Yeah, relax, I'm almost finished. Christ, it's the twenty-first century. You do know they have these things called unlimited plans, right? Anyway, gotta go."*

"Oklahoma?" Kelly asked. "What is she doing there?"

"No idea, but the timestamp on this message is from yesterday. If I know Sally, she's already on her way if she's not back already. That means I need to get there and find out what happened before anyone else gets to her first."

14

SPARK OF INSIGHT

I quickly brought Tom up to speed on what I needed to do, making it a point to grab Thundersmite from my tent and stuff it into the carpentry holster I'd picked up during one of our supply runs.

I wasn't sure if trouble would be waiting, but this time I planned on being prepared for it.

Tom, of course, wanted to come along, but I quickly ixnayed that. Tina was here which meant this was where he needed to be. That, and I could make the trip a hell of a lot faster with Kelly than I could with him.

Ignoring his bitching, I headed off to rendezvous with Kelly. Minutes later, I stepped through the magical barrier, surprised to find her waiting for me alongside Veronica.

The younger witch was wearing a jacket with her auburn hair up in a ponytail. Though she didn't appear to be in any obvious pain, her eyes had the sunken look of someone still on the mend.

"Hey," I greeted, enjoying how my headache had once again miraculously cleared up. "I thought you were still on bed rest."

"I'm almost all healed up," she replied.

"*Almost* being the operative word," Kelly chided.

"I'm well enough to come with you guys if you need me."

"No, and that's final. Besides, I need you to stay here and keep an eye on things."

"You mean you need someone to make excuses in case Liz asks what you're up to."

"That too."

Veronica let out a sigh. "Fine, but I want you both to promise to be careful."

"Relax. I left Vince a message. He knows we're coming. We'll have plenty of backup if we need it, not that I think we will."

"Okay, but what about getting back?"

"It's the city. Like I'll have any trouble finding someone to give me a boost."

I raised an eyebrow at that, but kept my mouth shut as they went back and forth, their banter sounding more like a married couple than Kelly did with her husband.

Finally, Veronica seemed to sense she wasn't going to convince her friend to let her tag along. She threw one last look my way, as if hoping I might step in, but I pretended to be engrossed by a nearby plant instead. No way was I getting in the middle of this.

Either way, she was apparently in good enough shape to help Kelly as she prepared to zap us back to the city, albeit I'd seen Christy do it enough times to guess it was pretty generic as far as Magi spells went.

I was far more concerned with keeping my lunch down as light flared around us. Then our particles were scattered to the ether before reassembling again inside Christy's apartment. I felt a momentary twinge in my head as we appeared, but thankfully my stomach seemed to be in a cooperative mood this day.

Everything appeared to be the same as when I'd last been there – the front door still locked and all. Nevertheless, we decided a quick spot check made sense for paranoia's sake. First, though, I helped myself to some pig blood I'd had the foresight to leave in the freezer.

"Eww," Kelly said, seeing me take a bite.

"Oh come on. It's no different than a popsicle."

"And if that's not a good argument for cutting back on dessert, I don't know what is."

Everyone's a critic.

I downed my snack while checking the adjoining apartment, finding it blissfully free of werewolf shit, giant monsters, or anything else suspicious.

"All's good on my end," I said when I was done.

Kelly stepped out from Tina's bedroom, closing the door behind her. "Clear here too."

"Oh hey, what did Veronica mean about needing a boost to get back?" I asked, making idle chitchat as I tossed the empty freezer bag in the trash. I turned to find her glaring at me from the living room. "What?"

"Don't you start with that trash witch crap too. Liz breaks my balls enough with that shit."

"Wait. What trash witch crap?"

"About me being a catalyst witch, duh."

That term sounded vaguely familiar, but no more. "I have no idea what you're talking about."

She fixed me with an incredulous look. "You're kidding, right?"

"About what?"

"It's just ... this is something we usually don't talk about with outsiders, but, well, you and Christy. I kind of figured it had come up at some point. You know, pillow talk."

"Not that I'm aware of." Okay, maybe that was a bit of a lie. Christy had tried on a few occasions to explain the details of witch culture, but I can't say I paid much attention. Magi politics held about as much interest to me as watching paint dry.

Kelly inclined her head as if mulling it over. "I guess it doesn't hurt to tell you. After all, Sheila knew and she was technically the last person in the world who should've. First up, spoiler alert. This isn't common knowledge and I'd prefer it remain that way."

"Kinda already figured that."

"Fair enough. So here's the thing – Magi like Christy and

Liz are the real deal. We're talking wicked witches of both the east and west."

"Yeah, and...?"

"They're more the exception than the rule, because they can do magic by themselves."

"So?"

"So, most of us can't."

"Seriously?" I replied.

"Not alone anyway. We need to ... *sync* up with another witch or wizard first."

"But I've seen you do plenty of..."

"No, actually you haven't. Anytime you've seen me cast a spell there's always been another Magi close by – whether it's been V, Christy, Liz, or someone else."

I considered that, not that I could pretend to have an ironclad memory. I supposed it was possible, though. "You really can't do magic by yourself?"

"Just little parlor tricks. But the real stuff, no. I'm like a spark with no fuel source, or vice versa. That's why they call us catalyst mages. Alone we can't do much, but together it's like a chemical reaction and ... *boom*, magic."

I was about to comment on that being nice to know should it ever come up during *Trivial Pursuit* night, however, then realization hit me. "Hold on. Are you saying we're fucked if we need to vacate the premises post haste?"

"Possibly, but probably not. The good thing about cities like New York is there's usually plenty of latent catalyst mages around. It's not all that uncommon to be walking down the street and feel a random jolt from one."

"Latent...?"

"Means they have the ability, but it never activated for whatever reason. They can't do any magic, at least not purposefully, but they can subconsciously provide that spark to others." No doubt sensing I wasn't entirely following along, she added, "Think of it like latent mutant genes in comic books. It's why Bruce Banner turned into the Hulk after getting irradiated, instead of dying from cancer."

"Ah, I get it now."

Now that she'd mentioned it, it seemed almost obvious – like all the clues in *The Sixth Sense* leading up to the big reveal, but not realizing it until after the fact.

Thinking back on things, run-ins with solo mages had actually been pretty rare. I'd merely assumed it was because they were douchebags who liked ganging up on people like me. But if what Kelly said was true, it was actually due to them needing a magic buddy in order to be a threat. That still made them dicks, but at least explained why they always swarmed like hornets.

As for that latent part, something in the back of my mind was sorta nagging me, but whatever. Kelly was probably right. Christy had likely told me about this shit at some point, but my head had been too far up my own ass to notice.

I needed to do better if ... *when* we got her back. She deserved that much.

"All right, now I have a question for you."

"Oh?" I replied, glad to be pulled away from that chasm of despair.

Kelly gestured down at my waist. "What's up with hammer time? No offense, but you don't strike me as Bob the Builder."

I considered telling her the truth, but then remembered the warning I'd been given. Besides, I still wanted Thundersmite to stay a surprise until we needed it.

"This? Oh ... I grabbed it just in case. Guns and swords are one thing, but at least the cops won't give me shit for carrying a hammer."

"I suppose."

"Besides," I added, rambling unnecessarily, "there's a few repairs I wanted to make, y'know, if we had the time."

"Really? That's what you're worried about?" She shrugged. "Whatever. Just so long as we don't lose sight of our priorities. Speaking of which, have you given any more thought as to how you're going to mend the fence with Matthias Falcon?"

I hadn't. Truth be told, Sally's message had thrown me for

a loop. Kelly was right, though. I probably needed to focus on how we could get a certain little birdie back on our side. "Sorry, didn't mean to gut that witch in front of you. Hope she wasn't anyone you liked," probably wouldn't cut it as far as apologies went.

If only we had a peace offering or some other way to...

Hold on ! I turned back toward the other apartment. "Wait here."

"What for?"

"It's a longshot, but I might have something that'll smooth things over with Falcon."

After Christy's disappearance, Tom had taken over her room to be near Tina. Ed, Glen, and I, however, had moved into the adjoining apartment. Then, when it was time to bug out for Purgatory, we'd packed fairly light – meaning *it* was likely still there.

Now where is it...? Ah!

I searched through my dresser drawers, finding Falcon's vape pen in the second from the top. The dude was always sucking on the stupid thing, at least before the fight at Gan's. When all was said and done, I'd found it lying on the battlefield. At first, I'd almost chucked the stupid thing away as a petty fuck you, but then had hesitated instead – something telling me to hold onto it. I wasn't sure if it held any actual significance beyond him really loving a nicotine fix, but maybe I'd get lucky and it would turn out to be a birthday present from a loved one.

Either way, fool's errand or not, it seemed better than showing up at his doorstep emptyhanded.

I picked it up then turned back toward...

Ugh!

Another stabbing headache picked that moment to slam into my frontal lobe from out of nowhere, this one a doozy.

The fuck?

Could vampires get brain tumors? Goddamn, I hoped not. How the hell would that even work for the undead?

Whatever way you looked at it, though, something wasn't

right. Unfortunately, I doubted I had time to stop off for a CAT scan.

I paused for a moment, waiting for the worst to pass, then headed back to where Kelly waited, doing my best to ignore the five-hundred watt subwoofer currently dropping a sick beat inside my skull.

She raised an eyebrow when she saw what I was holding. "You got him a sonic screwdriver? I didn't realize we were dealing with a big Whovian here."

"Not quite. This is his vape pen." And now that I said it, it sounded incredibly stupid to me too. "Yeah, I know what you're thinking, but he always had this thing in his mouth, so I thought..."

"What? That he couldn't afford a new one?"

"Well, no, but maybe it has ... sentimental value."

I was fairly sure her opinion of me was dropping by the second, but rather than just call me a dumbass, like Sally would've, she held out her hand. "Here, let me check. Maybe there's an engraving."

As I handed it over two things happened almost simultaneously – my headache disappeared and there came a spark from the device as her hand touched it, like the damned thing was electrified.

Kelly took it from me then actually stumbled back a step, her eyes wide with surprise.

"Are you okay?"

"Holy shit!" she cried, seemingly unable to take her eyes off the vape pen. "What the fuck is this thing?"

"Um, I think Falcon normally keeps it filled with pineapple flavor."

"I'm serious, Bill. This ... thing ... it feels... Wow!"

"Are we talking headache wow here, or some different type?"

"Different, why?"

I waved her off. "Never mind. So, what is it then?"

"I ... don't know how to describe it. It's... Hold on. Let me try something." Before I could even ask what she was talking about, she flipped the device on then put it between her lips and took a suck.

Eww. "I would've probably washed that first."

She coughed a few times, obviously not a smoker, but then when she looked at me again I couldn't help but notice her eyes were glowing with power. "Kelly? Are you...?"

"I'm better than okay." She grinned at me then held out her hand. A moment later, a green fireball appeared above her palm – not dissimilar to the one Tina had conjured back when all this craziness had first started.

"I thought you said you couldn't do that without another witch."

She twirled her fingers, causing the fireball to grow to the size of a bowling ball before closing her palm and making it disappear. "I can't."

"Then how...?"

"This pipe," she replied, her voice full of awe. "I don't know what the fuck's inside this thing, but it's ... incredible. I don't know how to describe it any other way. It's like suddenly I feel like I could do *anything* I wanted. Hell, I'm pretty sure I could spar with Tina and live."

"That's ... something."

"It sure as hell is." She looked me in the eye, power continuing to radiate from hers as she smiled. "You know what this means, right?"

"Not really."

"You wanted some leverage for when we meet with Falcon. Well, I'm pretty sure we've got it and then some."

15

SMOKING ON THE WATER

K elly went to take another suck, but I stepped in.

"Maybe don't use it all up before we can offer it as a trade."

For a moment I saw the naked desire in her eyes. Strong as I knew Kelly to be, it was obvious this was a level of power she'd never experienced. However, before things could turn worrisome, she slipped the device into her purse. "You're probably right, but damn!"

It was hard to disagree. The question now was what the hell was it? I'd seen Falcon do some gonzo stuff with his magic, like turn a hotel suite into a magical sex grotto. Had some of his power rubbed off on the vape pen, sorta like how Tom's sword had absorbed faith magic from those who'd owned it before him? Or was something else going on here?

Either way, we'd found a proverbial genie in a bottle in the least likely place I'd have expected.

It was a stroke of luck better than I could have ever anticipated, especially since I'd been fully expecting Falcon to tell me to go fuck myself sideways with an unsanded broomstick.

But now we had something we could use to...

Buzz!

For a brief moment, my eyes turned to the door – remembering the apartment was currently wardless.

However, it was just Christy's phone ringing. Nevertheless, that stopped our discussion dead in its tracks.

"Do you think that's...?"

"Probably just some asshole worried about our car's extended warranty," I interrupted, leaving my hand hovering just above the receiver.

"Yeah ... probably."

I hesitated for two more rings before picking up. It wasn't that I was afraid I might recognize the voice on the other end, so much as I feared that I was getting myself worked up over nothing.

Finally, not wanting it to go to voicemail, I clicked the button to put it on speaker. "Hello?"

"...so, to sum up, Christy got sucked into an interdimensional abyss, Ed flew back home, and now Tom and I are living in the woods with Kelly. And yes, the reception there sucks, not that it matters much since most of our stuff got melted by a magical pyromaniac. I think that about sums it up."

There was a pause from the other end. "Well, I guess that explains why nobody's been answering their damned phone."

"Pretty much. So ... how's things with you?"

"Seriously?" Kelly snapped. "*That's* what you're going to ask her?"

"This is Bill we're talking about," Sally replied from the other end. "If he didn't say something stupid I'd be worried." There came the sound of muffled voices in the background. "Fine, I'll ask. Leslie wants to know if she can have the admin password for the Wi-Fi router."

"First off, no, and secondly I really wish you hadn't gone back to my place."

"I didn't have much choice. Nobody was answering over there, and last I checked my building is still a fucking crater."

"What about a hotel?"

"With what? I had just enough cash left for the cab ride

over. And then there's the little matter of having no ID. Hell, I'm lucky they let me on the damned plane."

"Okay, I get it. I'm just saying..."

"You don't have to tell me, Bill. I know. It was dumb to come here, but waking up in the fucking Ozarks with no memory of how I got there didn't exactly leave me with a lot of options for careful planning. Like, seriously, what the hell happened to me?"

I considered answering but hesitated. I doubted either the werewolves or their inbred leader Hobart were smart enough to tap this line, but the same couldn't be said of Gan's people. We'd already spilled the beans about where Sally was, which was bad enough since the little psycho had a mad-on for her demise. It was probably best to stop before I dug myself even deeper. "I'll tell you when I see you. We're heading over."

"We are?" Kelly asked.

"Not a great idea," Sally replied, "That guy who lives in the basement saw me coming in."

"Mike? Then that's exactly why we need to..."

"No, it isn't. Far as we know these mutts don't give a shit about me. So let's not give them a reason to. Why don't I wait for dawn to break, then I'll head over to you?"

"No can do. We're kind of on a timetable here, not to mention Christy's place isn't a good idea."

"I can meet you downstairs if you're worried about the wards."

"It's more the lack thereof that I'm worried about."

"What the fuck did you do?"

"Me?"

"Fine, you and that numbnuts friend of yours."

"I'll tell you when I get there."

"I just said..."

"See you soon!" I disconnected the call. Then, knowing how Sally could be, I unplugged it from the wall.

When I was done, I found Kelly staring hard at me. "I'm not one to call out plans as being fucking stupid, but..."

"Except it isn't. Hear me out. It's not that late yet and I

live on a busy street. The foot traffic alone will give us cover from any monster mutts wanting to leg hump us to death. And that's even assuming we're going to walk in through the front door, which we're not."

"You're not talking about the sewers are you?"

"Fuck no. Even if Mike hasn't scouted out the sewer entrance by now, a big if, I don't trust the tunnels these days. There's too much shit down there ... and not the kind you're thinking about."

"Fine. Then how?"

I gestured toward her purse. "Gee, I don't know. If only we had a magical hookah that could supercharge a witch with one quick suck."

Her eyes opened wide as she caught on. "That could work. Hell, I don't see why it wouldn't. Although maybe next time you can word it in a way that doesn't make it sound like a blowjob."

"Sorry, but you're either getting good ideas or eloquent speech from me tonight, not both."

"Sure you don't need another suck?" I asked as we stood in the magic circle inlaid into Christy's bedroom floor.

"You really enjoy asking that, don't you?"

"You want me to lie?"

"Fine. Then you should probably know I'm so juiced up from ... whatever the hell that stuff is, that I can't promise I won't overshoot and accidentally drop us on the moon instead."

"Fair enough. So, what do you think it is? I mean, do they make Red Bull for Magi?"

Kelly shook her head. "No idea. Some artifacts can supplement a mage's power – an Apollo's prism, Orbs of Amun-Ra, those sort of things."

"Familiar with them both."

"As I'm aware." She patted her purse. "But something that can actually boost a Magi's power? That's news to me.

Far as I'm aware, that's our real life version of the philosopher's stone – something Magi have wasted their whole lives in pursuit of, only to fail time and again."

"And yet you're apparently holding success right there in your bag."

"Tell me about it. Like I said, no idea what this is or why Matt Falcon had it. All I can say is that you'd better hope nobody ever figures out how to mass produce this stuff."

She didn't need to say any more.

When we'd reopened the Source after five years without magic, we'd inadvertently upended the power balance of the supernatural world.

But something like this could upset that balance even further.

The Magi had existed for thousands of years alongside the vampire nation and the Feet – basically acting as Switzerland to our Cold War. A ready supply of Matt Falcon's magical vape fuel, however, could easily cause them to rethink that position of neutrality.

It was a sobering thought.

Still, scary as that idea might be, that was a worry for another day. For now, Kelly was in charge of this high octane puff stick, which meant the advantage was all ours.

Now to hope she didn't end up addicted to the power this magical meth provided.

16

THE HANDYMAN CAN

We reappeared on the rooftop of my building, the clear night sky hopefully the only witness to our coming. Once again, I was left feeling fine from the trip – my stomach seemingly unbothered by being disassembled and reassembled at the molecular level.

I figured the roof was as safe a place as any. Both the building and apartment were partially warded thanks to Christy, albeit not nearly at the level as her place had been. Still, there was no point in setting them off, or potentially freaking out the tenants by appearing in the hallway.

As I popped open the trapdoor leading down, I found myself wondering whether Falcon's miracle vape could help in our quest to save Christy. I mean, heck, one puff and Tina could probably reach through reality itself.

Okay, that was probably both reckless and stupid on a number of levels. Regardless, I found myself wishing we didn't need to hand it back to Falcon.

As we climbed down, I tried to push that thought from my head. So long as we got the help we needed, there was no point in being greedy. I wasn't some paranormal power broker. I just wanted Christy back and for us to settle into our lives again.

Speaking of living, we also had to figure out a way to

make sure Sally could keep on doing so. Maybe it was selfish to say, but I needed my friend too.

Still, there was little doubt Sally had rolled snake eyes in the cosmic game of craps. First, she'd taken a bolt of eldritch energy meant for Gan. She'd awoken rejuvenated, her body once again that of a twenty-something year old. Her newfound youth, however, brought with it a few unexpected cosmetic changes – in the form of unnaturally green hair and eyes.

More worrying had been her new powers. Chief among them seemed to be a lethal allergy to both magic and stress. Too much of either caused her to *explode*, in a manner of speaking, expelling a shockwave of devastating force from her body.

Then there was the fact that she'd started speaking in tongues, proclaiming herself the herald of something called the Great Beast – apparently the extradimensional entity Gan had sold the world out to in exchange for magic's return.

It was that last one that was most worrisome. When last I'd seen Sally, she'd given in to her herald of Galactus persona, right before being whisked away by some mammoth airborne monstrosity straight out of *The Giant Claw*.

And now she was back, having returned from Oklahoma of all places.

Talk about weird shit, I considered as I stopped outside my apartment door.

"There a problem?" Kelly asked from behind me.

"Just wool-gathering." I lifted a hand to knock, but then hesitated. "Actually, maybe there is. Normal levels of magic don't make Sally go boom, but..."

"But right now I'm not normal?"

"Your words not mine. I mean, it's probably okay. She was able to be around Falcon without blowing up ... except for one time, but that was because he'd turned his home into a magical minefield. Chances are you're..."

She held up a hand. "I'll go wait on the roof just in case. If she's going to have a reaction, it'll probably be safer up there."

I nodded. "My property insurance thanks you."

"Just don't take forever."

"Don't worry. I won't."

"Oh, and I hope you were joking about those repairs, because I'm gonna be really pissed if we've done all this Mission Impossible shit just so you can replace some old drywall."

"Relax. I was ... mostly." I glanced down at the hammer as she turned and headed back up. Hopefully there wouldn't be a need for me to keep it a secret much longer, albeit I'd be more than happy if the mystery lasted long enough for us to all get back to Purgatory.

Purgatory...

"Fuck!" I'd totally forgotten about that. If Falcon's over-abundance of wards had set Sally off, then what the hell would Purgatory do? After all, the magic there was thick enough to cut with a knife. The last thing I needed was us reappearing back there, our mission a success, only for her to accidentally shred every last occupant like cabbage in a food processor.

"Goddamn it all."

I'd have to discuss it with Kelly before we headed...

"So, are you done talking to yourself like a dipshit, or should we give you another minute?"

I looked up to find the apartment door open. Sally was standing in the doorway, tapping her fingers against the frame as the Village Coven vamps gathered behind her with amused looks on their faces.

When last I'd seen her she'd just gotten her guts unzipped by Gan's sword. However, looking at Sally now, you'd have never guessed she'd so much as broken a nail.

Her green hair was up in a ponytail and she was dressed in a white blouse and tan slacks, looking less like she'd survived being carried off by Rodan and more like she was about to head over to a board meeting at Stark Industries.

I tried to play it cool in the face of her snark ... and failed utterly.

Instead, I wrapped my arms around her, fighting back

tears of joy. It had felt like I'd lost so damned much in the last few weeks – all the while trying to be cool and collected on the outside, yet a raw nerve, utterly unsure of myself on the inside.

The reality was, I'd held myself in check ever since getting that message from her – not quite willing to believe it was true. But now, seeing that she was not only back but okay, well, it was almost too much.

Fortunately, true to form, Sally was too cool to let me blubber all over her, especially in front of company.

"All right, enough," she said, gently pulling away. "I know how awesome it can be for someone like you to touch someone like me, but how about we head inside so you can bring me up to speed on everything else that's been happening."

A little orange kitten dashed around my legs like a maniac as I recounted the last week or so – my father having apparently dropped Petunia off without a care in the world that my home was full of strangers. Gotta love parents.

It's hard to convey my emotions as I told them all about the final minutes of the battle at Gan's. Up until right then, even thinking about those events had depressed the fuck out of me.

Don't get me wrong. Tom was my best buddy, the sort of friend I'd have gladly died for. He knew where all my Kleenex-wrapped skeletons were buried, but talking to Sally was like having my right hand back again – and not just for the purpose of more masturbation analogies.

I'd been as optimistic as possible around others when discussing our plans to rescue Christy. But, for the first time, I truly believed we had a shot at it.

That was the nature of our relationship. Sally and I had been through Hell and back when we'd faced off against the likes of Alex, Calibra, and Turd. With her by my side I felt like I could do ... well, anything really.

Go figure. Superman had Earth's yellow sun, while I had a snarky non-blonde with an attitude problem.

I'd considered sending the coven out for pizza or some other errand while we talked, but had quickly ixnayed that. Keeping them in the dark was stupid and selfish, especially considering my apartment wasn't exactly a safe house these days.

Looking around at their faces – Leslie, Jessica, Craig, Bethany, Oswald, and one other dude whose name currently escaped me – I realized that survival might be a longshot for us these days, but at least I could ensure they didn't die of ignorance.

"So let me get this straight," Sally said once I was finished. "That little bitch actually gutted me?"

"Like a fish. You seriously don't remember?"

Sally let out a sigh. "Not even a blip. The last thing I remember was Falcon's bitch aunt locking me in that crystal prison. Then Glen was at my feet with one of those magic orb thingamabobs. We used it to bust out and..."

"Then...?"

She shook her head. "That's it. Next thing I knew it was daylight and I was standing atop a hill, covered in more of that weird black gunk and surrounded by a cluster of broken trees."

"So what did you do?" Jessica asked.

"I picked a direction and somehow managed to not get shot by the owner of the first shack I came across. Fortunately for me, hillbillies apparently take strange-ass stories in stride."

"And there wasn't any sign of that bird monster?" I asked.

That earned me an eye-roll. "Pretty sure I'd have mentioned it if there was."

"Fair enough."

"So what happened?" Leslie replied. "Did it just drop you off in the woods and fly away?"

"That's assuming it was even real," Craig said.

I turned his way. "Trust me. It was plenty real."

"No, I mean, what if it was like a mental construct or maybe a solid hologram?"

"Then Captain Picard really needs to get the fucking holodeck fixed."

Sally shook her head. "All right, that's enough. The last thing I need is you two jacking each other off with Star Trek trivia."

"Okay, fine, let's just assume it was real," Jessica said. "But if that's the case, what did it want with you?"

Sally's eyes met mine and I gave her a look that hopefully conveyed my thoughts on the matter. Much as I wanted to bring the coven up to speed, there were perhaps a few things it was best to keep under wraps, at least until we knew more.

That Sally might be the herald of some godlike being called the Great Beast was probably one of them.

That right there was part of the problem. Sally, or whatever had been controlling her at the time, had proclaimed allegiance to the Great Beast – singular. However, so far as I knew anyway, there were possibly three of them to contend with – Godzilla, Rodan, and Anguirus.

Or, more precisely: Leviathan, Ziz, and Behemoth – the legendary beasts of the Bible, said to foretell the end times.

All things considered, I'd have rather had Godzilla. At least then we'd be fine so long as we remembered to avoid Tokyo.

I told the coven to get packed as I went downstairs to unclog the Cortez's garbage disposal – because fuck it, I might as well kill two birds with one stone.

My original plan was to take Sally back to Purgatory with us, but there was no reason to leave the coven in the line of fire, now that we had a safe haven to retreat to. Far as I knew, the wolves weren't after them, but I'd seen the kind of logic their leaders Hobart and Myra used. It was probably only a matter of time before they tried something stupid in order to flush out the rest of us.

That, and it wouldn't hurt to have a few more allies close by just in case anyone else decided to sell our asses out to Claire.

I still had no idea how they were going to accommodate Sally, but we could deal with that once we'd met with Falcon and then gotten the fuck out of the city.

I finished extracting hair, coffee grounds, and god knows what else from the disposal, gave it a quick test, then headed back up – taking a couple extra minutes to look around.

In some ways, abandoning this place felt like betrayal, and not just because I had paying tenants. No. This ratty Bay Ridge apartment building had weathered many a storm over the years – serving more than once as both sanctuary and shelter for us.

On the flip side, I had no interest in getting my ass killed over this shithole. Nostalgia be damned. Besides, I could probably make enough selling it in the current real estate market to afford my own compound in upstate New York. Something to consider.

I found Kelly waiting outside the apartment door as I reached the top floor, a grim look on her face.

"I thought you were..."

"Up on the roof?" she interrupted. "I was. Wait time is over. We need to go."

"Why?"

"Because I'm sensing another magic user in the vicinity and they're definitely not latent."

Fuck. "Are you sure?"

"Positive."

I'd had a nasty feeling that we weren't going to be able to pull this off without attracting undue attention.

All the same, this wasn't like last time. We came in knowing an ambush was possible. I had other vampires as back up, a witch who was currently amped on magical PCP, and a legendary weapon by my side.

That said, we hadn't reached the point of no return yet. We had one more advantage on our side. This was New York, and it was still early enough that the streets of Brooklyn were far from empty.

The first rule of supernatural fight club was not letting anyone else talk about supernatural fight club. That meant keeping our shit hidden from prying eyes. It was kind of like holy ground in *Highlander*, a tradition nobody cared to break.

So if Myra and her mongrel friends wanted us, they'd have to wait for it.

Too bad we had no intention of giving them the chance.

Eager as I was to test out my new toy, I'd happily accept a clean getaway instead. After all, I hadn't gotten this far by charging into the fray like some sort of half-assed hero.

I saw no point in starting now.

17

A DOGGONE SHAME

The plan was simplicity itself. I ordered the coven to dump their garbage and dirty laundry in the hall. No, I wasn't condoning them to act like fucking slobs, but I'd dealt with Hobart and his werewolves before.

Last time they'd been quick to gloat about being able to track our scents anywhere, so I figured some olfactory cover was in order. My hope was to confuse them long enough for us to reach the roof where Kelly could zap us over to Manhattan for our unannounced meeting with Falcon.

"Take only what you need!"

I stood at the door as the coven filed past, heading to the roof with their possessions in hand. Sally was the last in line.

"Is it too much to hope that you brought me a gun?" she asked.

"I have something even better."

"Oh?"

I handed her the squirming orange kitten. "Yeah, some pussy for you to play with."

She glared at me in return. "Next time I'm just gonna fucking stay in the Ozarks."

"You'd miss me."

"Only because you didn't bring me that gun I asked for."

Our banter aside, the plan was simple. Hell, even an idiot could've pulled it off.

So, of course it all went to hell within about twenty seconds of me climbing out onto the roof.

I was about to tell Kelly she was clear to get us the hell out of there. Before I could so much as get out the first word, though, a gust of tornado strength wind slammed into me, lifting me from my feet and sending me careening over the edge.

Sadly, I wasn't alone.

Time seemed to slow as I fell, giving me a moment to consider how much a fifty foot drop onto concrete was going to suck.

Fuuuuck!

A moment later, however, I realized I wasn't imagining it. I really was slowing down.

A powerful updraft rose to meet me and the others, a counterforce to whatever had knocked us over the edge like tenpins.

We all hit the ground with about the same impact as falling off a stepladder – not exactly pleasant, but far better than the alternative.

A moment later, Kelly landed on her feet next to me, obviously responsible for our miraculous save.

"Thanks for that," Sally said, pulling herself up and no doubt reaching the same conclusion.

Kelly nodded, inclining her head upward. "I had a bad feeling something might happen, so I had a wide area fist of force prepared just in case."

I stood up and followed her gaze. "Well, I for one am happy to be fisted."

"That was just the foreplay," Sally replied, pointing toward the roof of the building next door. "Pretty sure we're still in danger of being royally fucked."

She wasn't wrong.

Someone was peering down at us, an all too familiar face grinning beneath a pile of curly red hair – Myra.

"Y'all are dumber than a sack of shit, you know that?" she cried out. "Like we ain't had scouts scoping out the rooftop."

Grrr! I wasn't big on hitting women, even freakishly powerful ones, but in her case I was happy to make an exception.

Unfortunately, that would have to wait.

"Are you guys okay?"

"How the hell are they still standing?"

"Someone should call an ambulance."

"Fuck that. Call the cops too."

Shit!

I'd been right about there being plenty of people still out, more than enough for a crowd of gawkers to already be forming around us.

"What do we do?" Jessica whispered.

"Play it cool," Sally hissed. "Nobody's hurt, so they *obviously* didn't see what they think they saw."

She was right. We could still salvage this. "All right, everyone," I said in a voice louder than was needed, "pick up your bungee cords. That's enough practice for one evening."

The look on Sally's face said she was perhaps somewhat less than in awe of my lie. Sue me. I hadn't expected Myra to be so fucking reckless. Besides, Kelly could probably conjure a glamour that would give everyone reason enough to doubt what they'd...

"FREEWILL!" a gruff voice called out.

"Holy shit! Why is that guy naked?"

Or maybe not.

I followed the sound of the voice to see a man step out from a nearby alleyway. He was large, had a prominent beer gut, and was bare-assed nude.

"Hobart."

"You know this guy, Bill?" Kelly asked.

"Yeah," Sally replied, "we've had the displeasure of running into his naked ass before."

"Phrasing," I remarked, turning toward the werewolf leader.

"I see you remember me," he said with a grin, sporting a hefty timber of wood below his waist. *Eww!* "That's good. Because I sure as fuck remember you."

"Well, duh," I replied. "It's only been about two weeks since I kicked your buddy Jeb's ass. Even fuckers who drink wood alcohol for breakfast can remember that far back."

Sally stepped next to me, putting a hand on my arm. "Much as I appreciate talking shit to white trash, maybe we should relocate first."

She had a point there.

I had no idea what the fuck Hobart was thinking, attacking us out in the open like this. Nevertheless, I spied more of his naked buddies, stepping out from alleyways and stairwells up and down the block – at least half a dozen, probably more.

"We should probably consider making a run for it..."

Before Sally could finish, one of the gawkers still milling about started to disrobe right in the middle of the throng.

The fuck is wrong with these assholes?

"Are they really going to do this here?" Leslie asked.

I had no easy answer for her. Logic dictated that nobody should be this stupid. Yeah, shit had gotten weird five years ago – especially near the end when the battle between the vamps and Sasquatches had spilled over into Boston, but we'd all been facing the apocalypse at the time. Today was just a normal Thursday so far as I was aware.

Still, they hadn't done anything yet. So far as anyone here was concerned, there were just a bunch of nudists cavorting about. Not exactly common, but when you lived in the city long enough you learned to expect the occasional bit of weirdness.

I turned and looked back at my building, noting the vestibule was empty. Even so, heading back inside was a poor strategy. That douchebag Mike might very well be waiting to ambush us. And even if not, there were innocent rent-paying tenants inside.

That didn't leave us a lot of options since the sewers were out of the question. I'd seen firsthand what had taken up residence down there and wanted no part of it.

No. What we needed to do was lose ourselves in the crowd. Let Hobart and his bare-naked buckaroos try to follow. If they wanted to be cited by the NYPD for indecent exposure that was their problem.

"Follow me," I told the others. "They won't start shit so long as we're out in the..."

"MYRA, NOW!"

So much for that plan.

"Woo-hee!" came the cry from above. "Let's get this hoedown started!"

A blast of power shot from her location high into the sky. I could only watch in horror as the quarter crescent that had been looking down on us morphed into the vision of a full moon. Sure, it was only a glamour – an illusion – but the reaction it caused was far more real than I cared for.

"Oh my God! What's happening to him?"

"Stay back. I think he's got some kind of disease."

Those and several other incredulous cries rose from the crowd as Hobart and his buddies began their horrific transformation from man to beast.

"These don't look like any werewolves I've ever seen," Craig stammered as their bodies continued to grotesquely expand.

"Welcome to real life," Sally replied. "It's not like a Michael Jackson video."

Kelly glanced her way and sighed. "I'm guessing we're not going to solve this with a dance off then."

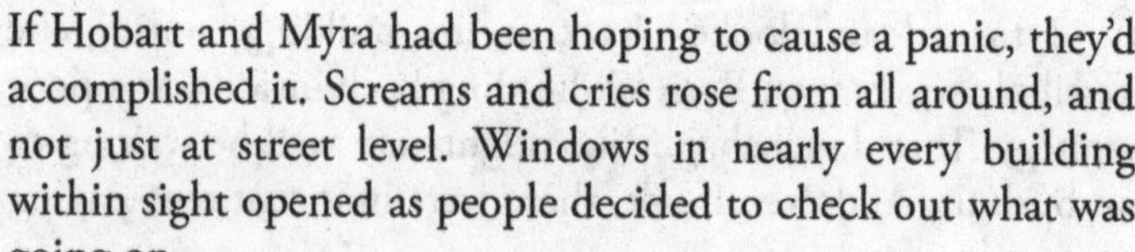

If Hobart and Myra had been hoping to cause a panic, they'd accomplished it. Screams and cries rose from all around, and not just at street level. Windows in nearly every building within sight opened as people decided to check out what was going on.

That wasn't all, though. Two gunshots rang out from somewhere close by, followed by a snarl of rage. I probably shouldn't have been surprised. This was New York, after all – the fuck around and find out state.

Any way you looked at it, the street had gone from a relatively quiet evening to total chaos in the span of minutes.

And that wasn't even the worst of it.

For every person with the common sense to run, another stopped to pull out their phone and record the craziness.

"We are so fucked," I muttered.

"Maybe not," Kelly replied, stepping in front of me and raising her hands. A bluish glow enveloped her arms. A moment later, there came cries of confusion and outrage as every cell phone in sight sparked and shorted out.

Including the one still in my pocket. "Ow!"

"Sorry," she said. "I figured subtle had gone out the window."

"It's fine. Think you got them all?"

"I highly doubt it. I can feel that rush starting to fade, but hopefully I got enough of them."

"Works for me. All right guys, do what you can to protect yourselves and Sally."

"I don't need protecting," she snapped.

"Sure you do. Because if anything happens to that stupid cat, I'm giving my mom your phone number."

"What about you?" Jessica asked.

"That's easy. I've got a bone to pick with a werewolf."

* * *

I couldn't believe I'd actually said that. I likewise couldn't believe I was leaving the safety of the crowd and heading straight toward Hobart – now a beer-bellied wolf monster over seven feet tall.

Still, crazy as it was for me to rush into battle, there was still a chance I could stop this before it turned into a bloodbath. If I could take out Hobart, the rest of his pound puppies would surely turn tail and run.

I had two things in my favor – a chip on my shoulder after my beatdown by Pam, and a little surprise strapped to my side.

I grabbed Thundersmite from its holster as I closed in on Hobart, who was standing there drooling as if in anticipation, or maybe just because he was about as smart as a fucking bulldog. Fortunately, I had the perfect chew toy to ram down his...

"Out of the way, buddy. I got this!"

Oof!

I was shoulder checked from my blindside. It wasn't a hard hit but it caught me by surprise, sending me sprawling. I hit the pavement, the hammer clattering out of my hands as some Punisher wannabe stepped in front of me with his gun drawn.

Fuck!

"Eat this, you ugly son of a whore!" he cried, opening fire.

Having fought these things, I knew they weren't invulnerable. Still, they were both tough and strong. They also had a nasty tendency to not stay dead, as I'd discovered during my last encounter with them.

In any case, the guy playing vigilante was in over his head.

I scrambled to my feet, determined to retrieve my weapon and ... get nailed again before I could so much as fucking move an inch.

Argh!

Sadly, this time it was no passerby, as a hairy two-legged truck slammed into me from the side.

The next moment found me rolling across the pavement with a different slobbering monster than the one I'd been targeting.

So much for the best-laid plans of vamps and men.

"Bill!"

"St ... ouch ... stay back!" I cried at hearing Sally's voice call out to me.

It wasn't that I didn't want her help. Fuck, I'd have been

happy to have it. It was more because this was rapidly becoming a somewhat *stressful* situation. The last thing any of us needed right then was her powers going off and leveling the block.

We were already at the point where I had no idea how we were going to contain this mess, but her powers would likely push us over the edge from unexplained incident to domestic terrorist watch list.

That was a worry for later, though. For now, it was all I could do to keep the werewolf's teeth and claws at bay – all while trying to ignore its red rocket poking me in the stomach.

Yeah, this was checking off boxes in way too many fetishes at once. It was time to see what I could do about the kink factor here.

Fortunately, experience had shown these things weren't exactly Rhodes Scholars. As the werewolf tried to snap at my face, I extended my claws and dug them into its arms – just barely holding it at bay. If I was going to wrestle with this thing, I might as well cheat a bit.

The beast let out a howl of pain as I ripped into its forearms, letting up the pressure just enough for me to shift our positions. I rolled with it, ending up on top – where its dick continued to stab into me. Goddamn, this thing needed to get laid, and no I wasn't volunteering. I liked doggy style, but this was a bit much even for me.

Instead, I bared my fangs and bit into its shoulder, taking advantage of the change in momentum.

I purposely made it a point not to swallow anything. Last time we'd tangled, I'd discovered a disturbing factoid about werewolves. Their blood gave me a boost much like vampire blood, save for one difference. I'd temporarily mutated into a freakish Brundlefly, halfway between vampire and werewolf.

And no, that hadn't been a good thing.

Needless to say, werewolf was off the menu for now. Instead, I tore a chunk out of its hide and promptly spat it out.

The werewolf opened its mouth and yowled in pain, letting its tongue loll to the side.

Now!

I let go of its arms and let fly with an uppercut – snapping its teeth shut onto its own tongue, stealing a move the Wanderer had suggested during my first battle with the wolves.

The effect was instantaneous. The wolf let out a surprised yipe as blood poured from its lips, leaving it wide open for me to grab the sides of its head and ram it into the ground repeatedly, hard enough to crack the asphalt.

After about four or five times, the wolf's eyes rolled back into its head and its arms went limp, allowing me to finally pry myself from its grasp.

Sadly, the wet squelch of meat from nearby told me I was too late to help my would-be savior.

Sure enough, I looked up to find Hobart-wolf, bloodied but very much still alive, as he rent the poor sap limb from limb.

And that was why you didn't send in Daredevil when you needed the Fantastic Four instead ... not that I was necessarily doing all that fantastically.

Speaking of teams, I dared a glance toward where I'd left the others and was pleasantly surprised to find the street not littered with piles of ash.

The coven had wisely put my building to their backs, while several members had picked up improvised weapons – broken bottles, chunks of asphalt, and a piece of wrought iron fence from the neighboring building. They were successfully keeping a trio of werewolves at bay, likely helped by the fact that strategy wasn't exactly the wolves' strong suit. Behind them stood small group of people, all of them protected by a purplish force dome.

So far so good, now where is...

There! Mixed in with the people the coven was protecting stood Sally, looking none-too-pleased to be benched. I knew she wasn't afraid to get her hands dirty, but it was for the best. The sky was currently clear with no sign of giant monsters, and I for one preferred to keep it that way.

Now to hope Kelly didn't inadvertently set her off, as I spied her a few yards away topping off her magic tank with another suck from Falcon's wonder pipe.

There wasn't much I could do about any of that, though. I still had Hobart to deal with and he wasn't alone. At least half his werewolf buddies were harassing pedestrians and cars alike – all of them too scattered for Kelly to protect.

"Come on, bite me! I want to be a werewolf, too!"

And apparently at least some of them were fucking idiots.

I turned to see a twentyish-looking girl with stars in her eyes and sawdust for brains approaching a werewolf that was busy gnawing on a parked SUV.

"No," I cried. "Don't do it!"

I was too late, though. In the next instant it swung one of its massive paws, sending her severed head flying from her shoulders and staining the sidewalk with her blood.

Shit!

I was rapidly beginning to see this wasn't like other battles I'd fought. Those had mostly been private affairs, closed to the public. But this was a brawl out in the open on the streets of New York, with creatures who seemed to have zero fucks to give when it came to subtlety. There was no doubt in my mind that the longer this went on the worse it would become.

"*Heh heh heh.*"

I spun at the sound of the huffing chuckle to find Hobart waiting for me, standing there staring – his teeth bared in what appeared to be a misshapen grin.

He was different than the others. Most of these things became little more than animals when they changed. Not Hobart, though. His eyes glimmered with intelligence, relatively speaking anyway. Let's just say I doubted he was in any danger of splitting the atom anytime soon.

Either way, a stupid dumbass still made for a pretty goddamned intelligent dog monster.

Although maybe not smart enough.

As I stared him down – wondering if I could retrieve my hammer before being torn a new asshole – my ears picked up something new.

Hobart likewise inclined his head as the sound of sirens began to fill the air.

About fucking time.

Don't get me wrong. As a vampire, I had zero interest in dealing with the cops. But the fact that New York's finest were on their way told me this battle was as good as done.

"Hear that?" I asked. "That means you and the Paw Patrol had better scoot your asses out of here."

In response, Hobart's flesh began to ripple. There came the sound of bones crackling as he shrank in size – the black fur upon his body receding like he'd bathed in a tub of reverse Rogaine.

Ugh! Gross as their transformation to wolf monsters was, watching it happen the other way around was even worse. It just looked ... nasty. If Hobart felt any discomfort, though, as his ugly dog face shifted back into an ugly human one, he didn't show it, continuing to grin like he knew a secret I didn't.

That probably wasn't too far from the truth as I still had no real clue where these fuckheads had come from or why they were after Ed.

I looked up as he finished his transformation, the sirens growing ever louder, noting that Myra's glamour was still hanging in the air. Interesting, as well as once again proving that Hobart was different than the rest. He could control it enough to revert back, even as elsewhere another of his buddies lifted a hairy leg to piss on the side of a parked coupe.

"Ready to put some pants on and call this off?" I asked.

"You know what we're after, Freewill," he replied. "You could end this in a heartbeat, if'n you had one. Just give us the Progenitor and we'll be on our way."

Good. So they didn't know Ed was gone. "I don't have him."

"But I think you know where he is."

"Maybe I do, but you and your *Hee Haw* huckleberries haven't told me why you want him."

"Ain't your concern. I did some digging about you. I know that you fought against the Top Coven back in the day."

Top Coven? It wasn't even worth correcting the idiot. "Yeah, so...?"

"So, we're looking to keep all that from happening again. You should be thanking us, boy. If we kill him it all falls apart."

"No it doesn't. Ignoring the fact that OG vamps don't need him to make others, he's not even the only one holding the keys to making neo-vamps anymore."

Hobart raised an eyebrow. "I got no idea what you're talking about with this OG and neo shit. All I know is that the Progenitor represents two things. He's the father of the new race of vampires and he's a symbol for the rest of you. Someone to rally behind as you build your new empire."

"Wait. Have you actually met Ed? Nobody's rallying behind his skinny ass."

He merely shrugged. "Maybe you don't know your friend as well as you think. And even if you're right, worst case is another dead bloodsucker. No skin off my tail."

Ignoring how disturbing he'd probably look with mange, I said, "You know, if you just tried talking to us instead, we could probably avoid all this shit."

"The time for words is past, Freewill," he snapped. "Where were your fancy words when the Top Coven was keeping us enslaved with their voodoo? Where were you when they were keeping us from being our true selves?"

"Top coven ... voodoo? Dude, I literally have no fucking clue what you're talking about." Red and blue party lights flashed in my periphery, telling me the cavalry had arrived. "But I suggest you end this now, unless you want to end up in the kennels at Rikers Island."

I turned my head partially, not daring to take my eyes fully off Hobart. He almost certainly knew that he'd lost this round, but I didn't trust him not to try for a cheap shot as a parting gift. "Hey, Kel," I called out. "Time for us to go. You ready?"

"I've *been* ready," she replied, still maintaining the magical barrier. "But what about the ... y'know?"

I had a feeling she was talking about the eyewitnesses. Unfortunately, I didn't see much we could do about that, other than hope their statements were either dismissed as hysteria or shunted over to Matt Falcon to investigate in his role as special consultant to the NYPD – ensuring the story got properly buried. Whatever the case, we needed to be gone and soon.

"Myra!" Hobart shouted, turning his head skyward toward the rooftop. "Care to show this shitkicker the error of his ways?"

She let out a cackle of glee in response. "With pleasure!"

What the?

I turned just as the first of the police cruisers screeched to a halt, not too far from where a werewolf was tearing into an unfortunate victim.

The cops scrambled to open their car doors, weapons drawn, just as a beam of red hot power lanced down upon them from above.

The fuck?!

I could only watch in horror as the vehicle exploded from the blast of death magic, incinerating the two officers inside, and leaving the car nothing more than a burning heap of slag as three more turned a corner and came racing our way.

A flash of light flared in the middle of the street. When it cleared, Myra was standing down at our level aglow with power.

"Like shooting turkeys in a barrel!" she cried.

"You get it now, Freewill?" Hobart gloated from behind me. "No more threats, no more warning shots. You're either going to tell me what I want to hear, or I swear to you on whatever unholy god you pray to that I will drown these streets and anyone who crosses me in blood."

18

AMISH ASSASSIN'S CREED

Before I could even think of a response, Myra fired a bolt of power at the next police car in line – blowing apart its front axle and sending it crashing into the nearest building.

It was … simply unbelievable.

Don't get me wrong, I'd seen my fair share of casual disregard for human life. That was, sadly, nothing new. But the previous generation of power brokers had always made it a point to ensure we remained in the shadows. Yes, there were back alley deals made with politicians and police alike, pulling the strings of government like puppet masters. But it had never been this blatant or careless, done with no regard to the fact that this shit was going to wind up on YouTube, TikTok, and every other social media site out there – assuming it wasn't already.

I'd joked with the coven a few weeks back about going public with a press conference, but it had been a crank. I wasn't insane enough to actually move forward with it, knowing there was no chance in hell of it actually making my life any easier.

Now, though, I was forced to wonder whether this was the moment that would change everything – the moment the world learned the truth.

All while I stood there watching with my thumb up my ass.

Some legendary vampire I was. More like a legendary joke.

"You see, Freewill," Hobart said from behind me, his voice growing gruffer as there once again came the ripple of flesh. "*This doesn't end until I say it does. And that won't be until the Progenitor's head is sitting on my mantle.*"

"You got that right," Myra replied, powering up again.

The two remaining police cars had stopped, blocking off the street from any other traffic that might've been insane enough to drive through this hell. They were no doubt even now radioing in for all the backup that could be provided and more.

Unfortunately, that left them sitting ducks for Myra's magic.

"No, don't!"

I kicked off in her direction as she loosed a spell, but barely made it two steps before Hobart fell on me, wrapping one massive arm around my neck and holding me there, forcing me to watch as...

As Myra's spell dissipated harmlessly against a wall of purple energy that appeared in front of the doubtless equal parts confused and terrified police.

"What if *I* say it ends?"

I looked to see Kelly striding forward, the grim expression on her face suggesting she'd had enough of sitting on the sidelines.

"Skedaddle, trash witch," Myra said, turning to meet her. "You don't want none of this."

"Really? I'd rather be a trash witch than a white trash bitch."

"A smart mouth like yours ain't gonna get you nothing but cut off."

Some sort of unspoken exchange seemed to pass between them, witch stuff I guessed. When it was over, though, only one thing seemed to have changed. Kelly was still aglow while the look on Myra's face had turned to one of confusion.

"How?" she asked. "Ain't no one else here and I turned off the spigot."

"That's for me to know," Kelly said, "and for you to get fucked!"

A blast of green flame shot out from her hand toward the other witch, telling me she was done playing games.

Note to self: stay on Kelly's good side.

Unfortunately, Myra was able to get a counter spell up in time to deflect the burst.

Regardless, Kelly seemed to have the redheaded witch at least stalemated for now, and just in time too as the police opened fire, forcing Myra to defend herself on two fronts.

Now to free myself before...

From over my shoulder, Hobart let out a low pitched howl.

The other werewolves which, up until now, had mostly been chaotically doing whatever the fuck they pleased, all lifted their heads – their ears perked up.

Then they stopped whatever they'd been doing and charged directly toward the police.

Shit!

Hobart wasn't playing. That meant it was time for me to stop fucking around.

I twisted my body, trying to use my vampire strength to flip him over my shoulder and ... mostly did nothing because I had no idea what the fuck I was doing. Goddamn, I really needed to take some self-defense classes again. Two or three Krav Maga lessons seven years ago weren't cutting it anymore.

Hobart chuckled as I struggled futilely, ignoring the pain as I dug my claws into his meaty arm in an attempt to pry the fat fucker off me.

"Hey! Are you going to let these assholes just piss all over your neighborhood? Don't just stand there, get them!"

Sally?

With Kelly otherwise engaged in a magic duel, the force

dome that had been keeping her and some of the other bystanders safe was gone. I looked to see my partner in crime not only directing the coven vamps, but also attempting to rally the people they'd been protecting.

Strength was on the side of the werewolves, but the numbers advantage was ours. Regardless, this was going to get ugly fast if someone didn't...

"AWWWWOOOOOOOOOOOOO!"

The howl echoed through the streets, but it had come from above. Had Hobart positioned another of his wolves up there to direct things?

The asshole's grip on me loosened as he backed up a step. I glanced over my shoulder to find him staring upward. Despite knowing I'd probably never get a better shot to retrieve my weapon, I followed his gaze.

Peering down at us was another massive werewolf, but this one was brown in color compared to the dirty black Hobart and his buddies seemed to sport.

Brown? Is that...?

The wolf wasn't alone either. Multiple figures stepped to the building's edge alongside it – people, oddly dressed ones from the look of it.

All of them, nearly a dozen, appeared to be wearing old-timey straw hats over bearded faces. Button down shirts and suspenders rounded out the parts of their attire I could see.

That wasn't all, though. Every single one of them was holding a rifle, which they quickly lifted and took aim with.

What ... the ... fuck?

In the next second, a round of firepower from above joined the barrage the NYPD was already unleashing.

Great, so we somehow managed to piss off the Amish too. This day just keeps getting better.

They weren't firing at us, though. Not only that, but whatever they were shooting from their weapons seemed to have more oomph behind it as screeches, yelps, and whines of pain filled the night sky as werewolf bodies were peppered from above.

I turned to meet Sally's gaze, but all she did was shake her head, apparently having no more of a clue than I did.

All I knew was that the tide had inexplicably changed – while also somehow getting even weirder.

From up above, my vamp ears caught wind of one of the marksmen saying, "Get going now, Michael. Take the others with you awhile and we'll finish things here. God's grace be with ye."

Michael?

The brown wolf leapt from the rooftop, landing nimbly in the street about halfway between me and where the coven was huddled. It took me a moment but then I realized it was wearing ... a backpack?

Sure, why not?

Though I had no way of being certain, I would've bet good money on this being the werewolf who'd saved our asses back at Pop's place.

Behind me, Hobart apparently concurred as he growled at the newcomer, having seemingly lost interest in me.

Pity for him as it gave me the opportunity to stop, drop, and spin myself around – just in time to deliver a right cross to the fucker's hairy crotch.

Hobart doubled over, his red eyes bulging from his skull as I found myself wishing I'd worn a pair of gloves. Oh well.

"That's how we do it here in Brooklyn, asshole."

There came a chuffing sound and I turned to see the brown wolf chuckle for a second or two before pointing down the road, as if telling us to go that way.

Though a part of me wanted to see a three way show-down between the police, werewolves, and a bunch of crazed farmers, I was forced to admit that a strategic retreat was for the best.

Sally seemed to concur as she led the coven over to where the beast waited. "You have our attention, Fido. Although I swear, if you fuck us over..."

Ah yes, we could always count on Sally to be the diplomat.

Fortunately, Leslie stepped in. "I think if he wanted to fuck us we'd already be bent over and cornholed."

"Probably a fair assessment." Sally turned back toward the werewolf. "Fine. Your move, furball."

The wolf chuffed again, then turned in the direction he'd pointed – which was the opposite of where the firefight was going on.

I had a feeling it was now or never because I could already hear the sound of more sirens approaching. Backup was on the way, which meant our escape route would almost certainly be cut off soon.

Soon, but perhaps leaving me just enough time for one last hit.

I took a quick look around the battle scarred street, spotting Thundersmite lying against the curb about five yards away. *Yes!*

Using my vampire speed, I raced over and picked it up. At this point I saw no reason not to use it. The cat was out of the bag for whoever was present to watch all this craziness go down. What was one more bit of insanity in a world gone batshit?

I turned grinning, imagining how awesome it was going to be knocking Hobart's stupid fucking head into next...

"Bill!"

Huh? I turned to see Sally calling for me, the squirming kitten still in her arms. "What?"

"Are you building a fucking bookcase or something? Let's go!"

"But..."

"Now, dipshit. You too, Kelly. Move it!"

Son of a...

It's like fate didn't want to give me the one bit of nerd-tastic joy left in my life – beating the shit out of an evil monster with a magic hammer.

Still, she had a point. With the situation escalating, it was high time to retreat rather than end up the star of tomorrow's headlines – asking if I, a mild-mannered Brooklyn man, could indeed be the reincarnation of Thor the thunder god.

Yeah, I could think of worse things.

That would have to wait for next time, though, as Kelly let loose with another spell – some kind of magical flashbang – that filled the street in front of her with near blinding light.

It was obviously meant to cover our escape by dazzling Myra, as well as everyone else present. That meant it was time to go. Not being a complete idiot, I stuffed Thundersmite back in its holster and followed.

Next time, buddy. I promise.

The brown werewolf quickly led us through a series of alleyways, away from the fight – Sally right behind it with me bringing up the rear.

The sounds of battle were still loud enough to ring in my ears when Kelly cried, "Everyone stop for a second!"

The werewolf turned and looked at her quizzically. In response, she raised her hands, mumbled something that I didn't quite catch, and then the air shimmered around us.

"There," she said, taking a deep breath but otherwise looking in decent shape. "I put up a glamour. It'll make us look and sound like a nondescript group of tourists to anyone on the outside. I just need everyone to stay close." Turning to the werewolf, she said, "I don't know if you can understand me, but I need you to..."

It's body began to ripple in response, followed by the distinct sound of flesh and bone rearranging itself. This werewolf may have looked a bit less mangy than its black-furred cousins, but its transformation wasn't any less gross to see as it began to shrink.

When it was finished, I found my eyes narrowing as they fell upon the sight of my downstairs tenant – Mike Walden – looking much the same as when last I'd seen him, except a bit more naked. Guess he was the Michael the Amish sniper had been speaking to.

Sure, he'd just pulled our fat from the fryer, but he was also the fucker who'd sold us out to Hobart and his mutts to begin with.

Maybe I wasn't going to have to wait to test out my hammer after all.

19

A TALE OF DOGGED
DETERMINATION

"Kelly, you got enough in you for another force field?" I asked, baring my fangs. "Everyone else, be ready. This is the fucker who's been spying on us."

"*This* is the guy?" Sally replied. "Oh, I so picked the wrong day to not be packing."

"Wait, Mr. Ryder." Mike held up his hands, which did nothing to distract from the fact that he was still naked save for the backpack around his shoulders. "You got it all wrong. I'm the one who helped you back at Pop Vesser's. Remember?"

"Oh, I remember all right." My hand dropped to my hammer, ready to bring the hurt down on this asshole if he so much as waved a pube in the wrong direction. "So what's the deal? Did you and your buddy Hobart set that shit up in advance to throw us off or something?"

"Hobart's not my friend, not even close. That guy is, well, he's a jackass. I've been working to stop him ever since I ... became like this."

"Oh really? So that's why you moved into my building?"

"I moved in because he figured out where you lived. Why do you think I've been keeping an eye on the street at all hours?"

"Because you're a fucking weirdo."

"No. I've been keeping watch for him."

"I hate to break it to you, Mikey, but you've done a shit job at it."

"I know and I'm sorry," he said. "I sometimes forget Myra's cagier than she looks."

"Oh, so you know her too?"

"We may have ... dated for a while." He looked down at the ground. "Heck, I was even thinking about proposing before things started getting strange."

"Offhand I'd say you dodged a bullet there," Sally remarked.

"Still remains to be seen if he's going to dodge another," Kelly added, nodding my way.

I held up a hand, curious to see where this was going. I wasn't quite ready to believe his bullshit, but seeing as he apparently had control over his transformation, much like Hobart did, it was obvious he could've ambushed any of us at any time had he wanted. "Go on."

"It wasn't always like this. Myra used to be a sweetheart."

"Yeah, bet she was a real peach."

"She was, at one time anyway." He shook his head. "It all started to change when she got her magic back. We started arguing more. She developed a real mean streak. Then I found out what I could do and..." Mike gestured toward his backpack. "Listen, mind if I slip into some pants? I'm getting a little self-conscious here."

"Fine. I'm tired of looking at your dick anyway."

"I'm not," Sally said.

"Really?"

"What? A girl can window shop."

I shot her a glare. "I don't want to hear a single word the next time I make a doggy style joke. Are we clear?"

"You're not the boss of me."

Mike was apparently used to dressing in stressful situations. As Kelly kept him in her sights, the threat of her power lingering in the air, he pulled out some clothes and proceeded to cover up. All the while, sirens, gunshots, and howls echoed in the distance, reminding us that shit was still going down.

Once he was done lacing his sneakers, he pulled a pill bottle from his bag, shook one out, and swallowed it before saying, "Come on. We should get moving. I know a place where we can hide over in..."

"Manhattan," I interrupted.

"Excuse me?"

"That's where we're going. And you're coming with us."

"But my friends..."

"Yeah, I'm sure they're a wonderful bunch of gun-toting Care Bears, but we have places to be and that doesn't include churning butter with a bunch of trigger-happy Amish fuckheads."

"Mennonite," he corrected.

"What?"

"They're Mennonites, not Amish. There's a difference."

"Who gives a fuck?"

"And they're not farmers. They're werewolf hunters."

Kelly threw me a look. "Mennonite werewolf hunters?"

"Don't look at me, I have no fucking idea."

Next to me, Sally shook her head. "Yeah, I definitely should've stayed in Oklahoma."

Kelly offered to teleport us to Manhattan, but she'd already expended a lot of power and I didn't want to risk her using up all of Falcon's happy juice before we could use it as a bargaining chip.

So we decided to do it the old fashioned way.

We caught a train at 86th Street, but had just barely pulled out of the station when the loudspeaker announced that service would be ending at our next stop – something about emergency track repairs.

That was bullshit, plain and simple. I had no idea what had transpired since we'd made a run for it, but it wasn't a stretch to imagine the authorities were locking Brooklyn down.

It made me wonder what the fallout would be, if any.

Much as I hated myself for doing it, I thanked my lucky stars that Gan had reinstituted the shadow treaty between the vampire nation and New York City. That meant the NYPD would likely be doing their best to cover this up. Sadly, that was going to be easier said than done this time. Regardless, I fully expected to see more rational theories pushed by those in charge – domestic terrorism or gang warfare – anything other than werewolves, vampires, and an invasion of gun-toting Mennonites.

On second thought, maybe they'd simply blame everything on that last group. That would certainly be interesting. None of that crap was our problem, though, at least not yet.

Thankfully, Kelly still had enough magical Viagra in her to glamour us so we could slip into the tunnel at the far end of the station. The trains might not be going any further, but that didn't mean we weren't.

I can't say I was happy to hoof it underground, but hopefully the giant cockroach monsters, proto-leprechauns, and other freaks that had been haunting the city as of late preferred to stick to the sewers instead of the train tunnels.

To help pass the time, as well as keep me from shitting a brick at every sound or drop of water, I figured this was our chance to continue our interrogation.

"All right, time to spill, Dog Boy," I said as we continued our trek. "Why do those assholes back there have a hardon for Ed?"

"Pop's boy, right? Okay, I just gotta warn you in advance, I don't know as much as you think I do."

"Yeah, well, we don't know shit, so anything is more than we're going on."

"I suppose that's fair." He took a deep breath, as if trying to figure out where to begin. "I used to think I was sick, growing up anyway. Hell, I thought my whole family was."

"Is that sick as in health issues," Sally asked, "or are you about to tell us your parents were brother and sister?"

He actually let out a laugh. "Contrary to what yinz might think, I don't actually know anyone who's married to a close relative."

"I have a second uncle once removed who married his first cousin," Craig offered. When silence met his confession, he added, "Sorry, just thought I'd mention it."

Sally let out a sigh in the darkness, her eerie green eyes aglow – which was doing little to make the situation less weird. At the very least, I could tell the coven vamps were nervous. I didn't think they were in any danger of scattering, but I couldn't help but notice that Sally, Kelly, and I had positioned ourselves at the fringes of this walking tour, just in case.

"Anyway, we had to take these pills, you see," Mike continued, "but not the stuff you get from the pharmacy. Once a month, like clockwork, some men would come to town in an unmarked van."

"Not suspicious at all," Kelly remarked.

"Afterward, there'd be a meeting called at town hall. We'd go and listen to the mayor talking these men up for their generosity. Then they'd hand out the pills, making sure we each swallowed one with a glass of water."

"And then...?" I prompted.

"And then my folks would usually take us out to Burger King, but I'm guessing that part's probably not super important."

Sally inclined her head. "And this didn't strike you as odd? The pills I mean, not family Whopper night."

Mike shrugged. "Well, it certainly does *now*. But back then it was just part of growing up. I mean, this happened as far back as I can remember. Heck, my grandpa once told me it had been going on for as long as he could remember too. The thing is, that's not the weird part."

"I'd disagree."

"Me too," Sally added. "I'm half surprised this story doesn't end with them locking the compound doors and handing out Kool-Aid."

"I suppose I can't blame you for that," Mike said, as we

continued along the dank subway tunnel. "But you see, all that stopped five years ago. No warning or nothing. One month the van didn't show and that was it."

I shared a not-insignificant glance with Sally. No way was that a coincidence.

"This was right around when the news was going off about the Strange Days. We all thought maybe something happened to delay them, that's all, but then days passed and still nothing. The mayor told everyone to sit tight and be patient. He was all smiles, like nothing at all was wrong, so we took him at his word..." He trailed off, shaking his head.

"Until?"

Mike let out an uncomfortable chuckle. "Until a week passed and his secretary found him swinging from a rope in his office. Safe to say, word spread fast. Panic set in, especially among the older folk. They figured the mayor knew more than he was telling us, and that's why he'd done himself in."

"So what happened?"

"A few more folks decided to go out on their own terms. But after that ... nothing. Nobody got sick, outside of normal ailments anyway. Months passed and people finally began to talk more freely. They'd bicker back and forth – some insisting we'd been cured, others claiming we'd been part of a government experiment that got shut down."

"Yeah, this is all fucking fascinating," Sally said. "But maybe let's skip the jamboree and get to the part where you grew a tail."

"I was getting to that," he replied, sounding not at all put out.

Either this guy was playing it close to the vest or he was one cool customer. Or maybe he was just a dumb hayseed who wasn't used to dealing with someone like Sally.

"Like I was saying, life moved on. I met Myra and we started dating. I got a raise at my job. Life was actually pretty good."

Sally chuckled. "The crazy ones are always the best lays."

I opted to ignore that one, lest it send us down a tangent

that would probably end with me getting decked. "So what then? She got her magic back and cursed you guys?"

"That would be a hell of a curse," Kelly replied. "Especially since nothing like that exists, far as I know anyway."

So much for that theory.

Mike nodded, though. "Myra got her magic back all right. Her coven did too. That was all news to me by the way. She'd never mentioned being a witch before then. And after ... that's when things started to change."

No shit.

"Now that she could do all the stuff she could before, all of a sudden I wasn't good enough for her anymore. That would've been bad, but I could have dealt with it. Not the first time I've been dumped."

"Sing it, brother," Oswald opined.

"Things got really weird, though, a few days later during the next full moon."

Finally we were to the interesting part.

He turned and looked my way. "Believe you me, that first time was something you don't forget – feeling my body change, like my whole skeleton wanted to rip itself out of my skin. And I wasn't the only one. I..."

He trailed off, cocking his head. In that same moment, I picked up a faint sound – like feet scuttling across the rocky ground. Could've been a distorted echo, nothing more, but I wasn't ready to dismiss it, not knowing what could be down here.

Fuck me! And just when we were getting to the good part. "Hold that thought."

"You heard it too?" he asked.

"Yeah. I'm thinking less talking and more hoofing."

"Just one quick thing," Sally said as we started double-timing it down the tunnel. "That pill you popped earlier. Is it the same those men in the van used to hand out?"

Mike let out a chuckle. "Nah, that was just a Benadryl. Keeps me from sneezing my head off."

"Oh?"

"Yeah, as luck would have it, I'm allergic to my own fur."

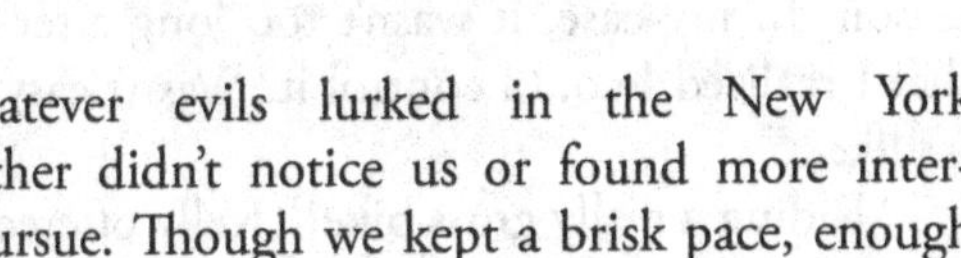

Thankfully, whatever evils lurked in the New York underground either didn't notice us or found more interesting prey to pursue. Though we kept a brisk pace, enough so that the non-vamp members of our party were breathing hard by the time we made it to Manhattan, we fortunately managed to avoid anything larger than the occasional sewer rat.

Mike was right, he didn't know much more, but what info he did have he seemed willing to share.

Turned out that he wasn't alone in experiencing changes during that first full moon. A not insignificant portion of the townsfolk had as well, including the mayor's younger brother – a fuckloaf by the name of Hobart.

Seemed the others were right in suspecting the mayor knew more than he was letting on, because Hobart was quick to organize the others as well as recruit Myra to his cause. It wasn't long before he was directing them to harass Pop Vesser, looking for Ed – the so-called neo-vamp Progenitor.

As to why that was, Mike claimed to have no idea as we emerged onto the streets of downtown Manhattan. It wasn't nearly as much as I'd been hoping to learn, but it was a lot more than we'd known up to that point.

As we started heading north, Sally turned to him. "So, all the rest of that shit aside, what's the deal with you and Hobart?"

"The deal? I mean, I've known the guy for years, sure, but we've never really been friends. He just always rubbed me the wrong..."

"That's nice," she interrupted. "Save the sob story for the Lifetime TV movie. What I meant is, what makes you two different? The rest of those chucklefucks barely looked smart enough to lick the bottom of a garbage can, but it was pretty obvious you two are in control."

"Yeah," I added. "Not to mention the fact that the both of you changed back despite Myra's spell still going strong."

Mike shook his head. "I'll be damned if I have any idea

why. All I know is that Hobart and me are different for some reason. In my case, it wasn't too long after that first change that I realized I could control it. Wasn't easy at first, but now it's like..."

"Riding a really gross bike?" Kelly offered.

"Something like that." He raised a hand to his chin. "I did overhear Hobart at one point, talking in third person and referring to himself as a Dominant, but I'm not sure if that was anything more than him stroking his own ego."

Sally let out a chuckle. "Guess we should keep an eye out for werewolves in gimp masks and ball gags."

"How about the phrase *wolves of men*?" I asked. "Does that mean anything to you?"

"Wolves of what?" Mike replied.

"Something our friend found in an old text. I forget exactly what it said, but..."

"Wherever Utu's shadow caressed the land, the wolves of men besieged the kingdom of Ib, seeking to lay them low," Sally said, rolling her eyes. "Some of us actually have working memories when it comes to important shit."

Mike shook his head, though. "What's an Ib?"

"So much for that question."

"Here's a better one," Sally replied, glancing my way. "Where exactly are we going?"

I stopped in my tracks. "The Lotte, I guess."

"You guess?"

"Well, yeah. I mean, that's where Falcon was last time."

"Hold on. Does he know we're coming to see him?"

"No."

"And you're not sure he's even there?"

"Not really."

"So let me see if I have this right. Your plan is for us to just march in there and confront this guy with a squad of vampires, a witch, a werewolf who may or may not be our prisoner, and..."

"The woman who threatened to shoot him in the face last time we spoke?" I finished for her. "Yeah, you might have a point there."

She shook her head. "Jesus fucking Christ. I'm beginning to think the only reason you don't want Gan to kill me is because no one else is stupid enough to be your babysitter."

"Sorry. It's been a stressful week."

"You're a fucking vampire. When is it *not* a stressful week?" She shook her head. "Seriously, Bill, this guy's a cop. Hell, he's *the* cop when it comes to weird shit in this city. Did you stop and consider that maybe, just maybe, he's already on his way to where we just came from?"

I opened my mouth then closed it again without saying anything. *Son of a bitch!*

The second the boys in blue realized they were in a shootout with werewolves, Falcon was probably the first person they called – meaning we could've just waited around the corner for him to show up.

This was precisely the reason why people needed to stop leaving me in charge of stuff. I had absolutely no talent for...

"He's not," Kelly said.

"Huh? Not what?"

"In Brooklyn," she continued, looking down at her phone – conveniently spared from her earlier EMP spell. "Remember what I told you earlier about Vince and the Order being in town?"

"Yeah."

"Well, while I was waiting up on the roof I shot him a text asking if he could find out where Falcon was and meet us there. Anyway, I just checked and it sounds like he's way ahead of us."

Thank goodness for competent friends. "He is? Awesome! Where?"

"Hold on," she said. "I missed a lot of messages while we were underground."

"The Order?" Sally asked.

"The Order of Saint Cyprian," I explained. "Think the Templar, but they hand out job applications before burning you at the stake."

I was about to say more, but a ding from Kelly's phone told us another message had arrived.

"Guys, Vince says Falcon is down at the docks off West Tenth..."

"I know the spot." I wasn't sure why he was down there in the middle of the night, considering the place was trashed. Either way, it was a far less conspicuous spot for a confrontation than a five star hotel. "Let's go..."

"That's not all," she said, staring at the phone. "He says something weird is going on there."

I shared a glance with Sally. "Of course it is."

So much for the rest of this night being all tea and crumpets.

20

THE FISH FRY OF DOOM

It was so goddamned tempting to just call the whole thing off and lay low until we could make our way back to Purgatory and regroup.

Too bad there were a couple of problems with that. For starters, I had a feeling Falcon was the key to us moving the needle again in our quest to find Christy. Secondly, he'd proven himself to be an okay guy. Despite how things had been left between us, I would've probably felt guilty if we just left him hanging.

It almost made me wish we'd brought Tom along, since he would've had no qualms with noping the fuck out of this mess.

Vincent hadn't been specific as to exactly what he meant by weird. That meant he and his crew were probably still outside the glamour Falcon had erected down at his dock headquarters – a smart move considering Matt had a tendency to boobytrap the place. Still, as a former Templar Vincent had seen some shit. So it was probably safe to say that when he said something was weird, he wasn't just talking about an impromptu wizard rap battle breaking out.

No doubt thinking the same thing, Kelly took another hit from the vape pipe of doom before I could stop her. The deed done, she directed us down a quiet side street in the financial district.

"You sure about this?" I asked her.

"One hundred and ten percent. Now I need everyone to move close together."

I found myself pressed up against Sally, Mike, and Jessica as Kelly began to work her newly enhanced mojo.

As the area around us began to glow, I turned to Sally. "Um ... try not to explode."

"Wait," Mike said. "What do you mean explode?"

"It's just something she has a habit of doing."

"Why?!"

Fortunately, Kelly's spell took effect before I was forced to explain. I figured either one of two things would happen. Either we'd arrive just fine, or her newfound power boost would react with Sally – resulting in a pile of innards and viscera showing up at the docks instead.

And then we were gone, our atoms disassembled across time and space as we zapped over to...

EAT OF MY FLESH AND GROW STRONG.

What the fuck? It was as if someone had broadcast a message directly into every single one of my scattered cells – causing the entirety of my essence to vibrate like a guitar string.

And then, just like that, all of my pieces slammed back together and I found my feet touching down onto the ground, but this arrival wasn't like normal. It was as if I'd been sitting in a car driving sixty miles an hour, only to be thrown out the door onto the pavement.

Needless to say, that didn't work out so well. I found myself falling face first to the asphalt, rolling several times before coming to a halt.

The fuck was that?

Had Kelly maybe put a bit too much into her spell? Or did Sally have a micro-episode mid-teleport, enough to send us sprawling but thankfully falling short of reducing us to human goulash?

"Get your fucking hand off my tits or so help me I'll end you right now."

Or maybe not. Sally's power tended to explode outward from her body, knocking people away from her – sometimes explosively so. If she was complaining about bad touches, though...

Sure enough, I peeled my face from the ground and saw that everyone in our party had been scattered, Sally included. It seemed Craig had landed atop her and was now busy trying to extract himself from her cleavage – albeit perhaps not as quickly as he could've.

The struggle is real, my friend.

At least we'd made it. We were in a lot next to one of the gentrified yuppie high rises that had been constructed down near the docks in recent years – the city's idea of making the area less shitty.

Not all of it had been developed, though. Further down near the water's edge one could still find old warehouses and derelict piers. A flimsy chain link fence separated one such property from the buildings around us, as if that would be enough to keep someone out.

What wasn't apparent to the naked eye, however, was the powerful glamour that hung over that section of the docks – not to mention the defensive wards that had been placed there.

It was the reason we'd landed here, well clear of any magical defenses that might be present. But if so, then why had we been knocked flat on our asses? And what the fuck had been with that weird-ass voice in my mind? It sure as shit hadn't been the Wanderer, unless he'd suddenly woken up totally bugfuck crazy.

That was something I most certainly didn't need in my life.

"Yo! You pendejos all right?"

I turned at the sound of the familiar voice, spying a masked form *looking* our way from the shadows. It was Char. She was a blind vampire vigilante who'd helped us out a few times, basically an undead Daredevil wannabe except a bit more profane.

She wasn't alone either as I realized others were behind her, all of them wearing blue cloaks.

"Kelly!" one cried, racing forward.

"Hey, Vince," I muttered as he ignored me to check on his wife. *Nice to see you too.*

"I-I'm fine," she told him from somewhere behind me. "Rough landing is all."

That was putting it mildly.

"Yo, Freebill," Char said, likewise heading our way, "s'up?"

"Nothing much, just picking gravel out of my teeth."

"That's nice. Mind if I ask you a question?"

"Knock yourself out."

"I don't pretend to know much about this magic crap, but was that spell supposed to work like that?"

I narrowed my eyes at her snark before remembering she couldn't see my expression. "Not really."

"Didn't think so."

As the rest of us got to our feet, the half dozen or so blue cloaks – obviously more of the Order – closed in and formed ranks. Fortunately, unlike the old days, they didn't immediately start beating us over the head with their rosaries.

Mind you, judging by the looks on some of their faces, a few of them wouldn't have minded.

Guess Vince had been successful in recruiting some of his old buddies, but I had a feeling it was going to take them a while before they were happy with the new rules.

At least nobody was any worse for the wear. Even Petunia seemed quick to shake it off, immediately finding an interesting looking pebble to bat her paws at. Mind you, Sally didn't look all too happy. It served as a reminder to be wary of her stress levels.

She noticed me staring and must've guessed what I was thinking because her expression softened a notch. "I'm fine. Not my first tumble in the dirt."

"Did anyone else hear a voice telling them to eat something?"

I turned at the sound of Mike's question. That he hadn't made a run for it went a long way toward telling me he wasn't responsible for either our rough landing or the creepy voice. That was good. I was still wrapping my head around Mennonite monster hunters. I wasn't ready to swallow psychic werewolves yet.

Nods went around all through the group ... at least until it was Sally's turn.

"What voice?"

"You didn't hear it?" I asked.

"The only thing I heard was the crunch of my ass against the asphalt."

I turned toward our resident power couple. "Kel?"

"I heard it," she replied, "but that doesn't mean I understand it. I ... don't think it was meant for us, though."

"How so?"

She shook her head. "It's hard to explain. Kind of felt more like an echo to me, or maybe some astral plane reverb."

"The astral plane?" Jessica asked. "That's actually a thing?"

"Oh yeah. The Magi use it as a shortcut to send ourselves places – kind of like a wormhole."

"And do you normally get *reverb* while traveling to the gamma quadrant?" I asked.

"Not really." She let out a laugh, but it was mostly bereft of humor. "I didn't know it was even possible."

That wasn't promising. Still, it sounded like an easily avoided problem. "Okay, next time we'll take an Uber." I turned toward Vincent. "What's the 4-1-1 on Falcon?"

He didn't seem in any particular hurry to stop fawning over his wife, but finally he seemed to accept that she was okay. "We think he's here."

"You *think* he's here?"

"It's more than that," he corrected. "We learned he wasn't in his room at the Lotte and chatter on the police scanner confirmed he wasn't picking up, despite numerous calls about some incident over in Brooklyn."

"That was probably us."

"So I figured. With those ruled out we came here next, where we met Ms. Reyes who graciously explained her acquaintance with you."

"Yeah," Char said. "*After* you putos almost gutted me like a fish."

"Please allow me to once again apologize," Vincent replied. "As I said, we had no way of knowing whether you were a threat."

She let out a snort. "Six fuckheads with swords, and yet one lone chica is the threat? If that ain't white boy logic I don't know what is."

It was also typical Templar logic as well, but now was probably not the time for additional sniping. "Okay, so let's get back to the part about Falcon being here."

Char nodded. "They're right, Freebill. Pretty sure he's in there. All I know is he hasn't walked out of there since I've been keeping watch, ain't zapped out either."

"How would you even know that?"

"He can't. Dude's upped security recently. Nobody can zap in or out, not even him."

"And you know this how?"

She let out a sigh, as if debating whether or not to tell me to go fuck myself.

"I like this one," Sally muttered, sidling up alongside me.

Char grinned, having obviously overheard. "Fine. Guess it don't hurt none. Bird Man helped me out a few weeks back. Some bad business over in Hudson River Park."

"What kind of business?" I asked.

"Normally I'd be split between it being the kind that's none of yours or that you wouldn't believe, but I'm guessing that last one don't count with this crew. Anyway, it involved those fish men we fought a while back, and some big-ass thing in the water they were carving up and feeding to folks."

"Nothing quite like New York when it comes to fine dining," Sally remarked.

"No shit. Problem was, this whale thing kept speaking in everyone's head, telling them to eat it and get stronger."

I shared a glance with Kelly. No way could that be a coincidence.

"I've been keeping in touch with him since then," Char continued. "We've been working to figure out what the fuck that thing is and how to keep it from snagging more folks."

"Snagging them, how?"

She shrugged. "Don't know exactly, but I'm guessing it ain't all that hard for something that can get in your head like it does. And once you accept a Filet-O-Fish from it, I'm pretty sure it just gets worse from there."

Sally nodded. "Hmm, I think there was something like that in an H.P. Lovecraft story." Then, before I could comment, she added, "I do read you know."

"Good for you, Ms. Librarian," Char remarked. "I'm more of a podcast girl myself. Go figure, right? Anyway, as I was about to say, things started getting weird with the bird guy about a week back. He got called in to check out that building that collapsed over in the Village. Something must've happened to him there. He wouldn't talk about it, but afterward he wasn't the same."

Sally gave me a not-insignificant look. That was her building that had collapsed and it had been no accident. Falcon's aunt had been directly responsible. Not long after, we'd found ourselves in upstate New York, storming Gan's compound.

"In what way?" I asked.

"Hard to say, but he definitely became a lot moodier. Started giving me excuses too. There were spots to check out where folks had seen something in the water, but he seemed too distracted to investigate. Kept telling me he needed to do more research and shit like that."

"What kind of research?" Mike asked, prompting us all to look his way. "What? Maybe he *really* was busy."

Char shook her head. "Nah, I'm telling you he wasn't himself. He was still all calm and British on the outside, but I could hear what was going on inside. His heart rate, his breathing, they were all off. Something has that dude seriously rattled."

I couldn't help but wonder if that flying monster had been the cause. I mean, it sure as shit had freaked me out. Still, Falcon hadn't hesitated to join in the fight against it. Those weren't the actions of someone who'd lost their nerve, unless this was some delayed reaction after the fact. "Is that why you've been staking out this place?"

"Don't get me wrong, it's not like I care about him or anything. Guy just did me a solid, so I was returning the favor."

"So what's he doing in there?"

"No idea. He's been getting a lot of shipments, though, trucks going in and out. I think he's rebuilding after that big scuffle we had down here last month."

"What big scuffle?" Mike asked.

"The kind that's none of your business," I replied.

"Yo, who is this dude anyway?" Char asked, pointing his way. "He smells kinda funny."

"We talking wet dog or flea bath?" Okay, that wasn't helping. "Sorry. Long story."

Char shrugged as if she couldn't have cared less. "Whatever. My point is, I was trying to figure out a way to sneak inside and check things out when these sword guys showed up."

"Why?" Kelly asked. "What changed?"

"Bird Guy's got his magic shield up around the place, but it ain't perfect. I don't get much, just the occasional whiff, but I noticed tonight that something don't smell right inside. Problem is, I can't just waltz in like normal."

"The defenses?"

She nodded. "Normally I can sense them no problem, but he's been adding more and more of these weird crystal things around the perimeter – too many of them. They cause my head to buzz which makes everything all fuzzy. And well, let's just say I'm not in the habit of wanting my ass blown off."

The more I thought about it, the more I had to wonder

whether the monster bird had been the cause of Falcon's paranoia or had simply reinforced it – after all, we weren't the only ones aware that there was more than one giant monster about.

Barely two weeks ago Ed and I had popped by here just as something massive had reared its ugly head – or tail anyway – crushing what had been left of Falcon's warehouse.

Char had been present, too, making me guess that the thing we'd seen that day was almost certainly the whale beast she'd just described – because I wasn't quite ready to accept that two megalodon-sized hell-beasts had taken up residence in the same river.

If they'd been actively investigating it, that also made me wonder whether that attack had indeed been as random as I'd assumed. Talk about a terrifying thought. What if the giant beast in question was intelligent enough to understand the concept of reprisal?

Fuck that noise.

None of that was my problem. I was here to get Falcon's help so we could access the Archives, nothing more. If he wanted a fishing buddy, he'd have to look elsewhere. Hell, his family was rich as fuck. He could probably hire his own private navy to take care of this, so let him.

All we needed to do was get in, talk to the guy, and maybe dangle his vape pen in front of his face as a bribe.

After that, we'd be on our way – easy as pie.

Or so I hoped.

21

ROCK AROUND THE
DOCK TONIGHT

I turned toward Sally, but she was way ahead of me. "I know the drill. Wait out here and play with your pussy."

I nodded. "Sorry, but if he has more of those orb things..."

"Which it sounds like he does." She nodded, clearly not happy with being sidelined, but also more than aware of what could happen. Back at Gan's it had taken only a single Orb of Amun-Ra to make her powers react, and now it sounded like Falcon was planting them by the truckload.

I turned to the rest. "Okay, we're not here Christmas caroling, so it might be best to keep the welcome party to a minimum. Kel, I'm thinking you, me, and..."

"If she goes then so do I."

"No offense, Vince, but the Magi and the Templar don't exactly have the best history."

"Then it's a good thing I don't represent the Templar anymore." At my dubious look, he took off his blue cloak and handed it to one of the others. "How about now?"

"Okay, I guess that works."

"Count me in too, Freebill," Char added. "Like I said, I owe the guy."

"All right, four it is then. I suppose that's not too obnoxious."

Oswalt raised his hand. "I'm kind of curious to see..."

"Overruled. Nobody else? Good. Sit tight and try not to do anything to make the locals call the cops."

"Way to rally the troops, Freebill," Char remarked as we turned toward the chain link fence separating Hipsterville from the derelict docks. "And this is why I prefer working alone."

"And here I thought it was your effervescent personality."

"What can I say? When you're this cool you don't need a posse."

The banter petered out as we stopped outside the gate. I took a quick sniff of the air, not noticing much out of the ordinary, but then I remembered what Char had said about something smelling off. I mean, to an outsider the whole city probably smelled funky, but she was clearly no tourist.

Fuck it. She might've attuned her senses more than me, but that didn't mean they were actually stronger. If she could sense something weird then so could I.

"Hold on a sec," I said, taking another whiff.

Once again, I didn't notice anything odd. I mean, yes, there was a briny underlayer to everything, but that didn't mean shit. Last time we'd been here there'd been a rotting sea serpent corpse lying in the middle of the dock – supposedly the river's former occupant, having been rudely evicted by whatever had taken up residence recently.

"You okay?" Kelly asked.

I nodded. "Yeah, let's go."

As usual, the gate wasn't locked. But then, it probably didn't need to be.

Continuing forward, the air began to ripple around us, telling me we were passing through the glamour that portrayed a picture of normalcy to the outside wor... *UGH!*

It was like someone kicked me in the fucking skull – from the inside. A migraine slammed into my head, even worse than the ones I'd suffered in Purgatory. *The fuck?*

"Wow," Kelly said a moment later. "That's a lot of orbs."

"Told ya," Char replied, seemingly no worse for the wear. "Bird Guy's been stockpiling them like they're Pokémon cards."

Kelly let out a whistle. "Trust me when I say that's no small feat. They're not exactly common in the Magi world. It usually takes a full coven a whole week just to charge one."

"Fascinating, I'm sure," I said, blinking the tears away so I could take a better look around.

At first glance, things didn't seem all that different. The pier itself was the same pitted asphalt as before. Thankfully, the river naga corpse was gone. Can't imagine that would've smelled all that pleasant after a week or two. As for the warehouse... "I thought you said he was rebuilding."

"And they say I'm the blind one."

A moment later, I realized she was right. Parked behind the remains of the ruined warehouse was a trailer, the same sort you might see at a construction site.

As I tried to focus on it, however, I felt another stab of pain in my frontal lobe. *Gah!*

"Most of the orbs are down that way." Kelly pointed toward the ruined warehouse. "I can feel them. He's got at least a dozen lined up along the water's edge."

That didn't sound particularly comforting.

"No, wait. There's more," she continued, "a lot more, but they've all been spent or are low on charge."

And just like that it immediately sounded worse.

"Why?" I asked, having a feeling I wasn't going to like the answer.

"Oh no, Bird Guy," Char said, more to herself than anyone. "Please tell me you're not doing something stupid."

I had a sinking sensation stupid was going to be too kind of a label. "All right, let's stop fucking around." I turned Kelly's way, forcing my agonized brain to focus. "The first time I was here, Christy did some sort of ... *thing* that exposed all the boobytraps and tripwires for a few seconds. I don't suppose you could..."

"I know exactly what spell you mean." She let out a nervous laugh. "I don't even need help for this one. This place is so saturated with power, I can pull the magic right out of the air."

Guess it was a good thing Sally had stayed behind.

Before, when Christy had done the spell, sigils and glyphs had appeared on the ground, attached to the lamp posts, and even hanging in the air – pretty much showing us a magical minefield of sorts. After Kelly waved her hands, though, it was like the entire pier lit up like a spotlight for at least fifty feet in front of us. It probably went even further, but that was as far as I could see. There were so many wards, I couldn't tell where one ended and another began.

If I really had acquired some sort of magic allergy from Ed's bite, well, this would certainly be the thing that set it off.

"The fuck was that about?" Char cried, shielding her eyes until Kelly dropped the spell.

I couldn't help but raise an eyebrow. "Wait. How did you...?"

"I can see some light if it's bright enough," she replied, shaking her head. "The fuck? Did someone accidentally teleport us to the surface of the sun?"

"You shouldn't be here!"

The voice thundered across the cracked asphalt as if we were standing atop a massive speaker. For a moment, I wondered if the voice we'd heard during our teleport was back, but then I realized I'd heard this with my ears. Well, that and the obvious British accent tipped me off.

The trailer door flew open, revealing Falcon ... or his dirty methhead cousin anyway. Even from across the pier, I could see the guy was an absolute mess. Usually he came across as a high class John Constantine with a porno-stash. Despite his family's wealth, he hadn't been all three-thousand dollar suits and ascots, but there'd been a disturbing amount of style to him, making his business casual look far better than it had any right to.

Not anymore. His shirt was untucked and his pants were wrinkled, as if he'd been sleeping in them for several days. His hair was unkempt and there were bags beneath his eyes.

Even his mustache seemed wilder than normal, as if he'd given up waxing it and decided to let it run free.

"Charisma," he cried. "You need to go. It's taking everything I have to keep it at..." He trailed off as his eyes landed on me. "You!"

Guess he was still miffed about that witch I killed. "Hey, Matt. So, how's things?"

He stormed our way, the magical death trap no doubt designed to allow him to pass unharmed. "You have a lot of fucking nerve coming here after what you did."

"Bill?" Kelly whispered.

"I've got this," I replied from the corner of my mouth before turning my attention back toward Falcon. "Listen, I'm really sorry about that. I ... panicked in the moment. I couldn't just let Ed die. Not like..."

"What in bloody hell are you going on about?" he snapped, stopping about ten feet away.

"Um, that witch I might have sorta..."

"This isn't about some damned witch! Everyone who was there knew what they were getting into. I'm talking about something far more serious, a breach of trust of the highest order."

Uh oh. I was afraid of that. "This is about the Archives isn't it?"

"Of course it's about the bleeding Archives, you git!" Spittle flew from his mouth, a far cry from his normal level of annoying refinement. "Do you have any idea how lucky you are that I figured it out before Marjorie or anyone else in the family did?"

"No, not really."

"You should count your lucky stars every Magi in Europe isn't out for your blood."

Okay, that definitely sounded potentially unpleasant.

"At first I thought Christine was to blame," he continued, starting to rant, "that she'd found a loophole we weren't aware of, some flaw in our security that was exposed during the last five years. But then I thought to ask one of the librarians to check the digital logs. And do you know what I found?"

I may have had a bit of an idea.

"I found someone had been using my password to access the Archives for nearly a month now – combing through manuscripts I know full well I haven't looked at." He narrowed his eyes. "You are aware that we have extensive files on you and your friends, yes?"

"You made that point pretty clear when we met."

"Enough for me to know the chances of Christine breaking through our digital safeguards were slim. But you, Freewill, you're another matter entirely, aren't you? A self-professed *hacker*, are you not?"

"Nobody actually calls themselves that." *Fuck it.* "What can I say, Matt? What you call safeguards, I'd call about as hard to get into as an open SSID with the default admin password."

"A what?"

"Exactly my point," I replied, allowing myself a small touch of pride.

"Pretty sure he wasn't applauding your skills there," Kelly said.

"Gotta take the compliments where I can." Okay maybe I needed to deescalate a bit. I was the one in the wrong here. Thumbing my nose at this guy's noob-level web skills was only going to make things worse – and I wasn't the only one at risk. "Okay fine. I admit it. We had too much on our plate, and no chance of solving it ourselves. So we came to you. Then you turned Christy down when she asked for access, so..."

"You thought you'd break into the most secure magic library in the world like some thief in the night?"

"In all fairness, your website sucked. An eight year old could've gotten into it."

He let out a huff of frustration and looked away. "So our brand new security consultant has informed me. Regardless, that doesn't give you any right."

"Wait, for real? You actually hacked this guy, Freebill?"

Char asked, a smirk on her face. "Goddamn, look at the cajones on you."

"Not helping," I hissed.

"Not really trying to."

Goddamn, it was like hanging out with Sally's younger, blinder twin. Time to refocus on Falcon. "Listen, I know what I did was wrong and in Christy's defense she said the same thing. But like I said, we needed help and..."

"And the Falcon Archives are the forbidden fruit that would tempt anyone," he replied, rubbing his eyes. "Of that I am well aware."

"Well, maybe not exactly..."

"Regardless, the fact remains, Freewill, that what you did could be construed as an act of war..."

"Hold on..."

"But as I said, fortunate for you I discovered this before my family did and was able to have those logs expunged."

"Wait, you did?"

"Yes, because the truth is you and your friends have helped my cause far more than you've had any reason to. So consider this my repayment in full. However, know this. Any trust I may have had in you is now irrevocably gone. As for Christine..."

"That's actually why we're here."

"Yes. Well, please allow me to offer my condolences. She may have made some mistakes but..."

"We need your help to get her back."

"Get her back? But she..."

"No, she didn't," Kelly interrupted. "We think ... *know* the Source took her somewhere outside our reality. We're trying to figure out where so we can get her back."

"Excuse me, and you are?"

"Kelly Schwarz ... Munroe. I'm a..."

"Kelly Munroe?" I replied. "You mean like..."

"Yes, like from *Congo*! Do we really need to do this now?"

I held up my hands. "Sorry." Geez, some people could be so touchy about their names.

"I'm one of Christy's coven," she continued.

"Ah yes," Falcon said. "The catalyst witch who married the Templar."

"Former Templar," Vincent corrected. "We are now the Order of Saint Cyprian."

Like that was relevant right now.

"Fascinating, I'm sure," Falcon replied. "Regardless, I'm not convinced I can be of help. And even if I could, now is not a good time. It's..." He trailed off, his eyes losing focus as he stumbled.

Fortunately for him, Char had Spider-man like reflexes – racing to his side just in time to keep his tired ass from spilling onto the asphalt. And yet according to her she didn't care.

She caught him then wrinkled her nose. "Ugh, when's the last time you showered?"

"My apologies, Charisma," he replied, ramping down the aggro by about three-thousand percent. "Alas, my current facilities are a bit lacking. A necessity I'm afraid."

"Forget showering, when's the last time you slept?" I asked.

"Sleep is not a luxury I can afford right now." He focused on me again, his eyes once more growing cold. "Now, for the last time, I really must insist that all of you..."

"We have your pen!" Kelly interrupted.

"My what?"

"Your vape pen I mean." She reached into her pocket then hesitated, as if unsure she wanted to hand it over. Credit to her, though, as she pulled it out a moment later.

Falcon's eyes immediately lit up at the sight of it. "Where did you get that?"

Guess it was my turn again. "You dropped it at Gan's. Must've been when that giant turkey attacked us. Anyway, I saw it and figured you might want it back."

"I ... I thought it lost."

"Well, it's all yours. It's the least I can do to try and make amends. If it helps, I really am sorry."

That was mostly bullshit, but hopefully none of his wards were designed to mimic a Zone of Truth spell.

Kelly stepped forward, her and Falcon's eyes both glued to the pipe in her hand. Go figure. I guess magical steroids was a popular flavor. "I have to ask. What exactly is in this because ... wow?"

"Oh no," Falcon replied, something akin to horror on his face. "Please tell me you didn't imbibe from that."

Huh. Ironic as he was way too ripe to be worrying about germs.

"Why?"

"You did, didn't you?!" Falcon snapped, backing up a step. "You fool woman!"

"I'll kindly ask you to apologize to my wife," Vincent said.

Falcon ignored him, though. "They'll be coming for you! They can sense her essence, you know. They know who's defiled it. They *always* know."

"Who?" she asked, echoing my thoughts.

"You have to understand, they've been searching for her remains for over three millennia. It is only through a complex and precise mix of warding incantations that I've been able to throw them off."

"Yo, Bird Guy, you okay?" Char asked. "You're sounding a bit ... how do I put this ... unhinged."

"I am not okay!" he snapped, his eyes wild. "I am..."

Unfortunately, he didn't get a chance to finish his spittle laden rant as the ground began to rumble beneath our feet – hard enough that Vincent put an arm around his wife to steady her.

Needless to say, it did nothing to make my headache any better. It...

Except that was a lie. In the space of the next few seconds the pain in my head decreased from an eleven to maybe a three – allowing me to think clearly again.

The instant migraine remedy coincided with a series of super bright flashes down at the water's edge, like a bunch of old-timey flash bulbs all going off at once.

"No!" Falcon cried. "Not now!"

Almost as if in response to his panic, the water began to

froth and churn. Then a bright blue glow became visible just below the surface.

Oh crap.

Falcon turned back toward us, naked fear upon his face. "You have to run! I thought it was sedated, but I was wrong. There's no way I'll be able to hold it. Not now."

"What did you do?" Char replied.

"You have to understand," he said, growing ever more unhinged. "After that fight, after seeing that thing in the sky, I knew I had to do something. I had to try and stop it from getting any worse, but I couldn't find it again. It's not alone, though. So instead I scried the entire river until I discovered *its* lair. Then I set a trap to capture it. I thought I could hold it until I figured out something, *anything* that might work to..."

"Captured *what*?" Kelly demanded.

Sadly, I had a feeling I already knew the answer.

"One of the great beasts of legend," he replied. "The almighty Leviathan."

22

FISHING FOR COMPLIMENTS

Eat of my flesh and serve. Eat and grow strong.

I just had to drag my friends here tonight, didn't I? It couldn't have been any other night. No, it had to be on the same day when Godzilla decided to emerge from the harbor and go looking for Matthew fucking Broderick.

The only thing that could make this worse was if it decided to lay eggs in Madison Square Garden for no fucking reason. Too bad I was fresh out of missiles or any other ideas for how to solve this.

"We ... we have to ... we need to..."

I wasn't alone in my despair either. It was pretty obvious that Falcon was broken, not that I could really blame the guy.

On the flipside, I couldn't quite believe he'd been insane enough to do this. I mean, my encounter with Big Bird up at Gan's was enough to make me happy to never ever see anything like that again outside of a Japanese movie. But Falcon was apparently cut from far more batshit cloth – having decided the best course of action was to cast his fishing line and hook the mother of all big ones.

Speaking of which, a wave of water washed over the pier as the ground beneath us continued to shake, sending a spray high into the air and soaking us all.

"Dear mother of God, this cannot be," Vincent said, eyes wide as his hand pulled a rosary from his shirt.

Huh. You'd think our group's resident Bible belter would be happy to meet one of the cast. Guess not.

I began to understand his terror, though, as something breached the surface. Triangular in shape with dark scaly skin, it continued to rise ... and rise ... and kept on going.

I made out glowing blue sigils etched into its skin, each of them at least ten feet high, like some kind of weird-ass nuclear tattoos.

Then, when a good forty feet of it was out of the water, it shifted a little, revealing a massive reptilian eye staring our way.

It's head. I was looking at this thing's fucking head – or at least part of it, which was fucking insane since I was pretty sure the water here was maybe twenty feet deep at most. That meant this monstrosity was either the world's most out of proportion bobblehead or some magical fuckery was afoot.

Sadly, I had a feeling it was the latter.

A part of me would've been fascinated to see the whole creature, on TV and from a great distance. After all, there was something cool about kaiju, or at least there was when they were more than a couple hundred feet from you.

What I could see, however, was more than enough to paint a nightmare picture. Think the Mosasaurus from *Jurassic World*, but a lot bigger, uglier, and sporting radioactive body art. It opened its mouth, revealing a triple set of serrated teeth – most of which were larger than me.

It made me almost long for the days when the biggest threat I had to deal with was the occasional Sasquatch.

Then, as disgusting black ichor drooled from the side of its mouth, it let out a low-pitched bellow, like someone strumming a massive bass guitar. I could feel the vibrations throughout my entire body. Weirder still, I could *see* them.

The air distorted around the creature's mouth, undulating as if superheated. Then the distortions began to radiate outward. It wasn't entirely unlike watching Sally's power go off, save it was a lot bigger and moving much slower.

"What the fuck?" Char cried, no doubt experiencing more sensory outrage than the rest of us. Can't say I envied her.

Slow or not, the distortions heading our way were too big to dodge.

As the shockwaves closed in, all I could think about was the devastation I'd seen Sally cause, more than enough to liquify a vampire a close range.

This was it. I was about to be reduced to pulp by the beast from twenty-thousand fathoms and there wasn't a goddamned thing I could do about it...

Except stand there as they passed harmlessly through us all?

Don't get me wrong, I certainly felt them. Like standing next to a giant gong that someone was beating. Worse still, as my body vibrated, I once more heard its voice inside my mind.

Serve.

Eat.

Grow strong.

I wasn't sure what it meant, other than doubting this thing was trying to advertise its new all-you-can-eat surf & turf bar.

Aside from being a bit uncomfortable, though, I felt fine. I certainly wasn't being blasted to pieces, which was nice. Likewise, my companions here on the...

Wh... what is that thing? What happened?

My eyes opened wide at the voice inside my head – one far more familiar than moby prick's.

Yo, Wanderer, is that you? You okay, man?

Unfortunately, he didn't appear to be in an answering mood, as my subconscious once again fell abruptly silent.

"No! Not that!" Falcon cried.

What now?

A mere instant later, his meaning became clear. The distortions coming from the beast hadn't blasted us to hell, but that didn't mean they weren't having an effect.

"Jesus fuck!" Char cried out as all the wards, glyphs, and

other defenses once more lit up like Broadway ... for a second or two anyway.

Then it was as if they simply disintegrated, blowing away like dust in the wind.

What the?

Was the creature somehow canceling out Falcon's magic? *Wait!* If that was the case then what about the glamour?

I turned toward the street in time to see more of those orb thingies explode. Then, the air around the entire pier began to distort. There came a brief flash of light and then ... nothing. It all looked the same.

To us anyway.

My eyes caught sight of Sally and the others who'd stayed behind, well away from the magic of this place. Too bad they likewise seemed to have caught sight of me.

Judging by the look on Sally's face and the way she met my gaze, I had a nasty feeling that the madness going on here was now in plain view for all the world to witness.

Well, isn't that just fucking wonderful?

On the upside, at least my headache was gone.

***

"I hate to break it to you, but I think the glamour's down."

"Really?" Kelly asked, rounding on me. "That's our biggest problem right now?"

"No, just saying..."

EAT OF ME AND SERVE!!

I dropped to my knees as the voice echoed inside my head again, this time about a thousand times louder than it had been before.

Guh! It was like a cockpunch to my cerebral cortex. "Anyone else catch the number of that bus?"

Silence greeted my entreaty, at least as far as voices were concerned.

The ground rumbled again as the sound of more rushing water met my ears. Almost afraid to look, I turned back that way – and immediately regretted it.

Everyone with me was staring in that direction, watching what was unfolding. Leviathan's head slammed down onto the pier, crushing Falcon's new trailer as well as the splintered remains of his warehouse. There it lay with its titanic noggin out of the water. Though I couldn't see the rest, I spied a frill rising from the Hudson behind it as well as a bluish glow beneath the water for what had to be at least two-hundred feet.

As if that weren't bad enough, much smaller figures were now scrambling up from the water. It was the apkallu – freakish fish men covered in razor sharp spines and glowing the same shade of blue as their big brother.

Oh yeah, we're fucked.

However, rather than charge at us, the scaly freaks converged on the big one, using their claws to rake chunks of flesh from the side of its head.

Eat of me!

I winced at the sound in my mind, although it wasn't as bad now. And at least I had the disturbing insight of knowing what the fuck it was talking about this time.

As I considered this, my four companions began walking that way.

"Um, guys, I think this is one clam bake we probably want to avoid."

If they heard me, they gave no indication as they continued to march forward.

Oh crap.

"Um, Kelly? Char?" *Shit!* "Yo, Falcon, tea and scones suck the big one!"

There was no response from any of them. They kept shuffle stepping forward as the apkallu continued carving fish filets from Leviathan.

Eat!

What was up with them? And then it hit me. I'd seen shit like this before. Hell, tons of times. Whatever was happening here, it wasn't too far off from vampiric compulsion.

So then why wasn't I being mindfucked too?

Is it because ... I'm the Freewill?

I'd always assumed my ability to reject being compelled was a vampire only thing. But maybe I was wrong. After all, I'd seen mages screw with other people's minds before. However, it was only now that I realized I'd never been among them.

Perhaps that wasn't a coincidence. Maybe my powers weren't as useless as I'd thought in this new 2.0 body.

"What the fuck are you idiots doing?"

Huh? I turned back to see Sally approaching. She'd crossed the street toward the pier, along with the others – including our new werewolf buddy.

"Don't come any closer!" I cried out. "This thing can screw with your..."

I quickly saw I was preaching to the choir. Sally hadn't been shouting at me so much as those in her contingent, all of whom now wore slack-jawed stares on their faces as if they were sleepwalking.

I wasn't sure how she was keeping her wits about her, but so long as she wasn't going all, "BOW TO THE GREAT BEAST!" on me, I wasn't about to question it either.

"Do what you can to stop them!" I shouted to her before turning back, only to find my group was still on the move – headed directly toward the worst seafood buffet of their lives. As for Leviathan, it continued to lie there, its massive reptilian eyes seeming to glare at us as its minions carved it up in earnest – doing relatively little damage to the monstrosity thanks to its sheer size.

Eat and grow strong!

"I've got something you can eat!" I shouted back before racing ahead and grabbing hold of Kelly.

I spun her back around toward me, seeing the glassy eyed stare on her face. I had no way of knowing how similar Titanosaurus's mind-control was to actual compulsion, but hopefully it was close – mostly because compulsion wasn't foolproof.

"Sorry, Kel, but you'll thank me if this works."

I slapped her across the face, hard enough for it to echo across the dock.

The result was almost immediate. Her head rocked to the side as she blinked and brought a hand up to her cheek. Fortunately, that was accompanied by her eyes clearing up.

"Wh ... what?"

"Are you okay?" I asked.

"Why did ... you hit me?"

"Because you were busy doing the zombie shuffle."

"I didn't ... realize you were into the rough stuff."

I couldn't help but laugh. "Good to have you back."

"What happened?"

"Gamera over there mind-zapped you. Now come on, we need to smack the others awake before..."

She grabbed hold of my arm. "It ... it won't work. I can still feel it. This close ... it's too strong. Going to ... take over again. We need ... something more."

Shit! I'd been afraid of that. Guess its compulsion was an upgraded model after all. "Can you apparate us out of here?"

"One or t-two maybe," she stammered, shaking her head, "but it's taking all I have just to keep talking. I could accidentally ... send us ... into a volcano or the middle of the ocean if I tried."

Double shit! That wasn't good. Back in my old D&D game, I'd once had the displeasure of being halfway through a wall when a Gaseous Form spell crapped out. Suffice to say, Dave had taken great pleasure in describing my horrific death in detail. Last thing I needed was to tempt fate trying it in real life.

But maybe there was another way. Maybe I could fight fire with fire. "Okay, how about this? Can you electrocute everyone here?"

"What?"

"I meant that stun gun spell you guys use. I need you to blast everyone with it. The guys back there too."

She thought about it for a second, her eyes momentarily glazing before clearing up again, then she nodded. "I can do that. Don't need as much concentration. But why?"

"Trust me. Just light everyone up and leave them twitching. I'll take care of the rest."

Fortunately, Kelly wasn't in a mood to argue. She took a deep breath and steadied herself, before noticing the vape pen still in her hand. Without hesitation, and with apparently no regard for Falcon's manic warning, she took another suck.

That was apparently all she needed to be in business again. Her body lit up with brilliant blue energy and she lashed out. There came the *crack* of power discharging and then Falcon, Char, and even Vincent collapsed to the ground. *Yes!* I turned back and was happy to see the others doing the same ... including Sally.

Oops, should have probably mentioned something about that.

Oh well, I could always beg for my life later. "Back in a second."

"Hurry!"

I put my supernatural speed to good use, racing to where the coven lay. They wouldn't be out of it for long. A vampire constitution was pretty good at shrugging off the effects of being stunned.

I knelt down, grabbed hold of Jessica's arm, and brought it to my lips before hesitating.

What a fucking joke I was. I'd promised them all that I wouldn't use them as my own personal battery packs, yet time and again I seemed to keep breaking that promise. And here I was about to break it again.

On the other hand, a fucking psychic kaiju was in the process of making landfall, so maybe, just maybe, I could save the self-recrimination for another day. A slippery slope was preferable to getting shit-stomped by a thousand tons of monster.

I bit her wrist, breaking the skin and letting her blood flow into me.

Please work! Don't let Ed have fucked this up for me too.

Thankfully, the next few moments proved that wrong as I felt my strength nearly double. *Now for the rest.*

I was quick about it – a sip or two from everyone, no

more. It wouldn't last long, but if this didn't work none of it would matter anyway.

By the time I was finished, they were already starting to shake off the effects of being zapped, but that was okay because I was now operating on a level several times higher than normal. I gave Mike a quick glance, mulling it over, but then decided against it. Whatever boost I got from him would likely be offset by me turning into a shambling dogman. No. What I had in me would have to be enough.

Without any further ado, I headed back to where Kelly waited, moving so much faster than before it was almost like teleporting. "Sorry for the wait. Are you okay?"

She shook her head. "Whatever's in this pipe is helping, but I won't be able to hold it off for long. It's really freaking strong."

"Well, then step back and watch the magic." I turned toward the monstrosity controlling my friends and random associates, forced myself to concentrate, and then shouted, "Stop obeying this fucking thing!"

And that's when I promptly remembered that I couldn't fucking compel anymore. *Fuck, fuck, fuck!*

Eat of my flesh and grow strong!

"NO!" I screamed in frustration, my anger boiling over. "Eat your own fucking ass!"

Guess I must've gotten its attention because a moment later the message changed.

Why do you fight me, sub-creature?

Sub-creature? "No offense, Zuul, but I like being in control of my own mind."

Was I actually having a conversation with this thing?

My flesh will give you strength you have never known.

Guess so. "Tempting, but I'm gonna go with you fucking yourself instead."

Have I mentioned that I'm delicious?

"What?"

Go on, try some. I bet you'll like it.

"What the fuck kind of argument is that?"

Nummy, nummy for your tummy.

"Are you fucking for real?"

Also, you'll get to be with your friends forever. Won't that be nice? Good food, good company.

Jesus fucking Christ. Was this thing giving me a sales pitch?

"Hurry, Bill ... I'm losing it," Kelly cried from behind me.

Oh yeah. This thing was busy running my friends' minds through a Cuisinart, yet there I was listening as it tried to sell me a timeshare.

Okay, so an anti-compulsion was out of the question. What did that leave me with?

I was currently hopped up on vamp blood, leaving me with power to spare – against a normal opponent anyway. I doubted Varan the Unbelievable over there would even feel my best shot, not unless I had a briefcase nuke...

Or a magic hammer!

Yes! This was it. This was that moment of destiny. We're talking like when Thor brought the hurt down onto Thanos, except this time I'd go for the head.

In all fairness, that part was actually fairly easy as this thing's head was the size of a warehouse.

So what do you say? it continued. *Care to take a bite?*

"Yeah, about that..."

All the cool kids are doing it. You want to be cool don't you?

For fuck's sake. Now it was an after school drug PSA. "You know what? You're right. Maybe I will have some."

Excellent.

I reached down and pulled Thundersmite from its holster. "But first, I think I need to work up a bit of an appetite."

With that, I called upon every ounce of vampire strength my legs had to give and sped forward – trying not to think about how absolutely batshit crazy this was.

Crazy, yet oh so awesome, assuming it worked.

Goddamn, this thing is big.

The closer I got, the larger Leviathan became, until its massive jaws were taking up nearly my entire field of vision.

At least my chances of missing were slim.

Now! Thunder ... thunder ... THUNDERSMITE!

I focused on the hammer, willing it to change. There came a flash of light. When it cleared, gone was the Home Depot special and in its place was a massive two-handed war hammer, glowing with power that was made for fucking up legendary monsters.

It was time to shit or get off the pot, and damn if I didn't feel the need to empty my bowels. I leapt, launching myself at least thirty feet into the air. Holding Thundersmite with both hands, I lifted it above my head as I began to descend.

Damnit! I really should've come up with a badass catchphrase ahead of time. Oh well, when in doubt, paraphrase something Thor might've said if he was only a bit cooler.

"Fuck thee verily!" I cried, bringing the weapon down onto the beast's snout with everything I had.

I'd rolled the dice. Now to see if I could score the critical hit of a lifetime.

23

THE DICE HAVE SPOKEN

Clonk!

Somehow the sound of impact was a bit less impressive than the fiery explosion of doom I'd envisioned.

Don't get me wrong, I didn't expect to vanquish my foe with one blow – as awesome as that would've been – but I certainly hoped to at least give it enough of a bloody nose to know that shit was about to get real.

But what happened instead was ... somewhat *less* than impressive.

Maybe I needed a better catchphrase, or perhaps I required more conviction of heart, or maybe...

Those thoughts trailed off as I landed on the ground, noticing the broken bits of metal that rained down around me.

Or maybe I needed to invest in a magic hammer that didn't break into a million goddamned pieces the first time I used it!

What the ever-living fuck?!

I looked down at the weapon's shaft still in my hands, realizing the rest of it had broken off on impact.

You've gotta be kidding me!

Oh, this was bad on so many levels I couldn't even begin to count them.

Even the apkallu had stopped what they were doing to stare at me with their googly fish eyes, most of their heads tilted as if trying to figure out what the hell I'd been hoping to accomplish.

"Yeah? Well ... fuck you too."

So that's how it's going to be, eh? the beast's psychic voice echoed in my head, sounding distinctly less friendly than it had moments earlier.

Uh oh. I should've figured, success or failure, I'd tick off the economy sized dinosaur with that stunt. I just hadn't counted on the failure part. I mean, it had been so perfect, a comic book moment if ever there was one.

And yet I'd fucked it up all the same.

The reject from Skull Island started to growl as I stood there, a low deep-pitched sound I could feel in my bones.

I backed up, trying to think of some way out of this shitstorm of my own making. *I just had to piss it off, didn't I?* In retrospect, perhaps not the best strategy I could've picked.

"Get the fuck out of there, Bill!"

It was Sally. Guess she'd finally shrugged off Kelly's spell. Too bad her advice was coming in a bit late.

"Bill can't come to the phone right now," I muttered as the gargantuan beast lifted its head, drenching me in a combination of seawater and black drool. "He's busy playing the bug on this windshield."

I could only watch as Leviathan reared up, its body rising high above me as it lifted an impossibly large clawed fin from the water. The intent was obvious. I was an ant and that was the boot.

And goddamn what a big boot it was. It made getting squashed by that river naga seem like a pleasant memory.

Vampire healing or not, there was no way I was going to survive being splattered across this thing's heel.

Much as I wanted to close my eyes, I couldn't look away from the monstrous appendage as it closed in – knowing full well at least some of the wetness in my pants was pee.

See you on the other side, guys. It's been real.

At least as far as failures went, this one was spectacular as...

"NO!"

What the?

In the instant after the voice cried out – Sally's, yet somehow not hers – I felt something push against my back, like a gust of wind except far more solid.

I stumbled a step before catching myself, then looked up to see a distortion in the air – some sort of shockwave – slam into Satan's salamander hard enough to actually push it back. It was an impossible amount of force against what I'd assumed to be an immoveable object, causing the beast to fall into the Hudson and sending a small tidal wave crashing over the pier.

In the next second, a wall of water washed over us, knocking first the apkallu and then me ass over teakettle.

Blood boost or not, I was sent tumbling backward until the torrent finally slaked. I spat out a mouthful of foul tasting water, only to realize I was leaning against something.

No, not something – *someone.*

Turning over, I saw my body was pressed against Sally's legs as she stood there, not only upright but somehow dry as a bone.

Neat trick.

Less neat was when she looked down at me. Her green eyes were ablaze with power and the look on her face was devoid of all humanity, as if she could've gladly murdered the shit out of me herself before casually moving on with the rest of her evening.

A moment later, however, she blinked and both the power and menace seemed to drain out of her.

"Are you okay?" I asked, spitting out more water.

"Um ... I think," she replied, looking befuddled. "You?"

"Better than I could be." I glanced around, seeing everyone else had been knocked on their asses. The apkallu had been scattered, but at least our friends further back hadn't been hit as hard. That was something. "What the hell was that?"

"Fuck if I know," she said. "I saw what was about to happen to you and I guess I got..."

"Angry?"

"More like annoyed, and maybe a little embarrassed too. What the fuck was up with that stunt you pulled?"

"I..." Thundersmite's handle was lying next to me, so I picked it up. "I was trying to use my magic hammer."

"Uh huh. Well, maybe next time try shopping for weapons at somewhere other than Party City. Now let's go. We need to get the fuck out of here."

You test my patience, Harbinger!

What the?

"Cancel that," she said. "We need to get the fuck out of here *now*."

"Wait, you heard it that time?"

"Unfortunately."

Interesting as that was, it would have to be a mystery for another day. I pushed myself to my feet and dared a glance back. Sure enough, the waters of the Hudson were roiling, a brilliant blue glow visible beneath it as if something massive were about to surface.

EAT AND GROW STRONG!

Leviathan had turned up the psychic radio to eleven again, loud enough to make it feel like my brain was trying to escape through my ears.

"Yeah, now would be a good time to..." The words died on my lips as I forced myself to turn away, only to see that what was going on behind us wasn't any more heartening.

Falcon was back on his feet, but it was clear the lights were on but no one was home. Same with Char.

I'd hoped the force of the wave would've snapped them out of it, but if so Leviathan had been quick to reassert its will.

"I ... I can't hold it much more," Kelly cried out a few steps behind them, still on her knees. "It's ... too strong."

"But…"

"She's right, Bill," Sally said, grabbing hold of my arm. "We need to go."

"Where?"

"Anywhere but here."

Couldn't really argue with that logic, although I wasn't sure there was anywhere in the city that would be safe if this thing decided to try its luck on dry land.

"Hurry!" Kelly said, beckoning us over. "I can … send … the two of you. Just enough … focus for that."

"What about you?"

She gave her head a single shake, telling me all I needed to know.

Shit!

"Bill…," Sally warned.

"We can't leave them!"

"And we can't help them if we're fish food. We need to regroup and come back later. You know I'm right."

A part of me was tempted to remind her she'd just given this thing an uppercut worthy of Gipsy Danger. Unfortunately, we both knew we couldn't rely on her powers, especially if she lost control and whatever was inside her took over again. Her alternate persona wasn't exactly sympathetic to our cause.

Much as I hated to admit it, she was right. There was no guarantee this thing wouldn't pull a Jonah and the whale on our friends the second we were gone, but then why bother going to all the trouble of controlling them? If it was simply hungry, it could've beached itself anywhere along the Manhattan shoreline and had its fill of New Yorkers.

That told me it had plans for them.

Mind you, that was human logic, which probably didn't apply to monsters, but Leviathan sure as shit seemed capable of rational thought at least based on the crap it had beamed into my mind.

As much as I didn't want to leave friends behind, I didn't see how we could help them.

Finally, and with no small amount of regret, I nodded to Sally before turning and heading toward Kelly. "We'll come back for you. I promise."

"You'd ... better," she said, the effort to remain in control obviously taxing her.

"Okay, we're ready. Send us back... No, wait!"

"What is it?"

"I forgot something. Just give me a sec."

I turned and raced to where Falcon was once more shuffling back in the direction of the apkallu.

Reaching him, I blocked his way and patted him down until... *Bingo!* I pulled his cell phone from his coat pocket and took a moment to look it over. Thankfully it was a high end model with IPX6 rating, meaning it was mostly waterproof.

"Sorry, Matt, but I need this more than you do right now." I grabbed his hand, quickly wiped it off on my shirt, then pressed his finger to the onscreen sensor – unlocking it.

It was a douche move, but it's not like I wasn't already on his shit list. And this would save me from having to hack the Archives again. Besides, there was little doubt in my mind we'd need Christy's help to save him from this mess. If so, then maybe we could agree it was a wash when this was all over.

Yeah, I was justifying a means to an end, but fuck it. We were running with our tails between our legs, but at least this way it wouldn't be for nothing.

That done, I headed back to where Sally and Kelly waited, the sound of the water churning behind me growing louder by the second, telling me the kraken was about to be unleashed on our asses again.

"What the fuck was that about?" Sally asked.

"Just saying goodbye. Okay, now I'm ready to..." I trailed off as a pathetic mewing caught my ear. *Oh crap!* "Wait!"

"What *now*?" Kelly growled, her eyes bloodshot, no doubt from the struggle going on inside her head.

I looked around for a second or two before spotting the

source of the sound. The poor little thing was drenched and looked absolutely miserable, but somehow Petunia hadn't been washed away. I'd be a real bastard if I left her behind, not to mention I'd have to hear about it from my folks.

I dashed over to where the coven was shambling forward and scooped the kitten up from amidst their feet. I turned, giving Mike one last glance – still not sure where he fit into any of this. Sadly, I had a feeling more answers wouldn't be forthcoming for a while. Now to hope this didn't further embolden Hobart to hunt my ass down.

Time would tell on that. For now, I once again made my way back to where Sally was waiting.

"Anything else you'd like to do?" she asked, looking none-too-pleased.

"Nope. Let's get going."

"Are you sure you don't want to volunteer at a soup kitchen, or maybe change someone's flat tire first?"

"Guys!" Kelly snapped. "Seriously now. Can we do this? I can feel that thing clawing at my brain."

EAT OF ME AND GROW STRONG!

Almost on cue, Kelly screamed out, cradling her head. Then, with no small amount of effort, she slapped herself across the face. When she looked at us again, I could tell there wasn't much of her left in there – a sliver of her personality fighting for control.

There was no time to worry about anything else. If we didn't leave right then, it wasn't going to happen. "Now!"

She hesitated for a moment, making me wonder if we'd waited too long. Then she began to cast the spell, biting her lip so hard that it started to bleed – her arms struggling to make the movements necessary, as if another puppet master were fighting for control of her strings.

I feared it wouldn't be enough, but then the air around us began to glow – the light becoming steadily brighter until I could barely make her out.

"Tuh ... take this, too!"

Just before I lost sight of Kelly to the nothingness of the

void, she jerked her arm and something came flying my way. I reached out with the hand not currently cradling an angry kitten and managed to catch it – realizing it was Falcon's vape pen in the moment before our atoms were scattered to the universe.

PART II

24

GETTING AWAY FROM IT ALL

It shouldn't have come as a surprise that being teleported by a witch only partly in control of her own mind would result in a bumpy ride. At least by then I was sort of getting used to being tossed around like a cucumber in a food processor.

Mind you, it didn't help that my head started pounding again the second I'd touched the seemingly cursed vape pen.

I landed off balance, falling and rolling in the dirt while trying to be mindful of my cargo. So, of course, the little ingrate rewarded my efforts by clawing the shit out of my arm.

Ouch!

When all was said and done, I picked my soaked and filthy body up and looked around. Gone was the opening attack scene from a Toho flick, and in its place was a peaceful forest.

Kelly had done it.

"You okay?" I asked Sally, who was likewise climbing to her feet – her green eyes glowing eerily in the darkness of the woods.

"Not the worst trip I've had as of late," she said, "but close."

She wasn't wrong, but there was no denying Kelly had saved our bacon. Now to make sure it wasn't all for naught.

"Here, take this for a minute," I said, handing the kitten over.

My hands were full and I needed to take care of something fast. I stuffed the pipe into my pocket, only to realize the headache disappeared the second it was no longer touching my skin. Something to remember. Then I secured Thundersmite's remains back in its holster before turning my attention to the remaining item in my inventory slot.

"What are you doing?" she asked, cradling the now purring kitten. Fucking traitor cats.

"Disabling the lock code on Falcon's phone before it can time out," I replied, clicking through the settings.

"*That's* what you went back for?" She let out a laugh. "Look at you being all black hat. Maybe you're more cut out for this vampire gig than I've given you credit for all these years."

"Considering this is almost certainly an act of war against the Magi, you might be right."

"Well, if they do decide to kill your ass, don't worry. I'll make it a point to always remember you fondly."

"You're too kind." Finishing up, I got serious again. "Do you think they'll be okay?"

Sally shrugged, continuing to scratch Petunia's head. "Okay is probably a stretch. But if that thing wanted them dead, I have a feeling it was more than capable of getting the job done."

"You probably have a point. Thanks for the save by the way. That was badass, although I'm not sure how you managed to smack that thing in the face without blowing me to bits."

Sally let out a chuckle. "Me neither. I just did it, I don't know how. That whole clusterfuck ... it was a lot more chaotic than it seemed."

"Yeah, I was there. Chaotic is putting it mildly."

"You don't understand. It was like there was an entire

conversation going on inside my head, and I was only one part of it."

"Let me guess. It was trying to convince you to eat its ass too."

She raised an eyebrow my way. "No. I think that was just you. Anyway, I'm not talking about that thing. This was more like arguing with my own subconscious, like it had a mind all its own. It kept telling me my destiny was a glorious one, that I'd been chosen as the Great Beast's harbinger and should embrace it. Thing is ... crazy as it sounds, it was starting to make sense there for a few minutes. Like it was trying to convince me to let it take over, and doing a pretty good job of it."

"Glad it didn't succeed."

"Yeah, well, it was touch and go there for a minute or two. But then you went and almost got your dumb ass killed, and at that point I managed to fight it back. So thanks for that, I guess."

"Likewise." I considered her words for a moment. "So let's back up here. That thing in the river seems to think you're its herald. So where does that leave your horrifically feathered friend?"

Sally shook her head. "That's kind of the problem right there. Don't ask me how I know this, but I kind of got the feeling my inner voice wasn't talking about either of them."

"What? Are you sure?"

"I'm not sure of anything, other than we're both standing in the middle of a fucking forest. Hear me out, though. Just be forewarned, this is going to sound crazy."

"Like being invited to dinner by the monster from a prehistoric planet isn't?"

"Point taken. Okay, so here's the thing. Remember when Leviathan mouthed off after I decked it, telling me I was pushing my luck? I felt the thing inside of me react to that, but it wasn't with fear. It was more ... indignance. Like, how dare you speak to me that way?"

"Huh. What do you think it means?"

"No idea, other than it's arrogant, which isn't exactly a first for any of us."

"True. I'm just glad it didn't take control. I've gotta think that a pissing match between whatever's inside you and Monstro out there wouldn't have ended in our favor."

"You're probably right, but then why didn't it – take control I mean? Think about it. Every other time the thing inside my head has decided to come out and play it's been able to push me to the side with no effort. But not tonight. So why is that? After all, it was almost a perfect storm with everything that was happening."

"Maybe you've gotten strong enough to fight it."

She waved a hand dismissively. "While I never discount my own awesomeness, I'm not so sure about that. I think ... maybe what happened at Gan's forced its hand, caused it to take a more active role sooner than it wanted. Don't quote me on this, but maybe all of that tired it out a bit. That's why it tried to negotiate tonight, rather than just shove me into a closet and take hold of the reins."

I couldn't help but laugh. These were strange days indeed if we were once again forced to give Gan credit for inadvertently helping us, by sheer virtue of being her crazy-ass self.

It was too bad that still left us in a heavy deficit when it came to winning this crazy game we seemed destined to play.

Especially now, because if Sally was correct then maybe we'd been wrong in our assumptions.

The badass monsters of the Bible – Leviathan, Behemoth, and Ziz – were all far too real. But, what if none of them were actually *the* Great Beast?

If so, then what else was waiting out there for us?

Talk about a recipe for a bad night's sleep.

"So where exactly are we?" Sally asked once the adrenaline rush of escaping Monster Island began to wear off.

"Offhand, I'd say the woods."

"Thanks. That's helpful."

"I'm hoping Kelly was able to drop us off close to Purgatory. Problem is one set of trees looks the same as all the rest to me."

"Well, if they gave out badges for uselessness you'd have definitely made Eagle Scout by now."

"Don't blame me. I didn't expect this night to end with us getting our..." I trailed off as the sound of skittering caught my ears. A moment later, Petunia hissed in Sally's arms.

"What is it?" she asked.

"Not sure. Maybe just a squirrel or a... Shit!"

I let out a less than manly scream as something furry scurried out from underneath a bush, then instantly felt foolish as I saw it was just a big racoon. Make that a seriously fucked up racoon – its jaw hanging open and both eyes practically bugging out of its skull.

Eyes?

Either this thing had a seriously advanced case of rabies, distemper, and a dozen other fatal diseases, or...

"Halt, strangers!" it cried out in a bubbling voice.

"Hey, Glen," I said, not bothering to hide the relief I felt.

The bloated little beast tilted its head up at me, its eyes bulging out even more as it took us in. "Freewill? Oh and Mistress Sally too. I'm overjoyed to see you both."

"What the fuck are you doing out here?"

"Oh, I volunteered for security detail. We patrol the forest around Purgatory looking for interlopers. As you can see, I found the perfect disguise. Tom says I blend in seamlessly with all the woodland creatures."

"That figures since he's a fucking moron," Sally remarked.

"It's so wonderful to see you in good health," he said to her, "especially after that nasty business at Gansetseg's."

"It's good to see you too, Glen."

"And might I add you're looking quite lovely this evening."

"Oh yeah," I said. "Sally always looks her best while grabbing her..."

"Don't make me regret not joining the other side." She

handed Petunia over to me. "There. Only pussy you'll be grabbing anytime soon, so I suggest you enjoy it."

"Ooh, is that Mistress Kelly in disguise?" Glen asked.

I glanced at the kitten then back at him. "No, it's just a cat. Why do you ask?"

"I was told she'd accompanied you on a snack run, and now you have a cat so I thought maybe it was her."

I tried to fathom his logic then decided it wasn't worth bothering. "It's ... a bit of a long story. I'll tell you on the way back. How far away are we?"

"Not far."

"Good. Then kindly lead the way."

"With pleasure."

Glen turned and started waddling, making me think this was going to take longer than it needed to – not that I was about to pick his gross new body up to speed things along.

Before we could get more than a couple dozen yards, though, I sensed someone else close by – a vampire if my nose was right.

"Greetings, Eric!" Glen cried a few moments later, as a man stepped out on the trail ahead of us. "I trust your patrol has been as invigorating as mine."

Eric? Oh yeah. One of Zoe's minions, the one with the staring problem.

I was right on the money, because his eyes locked on us as he approached – first on me then on Sally, narrowing with what I was sure was recognition. No big deal on my part since I'd already met him, but the way he was looking at my friend was setting me off for some reason.

"Where's the witch?" he asked, giving Glen a cursory nod before turning my way. "She was supposed to be with you."

I chose to ignore his attitude rather than add to an already bad evening. "We ran into trouble. She got ... delayed."

"Is that a fact?" He then turned Sally's way. "I see you changed your hair."

"Do I know you?"

"Oh, sorry," he said, his demeanor changing in an

instant. "You're Sally, aren't you? Saw your picture in the paper a while back in connection with that charity you run."

"Used to run." She glanced my way before adding, "Anyway, those days are behind me. Now if you don't mind, it's been a long night..."

"So I see," Eric replied, his nostrils flaring, no doubt telling his nose quite the story. "Well then, we should get back so you two can clean up and get some rest." He leaned in a bit closer, only for Petunia to hiss at him. "Cute cat."

"She's had a long night too."

"Seems to be a common theme. All right then, follow me. The barrier's only a couple hundred yards that way. We'll be through it before you can say..."

"Wait!" Glen cried, skittering to a halt.

"What is it, pal?" I asked. "You spot a trash can to root through?"

He shook his racoon head, his oversized eyeballs swaying side to side like miniature water balloons. Oh yeah, this was possibly his worst disguise yet.

"It's Mistress Sally."

"What about her?"

"All the Magi inside," he said. "Are we sure it's safe for her?"

Holy shit! He was right. I'd almost forgotten about that. "Thanks for the reminder, man. I must be more out of it than I thought."

"Why wouldn't it be safe?" Eric asked. "Purgatory takes in strays all the time."

Fortunately, Sally chose to ignore that remark. "I take it we're talking ambient magic here?"

I nodded. "A lot."

"Hold on," Eric interrupted. "What does ambient magic have to do with anything?"

I hooked a thumb Sally's way. "Too much can make her explode."

"Explode?"

"Yeah, big time."

"Hmm," he replied, looking her way. "Guess it's more than just your hair that's changed."

There he was again with that odd familiarity. Something was up with this guy. Perhaps it was time to take the bull by the horns.

"Hey, Glen, why don't you go ahead? Let Liz know we're out here and what the deal is. See if there's anything they can do to accommodate us, preferably without killing everyone inside."

"My pleasure, Freewill."

"Oh, and can you maybe take Petunia here with you? If Tom's asleep, just smack his ass awake and tell him to find a blanket and some cat food."

"Can do." The skin along the racoon's back split open, followed by some of Glen's slime pooling through the opening. "Just place her here on my back. I'll keep her warm and safe until then."

Jesus fuck! I was sorry I'd asked. "Um, okay."

I placed the unhappy kitten atop Glen's disguise. Once there, his slime surrounded her, holding her in place.

"There, all safe and secure."

Judging by the kitten's pathetic mewing, she had other thoughts on the matter. Guess my parents would be picking up one traumatized cat when they got back.

That done, Glen scurried away.

"That is one unhappy puss," Sally remarked as they disappeared into the undergrowth.

I couldn't disagree, but her discomfort was necessary. I wanted both hands free, just in case our little conversation with Eric went south.

Apparently he wasn't so stupid as to not notice. "I'm going to go out on a limb here and assume there's a reason you asked Glen to go ahead and not me."

"You'd guess correctly," Sally said, circling to the vampire's other side. "Especially since I'm pretty sure we're both aware that recent press photos don't exactly do me justice."

"You got me," he said, holding his hands up in mock

surrender. "Never even saw them. I'd just heard you'd become some sort of socialite."

"I prefer the term philanthropist."

"Can't say it really matters much to me. Not my scene."

"So what is your scene then, *Eric*?" I asked, hoping I had enough left for another throwdown, as my blood boost had worn off. "You Claire's ex-boyfriend or something?"

"Hardly. Whatever cause that witch and her sister serve is their own. I was more concerned by how badly they got the jump on you, being that you're the Freewill."

"Who's Claire," Sally asked. "And how badly did she kick your ass?"

"That crazed pyromaniac's sister, and it was more like a tie," I said before refocusing on Eric.

"I was likewise interested," he continued, "to learn someone else had apparently taken up residence in the Shining One's body." He paused for a moment. "Or should I say the Silver Eyes' body?"

Silver Eyes? There was a term I hadn't heard in a while. It was another name for Icons. Both they and Freewills apparently had a lot of monikers over the centuries. However, the only ones who'd ever referred to Sheila as that had been the...

"I'll admit, I wasn't quite this eloquent the last time you saw me. However, in all fairness, your language is a lot easier to pronounce with a human tongue."

"Wait. Who are you?"

He grinned. "An old friend. Just to be on the safe side, though, I hereby request the protection of parley as per the provisions set forth in the Humbaba Accord."

"Humbaba Accord? Hold on. Are you saying you're a...?"

"Yes. We've met before, although back in those days you knew me by another name. Perhaps this will ring a bell." He lowered his voice an octave before slapping a hand across his chest. "*Grulg welcomes you to Woods of Mourning.*"

25

OLD FRIENDS, NEW FACES

Grulg?!

Eric ended his Feet impression and started coughing. "Sorry ... not so easy to talk like that in this body."

I looked Sally's way, but she didn't appear to have any more clue than I did. Sounded about right considering this had come out of fucking left field.

Grulg had been the first Sasquatch we'd met at the ill-fated Woods of Mourning peace summit up in northern Canada. We'd gone there trying to avert a war between them and the vampire nation – and yes, it still sounded as fucking ridiculous now as it had back then.

Anyway, he'd turned out to be a fairly good guy. However, the same couldn't be said of his boss Turd – an ugly-ass ape looking to corner the maple syrup market by courting war with the vampires.

Trying to fathom the logic of that asshole's convoluted scheme still made my head hurt. Anyway, Grulg had stepped in to help us uncover the plot but then, just as it seemed all would be well, one of Gan's minions killed Turd's daughter – saving me from having to marry her as a condition of peace, but also bringing a war down on all our heads.

Not exactly our finest moment.

We ran into Grulg a couple more times over the next several months. Though we were on opposite sides, he had a strong enough sense of honor to help us – including at the very end, when we destroyed the Source and banished magic from our world.

In the space of minutes, vampires and sasquatches alike were cast out of our plane of existence, never to be seen again.

Or so I'd thought.

Obviously I was aware vampires were back, duh, but up until this point I'd hoped I'd seen the last of the Feet.

All of that said, I sure as hell didn't expect to find one wearing some regular dude's body.

"How the fuck?" I replied, gobsmacked. "You were…"

"Sent back home?" he interrupted. "Yes, along with so many others."

Fortunately, Sally was there to make up for my utter confusion. "You'll have to forgive Bill. Big reveals like this tend to cause his stupidity to flare up. Although, even I have to admit seeing you back as a vampire is a bit of a mind fuck."

He held up his hands in a placating manner. "Trust me, I get it. In fact, I'm not sure there's anyone in the world who gets it more. The thing is, after we went back home it all became clear."

"What did?" I asked.

"That vamps and Sasquatches were the same," Sally said, moving next to me. "At least at their core – their spirits, souls, or whatever the fuck you want to call it."

I nodded, remembering the history of our species that Calibra, former queen of the vampires, had shown us when we'd tried to storm her lair. The Feet were the physical manifestations of extradimensional nature spirits, whereas vampires were the result of those same spirits being forcibly melded with human souls.

That was why they'd hated us as much as they had. They considered us perversions of their true selves – *tainted* by human contamination.

"Precisely," Eric said. "Once we were back in ... *the Forest*, for lack of a proper name, all of that seemed to melt away. We were who, *what*, we used to be before this world set us at each other's throats. It put things into perspective."

"So ... you're saying *everyone* went back there?" *Yo, Wanderer, you listening to this? Any insight to share?*

Alas, my alter ego had once again fallen silent.

"Everyone who survived, that is. As for those who died before the Source could send them home..." He trailed off with a shrug.

Okay, that made sense. It meant assholes like Night Razor, Colin, or Turd didn't get to go back home and enjoy some woodland paradise after all the trouble they'd caused. More importantly, it meant I didn't have to worry about them showing up again.

Small victories and all.

Grulg here, on the other hand, was a different matter. "So how exactly are you a vampire now?"

"Sounds pretty obvious to me," Sally said. "Let me guess, once you were back home, all the differences melted away – physically anyway. So when shit started up here again..."

"Turns out it was pretty much a lottery," Eric – Grulg – replied. "I was walking along minding my own business, then the next thing I knew there was a flash of light and I was being sucked into this body – to find a very confused human half waiting for me, I might add."

"So then this Eric guy's in there with you?"

"Yes, although I seem to be the dominant personality. From what I can garner, he's a meek sort of fellow. All his memories are here – friends, family, that sort of thing – but I'm calling the shots for the most part."

That seemed to match up with what I knew about vampires. Two souls in one body, but it wasn't always an equal partnership. Hell, I'd learned that the hard way, having my own body hijacked on more than one occasion by Dr. Death, the fucker I'd previously *won* in the vampire lottery as Grulg here put it. "All right, I guess that makes sense. Nice to have you back, Grulg."

"Nice to be back," he said with a chuckle. "Probably best to call me Eric, though. It's less likely to freak people out."

"Fair enough," Sally remarked. "So what exactly is your deal here then?"

"My deal? Well, I suppose I'm seeing how the other half lives, so to speak. Mostly anyway. Personally I didn't care for city life, which is why I'm out here. I thought being in the woods would help me ease into my new existence, but so far it's a work in progress."

"How so?"

He shrugged. "It's this place. Purgatory is supposed to be a sanctuary for those who need it, but a lot of the old prejudices are still around just below the surface. Needless to say, not everyone was pleased when vampires first showed up, even if we've since proven ourselves."

I could see how that might be. After all, the majority of Purgatory's residents were Magi. And though vamps couldn't turn them, their blood worked just as well as anyone else's when it came to filling the old tank up. Considering all the families there, I could see how it might make folks uneasy to know their neighbors could potentially view their loved ones as walking juice boxes.

"So anyway," Eric continued, changing the subject, "you can imagine my surprise at seeing faces I recognized."

That made sense. At least it explained the staring. "Does anyone else know? I mean, Kelly was there when we..."

He shook his head. "She's had enough on her plate. Besides, five years is a long time. I wasn't sure whether people had changed or how they'd react to knowing who I'd been. I wanted to take a wait and see approach. Although, I guess I wasn't as subtle as I thought. You can't blame me, though. No offense, but I was surprised to see you both involved in all of this again."

"You're not the only one," Sally and I both muttered.

"I figured you two would be married and raising a couple of kids by now."

What?!

"And what exactly gave you that idea?" Sally asked, narrowing her eyes.

"No offense, but if anyone acted like a mated pair it was you two."

"We did not!"

"Yeah, you kind of did."

"Well, that's certainly a thought that makes me want to kill my brain cells with alcohol," she said, rubbing the bridge of her nose.

"Then I hope you like kombucha," I replied, "because that's mostly what they've got on tap."

"Eww, forget I said anything." She turned back toward Eric. "So, speaking of being involved again, is there any insight you can share on the various shit going on?"

He let out a chuckle. "That's the one problem with being a grunt in the woods. Nobody really tells me anything. I wouldn't even know what you're asking about."

"Werewolves," I replied, "giant Bible monsters, and crazed leprechaun cavemen. Any of that ring a bell?"

He raised an eyebrow. "I'm gonna assume it's a bit busy in the outside world."

"That's an understatement."

"Sorry to say, but the worst we've had to deal with here are the bad seeds you've already met."

"Don't remind me. So, anyway, I don't suppose you're interested in being part of the gang again? We made a pretty good team back in the day when it came to taking down Alex." I purposely left out the part where he'd been horribly tortured as part of that plan. "Won't lie, man. We could use all the allies we can get."

Eric inclined his head as if thinking about it. "You can count on me if you need some backup here."

"But...?"

"But, I'll be honest. One end of the world event was enough for me. I'm actually pretty content with how quiet it is here most of the time. Not sure I want to risk that. Besides, technically we were enemies last time around. Much as that's the past and things are different now, it's still ... kind of weird being one of you."

Guess I couldn't blame him. He was right. At best, we'd been reluctant allies. Besides, as deep in shit as I was right then, I can't lie and say an easy out wasn't tempting as fuck. If he was happy with his life now, I had no business dragging him back in.

Okay, so this was certainly an interesting development, but perhaps not a super useful one. Nice as it was to see Grulg both back and smelling a lot better than he once had, that's all it was – nice. In some ways it was like running into an old high school classmate. There was the whole, "Good to see you again," spiel but ultimately it didn't make much difference in anyone's life.

Fascinating as it was to know some of the vamps out there might have giant screaming apes inside of them, it was once again time to focus on what had happened to us and what needed to happen next.

Thankfully, we didn't have to stretch out our meet-cute for too long. Either we were closer to Purgatory than I realized or Glen was faster in his racoon getup than I'd assumed.

Either way, I soon sensed movement headed our way. I tensed up but then quickly relaxed once I realized the scents approaching us were familiar, albeit one was a familiar rotting corpse.

Speaking of which, Glen was the first to join us, still in his racoon suit but thankfully sans kitten. Hot on his heels were Tom, Veronica, and finally Liz – the welcome party seemingly limited to those in the know about the crap we were dealing with.

As Sally glared at Liz, forcing me to remember their last meeting had been less than friendly, Veronica stepped forward.

"Where's Kelly?"

I shook my head. "We ran into trouble and she was captured. Vincent and the others too."

"What? How?"

"I'm sorry, we tried to save them but it was too strong."

"What was?" Liz replied.

"Leviathan."

She raised an eyebrow. "We talking bad B-movies here or...?"

"The biblical sea monster. And yes, before anyone asks, it is absolutely fucking terrifying."

"I can't believe I missed that shit," Tom replied, sounding put out. "At least tell me you got to smack it with *you know what*."

Liz looked his way. "You know what?"

"I did," I replied, holding up the broken handle. "Not that it did fuck all."

"Okay, enough," Liz snapped. "We can catch up on the details later. I want to know what reason you had for going back to the city and why I was given the runaround about it."

"Or what?" Sally asked. "You'll torture it out of us *again*?"

Shit!

Liz opened her mouth then shut it, apparently thinking twice about what she was about to say. "I deserved that. Listen ... I'm sorry about what happened. It went ... further than I should have let it."

"Oh? So did you mean to stop before or after char-broiling my scalp?"

Liz took a deep breath, no doubt steadying herself. We probably couldn't afford to be doing this now, but I had the feeling we needed to nevertheless. If we didn't clear the air now, it would happen later, perhaps at a time that would fuck us all over.

"Do you want me to get on my knees and beg for your forgiveness? Because I will if that's what you want. Look, I'm not proud of what I did, but I can't change the past. All I can do is try to make amends for it."

"She really is trying," Veronica added.

Sally locked eyes with the elder witch for several tense moments, making me remember she'd shot people in the face for far less. Guess it was a good thing she wasn't currently armed.

"Oh, she's been taking good care of Cheetara too," Tom said, before turning my way. "Pretty sure your folks aren't getting that kitten back from her, though."

I shrugged, that being the least of my worries.

"Liz?" Eric asked uncertainly, but she merely held up a hand.

Finally, after way too long of a Mexican standoff, Sally backed up a step. "There was a time not that long ago when you'd be lying on the ground bleeding out." *Oh crap*. "But fortunately for you I understand a bit about making amends. Do right by my friends and I'll consider it water under the bridge. Do wrong by them, though..."

Liz nodded. "Understood."

I quickly stepped between them before anyone said anything to break the ceasefire. "Okay then. Now that it's settled, I'm sorry we left without telling you and I'm doubly sorry everything went to shit for our friends."

"You know," Liz replied, "if you'd told me where you were going then I ..."

"Would be Dragonzord's mind slave, too, right now," I interrupted. "Besides, Kelly was afraid you would've objected to what we were after."

"Which is?"

"This." I pulled Falcon's phone from my pocket, turned it on, and handed it to her.

"A cell phone? And it isn't even my birthday."

"Look what's on the screen."

She glanced down. "Okay, it's a webpage. So?"

Guess I needed to explain it. "You ever hear of the Falcon Archives."

"Of course. Every Magi knows about it. The question is, how do *you*? Last I checked, that wasn't the sort of news we shared with your kind."

"Yeah, well, the game has changed a bit. See, one of the reasons we left was to see Matthias Falcon. He's been helping us out down in the city."

"Okay, and?"

"That's his phone."

"Holy shit," Tom cried. "You fucking mugged the guy? Badass!"

"No, I didn't mug him! He just ... um... Anyway, bottom line is that's his phone and you're looking at the unlocked digital interface to the Falcon Archives."

"So what's in these archives?" Eric asked, sidling up alongside her to take a look.

"I need you to get back to your patrol," Liz told him, her eyes wide as if suddenly realizing he was still there. "Now."

"But..."

"That's an order!"

"You got it, boss," he said, backing away.

Oh yeah. The whole Grulg revelation had disarmed me to the fact that we'd just let him listen in on a bunch of shit we probably shouldn't have. Oops.

Liz waited for several seconds until she was sure he was gone, then her body suddenly lit up with angry red energy as she turned toward me again. "As for you, you'd better start explaining fast, and hope to whatever gods you pray to that I like the answer."

And yet she wondered why we hadn't said anything earlier.

26

A MOMENT TO BREATHE

Fortunately, this wasn't my first rodeo. That, and I was slowly beginning to realize how important the Archives were to the Magi community.

Not to mention how little sense of humor they had with regards to it.

Despite most of them seeming to have no clue what was contained within, they acted like it was their Holy Grail. And if so, then me having access to it was the highest form of heresy they could imagine – kind of like telling a devout catholic I'd picked my teeth with a shard of the one true cross.

Personally, I didn't get it. I wouldn't give a single shit if anyone declared they'd hacked the vampire nation's old archives. Heck, they could tell me they'd wiped their ass with Alexander the Great's ashes and I'd be fine with it. But I guess I'd always been disaffectedly agnostic when it came to most things. Needless to say, if I ever found myself human again I doubted I needed to worry about empowering anything with faith magic.

Regardless, I quickly brought Liz up to speed on the more pertinent facts surrounding our mission, while leaving out a few self-incriminating details.

Instead, I told her how our objective had been to speak

with Falcon about using the Archives, leaving the outcome of our discussion somewhat vague before Leviathan reared its ugly head and made it all a moot point. Being that I was the only one present who'd been privy to that part of the conversation, nobody could contradict me.

"So you stole it?" Liz concluded, looking less than pleased.

"I prefer the term borrowed, and definitely not mugged," I replied, throwing some side-eye Tom's way. "And only after I told him of our plan to rescue Christy and how the Archives were our best bet for success."

"And what did he say to that?"

"That's right about the point where we got interrupted by psychic Godzilla and about a dozen little Godzookies, if you catch my drift."

"And because of that you decided to…"

"Keep it from falling into Leviathan's hands? Exactly. I mean seriously, take a look at it. The guy obviously unlocked it for me before handing it over. Likewise, I'm pretty sure, as the ranking Magi here, he would've wanted me to pass it to you for safekeeping – which is what I'm doing."

Most of that was pure bullshit, something that would almost certainly come back to bite me in the ass at some point. But fuck it. I'd have stepped into Leviathan's mouth, crawled through his digestive tract, and then climbed out of his asshole if it meant rescuing Christy.

I wasn't going to let pesky things like respecting Magi law stand in my way.

"Bill's right," Sally said. "Matt unlocked it for him." It wasn't exactly an untruth, even if he wasn't what you'd call a willing unlockee. "So, are we good here?"

Liz let out a deep sigh, continuing to stare at the phone's screen. "If any of the grand mentors were to learn I have this…"

"We're not saying shit if you aren't. Come on. You're the one who just said she's trying to make amends. Well, helping us will go a long way toward that, and Bill just handed you the means necessary."

"I suppose..."

Veronica stepped in and put a hand on Liz's shoulder. "She's right. Kelly would want us to use it."

"Maybe..."

"And hell," I added, "while we're at it, there might even be something in there to save Kelly, Falcon, and the rest from that fucking sea monster."

I debated sweetening the deal, remembering what was in my pocket. It's not like the crazy power boost that came with it wouldn't be an added bonus. But then I remembered Falcon's unhinged warning about his magical Juul pod.

Considering his mental state at the time, I had doubts as to how real that was. The guy was pretty much off his rocker by that point. Nevertheless, I left the vape pen where it was, just to be safe. If there was any truth to Falcon's words, then it was best to be cautious – for now anyway.

I'd already handed over the Magi equivalent of the Ark of the Covenant. That was probably enough bombs dropped for one evening.

Besides, there was always tomorrow.

Thank goodness that was all the threats to my life that day or the next few had to offer. With Liz talked off her ledge, we were able to move on to less violent matters – like getting settled in before the sun came up and turned me into a pile of burnt wood shavings.

I was afraid the only way to accommodate Sally's strange powers would be for her to set up shop outside Purgatory's dome – which would leave her vulnerable to nutjob witches as well as defeat the purpose of bringing her there to begin with.

If so, my plan was to move my tent outside with hers. That wouldn't exactly be to my benefit, but no way was I leaving Sally on her own.

Fortunately, that turned out to be unnecessary.

Liz was able to recruit a few of her fellows to the cause

after making up some bullshit about Sally being allergic to high concentrations of magic – not unlike what seemed to be happening to me.

The barrier around Purgatory turned out not to be the issue – it was mostly just a specialized glamour, not nearly powerful enough to set Sally off. It was more the dozens of Magi in the main encampment that were the problem, along with all the whiz-bang magic they were constantly conjuring.

Fortunately, where magic was our bane here, it was also our salvation.

Liz and co were able to rig up a variation on the force fields I'd seen others use in battle. They essentially subdivided a small corner of Purgatory from the rest, putting up a dome within the dome, warded specifically to dampen any magic from getting in.

Yeah, it didn't make much sense to me either. But, so long as Sally stayed in her little slice of heaven and didn't venture into the main encampment, it kept her safe from outside eyes and left everyone else in a state other than being horrifically killed.

Win-win if you asked me.

As a bonus, I soon realized I didn't get headaches while in her little subdivision, so I uprooted and moved there, too, despite Sally's protests that she was quite all right on her own.

Fuck it.

Even had it not acted like magical Tylenol, I'd have still moved. Listening to her berate me for every little thing was preferable to being glared at by magical wankers any day of the week.

Hell, even Tom asked to join us there. However, warded undergarments or not, Tina was still a wildcard – and no way did I want her separated from her father again.

As for Petunia, well, she shit in Tom's sleeping bag her first day there, but there wasn't anything he could do about it because by then Tina was in love with the little fleabag. Again, both wins in my book.

All of it was minor, but I needed a few plusses in my column after our disastrous outing to New York. I'd lost friends, an entire coven, and the only lead I had as to why those werewolves were hunting us. That said, I figured I could forgive Mike being late with the rent, being that he was probably now employed scraping barnacles from the ball sack of a monstrous sea beast.

As the days passed and I awaited word from Liz on her progress, we settled back into our routine – meaning Tom and I went back to arguing over the price of snack food during our supply runs.

Though I can't say stepping out from Purgatory's protection didn't make me a wee bit paranoid, it was worth it since it allowed me to catch a few bars on my burner phone. First off was dropping a message to my parents, telling them I'd left on a last minute business trip for a new client – bringing Petunia with me to a pet-friendly hotel where we'd be for the next week or so.

That out of the way, I turned my attention toward keeping an eye on what was happening in the world.

None of it was promising.

The police had apparently failed to contain the news of what had gone down in Brooklyn. Not surprising, since you couldn't take a piss these days without someone putting it to music on TikTok, but still disheartening all the same. Footage was spreading like wildfire, along with a debate that didn't bode well for any of us – people once again seriously discussing whether monsters were real.

Likewise, despite the late hour at the time, footage of the debacle in Manhattan had likewise escaped into the wild. It was taken from a distance and thankfully less than crystal clear, but it was exacerbated by more eyewitness sightings of monstrous beings on land, sea, and in the air.

All of it served as a grim reminder that our little respite wouldn't last for long.

Bad things were afoot in the world. We could pretend that all was fine in our magical commune, but I had a feeling beneath all the serenity there was a powder keg slowly smoldering.

Call me cynical but, regardless of their precautions, I

didn't see how such a large grouping of supernatural weirdos like this could stay under the radar forever.

And knowing my luck, I had a feeling that if something was going to happen, it would almost certainly be a case of sooner rather than later.

"Hey, Cat! How was school?" I greeted as the tyke stepped into view, waving goodbye to some of the friend's she'd made here. It was a tiny slice of normal in an otherwise abnormal existence.

Tom was off on a daytime supply run with some of the others since the evening forecast called for bad weather. With the skies currently partly cloudy, that left me grounded. So Glen and I had popped by to keep Tina company for when class let out.

"Hey, Uncle Bill!" she cried, stepping past me and scooping Petunia up from where she'd been busy batting at one of Glen's eyeballs. "It was fun. But we're supposed to call it a gathering not class."

"Why?"

"I dunno." She instantly turned her attention to the purring kitten in her arms. "Such a good kitty. I missed you so much."

"I beg to differ," Glen bubbled, thankfully sans his raccoon suit. "She tried to use me as a litter box – twice. It was most demeaning."

I was sure it was. It had also been completely fucking hilarious.

Tina feigned shock, holding out the squirming kitten at arm's length. "Bad Petunia. No pooping on Glen."

"Thank you, Miss Tina."

"So, learn anything good?" I asked, pointedly watching my language since the swear jar was rapidly depleting what few funds I had to my name.

Tina put the cat down onto her cot then turned and sighed. "No. They only teach us baby stuff."

"Oh? Why's that?"

"Because of the other kids. Most of them can't do magic yet."

"Okay, so what kind of stuff did you learn?"

She rolled her eyes, for a moment looking like the petulant teen she would one day probably become. Then she held out her arms and spat out a few words in what I assumed were Enochian. A moment later, the air around us filled with a small shower of flower petals. "See?"

"Oh, this is most delightful," Glen opined.

"It's baby magic," Tina groused. "I can call lightning from the sky. Mommy showed me how. I can even hear the way the meadow sings, but all they let me do is conjure daisies. It's so dumb."

I was tempted to ask what she meant by the meadow singing, but figured it was some Magi thing I wouldn't understand. "Listen. We both know you can do more, but that's not the point. Remember what we talked about."

She nodded, looking none-too-pleased. "The others aren't allowed to know."

"They wouldn't understand. And with Aunt Kelly missing ... err ... still in the city, that's more important than ever. So for now anyway, maybe let's stick to the baby magic, okay?"

"I could make them understand, Uncle Bill," she offered. "I could reach into their heads and show them."

"Uh ... yeah, maybe let's not do that."

"Daddy said it would be funny to make everyone poop themselves," she replied with a giggle.

"Why does that not surprise me? Just remember that *other* thing we talked about."

She repeated it word for word. "Don't listen to Daddy unless another adult agrees first."

"Exactly."

"So, do *you* want me to make everyone poop?" she asked hopefully.

"Another time maybe."

"Who's pooping where?"

I turned at the sound of the voice to see Zoe approaching, blue cloak trailing behind her. With Kelly and Vincent both MIA, she was now in charge of security.

I threw Cat a look to hopefully let her know that it was time to act *normal*, then turned to the vampire. "Nobody. Just some potty humor."

"Good to hear," she replied. "Last thing I need is Ux complaining that he needs more warm bodies on latrine duty."

That lightened the mood, at least until Glen slithered forward and raised a tendril of slime in some bizarre semblance of a salute. "Mistress Commander Zoe, sir!"

"It's just Zoe, Glen. I keep telling you, this isn't the army. And I'm nobody's mistress."

"Just trying to pay my respects, Commander."

"Fine. At ease then." She let out a chuckle before unclipping the canteen at her side and holding it out to me. "Here. Thought you might be up for some refreshment."

"Thanks." I popped the cap, instantly savoring the scent of blood. "What's on tap today?"

"A blend of squirrel and rabbit."

"Yum, my favorite," I lied, taking a swig. It wasn't bad, good enough to keep the tank topped off, but I can't say it didn't make me long for better days. Creepy as it was to think, I missed the bagged human blood that the original Village Coven seemed to have in endless supply. Mind you, it was probably best not to consider where they'd gotten that blood from. Some memories aged better when coupled with willful ignorance.

"Anyway, I popped by because Liz was looking for you."

"Me?"

"Yeah, you and Tina."

I instantly perked up. That had to mean she'd figured something out. Either that or Tom had assaulted a vendor over the price of Pringles and needed to be bailed out.

"But first," she said, gesturing for me to follow, "do you mind if we have a word?"

I stepped away from the tent, curious. "What's up?"

"Nothing important. Just wondering if you've seen Eric lately."

"No, why?"

"I needed to discuss some upcoming shift rotations with him, but he's nowhere to be found."

"Purgatory is a pretty big place."

"Really? I hadn't noticed," she replied sarcastically. "Anyway, when I couldn't find him in his tent, I figured I'd … y'know." She tapped the side of her nose.

"Track his scent?"

She nodded. "Still feels weird to do that, like I'm half bloodhound, but yeah."

"I'm assuming no dice."

"Either he's not in Purgatory or he switched deodorants." She shook her head. "I just hope he didn't do anything stupid, not with the sun still out."

"He's probably just outside the dome doing a sweep. I wouldn't worry. The forest cover should be good enough on a day like this."

"You're probably right. Anyway, just figured I'd ask. You never know."

"True."

"C'mon, we should get going. Liz gets bitchy if you keep her waiting."

I had a feeling there wasn't much to worry about regarding Eric. His former life involved a lot of time spent in the woods. If anyone was okay out there, sun or not, it was probably the guy who was once a Sasquatch.

As for me, I had other things to worry about – like hopefully making some progress on the plan to rescue Christy.

27

WHERE IN THE WORLD IS CARMEN SOURCEDIEGO?

Rather than take us to Liz's tent, Zoe led us from the main encampment toward the direction of Purgatory that housed my and Sally's tents.

I can't say this bothered me much as I'd been feeling a pressure headache building ever since coming to meet Cat.

As we approached the secondary barrier, the one that filtered magic, I saw Liz waiting for us and she wasn't alone. Both Sally and Ux were with her.

"Aunt Sally!" Tina cried.

"Hey, Munchkin! Look at how big you've gotten!"

"I can do big girl magic now too."

"I bet."

"That's probably far enough," Liz said, holding up a hand before the tyke could pass through. "Zoe, do you and Glen mind watching her while we talk? I'll call you when we're ready."

Zoe shrugged. "Sure. C'mon, you two, let's go play for a bit."

"Ooh," Glen said. "Have I mentioned that I'm a master at hide and go seek?"

"I'm it!" Tina cried happily as she skipped off with them.

Once upon a time I'd have called anyone crazy for letting a vampire babysit a kid, but I guess times were changing.

That, and Tina was a walking talking Tunguska blast if she needed to be.

Either way, I doubted I had much to worry about.

In some ways, Purgatory was proving to be the dream some had professed for this new age of magic – casting aside the old rivalries in favor of cooperation. It wasn't perfect, far from it, but it might've been the closest I'd seen to date.

Enough of that for now, though. I was curious to see what Liz had for us.

"Took you long enough," Sally remarked as I stepped through the translucent barrier – my headache clearing up as I joined them on the other side.

"Figured it was a nice day to take the scenic route." I nodded toward the other two. "What brings you out here, Ux?"

"I invited him," Liz replied. At my raised eyebrow, she explained, "Like I told you, no secrets. I'm being upfront with everything I'm doing."

"Which is greatly appreciated," Ux said in his high-pitched voice. "I'll admit, it also gave me a welcome excuse to check on our newest resident, something I've been sadly remiss about. My apologies, Ms. Carlsbad."

"It's just Sally, and like I said it's all good. I appreciate the special accommodations."

"It is our pleasure. Purgatory is meant as a haven for all, even those who are unable to enjoy the company of the rest."

I was certain she had opinions when it came to *enjoying* the company of people she'd likely just barely tolerate on a good day, but I kept that to myself.

"All right," Liz said after a moment or two, "enough with the pleasantries. I'll get straight to the point. I did some research, and I think I found a tracking spell that will allow us to locate the Source, or *a* Source anyway."

Yes! I vaguely wondered if it was the same tracker Christy had found to help search for Ed, which had eventually led her to figure out there was a ley line beneath Gan's estate. But ultimately it didn't matter so long as it worked.

I glanced Ux's way to see if he had any reaction to this

news, but his long, reedy face was pretty much unreadable by human standards. It was like trying to get a handle on the emotions of a giant stick insect.

When no comment or critique came from him, I asked, "There's a *but*, right?"

"There always is," Sally remarked.

"You're not wrong," Liz said. "That's why I asked you to bring Tina here. She's essentially the fulcrum for whether this will succeed or fail."

"Go on."

"The reason is twofold," she explained. "Under normal circumstances, precision scrying requires a connection with the target. The stronger the connection, the better it works. That's why we usually ask for something like a tuft of hair or something that belonged to whoever we're looking for."

"Please tell me you're not sending me all the way back to Brooklyn for one of Christy's hairbrushes."

"No," she replied, much to my relief. "This isn't a normal scrying. You could hand me a pint of her blood and it wouldn't make a difference since she's not in our dimension."

"That's doubly true now," Ux added, "considering the circumstances."

"What circumstances?"

He stared at me with his oversized, unblinking eyes. "I know we were at odds with one another down below, Freewill, but you have to understand that many of those involved in that debacle simply wanted to go home to their respective worlds, nothing more."

I nodded. "So I've been told."

"Well, you see, that's part of why I founded Purgatory. Many who have attempted to return home since then have either been unable to, or have breached the veil only to never be heard from again."

"Why?" Sally asked.

"That's just it, we don't know. Some doorways that should be open again are not, and others ... the energy from them feels wrong."

"Wrong?"

"That's the best way I can describe it. It's like something is interfering, but in order to do so it would have to be unbelievably powerful."

Oh yeah, that didn't sound ominous at all. I mean, it's not like the return of magic had been interrupted by some ancient horror trying to claw its way through to our world. Oh wait, that's exactly what happened.

Fuck!

Liz sighed. "That's the reason why we need to locate one of the Sources. Pan-dimensional crossings have never been easy, mind you, but in the past they were possible with enough focus and effort."

"Like when Christy dragged Harry Decker's spirit back into this world?" Sally offered.

Liz narrowed her eyes my friend's way. "*Yes.* Just like that. Thank you for dredging up that painful memory by the way."

"Hey, you were the one who bailed on them, not me."

"Fair enough," Liz said through gritted teeth. Guess Sally wasn't one-hundred percent over the torture thing yet.

"Getting back to the point," Ux said, "attempting this rescue now is unwise at best, disastrous at worst."

"Which is why we need a Source," Liz continued, regaining her composure. "It serves as an active, stable connection to any of a hundred different realms, possibly more."

I made a hurry along motion. "And this requires Tina, why?"

"I was getting to that. Tina is still connected to her mother through some means I'm embarrassed to say I don't fully understand. Nebulous as that might sound, it means we can use her as the proverbial tuft of hair to find Christy. Since the process will involve reaching out beyond our plane of existence, that should also enable us to pinpoint the location of one or more Sources."

I shrugged. "I'm not even remotely following you here, but I'll take your word on it."

"Good, because I wasn't done yet."

"This next part is the one I'm uncomfortable with," Ux offered.

Liz nodded. "Finding Christy and reaching her are both going to require an inordinate amount of power, and it needs to be one we can control. Tapping into the Source itself for that is possible but..."

"Too risky." I waved her off, remembering what had happened to Christy.

"Exactly. We're dealing with the power of creation itself here. If I had several years to study it then maybe, but..."

"Then we'd potentially be dealing with another White Mother scenario here," Sally interrupted. "No thanks."

"I'd also kinda prefer we not wait several years," I added.

"Trust me, I get that," Liz replied. "We need to do this and do it soon."

Sally nodded, looking less than pleased. "And the kiddo is the only one with the power to do it."

"Not entirely true. A full coven of Magi could possibly attain the sustained power output we need, as well as a gathering of select other beings." Liz turned Ux's way, as if expecting him to have an opinion on this.

He fluttered his wings in response, the sound not a happy one. "If word of this gets out, others will wish to utilize the Source to try and find their way home rather than wait the current situation out. We could be risking dozens of lives, all of them desperate to try regardless of the danger."

Sally nodded. "It could cause a stampede of people throwing themselves into that damned thing and hoping for the best, which my gut tells me isn't likely to pan out."

"I share that opinion," he said. "Nevertheless, I am loathe to place such a burden upon a child's shoulders."

"What's the risk to Tina?" I asked.

"She'll be powering the spell and guiding us," Liz said, "but no way in hell am I letting her through. So the risk shouldn't be anything more severe than tiring her out, in theory anyway."

It was that *in theory* part I didn't like. However, I also

knew how badly Tina wanted to find her mother. God forbid we try to keep her in the dark on this and she found out. I had a feeling Purgatory would be lucky if all that was left was a smoking crater in the ground.

"Someone needs to find Tom," Sally said. "He's her father. I can't believe I'm the one saying this, but it has to be his decision." She thought about it for a second, likely coming to the same conclusion about anyone standing between Tina and her mom. "Hers too."

Ux nodded. "He should be returning soon. I'll inform the guards to send him here at once. Now if you'll excuse me, I should get back. I need to meditate on this, see if I can set my soul to ease."

The tone of his voice as he turned to leave told me he didn't have high expectations on that one.

Go figure, neither did I.

⟵———✳———⟶

"How long's it going to take?" I asked once Ux was gone.

"The tracking spell?" Liz replied. "Assuming everyone agrees to at least that much, not long. I already have most of it prepped."

"Anticipating a yes?" Sally asked.

Liz nodded. "No offense, but I'm rapidly beginning to understand how hard it is to dissuade your circle of friends once they set their mind to a task, no matter how crazed it might be."

"Sounds about right. Picking insane, unwinnable fights is pretty much our calling card."

"Considering your little detour to Manhattan resulted in us gaining access to the single most well-guarded secret of the Magi world, I'm in no position to doubt you."

"About that." I hooked a thumb back the way Ux had headed. "Does he know?"

"About the Archives? Are you fucking kidding? Absolutely nothing good will come out of that. Christ, do you know how much stress I'm under right now? I've been popping CBD gummies like candy ever since you handed it over, and I'm still so fucking wired *I* could probably power this damned spell alone."

A part of me considered fetching the vape pen from my tent so she could try. I couldn't do that, though. Liz was doing right by us. It would be the height of assholeness to let her juice up knowing there was at least a chance Falcon's unhinged prognostications had some merit to them.

Mind you, if I got the sense that Tina was in any danger, for even a second, then I had a feeling my tune would quickly change.

Speaking of stuff from that clusterfuck down in Manhattan, there was something else I had a few questions about. Since Liz was here now and we probably had some time to kill until Tom returned, it was probably as good a chance as any.

"Wait here. I'll be right back."

Fortunately, our tents were only about a dozen yards away, meaning it took no time at all to duck inside and retrieve Thundersmite's shattered remains. Then, despite my misgivings on using it, I decided to grab the vape pipe anyway, stuffing it in my pocket just in case. After all, we were on the cusp of starting a journey that could very well lead us down strange and seldom traveled roads. Better to be overprepared.

"Mind looking at something for me?" I asked once I returned.

"I already told you, she doesn't want to see your dick."

I flipped Sally the bird, then handed Thundersmite's pieces over to Liz.

"What's this?" she asked.

"A magic hammer, or it was anyway. It broke into pieces when I tried to use it."

"Bill tried to play carpenter on a King Kong sized nail, if you catch my drift."

"Not really," Liz replied, sounding confused, "but okay, let me check it out."

"Tell her how much you paid for it," Sally pestered, no doubt enjoying this.

I knew I should've kept my mouth shut around her. "No."

"Aw, come on. I want to hear again how you cleaned out your bank account, including the little windfall you got from Village Coven."

"Little being the operative word," I snapped, "since you kept most of it for yourself."

"Oh please. I gave you more than enough to ensure you could live comfortably sans gainful employment."

"I still work, you know."

"No. You take a cakewalk consulting gig every few months to keep from getting bored. That's not work."

"Could you two maybe shut up for like three seconds here?" Liz barked. "I mean, what is it with the constant nonstop sniping? Seriously, just fuck and get it over with already."

That pretty much stopped us in our tracks, for a second or two. "It's not like that."

"Yeah, I'd sooner sleep with a werewolf than with him."

"Too bad they'd need a distemper shot right after."

"Still better than listening to you jack off in your tent every night."

"I do not jack off in..."

"Enough!" Liz interrupted. "I see what the problem is here."

"We're not..."

"I'm not talking about you, I'm talking about *this*." She held up Thundersmite's handle. "The good news is that it's definitely magical."

"And the bad?" I asked.

"It's shit magic."

"Wait, what?"

"Exactly what I said. It's a piece of crap replica with some simple transmutation enchantments. A second year novice could do better."

"What do you mean by replica?"

She turned it over and pointed to a stamp on the bottom I hadn't noticed before. "See? Made in China. Hell, even I can tell it's made of cheap-ass aluminum."

Needless to say, Sally found this revelation absolutely hilarious.

Me, not so much. "That can't be right. I was told it was a legendary weapon."

"By who?"

"The ... guys who sold it to me."

That caused Sally to cackle even louder. "Oh, this gets better by the second."

"Don't you have a webcam you should be shaking your ass in front of?"

"At least I can still afford one."

I turned back toward Liz, my self-esteem slowly crumbling. "Please tell me you're joking."

"Afraid not." She shook her head. "So, who exactly sold you this thing?"

"These two gremlin dudes."

"Gremlins?"

"Yeah. Their names were ... um ... Beef and Queef, I think."

"Hold on," Sally replied. "You cleaned out your entire savings account for some dickhead named Queef?"

And now I felt even stupider.

"Back up a second," Liz said, looking confused. "You don't mean Be'af and his partner Kwe'af, do you?"

"Yeah, isn't that what I said?"

"Not even close. Anyway, one's tall and creepy with blue skin. The other is..."

"Short, hairy, and equally skeevy? Yeah, that's them."

Liz's eyes opened wide. "That can't be possible."

"Why not?"

"Because those two fucked with a grand mentor a long time ago, back during the Dark Ages, and ended up getting cursed for it."

"What kind of curse?"

"The kind to make them invisible to all other living beings for the rest of eternity."

"If that's the case then how do you know about them?"

"Because something went wrong. The curse worked for everyone *except* the Magi. In fact, we're the *only* ones who can still see and hear them. As far as the rest of the world is concerned, they might as well not even exist."

28

THE SOURCE OF ALL OUR TROUBLES

"Then I guess their curse is either broken or eternity is shorter than you think, because I saw those two assholes just fine."

"If so, that's a new development," Liz replied. "Probably not a good one either."

"Why? Are we talking a couple of powerful demons here or...?"

"Worse. They're scam artists." She shook her head. "I'm sure you don't want to hear this, but they make a living brewing subpar potions, offering shitty hexes, and ... reselling mildly enchanted junk."

"Behold the mighty Freewill," Sally said with a smirk, "wielder of mildly enchanted junk. You should put that on your business cards."

I wasn't sure whether to feel stupid or pissed off. I mean, it was one thing to trade one's earthly possessions for the *Infinity Gauntlet*, but instead I'd given everything away for the equivalent of the major award from *A Christmas Story*.

No way was Tom *ever* letting me live this one down.

"Guess I should spread the word to be on the lookout," Liz remarked.

"Hold on. If these guys are so infamous, then how come I've never heard of them?"

She shrugged. "We don't talk about it much because it's our problem to deal with, or at least it was until now. Besides, it's usually not that big of a deal. We warn new initiates about them when we can, end of story. If we're too late and they get to them first..."

"Then what?"

"We have a laugh over how the newbies got fleeced." She let out a whistle. "I gotta say, though, I'm aware of some of the scams they've run, but I've never heard of anyone being taken as badly as you were."

"Call it Bill's special talent," Sally said, still looking way too smug for my personal gratification. "When he fucks up, it's epic."

I turned away, thinking of all the horrible things I was going to do to those fuckheads should I ever see them again. Hell, it was almost worth it to call Gan and tell her these two had scammed her little Freewill love muffin. Let them deal with *that* fallout.

No. That would almost certainly come back to haunt me. Some deals with the devil just weren't worth it, although this one was kinda close. "Listen. I don't suppose we can keep this between ourselves."

Sally's response was a wide grin. "What do you think?"

I had a feeling that was going to be her answer. No doubt about it. I'd be eating shit on this for some time to come. Still, there was one upside. "At least tell me this means their dire prognostications were nothing more than bullshit."

"Why, what did they say?" Liz asked, a mix of humor and pity on her face.

"Some crap about me having an important destiny, and that tons of enemies would be hunting me down."

Sally let out a sigh. "They probably weren't wrong on the enemies part."

"Don't remind me. But these guys went so far as to cast some kind of..." I trailed off as the sound of footsteps approaching caught my ear.

"Some kind of what?" Liz replied.

Before I could answer, a voice cried out, "Time to get this show on the road, bitches!"

I turned to find Tom, Glen, and Tina heading our way.

"We ran into Ux on the trail," Glen explained. "He let us know the marvelous news."

"Hell's yeah," Tom replied, approaching the secondary barrier. "Let's show this Podunk campsite what a real witch can do. Right, Cheetara?"

"You got it, Daddy," she replied brightly from alongside him ... just as he stepped through the magic shield without a second thought.

Oh fuck.

"Wait, stop!" Liz cried, but she was too late. Tina was already through, which meant an empty bank account was about to become the least of my worries.

I hit the deck, hoping everyone else was smart enough to do the same.

A second passed, then a few more, until Tom finally said, "Oh shit. I forgot about that. Sorry."

I looked up to see surprise plastered on Sally's face. "Um ... are you okay?"

After a moment she nodded. "Yeah, I think so. No thanks to dipshit here."

"The wards on her clothes," Liz said, looking like she'd had about ten years scared off her life. "It must be. Guess they're doing their job."

Tina for her part looked nonplussed. "Does this mean I can play with Aunt Sally again?"

"I guess," I replied. "Just as soon as I kick your dad's ass for scaring the crap out of us."

"You said a bad word, Uncle Bill."

"Are you for real?"

"Bad words are never good," she replied solemnly.

"But Sally just said..."

"How about this, kiddo?" Sally interrupted, leaning

down. "We can play together, but only at a distance. That way we don't catch each other's cooties."

"Especially not Aunt Sally's," I remarked. "Because then you'd need a shot of penicillin."

Tina chuckled. "What's penicillin?"

"It's medicine to keep your dick from falling off."

"Silly Daddy! I don't have a birdie."

Liz shook her head. "I swear, I will never understand how child services hasn't been called on any of you."

She probably wasn't wrong. Still, I turned to my friend. "You're early."

Tom nodded. "We called it a day. There's some shit going on out there. The cops have traffic stopped in like a dozen different places."

"Oh, what for?"

"No idea. Probably some farmer lost his favorite fucking sheep."

"Maybe. You get those jalapeno chips I asked for?"

"They were all out. Barbecue okay?"

Liz threw us a piteous look before turning to Glen. "Where's Zoe?"

"Oh, she returned to her duties after Tom arrived."

"Is she still looking for Eric?" I asked.

Glen raised two tendrils in a semblance of a shrug.

With the small talk rapidly petering out, Liz proceeded to bring Tom up to speed on the plan as well as the risks involved. Go figure, but the retelling went a lot quicker this time – my best friend not being overly concerned with any details he didn't deem sufficiently interesting.

"You understand what I'm saying, right?" Liz finally asked. "The risks should be minor, but they're not entirely negligible."

"What she's saying, sweetie," Sally added, her focus squarely on Tina, "is you don't have to do this if you don't want to."

Tina nodded, looking as if she was taking this far more seriously than her father. "Will it help save Mommy?"

"We hope so."

"Then I want to do it."

I turned to Tom. "What do you think?"

"Fuck yeah, let's do this."

Liz gritted her teeth, her opinion of the new Icon obviously not all that high. "This first part should be relatively easy – locating a Source we can hopefully utilize. After that is where it gets…"

Tom waved her off, though. "Not a problem. Tina's a world class badass just like her dad. And if anything goes wrong, I'll be there. All I have to do is wade in and *boom*! No more jizz pool, because I am a Source-closing motherfucker."

Unsurprisingly, Tina didn't have any comment on her father's use of language. Liz, however, looked like she had one – reminding me of the lengths she'd gone to while trying to bring back magic. Yet here was Tom, boasting about how he could shut it all down again if he wanted to.

Oh yeah, probably best to address that before we went totally off the rails. "Let's try to avoid that except as an absolute last resort."

"Yeah," Liz said, "especially since some of us will likely be inside at the time."

"You can't just find her and reel her back in?" Tom asked.

Liz blew out a sigh. "It's not a fishing trip, genius. It doesn't work that way. Someone will need to extract her."

"I figured as much," Sally said, "which, of course, begs the question of who'll be going on this little vacation to oblivion."

I was in the same boat, having assumed this would be a rescue mission from the start. Nevertheless, she had a good point. We needed to figure out who was going, especially since we'd come back from New York with fewer allies than expected.

Fortunately, I was certain on at least a few of those details. "I'm in. No question about that. You're not, though."

Sally narrowed her eyes at me. "She's my friend too."

"I'm not questioning that. It's more what'll happen if we try throwing you into the magical black hole."

"I'm going too," Tom stated, raising his hand to volunteer.

"No, you're not either."

"Fuck you, dude."

"He's right," Glen replied. "If you go, then you can't be here to heroically guard Miss Tina."

"Oh yeah," he said, sounding crestfallen.

I nodded. "There's also the wee problem of your aura being anti-magic. If you try to follow, you might inadvertently destroy it all."

"Which we don't want," Liz pointed out, holding up a hand. "All right, why don't we figure that part out later? Let's find a viable Source location first, then decide who it makes sense to send. Fair?"

There didn't seem to be any dissent on at least that one.

"Okay, then. Let's do this."

⬦————⟁————⬦

As the afternoon gave way to evening, we helped Liz with the prep work for the spell, which mostly involved us moving shit to where she told us to put it. It didn't seem particularly complex, but that didn't mean there weren't some convoluted parts to it all. Because why would anything be straightforward in life?

For starters, we needed to do this outside Purgatory's walls, otherwise Tina's full power could set off some safeguards they'd apparently put in place. However, because of that, Sally needed to watch the fireworks show from inside her little slice of heaven, lest my goddaughter cause her to explode and violently kill the rest of us.

That wasn't all, though.

Tom wanted to be by Tina's side, as was his right as her father, but he couldn't be too close since his power fucked with magic. So that left him stuck on the inside, too, as Liz wanted to be right up against Purgatory's barrier in case we needed to hoof it back inside for any reason.

About the only person who didn't have to play this game

of Twister was me, since I was a vampire and little more than a bystander. That was fine, though, since it let me quietly seethe some more at being taken to the cleaners by those two asshole gremlins.

I couldn't help but remember the time in Dave's game when my character Kelvin Lightblade spent a hundred-thousand gold on a magic ring. Not only was it cursed to only work when worn on my dick, but it got one size smaller every time I expended a charge – the fucking prick.

I swore I'd never fall for that again, only to find myself once again burdened with the shrinking cock ring of life.

Maybe that's why the Wanderer had been so quiet. He'd figured it out and was avoiding my stupid ass. Either that or he'd simply died of embarrassment.

Regardless of any of that, though, Liz was ready soon after nightfall. It had continued to cloud up and the threat of rain was very much still in the air, but for the time being it was both quiet and still.

Sally and Tom were inside Purgatory, invisible to us even if they were only a few feet away. That left Glen and I as security, just in case – which meant me standing guard, while he bemoaned not bringing his camera.

I didn't really understand the casting portion, other than it vaguely resembled the times I'd seen Christy perform a scrying ritual. There were words, hand gestures, a stylized circle in the dirt, and various accoutrements – all shit I didn't know or care about, at least until Liz gestured for Tina to join her in the circle.

"Now, child," she said not unkindly, "focus. Concentrate on the circle and think of your mother's love for you. Reach out across the ocean of time and space and try to find her essence. As you feel for her, allow me to guide your hand so that we might locate the egress from this world that will lead us her way."

Unsurprisingly, her words were far more flowery than they really needed to be, but that was the Magi for you. Some of them really got off on their ceremonial bullshit, and

Liz was apparently old school when it came to this sort of thing.

She wasn't the star of the show, though. Tina was, and that became apparent mere moments later as her body began to glow. It was as if the wind whipped up, causing her hair to fly around her head as her eyes lit from within. Crackles of energy began to dance across her body, like a miniature lightning storm.

Fucking A. It was like Gohan's first transformation into Super Saiyan 2, except live and in person.

"Ooh, this is most exciting!" Glen bubbled from alongside me.

He wasn't wrong.

Apparently I wasn't the only one trying to contain a minor freakout as the look on Liz's face told me she hadn't been expecting this.

"Dear goddess, her power."

There came a spark from close behind them and for a second, no more, a portion of the dome around Purgatory winked out, momentarily revealing both Tom and Sally – their eyes wide as they watched the little sorceress of Grayskull spread her wings.

"Too much!" Liz shouted, no doubt realizing the danger. "Focus on keeping it in the circle!"

"Sorry," Tina replied, not sounding bothered in the slightest.

And Liz was worried about tiring her out? From the sound of things, Tina not only had enough to locate one of the remaining twelve Sources, but she probably could've found every lost set of car keys on the planet as well. My goddaughter's power was truly awesome to behold, not to mention pant-shittingly terrifying.

A few more seconds passed, then the air within the circle began to glow red around them as lines and dots appeared – seeming to form a pattern.

Almost like ... a map.

"It's working," Liz said. "Keep going."

"I ... I can feel her!" Tina shouted.

Any thought I might've had as to whether that was simply a figure of speech evaporated a moment later as a voice cried out from seemingly nowhere.

"*Is that you, baby girl?*"

Holy shit! The voice was echoey and full of reverb, like a bad radio connection, but there was zero doubt in my mind that it belonged to Christy.

"I'm here, Mommy!"

Tears sprung to my eyes as I realized what we'd done. Tina had reached out across time and space to her mother. There was absolutely no doubt about it. Christy was alive!

If that didn't motivate us to get off our asses, I didn't know what would.

"Hold on to her, kid!" Liz screamed, gesturing with her hands until a spot on the spectral map began to glow brighter than the rest.

"Is that it?" I asked. "Did you find one?"

She shook her head. "No good. It's too far."

It was a strange thing to hear from someone who could teleport wherever they wanted, but I guess I had to trust her on that.

"It's ... somewhere in eastern Africa. Beneath a mountain range, I think."

Okay, maybe that *was* a bit far.

"Keep holding," she told Tina. "I'm going to try again."

In the meantime, the reunion between mother and daughter continued.

"I miss you, Mommy."

"*I miss you too.*"

Again, some of the lights on the magical map grew brighter than the rest. "Better this time," Liz said, her eyes likewise lighting up as she apparently did some sort of eldritch GPS voodoo. "West of here. Oklahoma maybe. Looks like somewhere deep in the Ozarks."

The Ozarks?

Wasn't that where Sally had woken up after her little ride atop the flesh and blood Millennium Falcon? Hell, if I'd have known that, we could have simply come to her instead.

"I ... I think I can do better," Liz said after a moment. "How are you holding up?"

"I'm okay," Tina said, sounding no worse for the wear. "We're coming to get you, Mommy!"

"Nuh-no! I need you to ... isten to me, honey."

"Oh my Goddess!" Liz cried. "There's one right underneath New York City. Pretty deep from the look of it, but I don't think we're going to do better than that."

She was probably right. At the same time... "Um, you do remember that's the place with the giant fucking monster, right?"

"Is ... is that your Uncle Bill, sweetie?"

"Yes, Mommy. He's saying bad words again."

Son of a..

"Ooh, tell Madam Witch I'm here too," Glen said.

I glanced down at him. "Really?"

"Bill, if you're listening. Don't le... cuh ... come for ... here."

"What?" I replied. "You're breaking up."

"I'm losing her," Tina said. "Don't go, Mommy!"

"Christy!"

Liz's eyes suddenly opened wide as yet another part of the spectral map began to glow, this one brighter than the rest. "Holy shit! This can't be right."

"...ot here. ...repeat ... do ... come ... east is here."

"Mommy!"

It was obvious that the spell was losing cohesion, whether because of Tina, Liz, or perhaps interference on Christy's end.

Liz, for her part, seemed far more exhausted than my goddaughter, sweat practically pouring down her brow. Just before the light show ended, though, she cried out, "The Source! There's one right below us!"

There is?

29

SERPENT IN THE GARDEN

The spell collapsed and so too did Liz, or she would have had I not caught her.

"Thanks," she wheezed, "but I'm okay. Check on..."

"Tina's fine. Aren't you, Cat?"

She was wiping her eyes, no surprise there as I probably needed a tissue or two myself, but she otherwise seemed fit as a fiddle. "Let's go find my mommy."

"That's my girl," Tom said, stepping through the magical barrier now that the spell was over. "You heard Christy. We head east from here."

I threw him a look. "Pretty sure she's not in the middle of the Atlantic, dude." Then I turned my focus back toward Liz. "I'm more interested in what you meant when you said one of the Sources was below us."

She stood up on her own accord although she still looked winded. "Damn, even with her powering things that took a lot out of me. Anyway, I said exactly what I meant. That last blip. I don't know if you saw it or not, but it was right here in this spot."

"Are you sure you didn't read it wrong? Maybe you were picking up the one that used to be under Gan's estate. Her place is only a couple hours away."

Liz shook her head, though. "I know what I saw and I can read a map."

"Okay, if you say so. But why would she put two of them so close together?"

"Why the fuck does Gan do anything?" Tom countered. "Because she's Gan and she's fucking nuts."

That was a good point. Trying to figure out her apeshit crazy mind was like untangling a box of spare ethernet cables.

"Anyway, it's not outside the realm of reality," Liz continued. "This area is littered with cave systems. Still, it's crazy to even consider. Think of all the trouble we could've saved ourselves if we'd known that all we needed was a couple of shovels and the will to dig."

Tom shook his head. "Anyone else find it a weird coincidence that you just so happened to pick a spot for your hippy farm that was right above a fucking hell gate?"

Liz glared at him. "First off, Purgatory is not a hippy farm. Secondly, I didn't pick this place. Ux did."

"Did he ever mention why?" I asked.

"He said something about it just feeling right. Like he could sense his ancestors talking to him..." She trailed off, letting out a heavy sigh. "Which means it's possible they could have been, especially if we're right over one of those things. Son of a bitch."

It was like buying a house, only to discover later that it was sitting atop Three Mile Island. "But if that's the case then why hasn't Gan made a move? You'd think she take steps to ... I dunno ... evict you guys."

"Not really," came a tinny reply.

I turned to see something sticking out from the barrier about twenty feet away. It looked like ... the end of a toilet paper tube? "Sally?"

"Sorry," she said, her voice echoing slightly. "Figured this was the easiest way for us to talk without endangering anyone. Anyway, think about it, Bill. Hiding in plain sight makes perfect sense. Had she tried booting everyone, that's when folks would've gotten suspicious. But as it is, if we hadn't done that spell we'd have never been any the wiser."

"I guess that makes sense," Tom remarked.

"Trust me, it does. I've hidden enough bodies to know. Um, maybe pretend you didn't hear that part, kiddo."

"Okay, Aunt Sally."

"If that's the case, though, then we might have another problem."

"What now?" I asked.

"This is Gan we're talking about. I don't mean to drop more shit on our shoulders, since we're already weighted down, but I'd bet good money she has people on the inside here, keeping an eye on things just in case."

Fuck! I turned to see what Liz's reaction was.

"Ux is not going to be happy about this," she said. "We've built a community of trust here. But if what you're saying is true ... then we might not be able to trust anyone."

"Welcome to my former life," Sally replied. "We'll just have to keep this on the downlow for now. Find a way to access the Source without..."

"Without what?" I asked after she fell silent for several seconds.

"Is it supposed to be doing that?"

"What are you talking about?"

"The barrier. Is it supposed to be flashing red like this?"

Red?

"Oh, that must be the perimeter alarm," Glen said.

Liz nodded. "Yeah, we modified the barrier after the incident with Claire and Pam. It's supposed to let us know if any outsiders approach..."

Almost as if on cue, I caught the sound of faint movement in my ears. Turning, I saw nothing but the dark forest around... Wait. The air shimmered about ten yards away. A moment later, I realized it was doing that in almost every direction. "Um, guys?"

"I see it," Liz said. "It's a glamour. Someone put one up around us."

"What? How?"

"It must've been while we were focused on the tracking spell."

"But why?"

Sadly, that part was answered as the glamour dropped, revealing the woods beyond weren't nearly as empty as we'd thought them to be. I caught a quick flash of red light, then my vampire-powered eyes saw them. Armed and uniformed figures – peeking out from behind trees and beneath bushes – creeping into position in what seemed like teams of two.

What the fuck?

"Over there, officer!" a female voice shouted. "It's them! The ones I told you about!"

I followed the sound, my eyes cutting through the darkness until they came to rest upon the smug face of the slender brunette pointing our way.

Claire!

The sound of muffled cursing caught my attention, followed immediately by a digitally amplified voice which cut through the air.

"State Police! Drop your weapons and get on the ground!"

◆——————⟡——————▶

A good citizen with nothing to hide would've probably surrendered. Needless to say, we didn't waste a hot second beating feet back inside the barrier.

Not a moment too soon as there came numerous flashes of light along with the boom of sound outside, followed by the forest beyond filling with smoke – flashbangs if years of action movies had taught me anything.

Our little disappearing act caused some confusion among the interlopers, but not for long thanks to our buddy Claire.

"Don't be fooled," she cried out, her voice amplified in a way that was almost certainly magical. *"It's just an illusion. They can do that. These are the same ones responsible for what happened in the city. Don't let them get away."*

It was only once we were back inside that I realized we hadn't properly prepped for Sally. Fortunately, she was on the ball, having quickly backpedaled to about thirty feet away to give us some space. Judging by our current state of continued living, it was probably a safe distance – at least so long as Tina didn't go nuclear.

Sally might've not been going off, but the barrier was – lighting up like a Christmas tree.

"Will that hold them?" I asked.

Liz shook her head. "For a few minutes maybe. It's meant to hide us not keep an army out. That would require a lot more Magi than we have to man it."

"Wonderful."

Outside, Claire was continuing to direct the police. That was bad enough, but then I saw Pam step out from behind some trees and join her – still maimed as fuck and with fire dancing around her fingertips in plain view. However, nobody appeared to be paying her the slightest bit of attention.

Something was definitely not right.

"Why the fuck are those assholes listening to her?" Tom griped. "Is she banging half the force or something?"

"It's mind magic," Liz said. "Gotta be."

"She's controlling that many?" I asked, a chill creeping down my spine.

"She doesn't need to control them so long as she can give them a push in the right direction. You heard her. She told them we're responsible for what happened down in the city."

"Well, she's technically not wrong," Sally replied from a distance.

"She is if she's fingering all of Purgatory," Liz snapped. "What do you think their reaction will be once they get in here and see what this place really is?"

Oh crap.

"She's going to burn this whole place down around us," Sally said matter of factly. "It's what I would've done."

Remembering Pam's specialty, I replied, "You have no idea how right you are."

I couldn't even say this was personal. Those two had been ostracized from the community for what they'd done to Kelly and Veronica. Now they were taking their revenge on the whole damned place. Tom and I were probably just icing on the cake for those two nutcases. "What do we do? Fight or...?"

"We evacuate," Liz said. "That's what we do. You heard them out there. Claire gave them away before they were in position, otherwise we'd probably all be getting tazed right now. So we use that to our advantage and run."

"Run?"

"Do you honestly think we didn't plan for something like this?" she replied. "Every major Magi community since the Inquisition has had contingency plans in place. It's how we've managed to survive. It's one of the first things I insisted on when Ux agreed to give me a second chance."

"You did?"

"Yes. I'm not an idiot. A place like this is a tinder box waiting to happen. So, we made sure to have a fire escape. Now we need to make sure it works." She turned to Sally. "I don't suppose there's any chance you can hold it together around the others."

Sadly, she shook her head, just as I knew she would. "I don't know. We probably shouldn't chance it, though. Leave me here."

"We're not going to let them..."

"I don't even know if it's possible for them to kill me," Sally replied. "I honestly don't. What I do know is this. Even if those assholes manage to take me down, it won't be pretty. Trust me, you don't want to be around for that."

"Fuck that noise," I said. "I'm staying."

"Me too," Glen bubbled.

"Tom, take Tina and..."

"No," Tina replied.

"I'm serious, Cat, you need to go."

"I can help Aunt Sally."

Sally smiled at her, even as the voices outside grew louder and the flashlight beams drew ever closer. "Oh, pumpkin, I wish you could."

"I can. Watch."

Tina's eyes flashed with power, glowing bright purple. Then she waved a hand and a translucent dome of energy of the same color flashed into existence around Sally, surrounding her completely.

My eyes opened wide as I prepared to hit the dirt with as many of my friends as I could grab. However, once again nothing happened.

"It's like the spell around here," Tina explained. "Magic to keep other magic out."

"You can do that?" Liz asked, sounding amazed. "It takes four witches on a rotating shift just to maintain the static one we have up."

Tina shrugged as if to tell her it was no big deal, then she turned and walked up to the barrier she'd just conjured. "Stay close, Aunt Sally. It's harder to do if I don't know where you are."

"Sure thing," Sally replied, as gobsmacked as Liz. "You got it, kiddo."

"That's my girl," Tom proclaimed before turning Sally's way. "Now, so long as you don't lose your shit, we'll be golden."

"Oddly enough, the longer you talk the harder it is to hold my temper," she replied.

"Fuck it," Liz said. "Whatever works. Follow me and ... I dunno, try not to kill anyone."

Despite the urgency of what was going on outside – and judging by what my ears were telling me, there were a lot more cops than I could see – we were slow to step through the secondary barrier. You couldn't really blame us. Bullets sucked, but they were a mosquito sting compared to the lawnmower blade that was Sally's power.

Nevertheless, Tina wasn't shitting us. We stepped through and then, finding no issues other than my headache returning, hurried down the path toward the main encampment.

It wasn't long before we heard the sounds of chaos and panic ahead – definitely hinting at the invading force being larger than any of us expected.

"I'm thinking those traffic stops you saw weren't just to ticket drunks," I said to Tom.

"Already reached that conclusion, man. Guess luck's with me that we didn't get caught."

"Yeah. Luck. That's one word for it."

"Nobody likes a negative Nancy."

"Nancy can go fuck herself."

"Ooh, you said..."

"Not now, Cat."

Up ahead, a figure stepped out onto the path, turning our way. It was Zoe and she didn't look happy. "What the hell did you do?"

"Us?"

"Yes, you and your friends. Nobody bothered us out here until your little zoo crew arrived. Now look at it."

"Calm down," Liz said.

"No, I will not calm down, Liz. Think about it. They got back from doing God-knows what in the city. Kelly and Vincent are still missing. And now we're surrounded by the cops. No way is that a coincidence."

Well, when she put it that way...

"Oh, fuck this noise," Tom said, stepping forward. "As your Blessed One, I command you to cut the shit."

"Yeah," Glen echoed. "Bark! Or, um ... I mean squeak, Commander."

Zoe glanced his way for a moment before opting to focus on Tom. "I already told you that crap doesn't work here, bitch."

"Who are you calling a bitch, bitch? Now get out of our way. We don't have time for this shit."

"You're not going anywhere until you answer me."

"Yeah? Well, how's *this* for an answer?" Tom replied, igniting his aura.

"That's how we're going to play it, huh?" Zoe asked, drawing her weapon.

"Yep. Hard and fast," Tom said, "just how your mom likes it."

"My mother is dead, jackass."

"So? I own a shovel."

"I had her cremated."

"And a bottle of glue."

Jesus fucking Christ.

"Enough!" Liz shouted, red power flaring around her – causing me to wince from what felt like a sudden railroad spike to my frontal lobe. "And I mean from both of you." She stepped forward and faced Zoe, her power cancelling out where it touched Tom's aura. "Whether they have or haven't done anything isn't for you to decide. They were welcomed to Purgatory just like anyone else, and until they do something that blatantly destroys that trust we will treat them with respect. Do I make myself clear?"

"But..."

"No buts. Now isn't the time for us to fall apart. I'm vouching for them – *me*. If you don't think that's enough, take it up with Ux. Otherwise, knock off the crap so we can try and save everyone here."

"Yeah," Tom said smugly. "You tell her."

She immediately rounded on him. "Will you please shut the fuck up and try to have one tenth the decorum your predecessor had? Even if it's just for thirty fucking seconds."

"Well, damn," Sally muttered. "I may have to revise my assessment of her after all."

She wasn't fooling. It was one thing for Liz to tell us she was trying to make things right after the shit show that had started this whole mess, but to walk that walk was a whole other matter entirely.

Although maybe I'd save my praise for when I wasn't in danger of being dragged off to prison.

Uncomfortable seconds passed until finally Zoe sheathed her sword. "Fine. I'll follow your lead, but I am not leaving your side or letting them out of my sight."

"Fair enough," Liz said. "Let's move. We've got a lot of work to do."

Zoe brought Liz up to speed as we neared the main encampment. Far as she and the other guards could tell, the police had come in force, enough to cover Purgatory on three sides. Fortunately, the slice of forest they'd carved out here for their home was significant, leaving open a route for escape, albeit one that probably wouldn't stay clear for long.

At least Liz wasn't a one person show when it came to running things here.

I spotted Ux along with others from the leadership council doing their best to keep everyone calm while directing them where to go. Liz was right, there obviously was a plan in place here.

"Next!"

I turned at the sound of the voice, catching sight of Veronica. She was hustling a family toward a spot in between where four other Magi stood. As they stepped forward, the mages began to gesticulate. Then, high above, a hole opened in the semi-translucent barrier, revealing the cloudy sky sans any filter.

"Go!" Veronica cried.

A moment later the family vanished in a flash of light.

I turned to Liz. "Are they...?"

"Yeah. They're opening the barrier at regular intervals to let people out, or at least those capable of sending themselves via magic. Once they're done, they'll..." She trailed off as a massive ball of flame dropped through the still open hole in the barrier. "Oh God no!"

It hit the ground before everyone there could run for cover, incinerating two of the mages who'd opened the way. Thankfully, Veronica wasn't among them.

Regardless, the attack went a long way toward undoing the otherwise organized evacuation, as screams filled the air.

"It's Pam," Zoe cried. "Goddamn it! I knew we should've updated the protocols after we booted them."

"Go help Ux maintain order," Liz told her. "I'll..."

"I told you I'm staying by your side. That's non-negotiable."

"Fine. Then we'll both go." She turned to face me. "Keep

your friends safe. Meet us at the western garden before the barrier drops for good."

"Wait, we're not leaving too?"

"No."

"Why not?" Tom replied.

"Because we can't let an opportunity like this pass," Sally said.

Liz nodded. "She's right. The Source, it's right beneath our feet."

"It's our best bet," Sally continued. "Even if Gan has people on the inside, which I guarantee she does, they're probably distracted right now. Don't think for a second we're going to get so lucky if we go searching for another of those goddamned things."

She was probably right. Oh who was I kidding? This was Sally. Of course she was right. And I'd have realized it, too, if my head was screwed on straight. Crazy as everything was, this was still our best shot for attempting the rescue without having to fight our way through an army of hired mercenaries – undead and otherwise.

"Do we have enough people for that?" Tom asked.

"We'll have to make do with who we have."

Liz nodded before turning and gesturing for Zoe to follow her, barking instructions at people along the way in a bid to reclaim order.

I guess she really did care about this place.

Alas, I was a bit less generous when it came to those outside my circle since most of them tended to treat me like a piece of shit. Most wasn't all, though. I glanced over to where Veronica was still trying to help people. "I'll go get V. The rest of you..."

"The barrier's been breached!" someone cried from elsewhere. "Form a defensive line!"

"No!" a reedy voice shouted – Ux's. "Do not fight back! Don't give them a reason to..."

He was too late, though. The night sky lit up bright blue, illuminating the forest to the south of where we stood. Stun spells. Unfortunately, the gunshots that rang out in response were almost surely not of the nonlethal variety. *Fuck!*

"Petunia!" Tina cried.

"Huh, what?"

"She's all alone in the tent!"

"Who gives a...?"

I was a bit too slow, though, as the tyke turned and took off into the crowd.

Double fuck!

"I'll go with her," Glen cried, slithering in her wake. "Out of the way. Bark! Bark!"

Triple fuck!

"I gotta go with them, man," Tom said.

"I know." I turned to Sally as he raced after his daughter. "You too. Go."

"Are you sure?"

"You need to stay close to her, and someone needs to keep Tom from doing anything stupid."

"I don't get nearly enough hazard pay for that."

"Join the club. I'll grab Veronica and meet you guys at wherever that garden is."

"All right," she said, turning away. "Just make sure to follow your own advice and don't do anything dumb."

She didn't wait around for an answer. Probably a good thing, since I really wasn't in the mood to lie given how quickly the situation seemed to be turning into absolute shit.

30

A WAR IN HEAVEN

As I made my way to where Veronica was still valiantly organizing people, I quickly realized her efforts were doomed.

Pam may have killed two wizards, a drop in the bucket to Purgatory's magical population, but the effect it had went far beyond them.

Where before the evacuation had been orderly, now it was descending into pure chaos as panic set in.

It was kind of crazy to watch. Had this been a vampire settlement back in the old days, every single resource would've been directed toward repelling the invaders in the most bloody way possible.

And by that I mean everyone would be compelled to fight.

I assumed the same or similar would be true of the Magi and the other magical what-the-fucks of this place. After all, a good chunk of the mages I'd met during my time had been more than happy to shoot first and ask questions never. Hell, even those I was friendly with hadn't been hesitant when it came to fighting back.

But here I was seeing a side of the Magi community I hadn't before. I'd assumed that when the shit hit the fan, everyone would throw down their garden hoe and become

Gandalf the Grey. Not so. From the look of things, those were in the minority. Most of the people here appeared to want nothing more than to get their loved ones to safety – the fear on their faces speaking volumes.

I wasn't sure I could blame them.

A mixed contingent of blue cloaked defenders were spreading out to do what they could, but I could tell by the sound of weapons firing that they were outnumbered.

For Christ's sake, you would've sworn Claire had called in the fucking National Guard. Of course, considering the mess we'd left behind in the city, maybe I shouldn't have been so quick to dismiss that idea.

Had all the residents here made a coordinated stand against them this would've been a piece of cake. Instead, things didn't look good.

So it was probably time to make our move before it got even worse.

I reached Veronica just as she was helping an older man to the spot where he could beam out, another pair of mages having stepped in to replace those who'd fallen.

"Hey," she said, obviously doing her best to keep it together. "How are you holding up?"

"Me? This is a slow Tuesday compared to Manhattan. How about you?"

"I'm scared, but otherwise okay. Any idea what's happening besides the obvious? Nobody seems to know."

"Claire and her whackadoo sister, that's what. I'm guessing they called in a not so anonymous tip on us."

"That bitch."

"Yep, pretty much my thought too."

"Go!" she cried, momentarily turning her attention back to the old man – watching to make sure he zapped away before the barrier once again closed above us. "Where are the others?"

"Kitten hunting."

"What?"

"Don't ask. It's too convoluted. Listen, I need to know whether you're still with us."

"I'm here aren't I?"

"I meant the plan to rescue a certain someone. It's going down *soon* ... and by that I mean tonight. Not gonna lie. We could really use your help."

"Of course I'm in. But how? I thought we didn't know where..."

"We do now. Turns out one of the Sources is right beneath our feet. And yes, I'm sure of it. Problem is, we probably aren't going to get a better chance at this. That's the Cliff's Notes version. Any questions?"

She shook her head numbly.

"Good, then I need you to come with me to the western garden. That's where we're meeting up."

"Fine, but first I need to finish here."

I was afraid she'd say that.

Tempting as it was to toss her over my shoulder and carry her kicking and screaming with me, that wouldn't win me any points. So instead, rather than argue, I joined her – ushering people into the makeshift sending circle post haste, while keeping my eyes and ears peeled for the battle going on not too far away. Go figure, none of it was easy with a headache continuing to pummel my brain.

Playing Rescue Rangers was most certainly not my forte. I was used to running pretty lean during times of crises. When the shit hit the fan, my face was usually in the way. When things got tough, there was a small circle of people I knew I could count on and that was it. That meant watching out for them and letting everyone else go fuck themselves.

It was weird to be part of an effort like this, helping people who, just a few years ago, I wouldn't have pissed on had they been on fire.

Weird, but not entirely unpleasant as I helped a family carry their three small children into the circle next.

"Thank you," the mother said as they readied the spell to escape.

"No problem."

"I-I'm sorry, by the way."

I turned back toward her, half-expecting to be blasted

where I stood – as that's what usually happened when someone said something like that. Instead, I found her just staring at me. "Sorry? For what?"

"You probably don't remember, but I was there five years ago – with the White Mother, fighting against you and the other vampires."

"Oh, that? Don't worry about it. We're talking ancient history. No big deal."

"It *was* a big deal, though. Leaving that place without my magic, I thought … I hated you. But then I met my husband not too long after and we started a family. It put things into perspective. I … just wanted you to know that."

"Well … I…" Her words had caught me off guard. I was used to Magi calling me a filthy bloodsucker, usually while trying to turn me into a puddle of burning goo. That was the sort of shit I could handle. They fired death magic at me, in return I broke their clavicles. It wasn't what you'd call a healthy relationship, but at least I understood it.

This here, well, it was throwing me for a loop, to the point where I didn't have any idea how to respond. I mean, "Thanks, hope you don't die," didn't seem to cut it.

Fortunately for me, the assholes crashing this party picked that moment to make their presence known. A beam of angry green magic slammed into a cluster of tents maybe thirty feet away, turning them into burning confetti.

That served to break the impasse, while also sparing me from having to say anything that might fall under the banner of touchy-feely.

"Go, now!" I shouted at them. "We'll hold them off."

That was cutting a check with my mouth that my body wouldn't be happy to cash, as the sound of bullets whining through the air caught my ear.

Veronica turned and raised a barrier of purplish force behind us, wide enough to shield the family as they zapped away to hopefully much greener pastures than these.

"How many more?" I asked.

"Looks like two more families. Then the mages working the barrier."

"What about the Order of Saint Whatthefuck?"

"Don't worry about them. They know what to do ... I think."

That was good enough for me. Two more families and some assorted spellcasters, then we could make a run for it.

The smart move would've been to stay put and continue hurrying folks along, but that last blast had been too close for comfort. Not only that, but it was killing magic – meaning either Claire or her crispy critter sister were near.

My hope was that the police wouldn't open fire on those simply fleeing this mess but, with them engaging the Order as well as being semi-compelled, there was no telling what might happen. Even if not, I had to assume the psycho siblings were happy to flash fry anyone they could. I knew Veronica was good, but she wasn't at one-hundred percent. Hoping she could take the brunt of their assault seemed like putting all my eggs in a leaky basket.

That meant getting my hands dirty so as to buy her a bit of time.

I swear, one of these days I was going to wise the fuck up and join everyone else in running for the hills. But apparently not today.

I couldn't help but think of that witch and her children, all of them younger than Tina. The way she'd looked at me when she'd apologized...

Goddamn it!

It's not like my other friends weren't still out there. There was no point in getting to the garden early then standing around waiting with my thumb up my ass. Besides, I couldn't pretend a little payback against those two crazies wouldn't soothe my battered ego.

This time I wasn't going to let silly things like my conscience hold me back – hopefully.

"Finish up here, I'll keep them busy."

"Are you sure?" Veronica asked.

"No, but it's been a few hours since I've done anything cataclysmically stupid and I have a quota to meet."

Thank goodness I'd accepted Zoe's rabbit smoothie earlier. My tank was mostly full as I took off in the direction that last blast had come from – a good thing, as my ears picked up the whine of bullets. I had no idea if anyone was purposely aiming at me, but that wouldn't matter much if I got pegged. It's not like good intentions would make it hurt any less.

Mind you, that was still better than being caught by the blast of red hot energy that lanced out at me from a nearby stand of trees.

Fuck!

I leapt high, clearing the blast radius as it sent a shower of rocks and dirt flying.

At least now I have a direction.

I wasn't the only one who'd noticed, though. A bolt of blue electricity shot toward the trees, coming from somewhere off to the side. I turned that way to see two of the Order closing in.

Yes! Some backup.

The one in the rear drew a sword as he waved to me – a vamp from Zoe's unit if I recalled correctly. Jared, I think. "We've got this, Freewill!"

"Let's do it together," I called back. "These two are dangerous as..."

"You have no idea, honeybun."

What the?

The air to the duo's immediate left shimmered and then Pam appeared. In the next instant, the two defenders were engulfed in a burst of pure hellfire.

So much for having backup.

There was no doubt the attack had been fatal. The mage crumbled to the ground aflame, while the remnants of the vampire's cloak collapsed around his body as he turned to dust. *Shit!*

"You still owe me your eyes, Freewill," Pam cackled, her voice slurred thanks to her ruined face.

So much for this not being personal.

"And when I'm done with you, I'm cutting that other bitch's heart out. I aim to finish what we started."

Other bitch? Wait. Did she mean Veronica?

All at once it became personal for me, too. Saving my own ass was one thing, but I took exception to my friends being targeted, especially since I was currently running low on them.

It was time for round two with Firestarter here.

I leapt through the smoke rising from the remains of the two blue cloaks, sadly catching a good whiff of dead mage. Kinda smelled like burnt bacon.

Fortunately, it provided me with just enough cover to dodge Pam's first attack, a bolt of flame that would've surely turned a bad day even worse. Now I needed to close the gap between us before...

Now!

I leapt to the side just as a beam of green energy slammed down where I'd been about to step, sizzling a small crater into the ground. To my credit, I'd made it a point to remember Claire and mind my peripheral vision, knowing she was likely to try something like that. Fucking tag team witches.

"Don't kill him yet!" Pam shouted. "I'm not done playing with him."

I narrowed my eyes as I considered her words. There was an opportunity to be had there, but I had to be willing to take it.

And that meant pushing the stupid thoughts from my head that had hampered me during our first battle. Yes, Pam was young, and yes she was someone's child. But she was also a fucking unrepentant murderer who'd made the conscious decision to turn on both the people and place that had taken her in.

"Ah, did that make you mad?" Pam mocked as she hurled another fireball my way, a small one obviously meant to maim instead of kill. "Come here and mommy'll give you a hug."

"No thanks. My folks actually love me. Yours were probably just waiting for an excuse to dump your ass off at the home for wayward trash witches."

"I am *not* a trash witch!"

I'd said that without much thought, a weak-sauce insult if you asked me. Apparently it was a bigger deal in the witch world, though, despite its lameness. Maybe their version of calling someone a cuck. Either way, I'd definitely touched a nerve.

As if accentuating that point, the ground beneath my feet erupted in fire – melting the soles of my sneakers before I could course correct around it.

I stumbled for a moment, turning my head as I righted myself, then caught sight of Claire headed this way.

About damned time.

Now it was up to me to keep the pressure on and not screw this up. "Sorry, didn't catch that. Trashy McTrash Witch says what?"

In response, Pam pulled out a butterfly knife similar to the one she'd introduced me to last time – the blade instantly heating up red hot.

Sadly, I knew what I had to do if I wanted to win this.

Oh yeah, this is gonna suck.

I stepped in as if to attack, causing Pam to lash out at me. The blade slashed a line across my stomach, cauterizing the wound as it went and reminding me why it was a good thing actual lightsabers weren't real.

I stumbled back a few steps with my hand over the wound. It stung like a motherfucker and smelled like someone had left pork roll in the frying pan for too long, but fortunately it wasn't deep.

Now to just hope it looked more serious than it was.

There!

Pam stepped forward, no doubt sensing an opportunity to carve her initials in me. In that same moment, I caught a flash of blue light in my periphery – Claire preparing to double my displeasure.

Too bad for her that was exactly what I'd been hoping for.

Using every bit of speed at my disposal I lashed out and grabbed Pam, even as she buried her blade in my bicep – *Motherfucker!* Then I dragged her forward as I spun, putting her between me and...

ZAP!

I caught a piece of it, more than enough to make my teeth chatter, but Pam took the bulk of the stun spell. Whatever attack she'd planned scattered to the wind as she fell limp in my arms.

Sadly, I knew I couldn't leave it at that – not even if I wanted to.

Pam was a wolf in sheep's clothing, the kind who'd stab you in the back for showing the slightest bit of mercy – as I'd found out. Perhaps in a saner world she could've been helped, but here in the shadowy underworld of the strange and weird she was little better than a rabid dog.

And I knew far too well what they did to rabid dogs.

I looked up, meeting Claire's eyes as she ran my way, knowing my best shot of winning this was to do something that would make her lose any semblance of control.

So I bared my fangs as I tilted Pam's head to the side. Then I buried my teeth in her neck, hoping her crazy wasn't contagious.

"Pam!"

Too bad for Claire, I wasn't done yet. Knowing her eyes were locked on us, I grabbed her sister's chin and yanked – snapping her neck in one fluid motion.

Pam dropped to the ground as I stood there hating myself for what had to be done to bring this fight to an end.

Goddamn, some days this job really sucked.

31

THE RABBIT HOLE

To say that Claire lost it would be an understatement. She seemed used to her crazy sister getting uglied up in new and interesting ways, but had apparently assumed being a murderous sociopath was a survival trait.

My hope had been to purposely set her off, to make her so angry and outraged that she'd be sloppy as hell in her next move – allowing me to quickly finish this.

As I extracted Pam's knife from my arm, however, Claire let out a primal scream that was equal parts anguish and rage. Then, as a bright swirl of energy gathered around her, I realized that maybe, just maybe, I'd taken things a wee bit too far.

"I'll fucking kill you, you son of a bitch!"

Yeah, I might've overplayed my hand by taking a drink first.

Claire's next move was definitely sloppy, but the torrent of magic that poured forth from her was of such intensity that I had no choice but to run for cover.

She must've thrown every last bit of energy she had at me, because it felt like the slow motion escape of the hero in an action film – the ground literally exploding behind me with every step I took.

Ow!

Just my luck, a bullet picked that moment to nick me in the side as I ran, but I had a feeling that was the least of my worries. I had to trust in my vampire healing to keep my insides intact while my feet did all they could to keep me from reliving the nuke scene from *Terminator 2*.

Finally, I managed to leap behind a nearby copse of trees, landing in the dirt behind them and covering my head, hoping I wasn't about to have a couple tons of wooden stakes dropped on me.

As if that wasn't enough, in that same instant the pain in my head seemingly tripled – making me almost look forward to being engulfed in death magic.

That didn't happen, though. Instead, silence descended. Well, okay, not actual silence. The cops were still engaged in a fight with the Order, meaning it was noisy as hell. But the sounds of destruction from Claire's grief-powered onslaught died away to nothing.

A few moments later, the thrumming inside my head dialed it back to manageable levels. Chancing a look, I crept around the nearest tree and took a peek, ready to duck in case Claire had anything left in her.

She continued to stand where she'd been, silhouetted against the dark forest, but something had changed. A burning form lay at her feet – a body by the look of it.

But who...?

Wait, something's not right here.

Okay, maybe that was an understatement. I closed my eyes and shook my head, taking a moment to try and clear my thoughts. Then I looked again, my vision a bit clearer this time, and realized I was wrong. It wasn't Claire standing over a body.

It was Veronica!

Holy shit! While Claire was busy blowing her load at me, V must've come up behind her and finished the job – in a very final way by the look of things.

That was unexpected to say the least. Kelly had never been afraid to throw down, but Veronica had always struck me as being more on the gentle side. Apparently not anymore, though.

Now to hope she hadn't picked up a taste for blood and was thirsty for more.

I stepped out holding my side with one hand while waving with the other, hoping she realized it was me. However, she merely stood there staring down at the vanquished witch.

"Hey," I said, carefully approaching her.

She turned my way, her face unreadable. "I saw what you did."

Crap. "About that. I'm sorry, but it was either her or..."

"Thank you."

"Excuse me?"

"They were the ones who hurt me. Then, afterward, they tried to do the same ... worse to Kelly. They claimed to be victims seeking justice, but they were little more than monsters." She let out a mirthless chuckle. "And now I guess I am too..."

"No. You're not," I snapped, interrupting her. "You stayed and helped those people escape. Wait. They did escape, right?"

A ghost of a smile appeared on her face. "Yes, they all got out. The barrier mages too. They wanted me to come with them, but I figured you might need some help."

"More than I realized."

"The funny thing is, after the others were gone it was just me out here. I tried to sync up with Claire – use her power against her."

That sounded familiar. "Sync up?"

"It's a..."

"A catalyst witch thing, right?" I replied. "Kelly explained it to me."

Veronica nodded. "We're not supposed to talk about it with others, but that's Kelly for you. Anyway, I figured there'd be some irony in using Claire's own spark against her, but there was nothing there. She'd used up everything she had trying to get to you."

My hand dropped to my pocket wondering if ... nope. The vape pen was still there. "Then how...?"

"No idea. Maybe one of the Order was closer than I thought. Either way, I synced up with *someone* ... and now it's over."

Fascinating as this all was, she wasn't quite right on that as the sounds of battle continued to ring out from all around us. "Uh huh. Not to take away from the moment, but what say we get our asses moving to the western garden before this spot turns into the Alamo?"

She looked around as if suddenly realizing we were still in the middle of a Branch Dividians-sized raid. The only thing keeping us from getting swarmed was the chaos of so many people scrambling about over such a large area, but it was a fool's errand to think it would last forever. We needed to...

A strange shimmering appeared at the edge of my vision, catching my attention. I turned to look, only to realize what was happening. The massive glamour that kept Purgatory hidden from the world was finally collapsing. With the police inside and the evacuation ongoing, there was apparently no point in pretending anymore.

As the first drops of rain from the impending storm hit my face, I realized our time was up. "You good to go?"

"No, but that's never stopped me in the past. So let's see if we can find the others."

Thankfully, the western garden was home to a sizeable crop of corn – the stalks nice and tall, whether through magic or simple TLC. Together with my vampire senses, it served as good cover both from the police as well as the rain.

Even better, with the glamour shield down and evacuees scattering to the wind, my headache had up and disappeared – a small but welcome victory.

I'd told Veronica to stay behind me. With no other Magi in the area, she might as well have been a normal human right then. However, I comforted myself in knowing that I still had Falcon's vape pen in case we needed it.

I'd been lucky to grab it when I had. The damned thing was far too potent to have left behind when the shit hit the fan. I could only imagine what police forensics would've made of it.

Still, for now anyway, it was a last resort – Falcon's warning still bugging me like an earworm. Sadly, it was a last resort we might need soon, as the sound of footsteps headed this way caught my attention.

Please be friendlies.

I'd already gruesomely dispatched one person this night. She'd deserved it, but I didn't care to add any names to that list who didn't. The police were just doing their job, even if Claire's magic had ensured they were a wee bit *overenthusiastic* about it.

Fortunately, despite the rain my nose recognized Tom's overly familiar scent a few moments later, followed by that of my goddaughter.

I let out a heavy sigh I didn't realize I'd been holding, then nodded to Veronica to let her know it was okay. As I turned to move, though, she put a hand on my arm and called out, "It's us! Don't shoot."

Probably a good idea considering Tina could've razed this entire garden to ash if we accidentally spooked her. "Yeah, what she said."

We made it to the edge of the corn where, much to my surprise, I saw the entire group from earlier was headed our way, Liz and Zoe included. That was good. No waiting for stragglers. Sally's personal barrier was still up, too – a double bonus. Hell, they even had the stupid cat with them, huddled unmoving in Tina's arms.

Bringing up the rear, waddling along with a disturbingly unsteady gait, was Glen, back in his vile racoon costume for some unexplained reason.

"Took you guys long enough," I said, stepping out.

"Dude," Tom replied, looking less than pleased, "have you ever tried catching a freaked out cat in the woods during a rainstorm, all while avoiding the cops? Because trust me, it ain't easy."

"Sorry. Didn't realize you guys had it so hard. We *only* had the Sabrina sisters to deal with. Nothing important like corralling a kitten."

"I'm gonna tell your mom you said that."

"Fuck you." I pointed to the sword hanging off his back. "It couldn't have been all that difficult if you had time to stop and grab that."

"It was on the way."

"Be nice, Uncle Bill," Tina said, cradling the kitten. "She's really scared."

She was probably right. Petunia looked like she was down eight of her nine lives, practically comatose in my goddaughter's arms.

Fortunately, Liz stepped forward before we could follow this tangent any further. "I'm glad to see you're both okay."

"V pulled my butt out of the fire, literally."

The elder witch nodded, her expression grim. "Listen, I hate to ask this, but what about…?"

"Neither Pam nor her sister will be bothering us again." I'd considered saying something glib, but decided present company warranted a bit of diplomacy.

"I'm sorry it came down to that, but I guess they were too far gone to save."

Yeah, just a bit, although I kept that part to myself. "How'd things go on your end?"

"The Order did their job," she said solemnly.

"Not well enough," Zoe replied. "I counted at least twenty arrests, and several more injuries."

"Nobody could've foreseen this." Liz put a hand on her shoulder. "You should be proud. Thanks to your team, Ux is leading the majority of the families here to safety. You should go. You can still catch them if you try."

Zoe shook her head. "Don't worry about them. They have protection. I gave the word for the rest to fall back and rendezvous with the main group. Besides, I already told you

I'm not leaving your side." She took a moment to glare at the rest of us, specifically Tom.

Like we really needed more posturing. "Are they going to be okay?"

Liz let out a sigh. "Hopefully. They have casters at their periphery casting glamours as they go. With the sisters no longer a consideration, there should be no way to easily track them."

"Guess that's as good as we can hope for."

"I suppose."

"All right then," Sally said when nobody else spoke up. "Looks like that leaves us the last ones left at the party. So what now? Do we stand here shucking corn in the rain until a better idea hits us?"

"Is this really the time for jokes?" Zoe admonished.

Guess we had a wet blanket along for the ride. *The boring way it is then.* I turned to Liz. "You said a Source was somewhere below us. So how do we find it? Purgatory isn't exactly small and there's still plenty of cops combing the woods."

She shook her head. "Hate to say it, but I was hoping we'd have more time to figure that out. I tried to pull Ux aside to ask if he knew anything about the cave systems in this area, but..."

"Let me guess, things were a bit hectic for a lecture on spelunking."

"That's putting it mildly."

"Hold on," Zoe replied. "You said a source. Of what exactly?"

I shrugged. "Not much, just all the magic in the cosmos."
"What?!"

"Exactly. No offense, but we weren't planning to drag you into this. Since you're here, though, congratulations. This is where you learn that shit only gets weirder the more you follow the rabbit hole. We'll explain as we go ... as soon as we know *where* we're going."

"We could try dowsing for it," Veronica suggested.

Sally raised an eyebrow. "Dowsing? We're not digging a well here."

"Could work," Liz said before turning to face the rest of us. "It's actually not as crackpot as it sounds. Dowsing is a form of low level scrying – an attempt to *see* what's beneath the ground, or at least it is when it's not being used by charlatans."

"Huh. Who'd a guessed?" Sally replied.

"Only problem is it's a bit slow. I could try reworking that tracking spell from earlier, see if I can refine it a bit, but that'll still take time. Either way you look at it, we're dealing with a needle in a haystack situation that..."

"That way." Tina turned and pointed – to the northeast, if I had my bearings correct anyway. "That's where the meadow sings the loudest," she explained. "That's where I can hear Mommy's voice the best."

The meadow sings... Holy shit. If what I was hearing was correct, Tina knew – she'd known all along.

"That's sweet, honey," Zoe said, "but the adults are..."

"Going that way," I interrupted.

"What?"

"He's right," Liz said to the confused vampire. "We follow the girl."

Sally nodded toward Purgatory's security chief. "It's like Bill said. Welcome to the edge of the rabbit hole, Alice. I should warn you, though, we're fresh out of red pills and parachutes."

32

A HEAD OF THE CURVE

With both Tina and Liz around to sync up with, or whatever they called it, Veronica was good to go – giving us three mages to conceal our little party as we traipsed through the land that had been Purgatory.

The fireworks seemed to mostly be over, replaced instead by a constant downpour that simply added to the bleakness of it all. We passed groups of police reading cuffed prisoners their Miranda rights. I could tell Zoe wanted to stop and help them, but there wasn't much we could do without completely blowing our cover.

Liz put a hand on her shoulder at one point. "They're choosing not to resist. We need to respect that."

"But we can..."

"Yes, we could, but someone will almost certainly end up getting hurt if we do."

"I don't get it," Sally said, her voice barely a whisper as we walked. "They're Magi, right?"

"Magi, yes, but not battle trained." She chuckled humorlessly. "Don't worry too much. I'm pretty sure most of them are just waiting for the excitement to die down. I wouldn't be surprised if by tomorrow a good chunk had managed to slip out of their holding cells unseen and with no record of them ever having been there. Not all, but most. As for the rest, we'll see what we can do once we're done."

"The rest could be up on murder charges by then," Zoe pointed out.

"Not likely," the witch replied. "Things are going to be a mess, no doubt about it, but it's going to be really hard to make any of it stick. The reality is, outside of any old warrants they might manage to dig up, I doubt the authorities have much in the way of actual charges here – especially with Claire out of the picture."

"So we let the system work its own magic?" Sally asked.

"Pretty much."

It wasn't fancy or satisfying, but she had a point. The police had been tricked into coming here via a mind-whammy disguised as a hot tip. However, there was no way to prove anyone here had been in the city when all that shit had gone down. All they had to do was bide their time and hope nobody tried to pin the deaths here on them – probably not an easy thing unless they were planning on charging people with inducing spontaneous combustion.

Either way, we had a choice – get involved and almost certainly make this worse, or keep walking and focus instead on rescuing Christy.

Maybe it was me being selfish or the fact that we were finally so close, but I didn't have a single moment of doubt in that regard.

Sadly, it was obvious the remains of Purgatory wouldn't be left alone as we continued onward. Though freed of their magical compulsion, the forces present didn't sound all that forgiving at finding a tent city here in the forest. Those who weren't busy dealing with the arrestees, were knocking down everything in sight – destroying the homes of people who'd just been trying to survive.

Eyes on the prize, Bill. Keep focused.

It wasn't easy watching the destruction of what had been a thriving community only hours earlier – especially knowing Zoe was at least partially right in blaming us for it. At the very least, the chaos we'd caused in the city had given Claire a catalyst for revenge.

Fortunately, Tina soon led us further into the woods, away from the various encampments. There, outside of a few teams still looking for stragglers, we were mostly alone again.

Finally, Tina stopped and looked about. "The singing, it's loudest here."

"That's my girl," Tom said.

Sally glanced his way before rolling her eyes. "I don't suppose anyone brought a shovel."

Liz shook her head. "If we can figure out how far down it is, I might be able to send us there. We just need to be careful, otherwise..." She trailed off, likewise turning in Tom's direction. "Or that *would've* been a good way if we didn't have the Icon with us."

Shit! I turned to Sally. "What was that shovel idea again?"

She let out a sigh that spoke volumes toward her opinion of my intelligence. "All right, let's think this through. Gan had people present at every spot where she opened one of these things, right?"

"A few mages and at least one vampire each," Liz confirmed bitterly.

She was talking about the so-called Last Coven, of which her late boyfriend Komak had been a member. They'd been the last of the ancient vampires, who Gan had casually sacrificed in order to push the doors of magic open again — leaving her the only vamp left in the world over a century in age.

"Not quite," Sally corrected. "They only became that *after* the Source reopened. Before then they were just regular people. Which means they needed a regular way to get down there."

"You're right. They wouldn't have been able to send themselves, not with magic being so unreliable at the time. It would've been too risky."

Yeah," I added. "Gan's never been shy about throwing lives away when it suited her, but she needed those vamps as her promised sacrifice. She wouldn't have taken stupid chances. That means there's gotta be a way down."

"Holy shit, that actually makes sense," Tom replied.

We then stood there for a few minutes, feeling smug in having figured it out, at least until Sally asked, "So how do we find it then? I doubt that bitch left a neon sign pointing the way."

Zoe shook her head. "This is crazy. Even if there is a cave below us, it could snake for miles before touching the surface. So, what now? We blow random holes in the ground, hoping to find...?"

"Glen," Tom offered.

I turned his way. "What about him?"

He ignored me, though, addressing the creepy raccoon with the bugged out eyes. "Remember that thing you did in the sewer? Could it work here?"

"What thing in what sewer?" I asked.

Tom shrugged. "It was maybe a month back. You were busy, so Glen and I had to take care of a problem involving vampire goldfish."

"Did you actually just say vampire goldfish?" Zoe replied, echoing my thoughts.

"Ooh, it might very well work," Glen bubbled. "Good thinking."

I stepped up to them. "Okay, let's back up a second. What the fuck are we talking about?"

"It's a survival trait of my species, Freewill. Very useful to have back home in case any mucus-crawlers might be burrowing up from below."

"I'm not even going to pretend that made sense."

"By undulating my vacuoles I can send a low frequency pulse straight down. Normally we use it to sense the movement of predators, but I might be able to pinpoint the location of anything hollow."

I blinked a few times, letting this sink in. "Then why didn't you just say so? Get to ... um ... undulating."

"With pleasure."

Glen puked himself out of the racoon's mouth, a

disturbing sight as he had to distend the creature's jaw to allow himself egress. That done, he pooled there in the mud, his two dozen eyeballs blinking every which way.

"And...?"

"Doing it now, Freewill," he said. "I must say, the rock strata beneath us is quite fascinating. There's sandstone, a layer of granite, and..."

"Maybe save the geology lesson for another day," Sally remarked.

"Sorry. Ah, yes. I'm sensing an open area below – a tunnel – large enough for your kind to comfortably traverse. Ah! It appears to slope upward in that direction." He extended a tendril and pointed it to the right.

I turned to follow, trying to see if I noticed anything through the fairly dense forest.

"Hold on, there's a large outcropping that way," Zoe said. "About a hundred yards. Eric and I scouted it a few weeks back as a possible lookout location."

"That's gotta be it," I said, hoping she was right, because otherwise I had no idea what options we had left.

<—————— ⚬ ——————>

You'd think setting eyes upon one of the portals of creation itself – the very thing that connected this world to so many others would be an awe-inspiring experience.

But no, it still looked like a pool of glowing orange jizz to me.

Of course, I might've been jaded. I'd seen the original in all its glory. It had been a massive underground lake, like heatless magma, surrounded by rocky abominations and a giant statue of their crazed vampire witch queen.

Comparatively speaking, this was more like an off-color backyard swimming pool.

We'd gotten lucky in our exploration, finding a narrow crack after searching the outcropping Zoe had led us to. With a bit of magical help, we widened it enough to allow passage for those of us who weren't wearing size thirty-two jeans and below. Soon, we found ourselves in a natural tunnel sloping downward. It wasn't long before green flecks of light could be seen coming from the walls – the ley line Gan had tapped to open up this Source.

I won't lie. It was a bit nerve-racking to be in an enclosed space with both Sally and one of the arteries connecting magic to the rest of the world. Fortunately, whatever Tina had conjured around her seemed to do the job as we remained unexploded.

Less than an hour after descending, we rounded a corner and found ourselves facing a wide cavern with an ominous orange glow emanating from within.

Well, that and a whole bunch of security cameras pointed our way.

Fuck!

Leave it to Gan. This particular Source had been left unmanned, no doubt thanks to the fuckery that had happened above, but that didn't mean it had been abandoned.

Liz powered up to blast them to ash, but I stayed her hand. It was already too late anyway. Our presence had almost certainly been noticed.

So instead I hooked a thumb toward where Tom stood, hoping these things picked up audio too. "You even think about fucking with us and there'll be one less Source in this world. How many more do you want to lose?"

I then turned toward Liz. "*Now* you can blast them."

She did, taking them out with a blue sizzle of power. However, after she was done I found her ire directed my way. "I thought we'd agreed..."

"It was a bluff, okay? I'm trying to buy us some time here. It's not like we have a lot of room to dodge bullets if she decides to send a response team."

"Fine," she said, storming past me. "Just so long as we're clear on this."

"Relax, Hermione. I'm not trying to fuck with..." I started to follow, but instead found myself on my knees as I tried to step past the threshold into the cavern. "Uggghhh!"

It was the same as it had been in Purgatory, only a dozen times worse. In the space of a second, it felt like my brain was trying to gnaw its way out of my skull. *The fuck?*

"Are you okay?" Tom asked.

"N-uh ... no!"

Sally stepped to my side. "What's wrong?"

"Head ... feels like ... it's about to explode."

"Oh shit," Tom cried. "Gan!"

"What about her?" Sally asked.

"She must've planted a bomb in Bill's skull to keep him from touching her shit."

It was a good thing I was too busy listening to my neurons shriek to smack him upside the head. On the flip-side, considering what she'd done to Ed, perhaps it was best to not dismiss such theories so quickly.

"Is Uncle Bill okay?"

"Of course he is," Glen replied. "The Freewill is truly impressive to behold. Why, I bet he shrugs off whatever evil is afflicting him. Yep ... any second now. I'm sure it'll be glorious."

Jesus fucking Christ! I really needed to find friends who weren't complete morons.

"Oh yeah," Tom remarked. "You've been complaining about headaches, haven't you?"

"Thanks ... for ... noticing, dipshit."

On the upside, at least Tina didn't harangue me about my language.

Liz leaned down over me. "Hold on, headaches? I didn't think vampires got those."

"They don't," Sally and Zoe both confirmed.

While everyone else was debating the impossibility of vampire migraines, Veronica leaned in and placed her hand to my head, just as her body started to glow softly.

"Stay still. I'm going to try a little healing magic on you. Not my specialty, but let's see how it goes."

"I can help," Tom offered.

"Nuh-no!" I cried. "You stay the ... fuck ... back."

The last thing I needed was that idiot accidentally setting me on fire – *again*.

I could only hope that Veronica's touch was somewhat less painful, but there wasn't much I could do to stop her from...

CRACK!

As she tried to do whatever she had in mind, there came a sharp crackle of power – like an overly aggressive static shock. I didn't feel anything, at least anything worse than I already felt, but Veronica fell backward onto her butt.

"Ow!" she cried, waving her hand.

"What the hell was that?" Liz replied. "Some kind of vampire feedback?"

"I don't know." She shook her head. "I ... I only touched him for a second, but..."

"But what?"

"It's hard to say, but I think someone warded his mind."

The fuck?

"I knew it," Tom stated.

"Knew what?" Sally asked.

"It's Christy. She knew you were surfing Pornhub, dude, so she must've..."

"Here's an idea, meatwad. Go stand in the corner and try not to be stupid. Adults are talking."

"Is she always like this?" Zoe asked her.

"Only twenty-four-seven."

I was so glad they could find amusement from my pain.

Taking matters into my own hands as the others conversed, I did an about face and crawled back toward the tunnel leading in. Sure enough, the moment I crossed the threshold the headache faded away, like some invisible line in the sand.

What the hell was going on? "W-what do you mean someone warded my mind?" I finally asked.

"It sounds strange," Veronica said, "but I know what I felt."

"Which brings us back to who would do that to Bill and why?" Sally replied.

"Claire," Liz remarked. "Had to be. There's no doubt she had some talent with mind magic."

"To what end, though?" Zoe asked. "If she was trying to kill him, well, it seems to me there are more efficient ways."

Tom shrugged from off in the corner where he'd been banished. "Never discount the power of spite."

He wasn't wrong, but it seemed a lame form of spite – *unless* she'd actually meant for my head to explode but my vamp healing was somehow keeping my skull from splitting apart.

Veronica shook her head, though. "When would she have had the chance? Correct me if I'm wrong here, I'm no expert in this field, but that doesn't seem like the sort of casting one could do in the middle of a fight – at least not without it being obvious."

She wasn't wrong. Claire had thrown everything but the kitchen sink at me, but at no point had she gotten close enough to putz around in my brain.

Liz and Veronica shared a glance, before the older witch said, "Let me take a look. It's not my specialty either, but maybe I can..."

"I'll help," Tina offered. She handed Petunia over to her dad then joined us outside the chamber.

"I appreciate the offer, kid, but this is complex..."

Liz was a second too late in finishing, though. Tina lifted a hand, one already glowing with yellow power, and pointed it at me.

There came a *snap*, *crackle*, and *pop* of energy, causing her to wince slightly, but that was all. Whatever had knocked Veronica on her ass was apparently nothing to my goddaughter because a moment later I felt her *presence* lightly tiptoeing around inside my mind.

Oh yeah, this isn't weird at all.

Liz wasn't having any of it. "You need to stop before..."

"Don't," I warned. "She's already in my noggin. Can we maybe please not startle the insanely powerful child while she's dragging her fingernails across my frontal lobe?"

"Go, Cheetara," Tom cried. "Just try not to give your Uncle Bill any more brain damage than he already has."

I flipped him off, my skin crawling with the sensation that the inside of my head had suddenly become a little girl's playroom.

The only question now was whether she was going to host a quaint tea party for her stuffed animals, or throw a temper tantrum inside my mind.

33

MULTIVERSE OF TOO MUCH MADNESS

"You really should ask someone's permission first before doing that," Veronica chided.

"I'm sorry. I just wanted to help Uncle Bill."

"Can we maybe save the lectures for *after* she's done?" I replied, wondering what was going to happen.

"Aunt Sally?"

"Yeah, sweetie, what is it?"

"Can you move closer to the magic?"

"You mean the Source? Why?"

"I need to take the bubble down so I can help Uncle Bill."

"The bubble? You mean the one around me? Wouldn't that be ... bad?"

"As in *really* bad," I added.

Tina merely shrugged, looking frustrated. A moment later, though, I got the weirdest sensation in my mind. Somehow I knew she wasn't struggling with the power, but ... she needed the extra focus to do whatever she planned on doing. She just couldn't come up with the words to properly explain herself.

I had no idea how I knew this but... *Wait a second*. Our minds were connected. Did that mean it was a two way street? Her in my head and me in...

She nodded at me, grinning as if we were sharing a secret.

Yep, definitely weird.

I tried to focus on that connection, to learn why she wanted Sally to move closer to the big glowing thing that would most likely cause her to explode us all into bite-sized chunks of goo.

And then the answer was simply there, as if I'd known all along.

Weird as fuck. "Do it," I said. "She needs to drop the barrier spell so she can focus on me."

"I kind of got that part already," Sally replied. "But isn't it dangerous to..."

"No. Go figure, but it's actually the opposite. The Source, it's connected to everywhere and everything."

"Yeah, and?"

"Including wherever the fuck your powers come from. The mix of energies... Tina's pretty sure it'll counteract itself without setting you off. She just can't articulate it."

"How the fuck can *you* articulate it?" Tom asked.

"Because right now she's having fucking milk and cookies inside my goddamned head."

Bad words, Uncle Bill, came her voice from within my mind.

"Don't start with me, Cat. I know how much I owe you. Oh, and don't peek at my memories. There's stuff in there you're way too young to see."

"Fuck," Tom replied. "There's probably shit there we're *all* too young to see."

"Not helping."

"Sorry."

Sally did as she was asked, the look on her face more than a little bit doubtful – echoed by the fact that everyone else, save Glen, backed the hell out of the cave first. Then, as she stood near the Source, its orange glow clashing with her bright green hair, the force bubble around her simply vanished.

My eyes opened wide, hoping Tina was right ... only to

find us all still in one piece a few moments later. Goddamn, she really was something else.

As I thought that, her expression changed, becoming serious and making me think I'd thought something that had offended her. Maybe I should've used goddessdamn instead?

Oh, Uncle Bill, she silently said, as if chastising me. *You let Be'af play in your head, didn't you?*

"Of course not! I didn't let him..."

Except maybe I had. I recalled him placing that pendant against my forehead, telling me it would keep me safe from my enemies.

Mind you, it hadn't done shit to that end. Since then, it had been one ass-kicking after another, all while fighting off a constant ... *headache.*

No fucking way. Had those sons of bitches not only scammed me out of every last red cent, but continued fucking me after the fact as well?

I knew I should've been more careful when they'd offered it up as a freebie. The fucking assholes.

"Cat, listen to me. I think there's something inside my head. Be very careful with..."

"Found it!" she cried.

Her hand flashed with bright light. When it cleared, she was holding the angel wing pendant. In that same instant, a very familiar voice cried out in my head.

Hold on, Freewill. I'm not sure that's wise to do.

Wanderer? I replied.

Of course. Wait. What happened? I feel strange. Tell me you didn't let them...

I'll explain it all later, buddy.

Happy as I was to have him back in my subconscious, I was too distracted by another strange sensation.

Back when Beef had touched me with that thing, I hadn't felt anything. It was like a non-event. Now it was like the very opposite.

It's hard to explain, but it felt like a door had been flung open inside of my mind. And inside that metaphysical room it was like there was ... a fire raging.

The hell?

However, instead of burning the shit out of my neurons, it just felt ... *warm*, like a toasty fireplace inside my head. Hell, there was no pain at all. My headache was completely gone, as if it had never been there.

That wasn't all that was strange, though.

I looked up to find Veronica and Liz staring at me, both of them wearing wide-eyed looks of disbelief.

"What the fuck?" Liz remarked.

Tina giggled from inside my head. *I'll shut this for now, Uncle Bill. You can open it later ... when you're ready.*

Then that weird warm doorway inside my brain simply closed – obviously Tina's doing, but I could somehow tell she hadn't locked it. No idea how, it was just a feeling. Then, before I could say or think anything further, I felt her pull away – the yellow glow around her fading.

"Your friend is nice," she said, fully in her own body again.

"That I am," Tom replied.

"Not you, Daddy. I mean Uncle Bill's brain friend."

In the meantime, Liz and Veronica both continued staring at me.

"It's not just me, V. You felt it too, right?"

The other witch nodded.

"Felt what?" Zoe asked.

"Him," Liz replied, tapping the side of her head. "Up here."

"He was reading your mind?"

"No," Veronica said. "It's ... hard to explain. We..."

"Don't talk about it with others," Liz admonished. "Anyway, it's gone now. Must've been a side effect of whatever the kid did."

"I don't know, Liz. I'm pretty sure I felt..."

"All right, enough with the hocus pocus," Sally groused from next to the Source, the glow making her look like she was about to go all Dark Phoenix on us. "If everyone is finished crawling around in each other's brains, then maybe we can focus on why we're here to begin with."

"Yeah," the older witch replied, throwing me another look. "You're probably right."

In the meantime, Tina was back to being her normal self. "Can I keep this, Daddy?" she asked, looping the necklace over her head.

"I don't know, Cheetara. It was in Bill's head, so it's probably all gross and shit."

"But it's made of brighdril."

"I have no idea what that is."

"Mommy told me it's super rare."

"Does that mean it's expensive?"

She shrugged. "I don't know. Maybe."

"Oh. Then yes, you can definitely keep it."

I got to my feet and took a tentative step into the Source cave again. This time, however, there was no pain, not even the barest hint of discomfort. There was more of that warmth, though, as if that imaginary doorway inside my brain was practically begging to be opened again.

How did we get down here? The last thing I remember was being back in the apartment.

Yeah, about that, I thought toward the Wanderer, *we probably have some catching up to do.*

I eagerly look forward to it.

Glad at least one of us was.

⟵———✹———⟶

Hours passed as Liz and Veronica worked to prep the incantation. Maybe it was knowing Gan was aware of our transgression or maybe it was the nervousness of wondering whether Sally would eventually overload and blast the fuck out of us all, but the rest of us were mostly quiet, keeping to ourselves as the witches worked.

At least it gave me time to bring the Wanderer up to speed, and for him to mentally berate me for most of it.

Eventually I looked up, noting the two witches seemed to be about finished, before realizing Tina had turned her attention toward the Source at some point. She stood there just staring at it, then stepped forward and reached a hand toward its strange viscous waters.

"Don't touch that!" both Tom and I warned.

She stopped barely an inch away. "I know," she said somberly, cocking her head. "I thought I would hear Mommy in this place, but I can't. Why not?"

"I don't know, Cat," I replied, sharing a glance with Tom. "But that's what we're here to find out." I realized the conviction was slowly draining from my voice. Now that we were here, I was having second thoughts.

Not about rescuing Christy, but using Tina as the catalyst to make it happen. Call me crazy, but I was getting disturbing White Mother flashbacks watching her stand there in front of the Source.

"It's probably just interference," Liz said, using a knife to finish etching a circle in the ground. "Focus and try to touch her with your mind. Once you do, hold onto it. We'll need that to guide us."

"Okay, I'll try." Tina continued to stare ahead, her hand hovering over the portal to infinity that looked like nothing more than the bottom of a jizz mopper's pail. "Wow. There's so ... *much* here."

Of that I had little doubt.

Liz turned to the rest of us. "While she's doing that, we should probably finalize who's going and who's staying."

"Like I said, I'm definitely in." It was probably the first and only time I had zero reservations about jumping head-first into what was almost certainly going to be horrific danger.

"Me too..."

"We already went over this," Liz snapped at my best friend before I could say the same thing.

"It's not fair," Tom griped. "Christy's my woman. Or at least she will be once she dumps Bill's ass."

I narrowed my eyes. "Are we really going to start that shit again?"

"There's never a bad time to remind you of that fact."

I half expected Tina to admonish me for cursing, but she

seemed mesmerized by the Source, mumbling instead, "So many worlds. So many lives. An eternity of possibilities."

"Um, is it just me," Sally said, "or is that not really something that should be coming out of a five year old's mouth?"

Tom hooked a thumb at himself. "She's a fast learner, just like her old man."

"In what universe?"

"Not this one," Liz interrupted, "which is the only one he's staying in."

"There's gotta be a way to…"

"There isn't! End of discussion."

"I'll go," Veronica said, looking up from where she was helping Liz to prepare.

I turned her way. "Are you sure?"

"Positive. They don't need me here for the incantation, and if I can help save Christy then I say let's do this."

I opened my mouth to argue against her, but then thought twice about it. "Okay, that's two."

"I'm obviously out," Liz remarked. "I need to stay here to guide the kid. That, and I seem to recall Christy threatening my life if she saw me again."

"Fair enough. Zoe?"

"Yeah, I don't think so. I still only have the vaguest idea what that thing is or what we're doing with it. I don't even know what this Christy person looks like." Then, as if realizing she was being a bit harsh in front of Tina, she lightened her tone. "Besides, we need someone to stand guard in case any company shows up."

"That's what I'm for," Tom said.

Sally let out a laugh. "I think she means someone competent."

Either way, it made sense. I had a feeling any intruders would be hard pressed to get past both of them in the confined space of the tunnel leading in. It was just like in *300* … minus maybe two-hundred and ninety eight.

Glen was next to slither forward. "I too would like to join in the effort to locate Madam Witch."

"Glad to have you aboard, buddy. That makes three.

That'll give us a chance to cover more ground ... assuming there is ground where we're going."

"Want me to see if I can send you home when we're done?" Liz offered. "A lot of the ways are corrupted right now, but I might be able to piggyback a spell off this Source and punch through."

"Why would I want to do that?" Glen replied, blinking at her with about five different sets of eyes.

"I thought that was why you were helping us back then. You said you wanted to go home."

"Oh, I did ... at the time. But now I'm living with both the Icon and the Freewill. It's far too wonderful to even think about leaving."

"You sure, Buddy?" I asked. "It's a chance to see your family again."

"Oh it's quite all right. My parents had been bugging me to conjugate my nuclei with one of the symbiotes I budded off from and, well, I'm just not ready for that sort of commitment yet."

"Um ... okay."

"Sounds like it's settled," Sally said through gritted teeth. "I guess that leaves me to watch the cat and keep it from wandering into the infinity pool over there."

The frustration in her voice was evident, which I could fully understand. In truth, there was nobody else I'd rather have watching my back during a crazed mission like this. Sadly, with Sally's powers in a state of fuckery and her mind apparently up for grabs for the Great Beast, whatever it might be, we both knew it was way too risky to...

"You're wrong, Aunt Sally," Tina said turning to face us, all trace of youthful exuberance gone from her voice. "You need to go too."

"I don't think you understand, Cat."

"No, Uncle Bill, I do understand. In fact, I understand all too well. She's a part of this. She's connected to it all."

I inclined my head. Sally was right earlier. All of a sudden, Tina didn't sound like her normal self. "Cat, are you okay?"

"I'm fine. In fact we both are."

"You mean you and your mom?"

She shook her head. "No. I mean me – both of us. I'm the Tina McIntyre you know, but I'm also her sixteen years from now."

Tom was the first to break the stunned silence. "Come again."

"The Source, of course," Tina said before cocking her head and smiling. "Yes, I know that rhymes. Now if you don't mind..." She then focused on us again, speaking far more articulately than she had any right to. "The Source isn't just a window to elsewhere. It also touches an infinite number of *whens* as well, at least for those of us strong enough to withstand the currents of time."

"Um, so is this the point where you tell us you need to kill Sarah Connor?"

She smiled, her expression almost disturbingly more mature than her five years. "Not exactly, father."

"Liz?" I asked.

She merely shook her head, though. "Don't look at me."

"This isn't about her," Tina said. "It's me. I did this."

"How?"

"And more importantly, why?" Sally added.

Tina let out a sigh. "To put it in layman's terms, the time out here isn't the same as the time inside there. While you were debating who should go and who should stay, I was reaching out, trying to find mother, and growing increasingly desperate at the effort. After all, I've heard her voice quite clearly before now."

I blinked trying to make sense of this. "Wait. Are you saying you're actually sixteen years older now?"

"Not quite. But there is a correlation to that time span."

"What kind of correlation?"

She inclined her head again. "One that's difficult to explain. However, as I – *we* – searched, I realized I could hear echoes of my own thoughts, except they weren't me as I am today. They were the thoughts of other Tinas from other times. Realizing I didn't have the mental maturity needed to properly think this through, I grasped hold of one of those echoes and pulled her – me – back to help."

Silence greeted this, at least until Zoe said, "So let me get this straight. You somehow met another you and decided to drag her back here?"

Tina nodded. "It's more complex than that. It's more like I fused my thoughts with a me from one possible future."

"I hope the rest of you realize how seriously messed up this is."

Oh, I most certainly did.

"So how does that work?" Tom replied. "Like, can you tell me the winning lottery numbers for the next decade?"

Son of a...

She chuckled. "Oh, father, you haven't changed. It's one of the things I always loved about you."

"Wait, why does that sound like past tense?"

"Anyway," she continued, ignoring him, "I know it sounds a bit extreme, but it worked. As I am today, I have all the magical potential needed to do this, but I simply lacked the emotional stability required to properly think things through."

I was tempted to point out that twenty-one year olds were a lot of things, but emotionally stable usually wasn't one of them.

"I finally realized why I couldn't hear mother. It's not because she can't speak to me, but because she won't. Her last words to us during the tracking spell, they were some kind of warning. She doesn't want us to go wherever she is."

"Then how are you going to...?"

She held up a hand. "She might be able to block her words, but her love, her feelings for us aren't so easily turned off. So I simply focused on that instead."

"So you're saying you found her?"

"Yes. I believe so."

"And what about the warning she was trying to give?" Zoe asked.

"Fuck it," Sally replied. "Wouldn't be the first time one of us played the self-sacrifice card, not wanting others to get hurt. I doubt this'll be the last. So we do what we normally do in a situation like this, pretend we didn't hear it."

Tina smiled, the wisdom in her eyes not even remotely matching the gap-toothed grin on her face. Forget the White Mother, I was starting to get shades of Gan here.

God this was messed up. Speaking of which... "Okay, so what was that shit about Sally needing to go?"

"Ooh, you said a bad word, Uncle Bill." She let out a laugh. "Sorry. Force of habit. Remember what I said about hearing echoes from my future selves? That's part of it. I don't know *why* she has to go, just that she does."

"Fascinating I'm sure," Sally replied, "but what's to stop me from exploding and killing everyone if I step into that mess?"

Tina shook her head. "So long as you're tethered to me here, I should be able to keep you stable."

"Are you sure?"

"Mostly. Few things are certain when it comes to the multiverse."

Sally blew out a breath and shrugged. "Fuck it. This wouldn't be the first time I've bet it all on *should and maybe*."

"Says you," I replied. "You're not the one who goes splat if things go wrong."

"That won't happen," Tina assured me.

"But you just said few things are certain when..."

"The energies inside the Source are the same that are bathing her now," she explained. "So long as I regulate it, Aunt Sally is no more likely to explode, as she put it, than you are."

Somehow that wasn't all that comforting.

"And what about you?" Sally asked next. "Are you gonna stay like this, or will you go back to being you when this is done? Because I'm pretty sure I speak for everyone, your mom included, when I say we're not ready to send you off to college yet."

That caused Tina to smile, for a second looking her age, before once again turning serious. "I believe so. I'm reasonably certain this is a temporary state, one that will end once I disengage from the Source. I doubt I'll even remember it."

"Reasonably certain?"

Tina shrugged as if that was as much as we were going to get.

"That's good," Glen replied. "I would miss all the wonderful baths you give. Ooh, I know. When this is all said and done, maybe you can give me and Petunia one at the same time."

"Yeah, I'm sure the cat'll love that," I said. "So okay then, where are we off to? Because I don't know about anyone else, but I'm thinking the sooner we do this the better."

"I can't say for certain, Uncle Bill. I can sense where she is and guide you there, but I don't have any insight into where *there* is."

Of course it wouldn't be that easy, but it didn't change my thoughts on the matter. Had things been as they were five minutes ago, I think I might've waffled for longer. Now, though, it wasn't just Christy we were after. We needed to get Tina back to the way she was supposed to be.

"All right! Last chance to back out, everyone." When nobody answered, I turned to Liz. "What's the good word?"

"Hell if I know. But I should be ready in a few minutes."

"Fine, then let's get..."

"There's one more thing," Tina said, grabbing hold of my arm. "You need to take Dad's sword with you."

"What?" Tom and I both cried.

"No fucking way," Tom said. "This asshole already destroyed one magic item. No way am I letting him make it a set."

"First off, eat a bag of dicks," I replied, before turning back toward Tina. "Second, you do realize me and that sword don't exactly get along, right? I'm basically gasoline and it's a lit match."

"I realize that," she told me, "but you still have to bring it with you."

"Why?"

"Because you're supposed to."

I couldn't pretend this upgraded version of Tina wasn't starting to creep me out. This wasn't the first time I'd dealt with so-called prophetic wisdom from an older mind stuck inside a child's body.

"No way," Tom stated. "How am I going to protect you if I give it to him?"

"You don't need it," adult Tina said, sounding way more reasonable than her father. "You're the Icon."

"I know that, but that doesn't change the fact that I can't..."

"Yes you *can*." She put her hand over his. "You can do this, Dad, because I believe in you. Even if you won't believe in yourself, know that I always will."

"I..." He let out a sigh, obviously touched, but too much of a douche to show it.

"Everyone has a crisis of faith from time to time," I told him.

"We're not talking about your dick here." Then, as if realizing what he'd said, he turned his daughter's way. "Pretend you didn't hear that."

"Don't worry. I won't tell Mom."

"Good. As for you..." He pulled the scabbard from his back and held it out to me. "I want that back in one piece, asshole. You got it?"

"Yeah, I ... ow!"

It perhaps wasn't as bad as it had been in the past, but touching the sword's grip was still like grabbing a hot pan from the oven.

"See?" Tom remarked. "It won't do him any good."

"He still needs to bring it."

"But..."

She turned to me. "You have to take it. She needs it."

She? "Why does your mom need...?"

"You have to trust me on this, Uncle Bill."

"Fine. But how am I going to...?"

"Here," Zoe said, stepping in. She removed her cloak and handed it over. "Wrap it in this, then we can maybe get this fucking show on the road already."

That problem solved, I slid the weapon over my shoulder, feeling guilty for taking it. "Why does Christy want this?"

"I don't know. She just does." Tina shook her head then gestured toward the portal.

"Fine then." Guess we could always ask when we saw her. "All aboard for the next train to infinity and beyond."

"Not so fast," Liz said. "Tina's going to guide you, but my spell is the thing that'll ensure you all get back."

"Got it."

"No, you don't get it, at least not yet. There's a few things we need to go over before I send you, at least if you plan on coming back alive. So get comfortable, kiddies, you're about to get a crash course in traversing the astral plane."

34

A BRIGHT SUNSHINEY DAY

Ugh, someone get the number of that bus.

I swear, it felt like that time Tom and I went to the Fireman's Fair, got hammered on cheap dixie cup beer, then decided riding the Gravitron would be a good idea.

I'd have called that one a lesson learned, except we did the same thing again the following year, this time on the tilt-a-whirl.

Hey, at least we were consistent.

Regardless, as the world stopped spinning, I began to remember what I was supposed to do. Or at least bits and pieces of it. At the very least, it had nothing to do with puking on shitty carnival rides.

Of course, it was still possible that might all change in a hot second, depending on what I saw once I finally cracked open my eyes.

First, though, I took a breath, noting the air smelled clean and fresh – a far cry from the garbage and exhaust fumes of Brooklyn.

I waited a moment to see if there would be any ill effects, like me getting high as balls or exploding from the inside out. No luck on the former, but good deal on the latter as my lungs seemed to be processing everything normally in this new atmosphere.

Sensation returned to my limbs, telling me I was either lying on soft grass or some really funky carpeting. Considering how my journey into the world of the weird first started seven years ago – with SoHo, shag carpet, and dicks drawn on my face – I found myself really hoping for the former.

My nose was already telling me the answer, though, which meant it was time to get this show on the road.

I opened my eyes and saw ... grass, disturbingly normal looking grass.

Pushing myself to my knees, I adjusted my glasses and looked around.

I was in a forest, surrounded by trees and vegetation on all sides. In fact, it wasn't too different from the woods surrounding Purgatory, or what used to be Purgatory.

Well, this is pretty fucking basic so far.

I wasn't sure what I'd expected, but it wasn't this. Years spent watching sci-fi and fantasy movies had left me anticipating either some bleak horrorscape full of acid-drooling vegetation, or a Willy Wonka-esque magical garden full of candy and topless nymphs.

Alas, there were no licorice trees or boobs in sight.

How disturbingly mundane.

I swear, as batshit insane as the supernatural could be, there were some parts that would've had to strive to reach mediocrity.

Looking up, I saw it was daytime. Fortunately, the sunlight – assuming such a thing applied here – was filtered through a thick canopy of leaves and tree branches far above my head.

That was a plus.

"What do you say we get moving?" I called out once I'd finally clambered to my feet.

Silence greeted my entreaty, at least when it came to getting an answer. My sharp ears picked up the faint sound of wind through the trees, the light rustling of branches above, and a few piercing whistles that sounded like birds.

"Hello?"

I turned and scanned my surroundings, seeing nobody else around.

"Sally? Glen? Anyone?" *Crap!*

Before panic could set in, I started searching – stepping around trees, looking in bushes and low hanging branches, even checking the ground for footprints – as if I were some half-assed Army Ranger. All to no avail.

Damnit! Why the fuck hadn't I brought Thundersmite with me? Being alone in a strange new land sucked, but it would've sucked a lot less with a giant war hammer by my side. Like an ... adult teddy bear of sorts, except more smashy.

Oh wait. That's because Thundersmite had turned out to be a piece of shit.

I glanced back, noticing Tom's sword still strapped to me, but there was little chance in hell of me pulling that out. No thank you. I checked myself for anything else, noting a bulge in my pocket that had nothing to do with my dick – the vape pen. Guess I'd forgotten to hand it over before heading out, not that it would do me any good here. Oh well, probably for the best. Last thing I needed was Liz having a wild hookah party while we were gone.

Liz!

Finally, the last of the fog cleared from my head and I remembered everything I'd been told. Liz had said it was possible, likely even, that we'd be separated upon arrival. She'd also specifically told us not to panic if that happened. That so long as we had our tethers, we'd be okay. Even if we couldn't find each other, our tethers would always lead us back to...

Shit! My tether!

I searched the ground again, once more seeing nothing but grass, leaves, and dirt. The fuck? It was supposed to be visible to me. Without it, I'd likely be lost forever, destined to wander the Abyss for all eternity as a wandering...

Wait a second.

I took a deep breath and focused, willing it to appear – also as I'd been instructed. I knew I should've written this shit down. But no, I had to be all gung-ho about there not being a second to waste.

Oh well. What was done was done.

Speaking of which, I envisioned my tether then opened my eyes to see ... more nothing! *Son of a...* Or at least that was the case until I glanced over my shoulder again.

Duh!

Of course it made sense that it would be *behind* me. I spied a glowing silvery strand of energy leading away from my body, weaving through the trees and disappearing off into the distance.

What the?

I followed the tether back to myself, seeing it snake up my ankle and disappear inside my pants, making it look like I was taking an infinitely long silver shit.

"You've gotta be fucking kidding me."

Good thing I was the only one who could see it. As I spun to get a better look, the strand of light shifted, moving with me so it always appeared behind my body. How the fuck was I supposed to follow it back if it was constantly...?

In the same instant that thought hit my head, the tether suddenly appeared in front of me.

Huh.

Come to think of it, Liz had mentioned that, too – that the tether wasn't a physical thing so much as a concept, my mental connection to home. If so, then maybe I was only able to follow it when I wanted to – the rest of the time leaving it to trail behind me like I was constantly crapping out magical Silly Putty.

That said, a part of me was tempted to follow it now, especially since I didn't like the thought of being alone wherever I was. The problem was I had no idea how long I could do that before it simply snapped me back to where I'd started.

If that happened, I'd be at square one again without

having even tried. No fucking way was that happening. There was simply no way I could look Tina – either of them – in the eye knowing I'd given up so easily.

Mind you, that didn't mean I couldn't hope for the best.

I cupped my hands over my mouth and shouted, "Christy, are you out there?!"

My own voice echoed back, as well as the sound of scampering from the underbrush, but that was all. Still, it had to be done, even if there was no way it could ever be that easy.

Guess it was the old fashioned way then.

"So what do you say, Wanderer? Any direction look better to you than the rest?"

My subconscious, however, was apparently in the mood to be as quiet as the surrounding forest.

Not again!

I rapped a knuckle against my forehead. "Yoo hoo! You awake in there?"

No answer. *Great.* Not only was I physically alone, but the spirit inside my mind was taking a siesta, leaving me with nobody but myself to rely on.

Just fucking wonderful.

Nevertheless, I wasn't going to get anything done by standing around. So I turned in a circle and then picked a direction, using the scientific method of randomly deciding that one way looked better than the rest.

The hard work finished, it was time to get walking.

I'd never been much of a survivalist. I had no interest in being a Boy Scout. Hell, as a child I'd treated any and all entreaties about camping as nothing short of hostile. Needless to say, that hadn't changed much since becoming an adult.

That said, I wasn't a fucking idiot. I'd watched enough horror movies to know how easy it was to walk in circles. So I popped the talons on my right hand and used them to mark each tree that I passed – a horizontal slash followed by a vertical one, making it look like a tic-tac-toe board. That way there was no mistaking it.

It slowed me down a little, but not by much, as it's not like I was sprinting mindlessly at top speed.

Much as I didn't like the wilderness, I had to admit it was peaceful – a far cry from the hellish landscapes I'd imagined.

My head finally clear, I considered Liz's advice as I walked – or her lack thereof.

Besides telling us about our tethers, her *masterclass* had pretty much consisted of warning us that different dimensions could have different effects on our minds and bodies. Translation: good luck, hope you don't turn into goo when you get wherever you're going.

Real useful. Like twenty years of D&D hadn't taught me that much already.

Anyway, aside from the Wanderer giving me the silent treatment again, so far everything seemed mostly normal. I could've been in another plane of existence, or I could've simply been in Pennsylvania for all I knew.

Every so often I stopped to call out Christy's name, each time to no avail. If she was playing Snow White in this enchanted forest, then I had to assume she'd found somewhere to hole up – hopefully minus seven horny dwarves to keep her company. I swear, it *almost* made me sorry I'd downloaded that porno a few years back.

I continued onward for what felt like a good hour or more – it was hard to tell in this place – seeing nothing but trees, bushes, and more trees.

Finally, I spotted something up ahead.

Double-timing it that way, I realized it was a clearing, a large one by the looks of it. Just ahead, the canopy of trees gave way to open sky – with what appeared to be bright sunlight streaming down upon it, giving it an almost magical quality compared to the relative gloom of the forest.

Magical for anyone but me.

I stopped just inside the tree line, making sure I was still protected by the shadows.

Craning my neck up, I spied the first hint that I wasn't in

Kansas anymore, or anywhere else on Earth for that matter. The sky was a clear blue with only a few clouds visible, but they weren't the normal fluffy white clouds one might expect. These were bright pink, as if made of bales of cotton candy. There was nothing ominous about them, but it reminded me to stay sharp as the normal rules didn't necessarily apply here.

Looking at where the sunlight hit the ground just a few feet in front of me, I took a deep breath. Years back there'd been an episode of *Angel* where the group had traveled to another world – one where sunlight didn't cause vamps to go poof.

Fiction and reality seldom mixed well, but I found myself curious nevertheless. Guess it was time to test just *how* different the rules of this land were.

I tentatively reached out, feeling the ambient warmth as my hand started to leave the protective cover of the...

And then I quickly pulled back as the most godawful stench imaginable hit me from out of nowhere, causing me to double over coughing. It utterly disrupted the pristine scents of the forest like a shit covered baseball bat to the forehead.

What the ever loving fuck?

Worse yet, it seemed to come from everywhere at once. The hell? Had I somehow found the diarrhea fairy's invisible summer palace, or was this an unfortunate world where sunlight smelled like rancid ass?

My eyes watered as the disgusting odor continued to assault my nostrils. Even breathing through my mouth didn't help as I could fucking taste it too. *Ugh!*

For God's sake, I couldn't remember smelling anything this bad for at least ... five years.

No way! It can't be!

Then, as if to answer my disbelief, there came the crunch of leaves from behind me, as if something heavy had just taken a footstep.

It's not possible. I have to be imagining it. There's no way it can be a...

"*T'lunta,*" a throaty voice growled, sounding as if its owner were gargling with broken glass.

Fuck, fuck, fuck!

I turned, praying to whatever gods existed that I was high on shroom dust. Regrettably, the creature looming above me was both way too solid as well as far too ripe to merely be a figment of my imagination.

It was titanic in stature – a nightmare given form – ten feet tall if an inch and covered in rippling muscle beneath matted brown fur. I was tempted to shit my pants then and there, realizing nobody would be able to tell with Sasquatch stink dirtying the air.

Oh, this was definitely not good.

But then the beast opened its mouth to speak, and it was the space of seconds for me to realize it was so much worse than I could have ever thought.

"*Turd remembers you! Turd hates you! And now Turd will finally have his revenge!*"

35

TURD IS THE WORD

The next thing I knew, a fist the size of a bowling ball hit me with an uppercut that sent me flying out into the clearing.

It gave me a moment to reflect upon things, being that my brain was currently too scrambled to worry that I'd soon be a pile of dust beneath the blazing sun of this world.

Turd wasn't the worst enemy I'd faced back before the original Source was destroyed, but he sure as shit was in the top three. And no one else – not Alex, not Calibra – could match him when it came to either size or stench.

I'd thought all of that behind me, though, because Turd was dead. I should know. I'd killed him – or at least Dr. Death had. With him in control, Turd and I had faced off in one final battle, the end of which had found the big ape dead from an acute case of shattered spine.

Regardless, he sure as hell seemed plenty lively for a corpse.

Maybe this was like what had happened to Tina. She'd told us the Source connected not only to other places but other times too. What if that had been Christy's fate – to be sent to the past?

Goddamn, I hoped not. The last thing I wanted to do was relive all that. And, well, let's face facts, dealing with the headaches of time travel, the butterfly effect, and other headache-inducing bullshit wasn't high on my priority list either.

But maybe none of that would be an issue as I landed hard on the grass, skidding to a halt beneath the open sky. Staring up, I waited for the *wonderful* sensation of my skin to start bubbling in the second or two before I became a burnt tater tot.

Wherever you are, Ed, I hope you're safe. But just know I'm coming back to haunt your stupid ass for fucking this up for me.

However, nothing of the sort happened. The sun, more a bluish white than the yellow of the one I was familiar with, was warm on my skin, but that was all.

Holy shit! I was actually going to be okay.

"You killed Turd! Now Turd kill you! Again, and again, and again!"

Maybe I was being a bit optimistic. On the upside, if Turd remembered his death then that probably shot down the theory of this being the past. Glass half full and all.

Add my pants to that, as Turd came storming out into the clearing. I sat up just as the big shit clamped a massive hand over my face and dragged me the rest of the way – leaving me dangling from his clutches.

"I ... don't suppose ... we can talk ... about this?"

"Turd not talk. Turd will laugh as he crushes stupid Freewill!"

Yeah, I kind of had a feeling it would be that way.

Um, Wanderer? I know I told you we'd catch up later, but if you have any suggestions, now would be a good time to share them.

"That'll be quite enough of that, thank you."

I sighed with relief at hearing the Wanderer finally speak up, or tried to with my face currently in a hairy vice – the stink of which implied this was probably the hand Turd used to wipe.

Oh dear God, let me die...

Wait! I'd heard the Wanderer's voice with my ears, not inside my mind. *What the...?*

"Turd remembers you! Stupid t'lunta from Woods of Mourning. Stupid t'lunta friends with stupid Freewill!"

Before I could begin to figure out what was happening, I found myself airborne again as Turd flung me like a sack of shit. I tumbled end over end, not eager to discover what hard object I'd smash into next, when suddenly my flight came to an abrupt halt as something – no, *someone* – caught me.

Strong hands grabbed hold of me before setting me back onto the ground. I shook my head to clear the vertigo that came from being used as a punching bag then looked up to see who'd caught me.

Holy shit! "James?"

"Wanderer will do," he replied with a nod – looking as solid and alive as he had five years ago. Hell, he was even dressed the same as I remembered, looking almost too good in a shirt, jeans, and bomber jacket, as if he'd stepped directly from an L.L. Bean catalog.

"No offense, but why aren't you inside of me?"

Okay, perhaps I could've phrased that better.

He raised an eyebrow. "You always did have a way with words, Freewill. Still, perhaps we can save the discussion about your sexual proclivities for a later time."

"I didn't mean it that way. How are you...?"

"My own person again? No idea. Let us assume, though, that it has something to do with this world, wherever it might be. Now, if you'll excuse me..."

He shoved me to the side, diving out of the way just as Turd came barreling toward us like a semi.

I fell, whereas the Wanderer landed gracefully, turning and attacking before Turd could change course. He landed two hard blows to the beast's kidneys, before ducking as Turd swung around with a massive backhand.

"Feels good to stretch my legs again," he said, somehow managing to evade the monster ape's much greater reach.

"Turd will stretch t'lunta's legs until they snap off!"

There was no doubt in my mind that Turd was more than capable of his threat as he shrugged off the Wanderer's next two blows. However, my inner spirit given physical form almost certainly had the edge when it came to fighting skills.

"A little help perhaps," he called out, as he dodged and weaved. "He's a worthy foe, no doubt, but between the two of us I'm certain we can put this brute down."

Color me doubtful on that part, but I also realized that standing around and watching was unlikely to win me any points.

I still had no idea what James ... err ... the Wanderer was or how he'd taken physical form, but being a vampire was apparently still part of the equation as he unsheathed his claws and raked them across Turd's thigh before sidestepping the Sasquatch.

In the next instant he leapt upon the bigfoot's back, just barely wrapping one arm around Turd's nearly nonexistent neck.

"*Get off Turd!*"

"Now would be a good time to try ... whoa ... something!"

Turd whipped around, trying to dislodge the Wanderer, before finally reaching up with both arms to peel him off.

If that wasn't an opening sent by heaven itself, I didn't know what was.

The impasse broken, I raced forward while willing my claws to extend.

Don't think about what you're about to do, just do it.

Easier said than done, but it was either take the low road or die trying. "Hey, Turd. Nuts to you!"

I slammed my hand into Turd's crotch, driving my claws deep into his jingle bells.

Needless to say, manscaping was not one of Turd's specialties. His pubes were the most ungodly greasy mat of hair I'd ever had the displeasure of running my fingers through.

Still, I held down my bile, digging ever deeper and giving

Turd the quickest most violent vasectomy imaginable. He threw his head back and roared in fury as I sliced up his hairy cantaloupes like the worst fruit salad in history.

I looked up to see the Wanderer – all but forgotten by our foe – trying to maneuver his other arm to snap the monster ape's neck, but he was just barely holding on. I had a feeling we'd need another tactic to end this, one that hopefully didn't involve me knuckle deep inside Turd's...

That thought trailed off as I felt a weird twinge inside my head. Not painful or anything, just ... weird. Like an awareness of...

"For fuck's sake. I can't leave you alone for five goddamned minutes."

What the? I turned at the sound of the familiar voice, catching a glimpse of ... dirty blonde hair at the edge of the clearing?

"So, can anyone join this party," Sally asked, her locks somehow back to their original color, "or are you too busy giving bigfoot a handjob?"

She wasn't alone either. Veronica stood by her side – looking the same as she had. Hopefully, she had access to her magic, too, because if so then maybe we could...

OOF!

Turd kicked out as I stood there gawking, sending me tumbling away – my hand covered in his junk juice.

At least I'd ensured he wouldn't be fathering any Turdlings anytime soon.

Sadly, the damage we'd done only seemed to further enrage the beast, which in all fairness wasn't entirely unexpected. After all, I'd probably be a wee bit ticked, too, if someone tried going all Wolverine on my family jewels.

Mind you, I'd also be doubled over crying. Turd, alas, wasn't nearly as sentimental. He finally dragged the Wanderer off his back, tossing the hapless vamp to the side as he turned his attention my way, his eyes red with murderous intent.

Oh yeah, I'd ticked him off real good.

"Not so fast, asshole," Sally cried as she and Veronica

came racing my way. "If you want to get to us, you'll have to go through him first."

"That's not how the saying goes!"

"Sue me for not being a martyr."

Turd turned her way. "*Ugly female t'lunta? Turd remembers you, too!*"

"Turd?" she replied, eyes wide. "You've gotta be fucking kidding me. Oh, and who the hell are you calling ugly?"

"Really?!"

"Priorities, Bill," she replied.

"Yeah, well, mine involve staying alive."

Fortunately, Veronica was apparently more interested in ending this than watching us argue.

"Child of the forest, please hear my words." She held up her hands in a placating manner as she approached the brute. "I am one of the Magi, neutral in your conflict. I bear you no ill will."

"*Neutral?*" Turd growled, halting his advance.

"Yes, as set forth in the provisions of the Humbaba Accord. Please cease this conflict and afford us the grace of parley."

"*Parley? Humbaba Accord?*"

Sally threw her some side eye. "Call me crazy, but I have a feeling that's not going to work."

Unsurprisingly, Turd threw back his head and laughed, quite the accomplishment for someone whose balls had recently been fileted. "*Stupid Magi! No Humbaba Accord here! No parley! Only death!*"

Yep, that went about as well as expected.

"Please," Veronica replied. "The Magi have been friends with the forest folk for eons. I ... I have no wish to hurt you."

"*No, but Turd wishes to hurt you. Turd wishes to hurt you all!*"

"That's it," I said, pushing myself to my feet, half amazed to find myself still able to. "I think we're back to dogpiling this asshole."

"Works for me," Sally said from my side. "Just like old times."

"Indeed it is," the Wanderer called back, rising from where he'd been tossed.

"Oh my God, James! I thought my eyes were playing tricks."

"Wanderer actually," he replied. "And no tricks, although it is rather curious."

"I'll say. You ... you look good."

I turned to her, not believing my ears. "Can you maybe flirt later?"

"You take all the fun out of life."

"*No!*" Turd slammed a fist into the dirt, causing the ground beneath our feet to tremble. "*Turd will be the one to have fun ... taking your lives!*"

Oh crap.

The ugly motherfucker took a step forward. I raised my fists, wishing we'd had the foresight to have brought a fuck-load of guns along for the trip.

Alas, all we'd brought was a sword to this ape fight.

I was contemplating drawing it – hoping that maybe whatever stopped the sun from hurting me here worked on it, too – when the very air around us became a loudspeaker dialed up to twelve.

"*ENOUGH!*" a spectral voice boomed, loud enough to cause the very trees to quiver. "*BRING THEM!*"

"*No!*" Turd cried out. "*They are enemies. They are t'lunta!*"

"*I SAID ... BRING THEM!*"

All at once, the fight seemed to drain from the hairy bastard. His shoulders slouched and he let out a heavy sigh, even if the murderous gleam never left his eyes. "*Freewill, others follow Turd. Follow now.*"

"Hold on..."

"*Follow,*" he repeated, turning away and beckoning us half-heartedly. "*Turd no hurt.*"

Okay, this had just taken an unexpected turn.

"Follow you where?" Sally asked the retreating Sasquatch.

"*Where else?*" he replied, looking like a huge child who'd been sent to bed without his supper. "*We go to see great Humbaba.*"

36

A HUMBABADINGER
OF A REVELATION

Under normal circumstances, following Turd anywhere wasn't something I'd have even remotely considered.

Sadly, with no idea where we were and no clue which direction to go, we decided to heed the scary voice in the sky. It was either that or wander aimlessly ... and possibly risk running into something even worse.

Turd himself seemed to have no interest in explaining things. If anything, he appeared to be sulking as he led us back into the woods, grumbling to himself as if he'd just been scolded.

It left us with no options but to huddle up and talk amongst ourselves.

"So ... um, anyone seen Glen?"

Sadly, nobody had any insight on that. I could only hope Turd hadn't run into him first and, I dunno, maybe eaten the little blob. Ugh. Talk about unpleasant fates. That was nothing more than pessimistic speculation, though. In truth, all we could do was hope for the best as we moved on.

"So you're the one inside Bill's head now?" Sally asked the Wanderer as we trudged onward.

"It would seem so," he replied, the grime he'd picked up from the fight somehow looking good on him. "Or at least I was until I found myself taking corporeal form in this place. And no, I am not sure how."

She appeared to consider this. "You're a spirit then ... not actually him."

"Quite the contrary, I very much am. We shared a body and mind for seven hundred years. I am every bit as much him as he was once me."

"And now you're a part of Bill." She turned my way, a strange look in her eye, at least until she added, "In that case, you have my condolences. I can only imagine the shit you've seen in that noggin."

"Oh, it's been quite educational. That much I can say." He shrugged. "At the very least, it's nice to stretch my legs again, doubly so since it seems we don't have to worry about bursting aflame beneath this world's sun."

"Tell me about it," I replied. "You think Ed's upgrade finally took?"

He shook his head. "I doubt it. More than likely it's something to do with this world and the reason you and I were separated."

"Speaking of which." I turned Sally's way. "I can't help but notice the new, or shall I say *old* hair color. Has anything...?"

"I'll stop you right there," she interrupted. "I feel fine. Right as rain as a matter of fact. Hell, I didn't even realize anything was different until I met up with Veronica and she mentioned it."

"Huh. So, what do you think will happen if we, I dunno, try to annoy the shit outta you?"

She grinned. "No idea, but you're welcome to try at your own risk."

Fair enough. "How about you?" I asked Veronica. "Any weirdness on your end since arriving?"

She averted her eyes, as if unsure how to answer. "Well, now that you mention it, there is..."

"Not now," Sally said. "Save it."

"Save what?" I replied.

Rather than answer, she gestured ahead of us. "It's

nothing that can't wait until we're out of earshot of our stinky tour guide up there."

"*Turd smell good,*" the Sasquatch growled. "*T'lunta and she-T'lunta stink!*"

"I suppose perception is nine-tenths of reality, fucked up as that might be."

"While we're on the subject of fucked up," I said, glaring at Turd's backside, "anyone have a clue as to how *he's* alive again? I can't be the only one wondering that."

The Wanderer shook his head. "Trust me, my friend, you are not. Alas, I can offer nothing more than base speculation at this time."

"Maybe this is some fucked up dimension where our worst fears come true."

Sally shook her head. "If that were the case, I'd be married to you and all of our kids would be as dumb as your meathead friend."

"Really? And here I figured it would involve being paid for lap dances in loose pennies."

"*Stupid t'lunta wrong. Turd not alive.*"

Huh? The monster ape's comment brought an end to our sniping. "What was that?"

"*Turd not alive,*" he repeated. "*Turd is dead because stupid t'lunta kill Turd and send him to this place.*"

"This place?"

"*Yes, stupid Freewill. You are here with those who are dead.*"

Turd refused to elaborate, threatening to smash my skull with a rock when I persisted. Needless to say, I decided not to push it.

That was fine. I had enough to think about as we followed our fragrant foe through the primeval forest – none of it good. If this was truly the afterlife, then who else might we be unfortunate enough to meet here?

I'd gotten lucky in my earlier adventures and had not

only survived umpteen million attempts on my life, but had helped return the favor to most of those who'd tried.

That was the problem. There was almost certainly no shortage of beings here who'd be more than happy to get medieval on my ass. Hell, that wasn't even taking into account Sally or the Wanderer. The latter had a body count spanning seven centuries. Considering his fighting skills, I doubted that was a small number.

And what was up with being summoned by Humbaba? From what I knew, he'd been the leader of the Sasquatches way back when the first accord was signed – creating the uneasy peace between the Feet and the vampire nation that had lasted for thousands of years ... at least until I'd fucked it up.

Aside from that, I didn't know shit about the guy.

Speaking of shit, I noticed the Wanderer's nose perk up a few seconds before it hit me as well. As bad as Turd might've reeked, something up ahead smelled even worse.

Make that some *things*. I may not have caught fire beneath this world's sun, but that didn't mean my nose hairs weren't in danger of spontaneous combustion from the stench we were heading toward.

"Be on guard," I whispered. "I think we're..."

"Not my first rodeo," Sally interrupted. "My nose might not be as good these days, but I have eyes."

I was about to ask what she meant when movement in my periphery alerted me. I turned to see nothing but trees staring back, figuratively anyway. Just as I was about to dismiss it as paranoia, though, I caught sight of more shadowy forms from the corner of my eye – ones that were gone the moment I turned to face them.

It wasn't entirely unlike our first visit to the Woods of Mourning, as Grulg had led the way to his village.

In a footrace, a vamp could outpace a bigfoot, but when it came to stealth the giant gorillas were all twentieth level rogues. That meant if they wanted to, they could be on us like white on rice before we could so much as shout a warning.

And sadly, despite Turd's claim that this was the land of the dead, the ghosts here were way too solid for my liking.

"I think we're almost there," Sally said.

Up ahead I spied another break in the trees. Unlike the last clearing, however, this one was far from empty. I caught sight of massive huts made of wood, bark, and other ... *gunk*.

It was a village, and it was most certainly not empty.

As if realizing we'd noticed, Turd stopped and raised his head. He let loose with a roar that sounded like the unoiled gates of Hell bursting open. If this fucker ever got tired of being an asshole, he had a future heralding the start of Armageddon.

On that unpleasant note, Sasquatches suddenly scrambled out from seemingly everywhere ahead of us – from within huts, behind trees, and more – a veritable army of them.

It was almost enough to make me tug on my tether just to see if it would pull me the fuck out of here as promised.

Doing that wouldn't save Christy, though, and if she was here among these monsters then it was more imperative than ever to find her. No way would I leave her in this prison, not knowing the warden's name was Turd.

I glanced at my colleagues wondering if they were as nervous as me. The Wanderer appeared cool as a cucumber, no surprise there. Same with Sally. She had on her game face, just like when we'd faced similar odds up in northern Canada. As for Veronica...

Once again I felt something strange inside my mind. Not painful in the least. More like an itch that needed scratching.

As I met the witch's eyes, I wondered if it was connected to the Wanderer being on the outside when he should've been settled nice and snug inside my noggin. Or maybe it was...

"Easy now," Sally said. "Never let them see you sweat."

I shrugged, trying to look calm and collected while probably failing miserably. "Meh. It's just another Feet village. You've seen one, you've seen them all."

That response apparently didn't endear me to our guide, as up ahead Turd let out a quiet snarl.

I tried to look past him, adjusting my glasses at what I saw waiting for us – two living walls of towering muscle and matted brown fur.

It was as if the entirety of the Sasquatch village had lined up in two columns as we approached, with Turd intent on leading us down the middle of this smelly gauntlet.

To say it made me feel tiny in comparison was no joke. Even the smallest of the Sasquatch lineup still towered over my head, with the largest of their number being Turd's size. Hell, I could only imagine what kind of sardine Sally must've felt like compared to these giants.

"*All dead*," Turd said as the two lines stretched ahead of us. "*All killed by t'lunta.*"

"*Not all*," one of the smaller beasts replied – *only* seven feet tall and possessing breasts so saggy I could've used them as sleeping bags. A female. She locked eyes with Turd and let out a snarl.

"*Stupid Bush*," the larger Sasquatch grunted, stomping past her.

I could only imagine that was some kind of Sasquatch greeting, akin to handing them a dead skunk.

Whatever the case, Turd gestured at another Sasquatch further down the line, this one also female, before turning toward me. "*Push*."

"Huh? You want me to give her a shove?"

"Oh we are so gonna fucking die," Sally muttered.

"*Push daughter*," the bigfoot snarled. "*Push promised as Freewill wife ... until treachery.*"

Oh fuck. "You do realize that wasn't my fault, right?"

Turd bared his teeth at me. "*Push death is Freewill's fault. War is Freewill's fault. EVERYTHING IS FREEWILL'S FAULT!*"

"Good job as usual keeping the peace, Bill."

Fortunately, the Wanderer was there to step in. "Please continue, Turd, as I believe you were commanded to."

Turd looked as if he would've liked nothing better than to rip the Wanderer's arms off and beat him senseless with them. Instead he snorted, dripping copious snot runners from his ample nostrils.

Eww.

"In case you're wondering," Sally offered, "Bill's still single."

That seemed to please the bigfoot princess about as much as it did me. "*Ugly t'lunta,*" she spat.

Guess I could chalk that up to another bullet dodged.

Turd continued down the lineup, pointing at various Sasquatches along the way. "*Wurt, Butt, Plug.*"

"Butt plug?"

The two Feet turned and snarled at me. Oh yeah, I was making friends all over.

"*Gut, Lurg, Muk, Cult, Zurm...*"

On and on he went, each one somehow more ridiculous than the last. "It's like the land of dumbass names."

The Wanderer glanced my way. "I know the vampire nation is no more, and thus I have no real authority to pull rank. Nevertheless, for the sake of our mission here, do shut up."

"Sorry."

I tried to hold it together, as Turd continued introducing Feet, apparently in some attempt to make us feel guilty or something. All I knew was that I managed to keep a straight face until he got to *Cum.*

Feeling the laughter starting to win out, I turned Sally's way to find the ghost of a smirk on her face too.

"Fine," she whispered, rolling her eyes. "I'll let you have that one."

At last some justification. At least I saw we were finally nearing the end, Turd having marched us through the majority of the oversized village.

Thank goodness, because the air was starting to get pretty

rank surrounded by squatch stank as we were. What I wouldn't have given for a good breeze right about then.

On the upside, it could've been worse. So far the only creatures I'd seen had been Sasquatches. No sign of assholes like Night Razor yet, not that I wasn't keeping an eye out.

My fears would have to wait, though, as Turd reached the end and stopped, his massive frame blocking the view until he finally stepped to the side revealing what lay ahead.

The fuck?!

I beheld a veritable mountain of furs, stacked high before us. Laid out at the periphery were piles of fruit, vegetables, and heaping mounds of – *ugh* – squirming grubs.

That was gross enough, but nothing compared to the titanic beast that lay atop it all. It reached a hand into the grubs, grabbed hold of what had to be hundreds of them, then popped them all into a cavernous mouth full of sharp teeth.

I had thought Turd was big, but he may as well have been a child compared to whatever the fuck this thing was.

"*Humbaba has summoned you,*" Turd said. "*Now Freewill and others will face his judgement.*"

37

THE HAIRY AND THE DEAD

Humbaba was not your normal garden variety Sasquatch.

Definitely not, as he towered over us while barely sitting upright.

The fucker must've been at least fifteen feet high standing up, maybe twenty - assuming he could even get up.

He was almost as wide as he was tall – a good chunk of it muscle, don't get me wrong, but plenty of it flab as Humbaba was obviously enjoying the good life.

It was like someone had crossed a *Star Wars* bantha with a Sasquatch, or maybe genetically engineered a larger scarier version of Ludo from the movie *Labyrinth*.

A set of curly ram horns sprouted from the sides of Humbaba's shaggy head, hanging over shoulders that were as wide as a bus.

Beneath them, two sets of arms hung – one of them busy feeding the gigantic beast, as the other two were scratching places I'd have sooner not thought about.

A pair of dinner plate sized eyes took us in as the monstrosity stared our way.

I wondered what was next, as this thing didn't look all that bright. Maybe it was gonna eat us or try shoving us up its...

"*Come forward*," it said, its voice like a bass guitar with vocal cords.

The Wanderer was first to do so, much like in the years prior to being stuck inside my head. He turned and gestured for me to step up next to him, as if I had a single solitary clue what to say to fat King Kong.

I hesitated for maybe a second – at least until Sally shoved me forward, because what else were friends for?

Humbaba turned to the elder vampire first. "*You are the one known as the Wanderer, yes?*" it asked, surprisingly eloquent compared to the dim bulbs it seemingly ruled over.

"I am."

"*There are many who call this place home who were sent here by your hand.*"

If he ruffled the Wanderer's feathers with the implied threat, my friend didn't acknowledge it. "I take no pleasure in having done so. But I feel no guilt either. I simply did what was needed to survive."

That was his answer? And yet *I* was the one they all seemed to constantly give shit to?

Humbaba appeared to consider this for a moment before replying, "*Well said, warrior.*"

Son of a... How come when he said stuff like that, it was all well and good, yet the second I opened my mouth everyone was all over me like a new suit? I swear, even the afterlife wasn't fair.

Speaking of unfair, I was next to get the stink eye from the mountain of moldy fur. "*You are the Freewill, he who broke my eternal covenant.*"

Eternal...? *Oh crap.* He was talking about the Accord, the one with his name stamped on the title. Figured. The giant sack of shit couldn't have started with something cool like asking if I was the badass who ended the war. No, he had to jump straight to the finger pointing.

"Listen, that wasn't really my fault. I..."

He silenced me by raising one of his truck tire sized hands. "*Be at peace, Freewill. I know that which transpired. I see much from my place here in the land of the honored dead.*"

Oh. Guess he was just tweaking my balls for... *Wait. Did he say* honored *dead?* "Can we back up a second here? I don't think I heard you right. This is the land of the what now again?"

He inclined his head, causing a swarm of flies to rise from it. *Eww.* "*This is the final dwelling place of those honored in life. It is where our most revered souls come to rest.*"

"Yeah, that's what I thought." I hooked a thumb at Turd. "No offense, but you might want to rethink the entrance exam, because your shithead buddy here was into some shifty business back in the day. Not outright saying he should be in Sasquatch Hell, but if it were up to me we'd be talking a lake of fire and a pitchfork up his ass."

Several grunts of surprise came from behind us, as Turd himself bared his teeth.

Hmm, perhaps I could've worded that a wee bit less aggressively.

"Way to go, Bill," Sally opined from behind me. "We can always count on you to snatch defeat from the jaws of victory."

If what I'd said had pissed off big ole Baba, though, he likewise had his poker face on. "*I am aware of the transgressions of my underling. However, one small lapse in judgement cannot undo centuries of honorable service.*"

"One small lapse? Are you fucking for real? This asshole started a war so he could corner the market on fucking maple syrup."

The Wanderer nudged me with his elbow, none too gently either. "Are you through yet, or is there more gasoline you'd like to throw on this fire?"

Oh yeah, I probably needed to remember I was surrounded by more than enough Sasquatches to pummel me into pizza sauce. "No. I think I'm good here."

Humbaba shook his head, a look of pity on his face. "*That is why Turd serves me in this world, his penance if you will.*"

Despite my better judgement telling me to shut the fuck up, I found myself ready to rant again. Getting to serve one's patron demigod didn't seem like a bad gig as far as penance went. However, I held my tongue as I took a moment to actually think about it.

Humbaba was an absolute mess. He was big, fat, sloppy, and apparently had an appetite to match his girth. It was easy to imagine Turd as his errand boy – constantly making food runs, only to be called back because Humbaba had ass mites in need of plucking.

There was also Turd to consider. The economy-sized prick looked none too pleased to have been relegated to the roll of divine gofer.

Maybe this was actually a case of the punishment fitting the crime. Like finding out Jeffrey Dahmer was in heaven, only to learn his job was to constantly wipe God's sweaty taint with his face. Maybe this wasn't as unfair as I'd first thought.

Either way, Humbaba seemed to be done with my shit as he looked past me. "*You seem troubled, child. Why?*"

To say his question was a wee bit stupid was being kind. I mean, for fuck's sake, we were surrounded by an army of monsters. Who wouldn't be troubled by that shit?

Apparently Sally, as she replied, "I'm just wondering when the other shoe's going to drop?"

"*Shoe?*"

Go figure, the Feet didn't know about shoes.

"Yeah," she continued. "We've already established the standards for entry here are ... flexible. So I find myself wondering who else from our collective repertoire of dearly departed enemies we can expect to see next."

"*Ah,*" the beast replied. "*A simple answer indeed. This world exists as a reward for my kind and other children of the forest.*"

"Exactly. And since, technically speaking, vamps and your kind are..."

Humbaba once again held up a hand. "*Alas, you need not worry. What happened to those who died while tainted by humans I cannot say, save that they are not here. All I know is*" *that the multiverse is vast and this world is but a tiny corner of a much greater whole."*

I decided to ignore that tainted part. Guess Humbaba was as much an asshole as the rest when it came to his tolerance toward people. "I think what he's saying is we don't need to worry about either the Jeffs or Colins of the world showing up."

She shrugged. "Small victories."

"I don't know. It would be kind of fun to rub Alex's face in it."

"He would not be here regardless," the Wanderer said.

"Huh?"

"If you'll recall, his fate, as well as Calibra's and so many others, was no different than my own. We didn't die. We were merely separated from those we were bonded to and sent back to whence we came."

I let that sink in, remembering what Eric had told us. He was Grulg but in a new body. That meant it was entirely possible that others had returned in new forms as well...

Fuck!

It made me hope that Humbaba was right and that the multiverse was indeed big, because I sure as shit didn't want to deal with any of those fuckers again. One go around on that carousel was more than enough, thanks.

"That does bring up a good point, though," the Wanderer said after another moment or two. "As one of the aforementioned spirits tainted by a human..."

"Really?"

"His words, not mine," he replied with an easygoing grin before turning to face Humbaba again. "How am I here now and why do I look this way?"

Humbaba nodded as if that were a wise question. *"You appear as you choose, nothing more nothing less. As for this place, all souls are weighed equally here. So it is that all souls must stand on their own."*

I guess that sort of made sense. No two-for-one specials in the land of the less-then-honored dead. At the very least, it explained how the Wanderer was here with us.

Still, this was interesting and all, but we hadn't come here for some half-assed intervention in Bigfoot Heaven. Fuck the Ouija board shit, we were here for a far more important reason.

Sally must've been of the same mindset because she beat me to the punch. "This is all fascinating, it really is. But we're here to…"

"*Seek out that which is like yourself, which does not belong here,*" Humbaba interrupted. "*I know.*"

That was kind of a rude way to put it, but not entirely incorrect.

"*Rest now,*" he continued. "*Then my servant shall lead you to that which you seek.*"

Once again Turd bristled, making me think his *reward* consisted of nothing but shit work. Amusing as that was, though, I could laugh about it later, once we were back home. "While I appreciate the hospitality, we're kind of on a timetable here."

"*Is that so? The eternity of one realm is but a blink of the eye to another.*"

"I have no idea what that…"

"*Rest!*" he repeated, putting an edge into his voice that suggested it wasn't optional.

"We would be honored and humbled to accept your hospitality," the Wanderer replied, glancing my way. "Wouldn't we?"

"Yeah, what he said."

And just like that, we found ourselves guests of Sasquatch Nirvana – a place I was fairly certain none of us wanted to be.

38

A LICH IN TIME

This might've been a different village in a whole other dimension, but I was unsurprised to find the amenities hadn't changed much since the last time I'd been an unwilling guest of the Feet.

We were shown to an oversized hut at the far end of the village. Unsurprisingly, the door was then barred and guards stationed outside for our *safety*. Bowls of fruit, nuts, berries, and, of course, grubs awaited us, along with a crude stone knife – no doubt for those fancy pants types who preferred to dice their grubs first.

I couldn't help but notice the spread wasn't all that fresh. Guess Hum*burger* out there got the choicest cuts and everyone else got whatever he didn't finish. It figured. No matter what plane of reality you found yourself on, it was still good to be the king.

Sadly, I didn't see many viable options other than to wait as we'd been told.

I'd done my fair share of plane-shifting in my old D&D game. One thing that was always misleading was scale. Sure, you might end up in a volcanic field or atop a cloud, but one needed to remember it wasn't like on Earth. On the Elemental Plane of Fire, for instance, a lava field might be as wide as our solar system.

In the game at least, every realm was an entire universe unto itself. I didn't know if that translated to reality or not, but if so then that meant Christy could be half a mile down the road, or a billion light years of forest away.

The tether spell, combined with Tina's connection to her mother, was supposed to help get us close – so we were probably at least within the same galaxy, if not zip code. Nevertheless, pissing off our hosts didn't seem wise. It probably made sense to play along for now and hope that Turd led us to Christy as per his boss's orders.

Yeah, it made sense to wait, but it didn't mean I had to like it.

"How long do you think we'll be here?"

"Longer than we want to be," the Wanderer replied, "although hopefully not longer than we have to be."

"Thanks, that's useful."

I wasn't too worried about Tina's batteries running out. Still, we probably couldn't afford an extended vacation at Club Turd. At some point the tyke would reach her limit. When that happened, we'd be snapped back by our tethers, or so Liz claimed. I didn't fancy the other option, which likely involved living out eternity on the forest moon of Endor with the Ewoks' larger, smellier cousins.

With nothing better to do, I plopped myself down on one of the crude benches and popped a few berries into my mouth, not thinking much of it until they hit my tongue. "Holy shit!"

"What's the matter?" Sally asked. "Don't tell me they're Turd flavored."

I shook my head, swallowing. "No. They actually taste good ... as in *really* good."

She picked one up, glared as if to let me know I'd better not be messing with her, then ate it. "I dunno. Seems pretty normal to me."

"Let me have a try," the Wanderer said, doing the same. "Huh. I believe the Freewill's right. These do taste considerably better than expected."

"I think Sally's tastebuds are just ruined by sucking on too many..."

"Finishing that sentence would be *really* bad for your health," she countered.

The Wanderer wisely chose not to acknowledge our banter. "Hold on. It's not that they taste better so much as they taste *normal*."

"Normal?" I replied.

He locked eyes with me. "Blood."

It took me a second but then it hit me. He was right. Everything about a vampire's sense of taste revolved around blood. It was the end-all be-all of our survival. When you were a vamp, nothing tasted nearly as good. Comparatively speaking, however, all the other culinary joys in life tended to be muted in comparison.

Human Bill used to think there were few things as wonderful as a good plate of nachos. Bill the vampire, on the other hand, found them to be almost as bland as a veggie platter – unless they were smothered in a healthy layer of fresh plasma.

The Wanderer was right. It wasn't that the berries tasted better. They simply tasted how I *remembered* them. I grabbed a handful of nuts and tried those, too, likewise savoring the strong taste.

As for the grubs, well, Sally was welcome to those.

"What does it mean? Are we ... more human here?"

He shook his head. "I'm not sure. There's sunlight and now this, but physically everything else seems the same. Otherwise our battle with our friend out there would have been over considerably sooner than it was, and not in our favor."

"So what's the deal then?"

"I can't be certain, but for the time being I think it means we shouldn't have to worry about snacking on any of the natives while we're here."

That was good. I'd tried Sasquatch blood once. I had no real desire to try it again. All the same, I didn't want to risk finding Christy just as my tank was running dry. There had to be a catch-22 here.

"Okay," I said. "Let's take stock. The sun isn't an issue here and it seems blood isn't either. My so-called inner demon is also now an outie. No offense."

"None taken."

"That's three differences right there. There's Sally's hair too."

She nodded. "Not to mention the fact that I didn't explode out there. Because believe me, I might've looked all calm and collected, but marching through that gauntlet had my stress levels in the red."

I pursed my lips. "Thanks for the warning, by the way."

"I figured you had enough to worry about at the time."

"Ain't that the truth. Okay, so since we apparently have the time, is there anything else I'm missing?" I looked at our small group before settling my eyes on Veronica. Unlike the rest of us, she'd had the good graces to keep her mouth shut throughout our audience with Humbaba. "What about you? Anything new and interesting going on with your magic?"

"Me?" she replied. "I'm ... not sure. And, it's not like I can really test it."

"Well, you *could*," Sally replied.

"Do you think that's a good idea ... I mean here?"

Sally nodded. "At this point I don't think it's going to get any better. We should probably put all our cards on the table while we have the chance."

"What cards?" I asked.

"Are you sure?" Veronica replied, ignoring me.

"Not even remotely, but I can't help but think we're gonna need every advantage we can get."

I chuckled. "Your optimism warms my heart. All right spill, what's the big secret?"

"*You are*, stupid."

"Me?"

Sally turned to the witch. "Show him."

I figured she'd make with some parlor trick, but instead she locked eyes with me. "Whatever you do, don't freak out."

"Why would I freak out?"

"You'll see."

Veronica lifted her hands and conjured a fireball above them – a big one, for a second or two anyway. The globe of pure flame expanded to a good four feet in diameter before she reined it in to about six inches.

Disturbing as that was in the closed space, however, I barely noticed it compared to the weird-ass feeling inside my own mind.

All at once it was like I wasn't alone, and I'm not talking about the Wanderer. This was different. It wasn't so much hearing voices in my head, as the feeling of someone creeping around up there – as if there were a door inside my brain and someone had just jimmied the lock.

It made me remember what Tina had done to me back in the cave. *What the fuck?* Was my mind some open book now – a witch playground where they could simply waltz in, shit in the sandbox, and then leave? If so, then...

"Easy there, Elphaba," Sally said, as I tried to process things. "You almost burned the damned hut down."

"I ... I didn't mean to," Veronica replied wide-eyed. "It just flared up."

"Was it...?"

"I don't know. I only put the tiniest bit of power into..."

Fascinating as their conversation might've been, it dissolved into little more than white noise as a series of random thoughts and memories suddenly appeared in my mind's eye, none of them mine.

No. They belonged to... "Holy shit, you did it with Kelly?"

"No way!" Sally replied, turning to face me. "She did?"

Veronica's mouth dropped open as if I'd slapped her, the fireball vanishing in a puff of smoke. "That's a private memory, asshole!"

"Then how come you just flashed it in my noggin like a movie projector?"

She shook her head, looking away. "That ... happens

sometimes when we get distracted or lose focus. Doesn't mean you're supposed to tell the world."

"How the fuck was I supposed to know that?"

"Oh? How would you like it if I told a certain someone that you still whack off while thinking about her? Yeah, that's right, it's a two-way street."

"Uh..."

Sally merely shrugged, though. "Like that's supposed to surprise me?"

I held up my hands. "Okay, let's back up a second here. What the fuck just happened?"

"We synced up," Veronica said.

As much as I wanted to make a bad sex joke, I couldn't help but remember I'd heard both her and Kelly use that term recently, and it had nothing to do with hooking up. "Synced?"

"Yeah, like we did when you were fighting Claire. I just didn't realize it at the time."

I backed away, trying to make sense of this.

"Finally figuring it out?" Sally asked, grinning like the Cheshire Cat.

I shook my head. "I'm not even sure what I'm supposed to be figuring out here."

"I'll keep it nice and simple then, so you don't give your-self a brain aneurysm trying to overthink it. You're one of *them* now."

"Them?"

"What's that phrase from the movie? Oh yeah." She dropped her voice an octave and adopted a bad accent. "Yer a wizard, Billy."

39

ELDRITCH ENDEAVORS

"**O**r a catalyst mage, anyway," Veronica was quick to add.

I shook my head and laughed. "This place might be screwing with us, but that's a whole other level of fucked up."

"It has nothing to do with this place," Sally replied. "V just said as much."

Veronica nodded. "Exactly. You were the one I synced up with back during that fight, the one who gave me the spark I needed to stop Claire. I just didn't realize... Wait. Okay, that's not entirely true. I'm pretty sure I didn't want to realize it."

"Okay, well, if that's the case then how come I didn't see any memories that time, like of you and Kelly...?"

She stopped me with a glare. "That's because I was in and out real fast, grabbing just enough to finish the job. I didn't consciously realize it until we came across you fighting that forest folk."

"A Turd by any other name," Sally remarked with a sigh. "Anyway, I was the one who suggested she not say anything at the time, not unless we really needed it."

"I have to ask," Veronica replied. "Did you already know?"

Sally shrugged. "I *suspected*. Let's just say I've been

putting the pieces together bit by bit ever since Bill explained how the sun was still burning his ass."

The Wanderer threw her a smile. "You always were a clever one."

"Flattery will get you everywhere."

"Get a room," I snapped, starting to pace. "What I want to know is why you didn't say anything sooner?"

"It's because I know you, Bill. You don't always make sound decisions while under pressure, and this is pretty much the first downtime we've had since I figured it out." She looked me in the eye. "Or are you going to lie and tell me this would've been a good bombshell to drop while you were trying to saw Turd's dick off?"

I opened my mouth to respond, but then just shook my head. Bitch she may be, but she had a point.

She turned to the Wanderer. "Pretty sure you'd have come to the same conclusion, too, had Bill not let those scam artists fuck with his head."

"They said it was for my protection!"

"So do the nice people on the phone trying to sell you an extended warranty." She waited a beat, almost daring me to say something before continuing. "That was kind of my first big clue, that you saw those guys when only the Magi have been able to before."

The Wanderer nodded. "I get it now. It was no coincidence that they showed up after our metamorphosis."

"Nope. They must've sensed Bill the same way they can sense other Magi awakening to their power."

I turned their way, trying to make sense of this all. "Okay, I get why they sold me Thundersmite. They're scumbags. But why fuck around with my head too?"

The Wanderer chuckled softly. "I'm afraid, my friend, the answer is all too obvious."

"Pretend I'm stupid."

"Why pretend?" Sally replied. "It's simple. The jig is up pretty quickly with other Magi. Those dirtbags might be able to scam them once, but there's a buddy system in place to warn people about them. That sound about right?"

Veronica nodded.

"Thought so, but you... They realized you were different, unique. Let's face facts, most witches aren't going to bother pissing on a vampire, much less spilling any of their Magi beans, no matter how trivial. But, that could change if they sensed what you were. Those two clowns weren't idiots. You're their new mark, so I'm willing to bet they scrambled your circuits for no other reason than a chance to show up again in the future and relieve you of more of your hard-earned shekels."

Son of a...

She grinned. "And here comes the realization part of our show, folks."

"Those fucking ass clowns!"

"Pretty much."

"Hold on. Cat's the one who pulled their crap out of my head. Does that mean she..."

"Almost certainly."

"Then why didn't she say anything?"

"She's five," Veronica replied. "Knowing and being able to explain something are two different things. She probably realized the rest of us would figure it out and be better equipped to soften the blow."

Okay, I guess that made sense. Sadly, that was about the only thing that *did*. "I still don't get it. All I wanted to do was walk in the daylight. How the fuck did Ed's bite turn me into a wizard instead?"

"I suspect," the Wanderer replied, "that it has something to do with you being a Freewill. Which, if I recall correctly, is exactly what I warned you about beforehand."

"Is this your *I told you so* speech?"

"Probably a fair assessment."

"Actually," Sally said, "it has *everything* to do with you being a Freewill. I mean, it makes such perfect sense it's almost ridiculously contrived."

"How so?"

"One word – Ib."

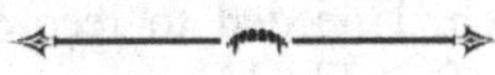

"Ib? Are you saying Calibra somehow did this?"

Sally stared hard at me for a few seconds before letting out a painful sigh. "How is it possible for one person to be so fucking stupid? No, forget I asked. I already know the type you keep as friends."

"Care to elaborate for the rest of us?" the Wanderer asked.

"Gladly." She turned toward me once again. "Remember when she gave us that history lesson about vampires?"

"Down at the Source?" I nodded. "Yeah. Hard to forget."

"Good. Then you must remember what she said about Freewills."

"Um ... I remember her pontificating about how awesome they were and that's why Alex had them all killed."

"I see. Fortunately for me, I have a memory that stretches slightly farther than the end of my dick." She held up a hand before I could comment. "Anyway, it was an offhand remark on her part. I don't think she meant to spill the beans. The thing is, she knew exactly what made some vampires into Freewills. It wasn't random or just dumb luck. She specifically said Freewills were, and I quote, *dormant catalyst mages*."

"She did?" Veronica replied, eyes wide.

"Yep. Heard it with my own two ears. Mind you, at the time I had no fucking idea what any of that meant, but you kind of filled in the final piece of that puzzle when you explained things right before we joined the fight with Turd." She turned my way. "Anyway, I'm willing to bet good money that Ed's bite somehow activated that dormant part inside of you."

Holy shit. Not only did that make sense, but it matched up almost perfectly with everything Kelly had told me. Had I not gotten bitten and become a vampire, I'd have ... gone on to live a normal life, never realizing other mages could tap into my noggin and use it like a battery pack.

I swear, next time a would-be world conqueror gave me a

big exposition speech, I needed to record that shit. Would have saved me a lot of grief had I remembered any of that.

There was one part still bugging me, though. "But that doesn't explain why the sun is still kicking my ass."

Sally shrugged. "Do I look like a genetic sequencer to you? Who knows? Maybe that part *is* dumb luck. I mean, it's not like what happened to Ed was exact science either."

"Fair enough."

The Wanderer reached over and put a hand atop Sally's. "I must say, I'm impressed. Your deductive reasoning is as sound as ever."

"Thanks. That means a lot coming from you."

"Hey, I'm impressed too," I replied.

"It means less coming from you, but thanks anyway."

I ignored the dig. My mind was too busy trying to make sense of this revelation. Calibra had been a witch first. She only became a vampire after fucking up a power play, something that had never been duplicated. She'd been unique all throughout our history – until today.

Now, I was a vampire who'd become a witch ... or wizard anyway.

It was absolutely insane. I reached for some nuts, almost grabbing a handful of grubs by accident as I tried to consider what this meant.

This was usually the part of the movie where the hero fell into an inexplicable deep depression, convinced they were a freak of nature.

But no. Fuck that noise.

Yeah, getting burnt by the sun still sucked, but screw it. I could always put on a hoodie. In retrospect, it seemed a small tradeoff for finding out I'd become motherfucking Dr. Voodoo.

It went even farther than that, though. There no longer needed to be any walls between my world and Christy's. Heck, I could join her coven if she wanted me to. Fuck it, I could apply for legitimate access to the Falcon Archives ... just as soon as I saved Matt and managed to convince him I hadn't hacked him *again*.

But whatever. I could figure that out later. I had magic now. I could do *anything*!

Speaking of which...

I turned toward where the others were still talking among themselves, setting my eyes on Veronica. "Do that thing again."

"What thing?"

"Where you synced up with my brain."

"Yeah, I think we've already shared enough..."

"Relax. I don't want any memories. Just show me how to do it."

"Why?"

"So I can blow some shit up, that's why."

I waited for that feeling of her creeping around inside my noggin again before realizing it wasn't forthcoming. "Well?"

"Call me crazy," Sally said, "but that's probably the last thing we need you doing right now."

"I must concur," the Wanderer replied.

From the look on Veronica's face, she was of the same mindset. "They're right. You need training first. You're just a novice. No, scratch that. You're actually worse than a novice."

"A sub-novice?" Sally offered. "Sounds about right for Bill."

"I'm not trying to be insulting, just truthful. Yes, some Magi come into their power later than others, but it's rare to see anyone develop it after the age of twenty. You're an adult, though..."

"Probably the first time he's ever been called that."

"And a vampire too," she added. "What I'm saying is..."

"I think I get it," Sally interrupted again. "The last thing we need is for your reckless ass to be running around acting like this is *Jackass* meets *Firestarter*."

"Fine," I replied. "I'll get trained ... later. I just want a little bit now, so I can try it out."

"I'd really prefer we didn't," Veronica said.

"You can pull the plug the second you notice anything amiss."

"I'm serious. I really don't think it's a good idea."

"Come on, please!"

"I..."

"How would you feel opening a PlayStation on Christmas morning, only to find your parents refused to give you the power cord? I just want to see how it feels."

Sally rolled her eyes. "Now you sound like my first boyfriend."

I ignored her, giving V my best sad puppy look, knowing that, in the past anyway, she was the most susceptible of our group to some browbeating. "Come on. Remember how we took down Pam and Claire. We're like ... a team now."

"I..." She let out a resigned sigh that told me I'd won. "Okay, fine. Just a little."

"Yes!"

Sally glanced the Wanderer's way. "Ten bucks says we live to regret this."

I threw them both some stink eye. "Your faith in me is astounding."

"Hey, I never claimed to be the Icon."

"And you never will be with that attitude."

40

WIZARD SCHOOLING

"JESUS FUCKING CHRIST! PUT ME OUT ALREADY!"

"Stop squirming!" Sally snapped, continuing to stomp on my burning hand. "I swear, being around you is like babysitting a brain-damaged chimpanzee."

As I continued trying to douse my hands in the dirt, I felt the equivalent of a door slam shut in my mind – a weird-ass sensation if ever there was one. I got the distinct sense the door swung both ways, but somehow also understood Veronica was locking it from her end.

"That's enough," she chided. "Like I said, you need training."

Fortunately, the moment our connection was severed, the fire I'd conjured and subsequently lost control of died down. "Ow! You can stop trying to break my fingers now. It's out!"

"I know," Sally replied, backing away. "That last one was for you being a dipshit."

I stood up, shaking my burnt appendages while I waited for my healing to compensate. Yeah, it hurt ... a lot. Nevertheless, I couldn't help but feel excited. Self-inflicted harm or not, I'd done it! I'd performed my first ever magic trick. Sure, spontaneous combustion probably wasn't particularly useful, but that didn't matter. I might've set myself ablaze today, but tomorrow it would be other motherfuckers who'd feel the burn. Eyes on the prize, baby!

Then, when I got good enough, maybe I could spend some time looking through Falcon's little black book learning all sorts of forbidden shit. Because fuck it, this was the first time I could remember in a good long while when I was actually *excited* to be a supernatural oddity. I had every intention of Doctor Stranging the shit out of this. But, unlike a certain five-thousand year old psycho named Calibra, I had no designs on ruling the world.

No. I just wanted to use my newfound powers to fuck up the assholes making life difficult for me. After that, I'd settle down with my hot witch girlfriend and we could use our magic to make everything awesome – and yes, that included sex.

"All right," I said, once my hands started to heal. "That was a good first try."

The Wanderer raised an eyebrow. "You have an interesting definition of good, Freewill."

"Aren't you glad you get to share a body with this putz once we get back?" Sally asked.

"Don't remind me."

I turned to them. "Are we sure that's what's going to happen?"

He nodded. "Not entirely. It's hard to be certain of anything these days, but I'd be willing to bet that's the case."

"Why?"

"Our tethers. Though they may have split, much like ourselves, when we got here, they originate from the exact same spot. Thus it serves to reason that when we're finally pulled back home..." He clapped his hands together to emphasize the point.

"If that's the case," Sally said, twirling a lock of blonde hair with her index finger, "then whatever happened to me is going to..."

"Reverse itself? Unfortunately, yes. Whatever respite you've been given in this place is temporary at best."

"Figures." She grabbed the stone knife, placed her hand

on the table, and proceeded to start stabbing the tip between her outstretched fingers – like Bishop from *Aliens*. "This is the first time in thirty-five years that I've almost felt like me again ... the me I was *before* I got sucked into this life. So what a surprise that it won't last."

"Just for the record," the Wanderer said, "there's absolutely nothing wrong with the you of the here and now."

Goddamn. It was almost hard to not hate someone who could be this freaking smooth with so little effort. Christ, from the look Sally was giving him back, I half expected her panties to explode off her body of their own accord. Once we were back together again, I really needed to convince him to feed me lines like that. Even with a steady girlfriend it never hurt to have one's own personal Cyrano de Bergerac to help grease the wheels of romance.

Speaking of greasy things, just then the door to the hut was unceremoniously pulled open revealing a mountain of matted fur and muscle.

Turd stepped inside, glowering at us all.

Feeling my oats at having discovered I was a vamp-mage, I grinned up at him and said, "Let me guess. Humbaba sent you to take our dinner order? Well, I'd like my steak rare with a side of... oomph!"

Instead, he clamped one massive hand over my face, lifted me up, and tossed me unceremoniously out of the hut.

Okay, maybe I deserved that one.

"*It time*," he growled. "*Follow Turd now!*"

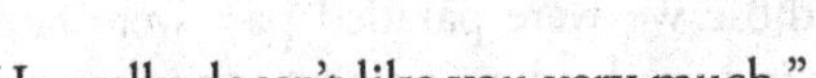

"He really doesn't like you very much."

"Ya think?"

Sally shrugged. "Just an observation."

We'd long since left the *comfort* of the Sasquatch village and headed back into the forest. I wasn't sure exactly how much time had passed as we were led through the seemingly endless woods, but when I looked up again I couldn't help but notice the sun was in the same spot it had been during our fight with Turd.

Definitely weird, especially since our stay in the hut had spanned several hours at the very least.

As the rest of us chatted among ourselves, I couldn't help but notice the Wanderer seemed deep in thought. "Something up?"

"Possibly," he replied, slowing his gait and keeping his voice low. "Have you noticed anything strange about this place?"

"You mean besides the fact that parts of it smell like a latrine and are populated entirely by Mighty Joe Young wannabes?"

The look he gave me implied that it was maybe best to shut up and listen. Jeez, some ancient vampire spirits could be so touchy when they wanted to be.

"It's not the denizens of this world that worry me so much as their number."

"Their number?" Veronica asked. "You mean how many there are?"

"No, how *few* there are."

"Few?" I replied. "Maybe your memory is going, but I seem to recall our buddy up there marching us past a small army on the way in."

"Exactly. There was a small army's worth, when there should be endless legions upon legions. Remember where we are. Humbaba was the leader of the Grendel some five-thousand years ago, back when we were in a state of open warfare with his people. That is a very long time – time enough for even an ageless species to have experienced countless casualties. Yet, it seemed that many of those we were paraded past were fairly recent additions, at least judging by their reaction to seeing you."

"Point taken, you don't have to rub it in. Anyway, Humbaba said this was the land of the honored dead. Maybe all the rest who died over the years were, y'know, assholes."

Sally shook her head. "I doubt it. I don't claim to be a scholar when it comes to Feet culture, but I'm pretty sure that so long as they did what they were told and smashed a few heads along the way, they got an honored tag slapped onto them. I mean, look at the shithead leading us. He fucked two nations up, good and proper, and yet his iTunes-loving ass still ended up here."

Guess Turd's ass was more into Spotify these days, as he lashed out and shattered a nearby tree trunk with his fist – the *crack* of wood like a shotgun blast.

"Uh yeah. Maybe we should dial it down a bit more," I whispered. "Don't want to distract our guide and end up being led someplace where he can beat us all to death in private."

"Fair point," the Wanderer replied as Turd continued leading the way. "And likewise we should perhaps keep the personal insults to a bare minimum."

I turned to Sally. "Yeah, be nice to me."

"Pretty sure he wasn't talking about you."

"Do you mind if we focus a bit here, please?" the Wanderer snapped, as if we were in his former Boston office chattering away while he tried to brief us on some matter of importance.

"Sorry. So what do you think it all means?"

He shook his head. "I'm not sure. It could be something innocuous. Perhaps these woods are full of similar villages, each hosting their own clan."

"Maybe," Sally replied. "But if that were the case then why is Humbaba in this one? You said it yourself, the guy's older than dirt. You'd think he'd want to surround himself with his buddies from back in the day."

"Maybe he likes them young," I offered. "A real pedo-squatch."

"Eww," Veronica said. "Like I needed to hear that. Maybe he's just a traveling demigod, moving from village to village, and we just happened to catch him at that one."

"Perhaps," the Wanderer replied. "Or perhaps there's something else going on. Something that's required the atten-tion of their more experienced members."

Sally turned my way. "He means warriors by the way, not dicks."

"You know me so well."

"Unfortunately."

The Wanderer pointed ahead past Turd. "Either way, I have a feeling we're about to find out."

I spied another break in the trees, but this one was different than the others. It wasn't merely some clearing. Judging from how far I could see to either side of it, it was as if the forest simply ended at that point.

However, it was what lay beyond that truly caught my interest. It wasn't some lush grassland or vast plain. What lay ahead was what could only be described as an apocalyptic wasteland of dirt and broken rocks, one that continued as far as the eye could see.

Maybe I should've filled up on those grubs after all.

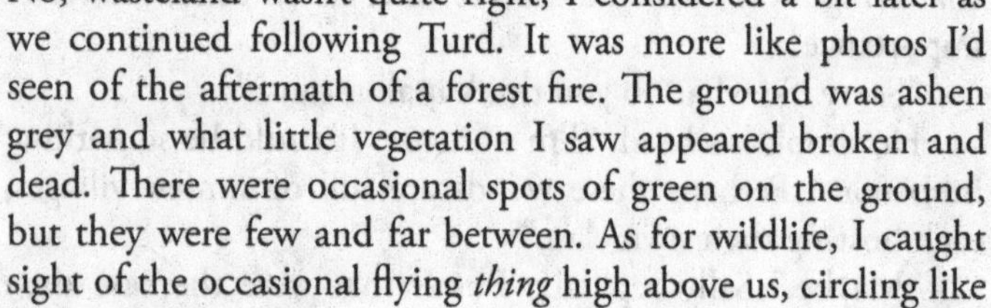

No, wasteland wasn't quite right, I considered a bit later as we continued following Turd. It was more like photos I'd seen of the aftermath of a forest fire. The ground was ashen grey and what little vegetation I saw appeared broken and dead. There were occasional spots of green on the ground, but they were few and far between. As for wildlife, I caught sight of the occasional flying *thing* high above us, circling like buzzards, but if there were any creatures living at ground level they were staying out of sight and giving us a wide berth.

Eventually, the pristine forest was so far behind us I could barely make it out whenever I took the chance to look back.

Though the land itself continued to be dead and barren, eventually the terrain changed – going from flat to rolling hills. Had the forest not ended, I could've seen this area being not dissimilar to the Appalachian mountains back home, minus the moonshiners and gun-toting rednecks.

However, something had caused the forest to stop growing where it had. And, judging by the occasional wisps of smoke I noticed from up ahead, I guessed it hadn't happened all too long ago.

I shared a glance with my compatriots, and the looks I got back told me they were likely thinking the same thing. It was time for someone to start asking questions.

Fortunately for me, being inside my mind hadn't caused the Wanderer to lose his natural affinity for leadership. He strode up ahead to where Turd was trudging along and muttering to himself – probably envisioning all the ways he'd love to rearrange our body parts.

"What happened here?" he asked.

"*War*," Turd replied, seemingly not in much of a conversational mood.

"War? With others of your kind?"

"*No.*"

"Then with who?"

"*Something*," Turd spat. "*Something that not belong here.*"

Oh boy. That didn't sound good.

"What do you mean?" the Wanderer persisted. "Where is it from?"

"*Other world. Not here. Enemy from other place. Not one of the dead.*"

Not one of the...? Did he mean Christy?

Holy shit! Was Turd trying to tell us that Christy had come here and decided to torch the fucking place?

If so, I needed to give her a high-five when we found her, because goddamn that was hardcore. I mean, I knew she was a badass, but I would've loved to watch her finally lose her shit with these assholes.

"*No more talk*," the ugly ape said, pointing ahead. "*Answers, what you seek, are there. Others are there.*"

Others?

I followed his gaze, at first seeing nothing but more ashen grey terrain. But then I realized there was something out there after all. I spied a small group of Sasquatch sized huts ahead – the same ashen color as everything around them, blending in almost perfectly with the ruined landscape.

That wasn't all, though.

As I tried to take it in, I spied movement among the huts. There was a figure there as ashen grey as everything else and ... wait. I realized it was simply wearing a cape or maybe a cloak of that color, as it moved between the huts until it finally stood there facing away from us.

In the next instant, the wind started up – not much, but just enough for me to catch a glimpse of black hair blowing in the breeze.

Christy!

41

THE WOMAN IN THE WASTELAND

"Come on!"

I didn't wait to see if the others followed or not, throwing caution to the wind and sprinting ahead.

Sure, it might've been a trap. Hell, it probably was, but it's not like I hadn't walked face-first into them before. I'd figure it out and deal with it.

But if it wasn't...

A part of me wanted to shout her name, but I'd played this game enough times to know that was a good way to get blasted by anything lying in wait. Besides, I wasn't alone. It was one thing to draw fire, but another to open my big mouth and get my friends napalmed in the process.

I mean, sure, they might hit Turd, too, but that probably wasn't a fair tradeoff – yet anyway.

Fortunately, I didn't have to worry about patience being a virtue because my vamp speed was more than up to snuff – quickly erasing the distance between us, even faster than I expected.

In short order, I began to make out more details – my footfalls made near silent by the dead soil beneath my feet.

The figure was clad in a loose fitting cloak. As for their hair color, I realized I'd been mistaken. It was mostly the same shade as Christy's, but I spied a white streak through it à la Cruella de Vil.

My heart sank, realizing it probably wasn't Christy after all. Not unless she'd decided to go the skunk stripe route in some bizarre attempt to make the hairy idiots of this realm think she was a living, breathing peace offering.

Come to think of it, that wasn't the worst idea I'd ever heard of.

I slowed my steps as rational thought once more took hold. This was the first non-ape we'd seen here, but that didn't necessarily mean it was human.

I knew how these things played out in horror movies. I might run up, blindly assuming she was who I wanted her to be, only to discover a giant pile of cockroaches wearing people clothes instead. So I decided to play it cautious, get close enough to...

However, I stopped dead in my tracks instead as I once more felt that strange sensation of a door being opened inside my mind. It was completely painless, but I still had a feeling it would take some time to get used to.

Either way, it told me the power was back on. Veronica had apparently decided to unlock her mental door and let me back in.

No, wait. It wasn't her. No idea how I knew that. I just did. This power was slightly different, almost imperceivably so, as if I was ... tapping into another source.

The figure inclined their head in that same instant, not only telling me who I must've synced up with – their term, not mine – but cluing me in on one other thing as well.

They knew I was there.

I opened my mouth to announce myself when, from the corner of my eye, I caught the barest hint of movement from inside one of the huts. Was something else here, too? Before I could turn that way, though, the dirt beneath my feet began to undulate and heave, as something clawed its way out from under me.

The fuck?

Yep, despite my caution, I'd walked straight into a trap. And now, thanks to my stupidity, I was going to be swallowed up by the motherfucking Sarlacc Pit...

"Bark bark bark! Halt, intruder!"

Or not?

The grey dust at my feet became the consistency of jelly as a dozen eyeballs all opened up in it at once.

"Glen?"

"Oh, hey, Freewill."

Before I could say anything, another voice responded – one which caught my full attention, driving everything else into the background.

"Hello, Bill."

As great as it was to find our lost friend, I turned to find the figure I'd spied now facing my way – her beautiful face a sight for the sorest of eyes.

It was Christy after all. It was actually her!

Everything else could wait. I stepped forward, slipping on Glen once before finding my footing and racing onward until I could grab hold of her in my arms.

Her face was weathered and dry, worry lines ran across her forehead as she stared up at me with wide eyes, but I couldn't have cared less. I pulled her in and hugged her tight, letting the tears fall freely as I held onto her.

"My apologies, Freewill," Glen said from somewhere behind me. "I thought you might be the enemy attempting a sneak attack. Can't be too cautious, you know."

Whatever he was babbling about could wait. First, I wanted to take in the sight of the woman I loved.

I pulled back, seeing her blurry form in front of me. *Duh!* I took a moment to wipe away my tears, clearing things up, only to realize I'd once again been wrong. What I'd mistaken for worry lines had been nothing but smudges of dirt. The weathering of her face as well as the white stripe in her hair were merely dust, nothing more. Aside from a change of clothes and needing a washcloth, she was exactly as I remembered her.

"I'm here," I told her. "Just as I..."

"Was explicitly warned against?" she replied, lightly slapping my arm. "God, you can be such a jerk."

I raised an eyebrow and grinned back at her. She truly was the most beautiful creature in this or any other universe. "Sorry, the reception kind of cut out mid-message. Besides, did you really expect me to listen?"

She shook her head, right before letting out a chuckle. "I guess not, especially since that's the same answer Glen gave me."

"What can I say? We're not particularly good listeners."

"I can see that. It's just..." She trailed off, inclining her head as she stared at me.

"What? I got a booger in my nose?"

"No," she said, looking away. "It ... must be this place. It's just a feeling, a Magi thing. Hard to explain to..."

"The guy who's about to kiss you?"

"No, it's... Wait. What?"

I leaned in as she turned back toward me, planting my lips to hers. The whole vampire wizard revelation could wait, this couldn't. For a moment, I got the sense that she was going to pull away, but then she leaned into it – her lips parting slowly as I...

"Bark! Bark! Bark!"

As I remembered I wasn't alone. *Shit!*

I stepped back and turned. Glen had shaken himself free of the grey dust, revealing his normal puke yellow color as he raised the *alarm*.

"Halt, stranger!"

"Knock it off, Glen," I called out, realizing there was one member of our party I'd never gotten a chance to introduce him to. "That's just the Wanderer. He's ... a friend."

"The Wanderer?" Christy replied, looking past me. "Hold on, isn't that...?"

"The vampire formerly known as James? Yes. And now he's the spirit inside of me, except here he's on the outside."

"He is?"

"Yep. Oh, and before I forget, that feeling in your head is probably me."

"How do you know about...?"

"I'm a catalyst mage now too."

"What?!"

"Um ... surprise!"

⊰————⟡————⊱

Yeah, I may have steamrolled Christy a bit with that last one, but there was no point in sugarcoating it since she could obviously sense me siphoning gas from her noggin.

Glen had apparently caught her up on some of what had happened, but the surprise in her eyes as the rest of the group joined us was all too evident.

Thankfully, Turd gave us a wide berth, glaring at us from a distance as we babbled like idiots, trying to bring her up to speed as quickly as we could.

Veronica, Sally, the Wanderer, Ed, and more. Christy may have only been gone for a few weeks, but it might as well have been a decade for all that had changed.

"I can't believe what I'm hearing," she said at last. "I'm so sorry, so sorry I wasn't there to..."

"None of that's your fault." I reached out and took her hand. "You didn't ask to come here."

"No, I just tempted fate by arrogantly playing with powers beyond my understanding."

Sally shrugged. "Who among us hasn't been guilty of that from time to time?"

I glanced her way before turning my focus back to Christy. "Whatever. The only thing that matters is there's a little girl who misses her mother and wants her back more than anything."

Christy raised a hand to wipe her eyes. "I know. If there's one thing I never doubted here it was that." She paused for a moment before continuing. "I swear, hearing her voice, knowing she could sense me – it was the only thing that kept me sane, at first anyway."

"At first?"

She nodded. "Let's just say there hasn't been too much time as of late to rue the hand fate has dealt me."

"How so?"

She seemed to consider her next words. "We'll get to that, I promise. For now, I'm still kind of stuck on you... I mean what happened to you. Ed's bite really did that?"

"More like it woke up something already inside him," Sally said.

Christy nodded. "So, if there were other Freewills out there, they'd likely be dormant Magi too?"

I hadn't considered that, but she was right. With Alex no longer around to cull the herd, it stood to reason that at some point another person with latent Magi genes could end up bitten.

"Probably," Sally replied. "Let's just hope Gan doesn't figure that out before her next recruitment drive."

Christy grimaced. "Don't remind me. I was really hoping you'd bring good news about her unexpected demise."

"Sorry. She's inconvenient like that."

"So I've noticed." She paused, as if realizing something. "Wait. You said Tom destroyed the Source beneath her home, but you needed one to find me. So then where...?"

"We found another," I said. "Turned out to be closer than you might think."

I took a quick glance around, checking to see if anyone was about to volunteer extra information. I wasn't trying to hide anything, but Christy had been sent here because she'd tapped into the Source with forbidden magic found in the Falcon Archives. I had a feeling the last thing she needed to hear was how those same Archives were also the basis of our rescue plan.

Some things could wait until we were back home.

"Hold on. Kelly and Matt were both captured by that thing ... Leviathan, right?"

"Unfortunately."

"Then who's running the incantation back home? Please tell me you didn't leave Tina…"

"Of course not. She's only five." *Going on twenty-one apparently.*

"She's the anchor for our tethers," Veronica explained, "but Liz is the one actually running the show."

Oh crap.

"Excuse me? Did you say Liz?" There came a crackle of red energy from behind Christy's eyes. "Are you telling me you left my daughter alone with that backstabbing bitch?"

Just for the record, I'd been planning on dancing around that answer, too, knowing how she'd react.

"She's not alone," Veronica explained. "Tom's with her. And you have it all wrong. Liz is … well, she's trying to make things right."

"Oh really? Was she trying to make things right when she shoved a gun in my daughter's face?"

Though my better judgement told me to stay the fuck out of this, I had a feeling it was going to be a sticking point otherwise. Besides, the last thing we needed was to get back home only to have Christy immediately kill the woman in charge of her rescue. "V's right. Liz has been going above and beyond the call of duty to help us, even risking her own life."

"You of all people should…"

"I know how you feel. I didn't want to believe it either, but it's true. You have to trust us on this. Trust *me* on this."

Christy narrowed her eyes but said nothing. I had a feeling that was my cue for an abrupt change in subject. "So, Glen, where have you been all this time?"

"Oh, you know, mostly ambling about," he replied, grey flecks of dirt still clinging to his slimy body. "I didn't see any of you around when I arrived, so I decided to go searching instead. By the way, you'll be happy to know this world is free of mucus crawlers."

"Good to know."

"Anyway, I meandered for a bit until I eventually sensed

the vibrations of distant footsteps. So I followed them. Imagine both my surprise and delight to find..."

"Me," Christy interrupted. "Isn't that right?"

"Oh ... yes, you're correct," Glen replied after a moment, blinking a few times. "It's been most glorious, especially since Madam Witch graciously accepted my offer to act as her bodyguard."

I couldn't help but feel a slight sting of jealousy that he'd gotten to spend time alone with her, while I'd been stuck getting the third degree from Turd and friends. Still, it wasn't like this was some vacation getaway.

"By the way, what did you think of my newest disguise? I couldn't find any dogs or racoons here, so I decided to become the ground instead."

"Gotta admit, one of your better costumes, man. You are certainly well-suited to being a pile of dirt."

"Thank you!"

"So, what was that earlier about sneak attacks? Has there been...?"

"I am happy to report that none have succeeded since I've been on duty."

"None have been attempted either," Christy added.

"About that." I hooked a thumb Turd's way. "Have these assholes been giving you any shit, because if that's the case I'll...?"

"Get your ass kicked again?" Sally interrupted.

"No!"

Christy shook her head, though. "Glen's not talking about them. If anything, the forest folk have been nothing but kind and welcoming since I arrived."

"Oh really? Then why are you all the way out here in this barren shithole?"

"Because I choose to be."

I took a look around. "Why? I mean, yeah, it smells better, sure, but the scenery kinda sucks."

"I'm not here for the view, Bill. I'm here so I can help defend their home."

I once more glanced Turd's way, catching the filthy shitbag with a finger knuckle-deep in one of his nostrils. *Eww!* "Against what – sentient bars of soap?"

"That isn't funny," she snapped. "Nothing the Great Beast has done to this world is."

42

THE POWERS THAT BEAST

"Great Beast? Are you saying Leviathan and its...?"

"No," Christy said. "You have it all wrong, Bill. The beasts of Genesis, powerful as they might be, are mere soldiers – avatars following the command of their true god."

Their true god... That didn't sound good, not good at all.

"Told ya," Sally said.

"No need to rub it in."

The Wanderer threw us a look before asking, "How do you know this?"

Christy hugged her cloak tighter despite the pleasant temperature. "From what I've been able to piece together, Gan woke this thing up when she was trying to reopen the Source – after a thousand years of slumber, maybe more. Hell, it could've been millions for all I know."

Oh yeah, this was getting better by the second. "Is it safe to say it woke up on the wrong side of the bed?"

"Without a doubt. I'm limited in what I can scry here, so I don't know for certain this is a fact, but Humbaba said that its forces have been working their way through other worlds, other universes – ravaging them like fire ants."

"Let me guess. Our world is one of the entrées in this seven course meal of destruction?"

She nodded. "More like dessert. Apparently our reality – our world in particular – is some sort of nexus point for the multiverse."

"Of course it is."

"It's why the Source functions as it does there, leading both everywhere and everywhen at once."

Goddamn. It was like a Jim Starlin comic, except in real life. Call me pessimistic but I had a feeling the Silver Surfer wasn't gonna fly in and save our asses at the last second.

"Okay, so the supersized ape with a side order of ugly told you this. Doesn't explain why you're out here, unless you're delivering a message to Mad Max."

"Doesn't it?" the Wanderer replied.

"He's right, Bill," Sally said. "Seems pretty clear to me."

And this is exactly why I used to leave the room whenever my mother put on *Murder She Wrote*. I simply wasn't good with vague hints. I preferred my clues spelled out in plain English.

Christy nodded. "That forest you came from, all of this used to be just like that. But now look at it, and this is just the tip of the iceberg. This blight spreads farther than the eye can see – all of it dead, along with so many who once called it home."

Dead? I was tempted to ask how that even worked for those who'd already kicked the proverbial bucket, but then figured that was one of those mysteries better left untouched. I had a feeling there was no way I'd like any possible answer. Leave that metaphysical shit to the philosophy majors, I say.

There was one tidbit there, however, that had me more concerned than the rest.

"That doesn't tell me *why* you're here. Yes, I get that you're here to fight that thing. It's your motivation that I'm not quite grokking, especially when Humbaba is back home stuffing his face with grubs."

There came a growl from behind us, Turd no doubt eavesdropping on our conversation. I flipped him off over my shoulder, not giving a single shit what his opinion was.

"Are you sure you don't want to insult his mother while you're at it?" Sally asked.

"Telling him his mom smells like week old dogshit is probably a compliment in their culture."

Christy let out a sigh. "Do you honestly think Humbaba wants to be back there on the sidelines?"

I shrugged, having no idea what she expected me to say. After all, he'd looked pretty comfy to me.

"The answer you're looking for is no," she continued. "Tell me, what does vampire history say about him?"

I had no fucking clue, but fortunately the Wanderer was there. "It tells us that he was a warrior without compare, unequaled among his peers in terms of battle prowess or bravery."

"Our history says the same thing," Veronica replied. "To be compared to the great Humbaba was the highest compliment one of the forest folk could bestow on another."

"You guys do realize that history is written by the victors, right? Just saying."

"Anyway," Christy continued, ignoring my interruption, "he was right there on the front lines when this first started. But this place, this world, it's ... attuned to him. He has essentially transcended from warrior to demigod."

I raised a hand.

"No, Bill, that doesn't make him a match against what we're up against, not even close. What it does mean, however, is that losing him could irreparably harm this reality."

"Fine. He's no match for the big bad, I get that. But neither are you." I hated to say it. After all, Christy was a badass when she wanted to be. But we were dealing with something that apparently called the monsters of the Bible its personal bitches. If that didn't describe something way the fuck out of our league, I didn't know what did. "You're with me on this, Glen, right?"

About a dozen eyes shifted focus from me to Christy and back again. "Well..."

"Seriously?"

If Christy was insulted by what I'd said, she didn't show

it. If anything, she let out a laugh. "The funny thing is, I pretty much said the exact same thing a year ago, when the Beast's forces first attacked."

"Wait. A *year* ago? But you've only been gone..."

"Time moves differently here, Bill," Sally said, fixing her gaze on Christy. "Humbaba even said as much."

The two shared a glance, some unspoken comment passing between them, before Christy turned her attention back toward me. "She's right."

Holy shit. An entire year in this fucking place? "I – I didn't realize... Oh my God, I'm so sorry. If I'd known..."

"You couldn't have known. Nobody could have."

"But..." I wasn't even sure what to say. "From hearing Cat talk ... I mean ... it sounded like you and she were in near constant contact."

Christy looked away, her lower lip trembling ever so slightly. "I suppose it was, for her. For me..." She shook her head. "It was long stretches of silence, broken up by hearing my baby girl's voice. It's... Some days it was the only thing that kept me going."

I reached over and put a hand atop hers, her once smooth skin now dry and chapped. No surprise there as I had a feeling the only moisturizer in this place came straight from a Sasquatch's ass.

She grasped hold of my hand for a moment, before pulling away to wipe her eyes. "You're sure she's okay?"

There was no doubt the situation back home was complicated, but I saw no reason to add any more burden to whatever was already on her shoulders. "She's right as rain. Her dad's taking good care of her, and her Uncle Bill's keeping the swear jar overflowing with cash."

"Her Aunt Sally too," Sally added.

"And me as well," Glen replied.

Christy nodded, gratitude showing in her eyes as she took a moment to steel herself again. "Anyway ... as I was saying, I told them there was nothing I could do against this thing that they couldn't."

"But I'm assuming you were wrong," Sally surmised.

"Stop spoiling her story," I snapped.

"Bite me, dipshit."

"In your dreams."

Christy smiled, our banter no doubt reminding her of better days spent in a world not populated by giant screaming apes. "Yes, I was wrong. I was very wrong ... which is also why I suspect Humbaba had you all sent out here to find me instead of the other way around."

"Not following."

"This is their Elysium Fields, their Heaven if you will," she explained. "The forest folk appear here much as they did in life – as spirits given flesh – but they've still passed on. They aren't alive. They lack that spark. Not so with us, though. We're all still brimming with life."

"Okay and...? I mean, yeah, the berries taste a bit better and it's nice to take a walk in the sun, but what of it?"

"It's far more than that, Bill. I don't exactly understand how it works, except that in a place such as this that spark of life makes all the difference. The dead may appear strong to us, but in truth they have nothing on the living. That's why I'm out here fighting. I'm one Magi, true, but here I might as well be an entire army."

"Now you're really losing me."

"Then now's the time to watch and learn."

She turned and pointed toward a rock formation about a quarter mile away. Before I could so much as ask what I was looking at, it exploded in green flames – leaving nothing but rubble behind.

Whoa!

"Back home, that would've taken nearly everything I have. But here? I barely even felt it."

My eyes opened wide as I realized not only what she was saying, but that I could still feel her in my mind, or the door leading to her inner spark anyway. If she could do that then maybe I...

Veronica, unfortunately, was more perceptive than I gave her credit for, turning to me and snapping, "No!"

"But..."

"I said no!"

"Let him," Sally replied. "I could use a good laugh."

Her derision served to sober me up, reminding me that I actually had no idea what I was doing. Hell, ever since arriving I'd been... "Wait a second. I'm not calling you a liar or anything, but our buddy Turd back there kind of kicked our collective asses shortly after we arrived."

Nods came from the others as they no doubt realized the conundrum.

Christy, however, remained nonplussed. "Did he hurt you?"

"Pretty much. I mean, he tossed my ass around like a freaking beach ball."

"But did he *actually* hurt you?"

"I..." I mean our fight hadn't exactly tickled but, aside from being bounced around a bit... "Not too badly, I suppose. I mean, I'm still here. But it's not like I kicked his ass either."

"Tell me, were you fighting him like you did back home?"

"Well, yeah. How else was I supposed to fight him?"

She grinned. "That's the problem. You know how strong you are back there, so you naturally assumed the same is true here."

"Not following."

"It's something you need to be made aware of. Or at least that's how it was explained to me." She snapped her fingers a few times as if trying to recall something. "What's the name of that stupid movie you made me watch? The one with the red pills."

"*The Matrix?*"

"Yeah, that's the one."

"You said you enjoyed it."

"Ah, the male ego," Sally remarked. "Is there anything in nature quite as fragile?"

"It's like in that movie," Christy explained. "Here, the living need to become aware that they can surpass their normal limitations, but once we accept that…" She turned to our blobby buddy. "Care to show them, Glen?"

"It would be my pleasure."

I wasn't sure what she expected him to do, except maybe ooze into a dead dog without making it look like a horror show. But since I didn't see any… *Whoa!*

Glen's body began to stretch and elongate, growing taller. Two leg-like appendages sprouted from his bottom. Arms and a pseudo head soon followed, until he was roughly the size and shape of a person – if that person were made of translucent yellow snot and had all their internal organs replaced by eyeballs.

"Isn't it great?" he cried. "I can pass as one of you here. It's the ultimate disguise."

"It's definitely … something."

He stepped in front of Sally and bowed, the jelly-filled head atop his form bobbing in a way most unnatural. "May I have this dance?"

"Maybe next time," she replied. "But points for trying."

A half dozen of his eyeballs turned my way. "See, Freewill? She was totally fooled."

"Um yeah, sure she was." I focused on Christy again before this could get any more disturbing. "Okay, so that was a neat trick, I suppose. Please tell me we can't all do that now."

"Fortunately not," she replied with a smile. "But your abilities here should all be greatly amplified, same as mine."

"But…"

"Let me ask you this. How long did it take you all to get here?"

"A while."

"I'll bet. And is anyone winded? V? Sally?"

"She's got a point," Sally replied, after nobody else said anything. "It's not like I'm even wearing good shoes for a nature hike."

I hadn't even considered that. We'd followed Turd for miles, but only two of us had vampire stamina to fall back on. *Wait a second...* "Hold on. Is that why he had us brought out here?"

She nodded. "I should have said something sooner, and I apologize for that, but what's done is done. You're all here now, so it's time for the whole truth. Humbaba's deepest hope, as well as mine, is that you'll be willing to help us. You see, as powerful as I might be in this realm, I'm still one person. At best, I've been able to slow the Beast's forces. But together we may have a chance of saving this place."

I understood what she was saying, but the truth was none of that mattered to me. I didn't give a shit about this land or its inhabitants. Nor did it matter in the slightest that my powers here might be kinda badass. All I wanted was to go back home so we could put this shit behind us.

Christy knew me way too well, though, because she wasn't done yet. She looked me in the eye as she dropped a cherry atop this doom sundae.

"Because if we can stop it here, then maybe, just maybe, we can keep it from invading our world next."

43

NEED I SÉANCE MORE?

I had zero interest in doing the Feet any favors. Far as I was concerned, this was their fight, not mine.

But Christy knew exactly the right bait to use. Ending this here and now, as impossible as it sounded, went beyond any anti-Bigfoot prejudices. If we could stop the Great Beast's advance, we could save Kelly, Vincent, Falcon, and the rest. We wouldn't have to worry about sea monsters in the Hudson. We wouldn't have to wonder if a 747-sized bird was about to drop ten tons of shit on anyone's head. Most important, though, it would save Sally – taking the target off her back that Gan had painted there.

It might even force whatever was residing inside her to vacate the premises. I wasn't sure what that would do – if it would leave her as she was now or cause her to revert back to her true age – but that didn't matter so long as she was safe.

It would also ensure Tina could grow up in a world that was sane ... or at least *saner* than what we had right now.

Let's be honest, there was also a wee bit of selfishness on my part. I wanted to get back to my life. Maybe Christy and I could find some spell in the Falcon Archives to turn lead into gold. Then, afterward we could spend our days practicing magic together and our nights cavorting naked beneath the moonlight – preferably without her coven there to watch.

Damn it all!

I glanced back at Turd, now engrossed with picking lice from his butt cheeks – using the same hand he'd used on my face earlier. I'd have loved nothing better than to know I'd ruined his heavenly reward, but the pros of this plan outweighed the cons. Besides, Turd would then have to live with the fact that he'd been saved by the Freewill, something that would almost certainly chap his hairy ass.

"We're in," Sally said.

"I was just about to..."

"I know," she replied to me, "but even if you weren't, I'm still helping."

"I concur," the Wanderer added.

I turned to Veronica, figuring if we were going to be marching to our likely deaths then there should at least be a consensus.

"We came here to bring Christy home. That's it. But if we can save our friends in the process then I think we need to take that chance."

Christy leaned over and put a hand on her shoulder. "Kelly's a fighter."

"I know. But if we're going to do this, we need to do it now. We have no idea what's going on back home. I doubt we have time for an extended siege or some hundred day war. We have to hit hard and we need to do it quickly."

The Wanderer nodded. "Well said. Though I will admit to enjoying having my own body again, there is little doubt that every minute spent here puts our friends back home at risk. That said, I am curious to know how we plan to strike this quick and decisive blow. A crushing victory against foot soldiers is all well and good, but it does not win a war." He turned toward Christy, raising an eyebrow. "But you knew that already, correct?"

"What are you getting at?" I asked.

"I believe Christine here knows a thing or two she still hasn't told us yet. Considering Glen's presence here when we arrived, she's had at least several hours to think this over and come up with a plan – more than enough for a clever soul such as herself."

Huh. I hadn't considered that. Needless to say, all eyes turned her way.

She looked down for a moment or two before smiling. "Apparently I'm not the only clever one here."

Sally elbowed me in the side. "She's talking about him, not you."

"Thanks for the clarification."

"You're right," she continued, ignoring our banter. "I *have* been giving this thought ever since learning you were all here, and there's only one possible solution. In order to win this, we need to take the fight to the Great Beast itself."

"So it's actually here on this world?" Sally asked.

"In a sense. Everything in existence, regardless of where it comes from, has a place of origin – and the pull from that place can be strong indeed."

"Meaning?" I replied.

"I assume ... *Liz* filled you in on your astral tethers."

I couldn't help but notice the way she gritted her teeth, so I opted to simply nod rather than say anything.

"The reason tethers work is because of that strong pull. In essence, you leave a small bit of yourself behind as an anchor. So long as you have that you can go back home at any time, but it also means that your stay anywhere else is only temporary. The inverse is traveling without a tether. That's how someone like Glen for instance is able to reside in our world. His whole being is there. However, minus that tether it's much harder to go home again – at least without help."

"Hold on," I interrupted. "Does that mean you're stuck here permanently?"

"No. But it's the reason I haven't been able to get back on my own. When it's time to leave, I'll need to hold onto one of you and let you carry me back – letting your tether essentially function as a bungee cord for us both."

I nodded. That info basically lined up with what Liz had told us.

"The principle mostly works the same for everyone, but according to Humbaba it's a bit different for godlike beings. The divine are so powerful that they rarely send the majority of their essence to another realm. So, for instance, you all might be ninety-nine percent here, with a small piece left behind as your anchor, but it's the opposite for something on that scale. In that case, what you're seeing is barely an echo of their true selves."

Sally nodded, apparently understanding more of this word vomit than me. "So what you're saying is that we're only dealing with a small piece of this asshole."

"In a sense, which works to our favor in terms of trying to fight it. But there's more. We use our astral tethers so we can go back home. Sever it and we're stuck. Divine entities use theirs to anchor that small portion of their essence elsewhere. They need it to stay there. Cut it..."

"And they're flung back to whence they came," the Wanderer surmised.

"Exactly. But none of that helps us if we don't know where it is – which is why I saved the best part for last. We can use another being's tether to pinpoint exactly where they are."

"How?" I asked. "I thought we were the only ones who could see our tethers."

She shook her head. "No. You can make it appear for others if you so choose. There just usually isn't a reason to."

"I can?"

"Yes, and once it's visible, a tiny bit of magic can keep it that way."

Fuck it. I looked behind me and focused, trying to see if I could make it visible for everyone else. *There!* Within seconds I could see it, but did that mean...?

"Wow, Bill," Sally said. "Looks like you're taking a giant silver shit there."

Guess that answered that question. I stopped focusing and turned back toward Christy. "Okay, so then what? How do we make this thing want us to see its tether?"

"We don't. But there's more than one kind of tether. A

being bound to its plane of origin will have one connecting it back home, but a soul bound to a stronger soul will..."

"Be fettered to its master," the Wanderer finished. "Are you talking about its troops?"

"In a sense," Christy said. "Yes, they're bound to the Great Beast, but we're mostly talking savage monstrosities here. They'd sooner gnaw off their legs than do our bidding, even under torture. Trust me on this."

Whoa. Hardcore.

"Fortunately," she continued, "not everyone bound to the Beast is a mindless foot soldier."

"How so?"

"Trophies it's taken as part of its ongoing conquest. In short, prisoners of war."

"So we need to break into a prison camp first?" I asked.

She shook her head. "What need are there for cages when one is inexorably bound to a creature such as the Great Beast? Just knowing you can't escape is prison enough. But therein lies opportunity."

Sally appeared to consider this. "I think I get it. We need to find one of these spoils of war and convince them to help us."

Christy grinned. "Way ahead of you there. The forest folk aren't our only allies here. There's another, who I know for a fact is more than willing to help us do whatever it takes to bring this monstrosity down once and for all."

"And?" I asked after a minute or two of silence. "How do we find them?"

"We don't. She's already here."

She?

"And is this special someone perchance invisible?" Sally replied, looking around.

"In a sense. When we learned you were all coming here, she thought it best to wait out of sight." Christy turned and met my gaze. "To give us a little time to get reacquainted."

"Okay, that's nice, I suppose."

I guess it was good that some reptilian horror had enough sense to not come plodding out until after Christy had a chance to soften the blow for us.

As for the reacquainted part, well, much as I'd have killed to get some alone time with Christy, that would have to wait until we returned home – far away from where I could smell Turd.

No offense to the big pile of shit, but his stench was a real boner killer.

Hell, I was half-surprised my nose hairs hadn't incinerated yet. Although, I guess that told me why I hadn't noticed we weren't alone. The reek of Sasquatch tended to blot out the scent of everything else.

"All right then. Bring them out and let's get this show on the road. The sooner we can end these Beast Wars, the sooner we can save Cybertron." Upon the resulting silence, I explained, "That's a..."

"Loser dork reference?" Sally replied. "Yeah, kinda figured."

Everyone's a critic. Rather than grouse, I turned toward Christy and nodded for her to continue.

She let out a deep breath. "Brace yourselves. This might be a bit of a shock."

Considering all the weird-ass things we'd fought against, I had to wonder what constituted a shock for her. Were we about to see some shambling abomination with a face made of tentacle dicks, or something even worse?

If so, it was probably a good thing Tom had stayed home, because he'd probably have way too much fun with...

Christy waved a hand and the air began to shimmer about twenty feet away. It was another glamour. Apparently she'd been holding it all this time with seemingly no effort on her part. Guess this place really did have her juiced.

As it dropped, my nose caught wind of another scent – one familiar enough that I recognized it even amidst the odiferous outrage wafting from Turd.

Tom?

A moment later I caught sight of shoulder length blonde hair over silver eyes, all atop a lithe frame clad in dull cosplay armor.

"Oh my God," Veronica gasped.

She was right on that front. *This* was the big surprise? Guess it was good that we'd minimized the canoodling, since the last thing I needed was to catch shit about it. "What the fuck are you doing here? You're supposed to be watching Cat!"

"The stupid truly does burn," Sally muttered from alongside me.

"What are you talking about? He's..."

And that's when it hit me. She was right, I was a dumbass. Tom couldn't have followed us here. His power simply didn't allow it.

But if he was still back home, then that meant I was looking at an honest to goodness ghost from my past.

"Sheila?"

44

EX MARKS THE SPOT

I realized my mistake, especially now that I had a moment to take a good hard look – and not be a moron about it.

Sheila was dressed the same as when last I'd seen her – right before Gan had struck. She was wearing the armor and cloak of a Templar warrior, although both were tarnished and torn, as if they'd seen too many battles.

That wasn't all that was different with the woman I'd once been infatuated with. Her hair was limp and brittle, and her skin was way too pale. The only thing about her that seemed alive were her eyes, still blazing like freshly minted silver.

Gan's intent had been to make her the final sacrifice for the Great Beast, to open wide the floodgates of magic once again. It hadn't just been because she was the Icon either, one of the few beings in existence that was a threat to her plans.

No. Sheila was my ex, something Gan simply couldn't abide – knowing that at one point I'd thought my entire future would revolve around her.

In the end, things hadn't worked out, but then neither had Gan's scheme. Through some means – whether magic, faith, or simple force of will – Sheila had dragged Tom's soul into her body, even as hers was ripped away.

377

Since then, her fate had been left a mystery. I'd hoped she'd moved on to her own version of Heaven, somewhere she could find the peace in death she hadn't been able to find in life. Sadly, that couldn't have been farther from the truth.

Christy's exposition about tethers hadn't been solely to bore us to tears. She'd been softening the blow, letting us know what to expect.

Sheila's final battle in life had ended in defeat to the Beast. As such, she'd become little more than a spoil of war. The mighty Icon, the very being who'd destroyed all magic in our world, reduced to little more than a trophy.

All of that passed through my mind as I tried to form the words to express what I was feeling. So, of course, what came sputtering out instead was, "Holy shit! It's you!"

What can I say? I always did have a way with words.

"Hey, Bill," she said approaching, a sad smile upon her face. "You look well. You all do."

"Um, you do, too, all things considered."

"Oh yeah," Sally muttered, "this isn't awkward at all."

"Sally?" she replied. "You certainly look different than the last time I saw you."

"Let's just say I had the mother of all chemical peels a couple months back. Did wonders for my skin."

"Months." Sheila shook her head. "It's been decades for me, maybe centuries. It's hard to tell. I've been dragged through so many worlds like a dog on a leash, seen so many of them fall. Muspelheim, Pitala, the Endless Dunes, the Jade Court, Hades..."

"I'm gonna assume that's a bad thing."

"Bad? I doubt even Gansetseg is fully aware of what she's unleashed."

I had my doubts there, but now wasn't the time. "So ... how have you been?"

"Oh for fuck's sake." Sally pushed me to the side and stepped forward. "Let's cut to the chase. The thing that's got you has got a hold of me, too, so if we can fuck up its day then count me in."

Sheila nodded. "You're the Earth Harbinger I've heard her bragging about."

"So it would seem."

"For the record, I'm glad it's you and not Gan."

"Not sure I'd agree, but I appreciate the sentiment."

"Hold on a moment," the Wanderer interrupted. "You said *her*, yes?"

"What else do you call something that proclaims itself the mother of all beasts?"

Guess that was a fair point.

If Sheila was curious as to how the Wanderer was alive again, she didn't ask. Guess when you were cuffed to an interdimensional hell-beast, the unexplainable became mundane. Either that, or she'd simply been listening in while Christy had her cloaked.

Speaking of which, she was probably who I'd spied skulking around inside the hut. Christy must've glamoured her at some point after Glen started barking his head off.

As I was considering this, Sheila backed up a step, a strange expression upon her face as she seemingly looked at us all in turn.

"What are you doing?" Veronica asked after a minute or two.

"Taking this all in." She let out a choked sigh. "I know it sounds weird, but I'm just trying to ... remember this moment. I know it hasn't been long for most of you, but it's been a near eternity for me and..." She trailed off for a moment, her silver eyes shining – not with power but from the tears gathering within them. "Well, I was starting to forget what some of you looked like."

My heart broke upon hearing her say that – not even close to understanding what she'd been through, yet knowing what was still to come if we failed.

I wanted nothing more than to comfort her, but held myself in check. Crazy as it might've sounded, I wasn't quite sure about the rules for hugging your ex in front of your current girlfriend, even knowing she'd been dragged through literal Hell and back.

Fortunately, the Wanderer was there to make up for my inaction. He stepped forward, hesitated for a moment – no doubt remembering how well vampires and her power used to go together – then put a hand on her shoulder. "Tell us how we can help."

If Sheila was still capable of bursting into white hot fury, she managed to hold it back. "By stopping it. That's all. I can't lie to you and say I share Christy's optimism, but I'm hoping you can at least slow it down, buy some time for the world to..."

"How can we help *you*?" I interrupted.

She turned and met my eyes. Despite everything, I couldn't help the flutter I felt in my stomach. "I'm dead, Bill. There is no helping me."

"Tell that to Tom."

"I get the impression he's a rather unique case," the Wanderer replied.

Sally chuckled. "He's unique all right."

"I'm serious."

"So am I," she replied to me. "I was sacrificed in the Beast's name. That carries a lot of weight among the divine."

"She's right," Christy said. "Think of it like a high stakes poker game. Winner takes all."

"Well, then how do we win her back?" I asked.

"I'm not sure that's even possible."

"Hold on here," Sally interrupted. "I don't mean to be the negative Nancy at this reunion, but if you're telling us this thing owns your soul lock, stock, and barrel, then how do we know you're not simply doing its bidding and leading our asses into a trap?"

Sheila inclined her head. "A fair question. Although, in that same vein, how do we know we can trust her harbinger?"

"Touché, although my current hair color suggests I'm on hiatus right now."

"Fair enough. Then I'll offer this in return. I have no doubt the Beast could control me if she so chose, but she's never tried to. Not even once." She let out a laugh devoid of any humor. "Call me cynical, but I think she enjoys giving me what little freedom I have. That's the only reason I'm even here. She gives me free rein in whatever world she drags me to, knowing I can run as far as I want but I'm still no better than a leashed dog at the park."

"Except that might be a mistake this time," the Wanderer said, turning Christy's way. "Correct?"

"I'm hoping that's the case. Far as I can tell, this is one chance in a million. Us, all here now."

I raised my hand. "Weren't you the one who tried to warn us from coming here?"

She turned away from me, sounding unhappy. "I did, and would do it again. One chance in a million is still terrible odds. And if faced with a choice between keeping you safe and dragging you all into ... this, *knowing* what's to come, there's no doubt which one I'd choose. What's done is done, though."

I couldn't help but feel my heart swell for her. Sheila had been my dream girl, but Christy was now my reality – and I was finally beginning to realize that was every bit as sweet as any dream could ever be. "Well, consider me glad that we're all too pigheaded to listen to reason."

"Same," Sally said. "We may be assholes, but we're each other's assholes ... even if some of us are full of shit."

I let out a laugh. "I'm not sure anything else needs to be said. So how do we do this?"

"By doing the most insane thing possible," Christy replied, "attacking it directly."

Sheila nodded. "That's my cue."

She took a deep breath and furrowed her brow. In the next instant, a thread seemingly made of crimson fire appeared around her neck – her tether. It ran down her body to the ground, where it led off into the distance.

"You're all connected back home," she said, "but I'm connected to the thing that would have me and all of creation call it master."

"Well then, what say we go cut this puppet master's strings once and for all?"

Wherever Sheila's tether was leading us, it apparently wasn't anywhere close.

The upside was the long walk gave us plenty of time to experiment with what Christy had told us about this place. The Wanderer was the first to try it out, because of course he was – taking a moment to steady himself before splitting a man-sized boulder in two with a single blow.

Watching him succeed while not breaking his hand in the process was enough to spur me on.

I'd like to say I got it right on the first try, but at least by my tenth I was able to free my mind enough to make good on it. Sure enough, Christy was right. Soon, I was punting heavy rocks off into the distance and smashing any tree trunks that we passed. I only wished someone would've thought to film this shit because it was badass as fuck.

More than once, I found myself glancing Turd's way as he trudged morosely behind us, wishing the fucker would start something. Oh, how nice it would be to rearrange his ugly mug without having to cede control of my body to Dr. Death.

Sadly, Turd was on his best behavior, so I settled for kicking his ass in my thoughts.

Soon, I found myself with Sally and Glen as marching buddies on this expedition. Christy and Veronica had paired off up ahead to discuss strategies pertaining to their amped up magic – both of them making it clear that I wasn't invited to the party until I'd been properly trained.

It gave me a moment to consider the vape pen still hidden in my pocket. I'd brought it here almost by accident, not knowing who back home to leave it with. Then I'd kind of forgotten about it once the threat of Turd and his buddies had been downgraded. Now, marching into battle, I remembered what it had done for Kelly back home. Here, well, there's no telling what it could do for me if we found ourselves in a bind. Still, tempting as it was to give it an experimental suck, it was probably best to leave it as an absolute last resort.

Ultimately, it was for my own good and I knew it. The last thing I needed was to blow myself sky high before our suicidal battle against an ancient god-beast had even begun.

Still kinda sucked, though.

As for the others, Sheila and the Wanderer had, well, *wandered* off to the side to talk about battle tactics, something I probably should've listened to had it not sounded dull as fuck.

That was fine, however. It gave me time to mull over some concerns I had – of which there was no small number.

◄———— ∕∕∕∕ ————►

"You okay?" Sally whispered as we continued trudging along.

"Yeah, why wouldn't I be?"

"Ooh, I know," Glen replied, having rolled himself into a ball to keep pace beside us. "It's because of the Icon – the old one, not the new one back at..."

"I get the picture," I hissed. "Okay fine. I'll admit to being a bit weirded out by all of ... this."

Sally, for her part, simply shrugged. "You didn't honestly think we'd zap in here, find Christy, then zap back home again with no problems did you?"

"Hoped for? Yes. Expected it? No. But this..."

"Is a bit of a mind fuck?"

"Pretty much."

"It's all very exciting."

Sally glanced down at the little blob. "That's one way of putting it."

"And might I add, your hair is a lovely shade of yellow."

She raised an eyebrow but apparently opted not to address that, turning back toward me instead. "We should probably be prepared."

"You think we're gonna be fucked over?"

"I'm hoping not, but..." She trailed off, letting me fill in the blanks as an uncomfortable silence set in.

383

The cliché response would've been to defend Sheila, to say that I trusted her – and in truth a part of me did. I knew her heart was always in the right place, but I was also well aware that the road to Hell was paved with good intentions.

In her case, those good intentions had not only broken my heart, but had indirectly led us to where we were today. She'd been the driving force seeking to reopen the Source. And though I'd believed her when she'd said her intentions had been pure, they'd still led to a lot of people being hurt or worse – including Sally, who'd been tortured nearly to death before we could rescue her.

Ironic that we were now relying on one of her torturers to hold the portal back home open. Life certainly seemed to enjoy throwing curveballs like that at us.

Still, Christy seemed to trust Sheila on this. Of us all she probably had the least reason to, considering that aforementioned road to Hell had led to Tina being threatened at gunpoint. That she was willing to forgive and forget carried a lot of weight in my book.

"Oh for Christ's sake, get going," Sally said, almost as if reading my mind.

"Huh?"

"I know what you're thinking, Bill. Go talk to her."

"But you said..."

"Even if she is planning to screw us over, that doesn't mean you shouldn't at least try to clear the air first. So go on. Besides, let's face facts. You probably won't ever get another chance."

"If you're trying to depress me, you're doing a hell of a job."

"We're marching off to ambush a god, about as batshit of a plan as they come. It's not depressing so much as realistic."

Sadly, I couldn't dispute her logic.

45

THE EXPOSITION
BEFORE THE STORM

It was all uphill from that point – literally.

Ahead lay a high ridge, beyond which smoke could be seen rising in several places. Unsurprisingly, Sheila's tether – still visible to us thanks to Christy's magic – led straight in that direction.

It wasn't all bleak ashen hellscapes, though.

To our left, way off in the distance, I spied trees – where the vast forest appeared to start up once more. I didn't pretend to understand the strategies of ancient gods hell-bent on conquest, but considering the wasteland upon which we now strode, I had a feeling that slice of Sasquatch Heaven was next on the Great Beast's hit list.

Despite Sally's insistence, I'd held myself in check for the past few miles. Now, with the end of our journey likely in sight, I had a feeling it was now or never.

Forcing myself not to wuss out, I headed to where Sheila still walked alongside the Wanderer – their strategy session seemingly long over.

"Hey."

"Freewill," the Wanderer greeted.

"Err ... I think Sally wants to talk to you."

"Oh, does she?" he replied with a knowing grin – the smug bastard. "Then heaven forbid I keep her waiting."

385

He dropped back, leaving Sheila and me alone ... to walk in uncomfortable silence, at least for a few minutes.

"So," she finally asked, "how's my body doing?"

"What?"

She let out a laugh. "I meant Tom. How's he doing in, well, me?"

"He cut his hair."

"Really?"

"Yeah, said it kept getting in his face."

"Never liked how I looked with short hair."

"Oh, I don't know. I think it's kind of cute ... for him that is. By which I mean it's not cute in the slightest."

She chuckled again. "Sorry, wasn't trying to make that awkward."

"It's not you. I mean, it's just weird."

She shook her head. "You have no idea."

"So ... what was it like?"

"Dying?"

"I was going to say body swapping."

"Oh. Kinda painful actually. Not physically, but up here." She put a finger to her head. "It's true what they say. Your life really does flash before your eyes in those last few moments. Can't lie and say I liked everything I saw."

"Pretty sure none of us would, and you're almost certainly the closest thing to a saint our group had."

"Don't believe the Templar hype. It was all a pack of lies to build up my ego and make me more of what they wanted me to be." She blew out a breath. "The funny thing is, it's all still there."

"What is?"

"That insane self-confidence. It never left. I know it doesn't sound like it, hearing my voice. It's been beaten down over time by the Beast, but it's there all the same — refusing to die. It's the reason I'm here trying to fight, despite knowing it's probably futile." She let out a bitter laugh. "The others, Komak and those other vampires Gan sacrificed, they broke a long time ago. They're little more than shells of their former selves, dogs groveling for whatever scraps our master will throw them. And yet here I am, still trying."

"Komak, eh? Liz won't be happy to know that."

"Might be best if you don't tell her."

"Agreed."

Sheila turned and stared at me, as if debating what to say next. "I ... never wanted to leave. I just thought you should know that. But I..."

"Had to?"

"The guilt was too strong. That's the downside of this blasted confidence. Once magic was gone and it turned off, all that was left was the guilt – slowly growing inside me, gnawing at everything, telling me it was all my fault. You ... you deserved better than that."

"Not entirely sure I agree. You could've at least told me. I'd have listened."

"I'm not sure listening would've been enough."

"I ... sorta get that now."

She nodded. "I really am sorry."

"I am too."

She turned and gestured Christy's way. "You know, it's funny. Back then, I never even considered you two might be a thing."

"Neither did I. It just kinda happened."

"No it didn't. There's more there than that and you know it."

I considered this. "Maybe."

"No maybes about it. I've had a long time to think about these things, trust me. It might be hindsight, but I see now how good of a fit you two were. She realizes it, too, even knowing that so much..."

"Hold on. Did you two talk about me while I wasn't here?"

Sheila grinned sheepishly as if I'd figured out something I wasn't supposed to. "Maybe. We had to do something to pass the time between apocalyptic battles. But anyway what I'm saying is, I'm glad you found each other."

I couldn't help but laugh, it was either that or break

down sobbing and, well, this really wasn't the time. "Now if I can only convince Tom of that."

"Sorry. That's gotta be a bit awkward."

"It is, for all of us, but I won't lie and say it isn't great to have him back."

"Has he...?"

"Started spending the money in your bank account like it was water? Unfortunately."

"I meant, has he told my family anything?"

"Oh?" I considered lying, but decided against it. "Yeah, he has."

"Do they ... know?"

"This is Tom we're talking about. He considers what the right thing is then does the opposite. Anyway, I know he's been in touch with your mother – but more about stuff like birthday and Christmas gifts. You ... well, know how Tom can be."

She opened her eyes wide. "Wait, so Mom thinks I'm okay?"

"Sorta."

"No, that's actually a good thing. I'm glad he did that – maybe not for his reasons, but I'm happy nevertheless. It's probably silly of me but I don't want her to worry."

"It's not silly in the least. Listen, how about I keep an eye on things, do what I can to keep him in check? At least that way I can keep him from taking advantage of her."

"I appreciate that. Can't say I won't mind having one less thing to worry about as we head into this fight." She paused for a moment before adding, "Listen, I'm going to warn you in advance, I might not be as useful in this battle as I'd like to..."

Wait ... useful? I tuned the rest out as I finally remembered the weapon still strapped to my back. Up until now, I'd no idea why I'd been asked to bring it, but suddenly that all became crystal clear.

"Would this help by any chance?" I slid the scabbard from my shoulder and carefully unwrapped Zoe's cloak from it.

Sheila's eyes immediately opened wide. "Is that…?"

"Your sword? Why yes. I do believe it is."

"But … how … why do you even have it?"

"Tina told me to bring it. I had no clue why at the time, but now… Call me crazy, but I think she might've known more than she was telling us."

"Do you think Christy…?"

I nodded. "Maybe. I guess it's possible she might've mentioned it last time they spoke."

If that was the case, then I had to wonder if Christy had also asked her daughter not to tell me the reason – since I probably would've freaked.

Either that or twenty-one year old Tina took after her mother when it came to thinking these things through. If so, it was nice to know she'd grow to have a good head on her shoulders. Now we just needed to get back and ensure we could be there to watch it happen.

"So, how about it?" I asked, holding the sword out.

"I … I can't," Sheila said, despite obviously wanting to take it. "It's not mine anymore."

"And yet it's here anyway, for you."

"It's… I'm not sure, Bill. My powers, there's still a spark there much like my confidence, but it's not like it is for you. You're still alive. I'm … barely a shadow of who I used to be."

"Then that's even more reason for you to take it. We're gonna need all the help we can get, and if this gives you the boost I think it will, then all the better."

"But…"

"To paraphrase what a wise little girl told her father not too long ago, even if you don't believe in yourself, I still do."

⊹─────── ∧∧∧ ───────⊱

Sheila took the sword, but didn't draw it – continuing to stare at it in its scabbard as if it were Excalibur and she was debating the odds of successfully pulling it from the stone.

There was still so much more to be said, but I'd done – maybe not the best I could – but at least I tried. Now it appeared that she needed some time alone to think things through.

That was fine, because she wasn't the only one I wanted to talk to before the shit hit the fan.

What's that saying about saving the best for last?

Or hopefully that was the case as Veronica saw me approaching and mouthed, "It's about time," before pretending she had other business to attend to.

Ah, such a subtle bunch of friends I kept.

"Did you say what you needed to?" Christy asked, looking at me from the corner of her eye.

"Sorta," I mumbled. "Listen, I'm sorry. I know I should've been here next to you this entire..."

She actually laughed at that. "There's nothing to be sorry about, Bill, and no you didn't need to be. V and I had stuff to go over and it's probably best that you didn't listen, all things considered."

"Yeah, but..."

She turned and put a finger to my lips, still continuing to smile. "You're here now. That's what matters."

"Yeah, I guess you're right. That, and there'll be time enough for us when we get back."

She looked away. "I suppose... I mean, you're right of course."

Goddamn, I couldn't wait for this to be over. It was obvious she was trying to carry the weight of this world on her shoulders, as if it was worth fighting for. I glanced back to where Turd continued trudging behind us, his jaw moving as if he were grumbling to himself. Yeah, things would definitely be better when we could finally put this shithole behind us.

"I know what you're thinking," she replied. "It really hasn't been all bad. I wasn't lying when I said the forest folk have treated me well."

"Yeah, but being stuck with them for an entire fucking year?"

She looked away again for a moment before saying, "Let's just say I won't mind sleeping in my own bed again."

"Oh yeah, about that..."

"About what?"

"We sorta had to ... abandon the apartment."

"I see Glen left out a few details." Christy fixed me with a look. "Care to tell me why, since it's fully warded against...?"

"*Was* fully warded."

"What do you mean?"

I told her about my little run in with Beef and Queef, feeling extra stupid now that I knew the truth. I expected her to lose her temper. However, as she grew more red-faced, I realized it was more with humor than anger.

"That is ... so them and so you."

"It is?"

"Yes! Even Tina knows not to talk to those two, but you ... well, I never would've even thought to warn you. So I guess it's just as much my fault as it is yours."

"Oh. Okay then."

"But it's still mostly yours, which only highlights my concerns right now. Listen, Bill, I need you to promise me that you're not going to mess with magic until you've had at least rudimentary training."

"Seriously?"

"Yes, seriously. We're going into a situation where V and I will need to remain open, and we aren't going to have time to babysit you."

"I don't need babysitting."

She inclined her head. "Yes, you do, and no I don't mean that in a condescending way. All new Magi do. I did, Kelly did. Even Liz did. Without it, accidents happen."

"Fine, I'll try not to..."

"I'm not done yet. It's worse for you because we both know you rely on your other powers to keep you on your feet. You pretend you don't, but you do. It means you take stupid risks that others wouldn't."

I opened my mouth to protest but then quickly shut it again. She was right after all.

"The last thing any of us, you included, need is for you to get cocky out there and think you're some dungeon lord casting a... What's one of those cockamamie spells from that game?"

"It's dungeon *master* and you're probably thinking about something like Power Word Kill."

"Goddess what a vulgar name. But yes. I need you to trust me when I say you require proper instruction. Magic isn't a game."

Technically, it *was* a game, too, but I had a feeling she wasn't in the mood to mince words. Besides, Tom was more the card collector.

I noticed the incline of the terrain. It wasn't going to be long now. Probably best to not argue over things she was right about anyway. "Fine. I promise."

"Good, because if I find you on fire of your own accord I'm not putting you out."

"Harsh."

She smiled coyly at me. "Sometimes you need a little harsh in your life."

"Yes, ma'am."

I meant that last part as a joke, but a pained look appeared on her face nevertheless – if only for a moment. It made me wonder if life in Sasquatchland was as wonderful as she claimed. I could just see Turd treating her like his own personal Cinderella, all while Humbaba stuffed his fat face with grubs.

"Are you really sure we need to do this?" I asked bluntly, not caring that Turd's ears were sensitive enough to overhear us even at this distance. "I mean, I could just grab hold of you now, give my tether a tug, and we'd be home again in an instant."

"So you want to hold onto me while tugging your tether?"

I raised an eyebrow. "I really have rubbed off on you, haven't I?"

"In a good way ... mostly."

"We wouldn't even have to worry about the others. That's the failsafe. The second Liz senses one of us returning with a *passenger* that's her cue to start recalling the rest."

"Smart of her," she said before turning serious again. "I won't lie and say I haven't considered it a hundred times since Glen showed up. A part of me would love nothing better than to cut and run."

"It's not even that. This isn't your fight."

"No it isn't, but it's *her* fight." She inclined her head in Sheila's direction, effectively shutting me down. "Besides, I wasn't lying about this being a one in a million opportunity. You have no idea how lucky we've gotten."

"You're gonna have to expound upon that lucky part."

"I've talked to Sheila. She told me about the other dimensions that have been overrun or are in the process of being. The Great Beast is frighteningly strong, no doubt about it – a primal force that potentially dwarfs the power of the known gods."

"Still not feeling particularly lucky."

"*Anyway*, as I was saying, it's powerful but its strength is still finite. From what she said, it sounds like it might be stretched thin right now. It's like a hungry dog trying to bite off more than it can chew. I was too late destroying its Harbinger here, but if we can banish it from this place then..."

I held up a hand. "Whoa, back up a bit. Did you say you destroyed its Harbinger? I thought Sally was..."

"She's the Harbinger of *our* realm."

"Meaning?"

"I didn't understand it back then, but being here has offered me some fresh insight."

"Spill."

"You're familiar with Lovecraft, right?" She thought about that for a moment before letting out a chuckle. "Never mind, stupid question. Anyway, I'm specifically talking about the so-called Old Ones he referenced."

Shit! "Are you saying the Great Beast is actually Cthulhu?"

"No."

"Oh."

"But Lovecraft's concept of the Old Ones being sealed

away by the Elder Gods is a good analogy, if not entirely correct. The Great Beast is an ancient primal power, older than recorded history."

"Let me guess, it tried to conquer all the other realms before a coalition of gods banded together to stop it once and for..." I trailed off as she stared at me, eyebrow raised. "What? That's a pretty common trope in gaming. D&D and Pathfinder both have it."

"Fascinating, but not even remotely where I was going."

"I'll be shutting up now."

She nodded once before continuing. "It wasn't a war so much as a preventative measure. The Beast subjugated its realm completely and utterly. It is, in effect, the one true God of whatever dimension it originated from."

"This story gets better, right? Because so far it sounds like we're on a suicide mission to punch out dinosaur Jesus."

Christy let out a sigh, letting me know to zip it again. "After becoming, well, God, the Beast – whether tired from its conquest or bored – fell into a deep slumber."

"And on the seventh day..."

"I somehow knew you were going to say that. Anyway, its minions, some of them nearly gods in their own right, began to pierce the veil seeking new worlds. The pantheons of the other realms recognized this as the threat it was and took measures to stop it. They effectively warded the multiverse against this creature, basically doing to reality the same thing I did in my apartment."

"Is this where you tell me it's my fault for undoing all of that too?"

I was only half-joking, but thankfully she giggled instead of nodding. "Technically, that one's on Gan's head. But it's also the reason the Beast was able to push open the Source but not step through in that moment." She let out a heavy sigh. "Much as I don't like giving her any credit, I think Gan knew that."

"So what about the Harbinger part?"

"I was getting to that. With the walls of reality hardened against it, the Great Beast is forced to share a portion of its power with a being already within whatever world it sets its sights on — one who serves to strengthen its hold there until such time as it can force its way through."

"So what you're saying is Sally is part Silver Surfer and part Keymaster of Gozer."

She inclined her head. "I suppose."

Guess it was a good thing I'd hosted so many movie nights back when magic was still gone. "So if that's the case, then what's the deal with Leviathan and his kaiju buddies?"

"Remember those minions I mentioned? They'd been slumbering in our world for eons until their master's voice awoke them."

Ah, that made sense. They were already there long before the doors were locked. It wasn't hard to imagine them occasionally turning over in their sleep and freaking out any cavemen who happened to notice. Guess that explained their cameos in the Bible. Now, we only had to... *Wait a second.* "Hold on, didn't you say you destroyed its harbinger here?"

Christy met my gaze. Her eyes weren't entirely unsympathetic, but they were hard as steel all the same. "I did. When one accepts the Beast's power, one also accepts an aspect of it into themselves. It's not entirely unlike when someone gets bitten by a vampire — except that what's inside them is a small sliver of a greater whole. And that sliver has but one purpose."

"Sally is still herself."

"I'm not saying she isn't. But she's not alone in her body either and what's inside of her is actively working against us."

I knew exactly what she was getting at. "Please tell me you're not siding with Gan on this."

"If that little bitch told me I needed air, I'd make it a point to stop breathing." She let out a snort before quickly turning serious again. "The thing is, she's not wrong either. Killing ... *stopping* the Beast's chosen harbinger ensures the wards put up against it remain intact. I don't know of any other way of putting this, Bill, but we need to keep it on the table as a last resort."

The world or Sally? It was the same question Gan had

put to me barely a month ago. The same one I'd told her to go fuck a duck with. Christy, however, at the time had cautioned that we might need to consider it, and Sally had agreed. Now we seemed to be past the considering stage. "And you know all this how exactly?"

"Humbaba..."

"No offense, but are we really going to take the word of some lard-ass Bigfoot whose idea of heaven is stuffing his face with bugs?"

"Do you really need to body shame him on top of everything else?"

"All things considered, I'm okay with it."

"Look, I know you don't like the forest folk, but there's no denying he's wise beyond comprehension – practically a walking version of the Falcon Archives, but with far greater breadth."

I considered commenting on that part but held my tongue. I was here to rescue Christy, not rile her up. There was more too. Gan threatening Sally's life was a slow Tuesday, nothing either new or interesting. But with Christy saying it now, I had to wonder whether I'd soon find my back against the wall – faced with the choice of killing a friend I'd have laid down my life for or sparing her, only to see all of creation become a nightmare version of *Jurassic World*.

"Wait, you said last resort."

Christy nodded. "I'm not ready to give up on her just yet. That's why we're doing this. Doling out a loss to this thing saves this world, yes, but it should also slow the Beast's progress and give us time to work something out."

And suddenly I found my motivation to fight renewed. I still didn't give a damn about Turd, Humbaba, or any of the other King Dongs that called this endless forest home, but I had no problem handing them a victory if it meant saving Sally too. "Why didn't you just say so?"

"I thought I did."

"Fine, then let's go kick this monster's ass. We have a friend who needs saving and you have a little girl who really wants to see her mother again."

Sounds began to reach my ears as we crested the rise – chittering, hissing, grunting, and other sorts of weird-ass shit. Whatever was waiting for us, there were a lot of them.

We crouched low as we reached the top, inching forward until we could see down into the valley beyond. What was there gave me reason to consider how fucking stupid this plan really was.

I could see just why the thing we were after was called the Great Beast. What lay below us wasn't some enemy encampment full of tents, latrines, and soldiers reading copies of *Stars and Stripes*. No, it was more like some crazed stampede had stopped for a momentary breather – save that the *cows* were all straight out of a nightmare.

I tried to take stock of the various monstrosities skittering around below – noting a good many of them resembled the cockroach-rat things I'd had the displeasure of meeting in the New York City sewer system. Then, as my eyes were sweeping over the horde of horrors, I almost shit a brick – spying the death god who'd once displayed a disturbing interest in using me as breeding stock.

"Jesus fuck, is that Druaga?! What the hell is that asshole doing here?"

Nearly eight feet tall, it was a drug-fueled horror mashup of a sleestak and a centaur. We're talking a towering mass of multi-hued scales, claws, and too many legs, topped by horns and two sets of gleaming red eyes.

"You're mistaken, Freewill," the Wanderer replied, his voice a harsh whisper. "That's not Druaga."

"The fuck it ain't."

"Look closer."

I did, only to suddenly feel even worse, if that was possible. The Druaga I'd spotted wasn't the only one. Scattered among the cockratters and other freaks were more like him, as if the fucker had an equally ugly extended family. "What the fuck?"

"Remember what I said about the Beast's minions,"

Christy replied, "how some were practically gods in their own right?"

"Are you shitting me? Seriously, are you telling me that the death god Alexander tried to woo was nothing more than this fucking thing's foot soldier?"

"Actually, if I had to guess, I'd say they appear to be officers," the Wanderer corrected.

"We're going to fight a death god?" Glen quivered. "I so wish I'd brought my camera."

I shook my head. "That's it, we're fucked. New plan because this one sucks."

"I hate to agree with Captain Bravery here," Sally said, "but he's right. Powered up in this world or not, how the hell are we going to make it through even five feet of that?"

"We're not," Christy replied.

For a moment I thought sanity had taken hold and she'd realized that it was best to just go home and pretend this had all been nothing but a bad dream. Instead, she turned toward the smelly asshole who'd been following us for hours like a forlorn puppy.

I'd been silently questioning why Turd had stuck around after leading us to Christy, as he'd done nothing since then but give us a wide berth and mumble to himself. I guess we were about to find out.

"In the name of Humbaba, lord and master of this land, I beseech thee. Help me free your people from this nightmare."

Turd lifted one corner of his mouth in a snarl, no doubt taking exception to the way she'd worded the request. Go figure. Here we were, risking life and limb to save his shithead friends, and he was giving us the stink-eye for it.

Then Turd threw back his head, opened his considerable jaws, and let loose with a godawful roar that was loud enough to echo across the valley below – turning heads, antennae, and other freakish appendages our way.

"Well, if they didn't know we were here before, they sure as shit do now," Sally remarked once Turd's cry finally died down.

I turned and narrowed my eyes. "Anyone else up for killing that asshole *again* before those things climb up here?"

Sheila, however, shook her head. "It's not us they should be worried about."

Before I could question what she meant, another roar rose in the distance – an answering cry to Turd's.

Then another joined it, and more followed. Soon, the air was filled with thousands of screaming cries, an enormously large counterforce. Either that or mating season in Sasquatch Heaven had just started, which was an equally terrifying proposition.

There was little doubt it was the former, though, as it quickly became obvious it was coming from the direction of the forest.

"An ambush?" the Wanderer asked, a trace of respect in his voice.

Christy nodded. "To buy us some time."

"How so?"

"From what I've witnessed, the Beast considers the forest folk beneath its attention. Expect it to hold back as its forces respond."

I grinned. "Sounds like another word for pussing out."

Either way, I felt a wee bit better at hearing that news. There were all sorts of reasons for a commander to hang back while their forces raced out to meet death, but most of them boiled down to excuses. It was the guys like Alex, the ones leading the charge, that worried me more.

Sure enough, the battle cry seemed to have grabbed the attention of the army below us. Plumes of dust rose from everywhere down below as the myriad nightmares wasted no time in charging forward to meet the challenge.

There wasn't much caution given either, as I spied multiple creatures outright trampled by their fellows. It was less an army and more like a living tidal wave.

"You should go join your people," Christy said from behind me, obviously talking to Turd.

Yeah, go do that. At the same time, I found myself hoping the Feet were planning to play to their strengths – drawing the enemy into the woods where they'd have the homefield advantage. I had a feeling they were going to need it.

I approached the drop off, listening more than seeing since the valley below was engulfed in a cloud of dust. It was crazy how quickly they'd responded, far faster than any human encampment could've mobilized under the same circumstances.

There'd been no orders or rallying cries. They'd simply all reacted ... like a swarm of hornets.

It made me wonder if that was something we could use to our...

"Bill!" Sally hissed. "Don't stand there like a fucking target. Get your ass down!"

"It's fine," I replied. "They can't see me down there with all the..."

I trailed off as a high pitched voice shrieked in my mind. For a moment, I wondered if it was some kind of magic thing either Christy or Veronica was doing, but then it solidified into coherent words.

Enemies... Die!

What the...?

A flash of multihued energy lanced up from the dust cloud below, causing me to remember one very important detail about Druaga – he was a mind reader. The things in the Beast's army might not be him, but it stood to reason they'd have similar abilities.

As the bolt of power struck the rocky ground, causing it to crumble beneath my feet, I had a moment to rue my faulty ass memory before I found myself tumbling down toward whatever horrors waited below.

46

NOT EASY BEING GREEN

If there was one upside to my descent, it was that the screeching inside my head drowned out the sound of my own screams.

At least it wasn't a sheer drop. I hit the slope and continued tumbling down. It wasn't exactly pleasant, but thankfully the ground was mostly covered in that same thick ash which seemed to make up a good chunk of this wasteland.

Then I hit the bottom where I eventually rolled to a stop – quickly realizing that I was mostly unhurt. At first I thought it must be due to my powers being amped in this place, but then I realized the ground beneath me was kind of spongey, akin to landing atop an ash-covered mattress.

That was a bit weird. It...

Die!

Shit! I'd almost forgotten about the Druaga cosplay winner out there. Unfortunately, I couldn't see shit. The dust cloud kicked up by its buddies as they'd raced into battle was now lingering in the air – giving me visibility for maybe ten or fifteen feet at most. Good thing I didn't need to breathe because I doubted this crap was particularly healthy.

The sound of the Beast's army thundered in my ears as they headed to meet the Feet, the ground beneath me jiggling like jelly from innumerable footfalls – a not even remotely pleasant sensation.

Crazy as it was, I found myself wishing the Sasquatches well. With any luck, we could cripple this invasion force from both ends. Now I just had to find out where...

Nope, scratch that. First I had to live, as another blast of prismatic energy came blazing out of the dust cloud. I barely had time to leap to the side before it gouged a chunk from the spot I'd been standing – drenching me in a foul rain of gore and ichor as...

Wait. Gore and ichor?

While I knew I should've been keeping watch for the mutant velociraptor with the laser beam fists, I couldn't help myself as I crept to the small crater Druaga-2 had opened up – realizing that it wasn't full of rocks and dirt so much as what appeared to be pulped flesh.

The fuck?

Then I saw it. Between all the gory mess I made out fingers attached to a dinner plate-sized hand, one still partially connected to a bloody hair-covered arm.

Holy shit!

The dead Bigfoot was entangled with more of its kind, too many to count as they were mutilated nearly beyond recognition – to the point where I couldn't tell where one ended and another began. That solved the mystery of why the ground was so spongey here.

It was a mass grave – piles upon piles of brutalized bodies, buried only by a thin layer of ash and sediment.

Oh my God.

I still had no idea how one killed something already in the afterlife, but that seemed kind of like mincing words. Everything I needed to know was in the ground beneath my feet, the multiverse's most morbid bounce house. And the Great Beast had parked its army atop it with apparently no concern whatsoever for how fucking sick in the head that was. It...

It was unfortunately a piss poor time to ruminate on such things as a reptilian hell-beast galloped out of the gloom toward me – its footfalls muffled due to us standing atop the memory foam of Satan's mattress.

Oof! I tried to brace myself but was too late. It barreled into me right before its two upper arms plucked me from the ground by the waist. Then the fucker squeezed me like a vice as it carried me off ... somewhere. It was hard to tell which direction.

Goddamn, the dust in this place wasn't fucking around.

Either way, I had more important things to worry about as its four red eyes glared at me from beneath a crown of horns. Its teeth were the more immediate problem, though, as I managed to grab its head just before it could take a chunk out of me.

Man, I was so fucked.

Yes you are. Now die!

The hissing voice inside my head served to remind me that I was dealing with a psychic dragonborn here.

Last time I'd dealt with Druaga, he'd been able to pick up seemingly any thought that crossed my mind – leading to a somewhat embarrassing scenario where he'd tried to barter me from Alex for the purposes of crossbreeding.

But maybe I could use that to my advantage.

As I struggled to keep the creature's teeth at bay while its claws began to dig rather unpleasantly into my back, I forced myself to focus, picturing ... um...

Screw it. I imagined what a female version of this thing might look like – basically just giving it long hair and tits. Then I pictured myself railing it from behind.

Within seconds, the Druaga wannabe slowed its gallop and tilted its head at me.

That's right, I thought at it. *Your mom likes it centaur style.*

Apparently that struck a nerve because it reared back and let out a hiss of rage.

Now!

With it distracted, I grabbed hold of its horns and twisted with everything I had – trying not to remember how I'd once attacked Druaga while bolstered on Alex's blood, only to barely budge the damned...

No! That was the wrong way to think about it. As the hissing inside my head grew ever louder, I tried to remember what Christy had said about *The Matrix*. I needed to believe in my powers here. *Red pill this, motherfucker!*

Crack!

In the next instant, I hit the spongey ground – the beasts arms still wrapped around me as it fell, pinning me beneath its massive body. I looked up to see the malevolent light fade from the creature's eyes, amazed to find myself not only alive but apparently the victor as well.

Either this thing was a pale imitation of its death-god cousin, or I was a lot more juiced than I realized. Goddamn, if it weren't for the fact that I'd have to consign myself to an eternity of smelling Turd funk, I'd almost be tempted to move here and become its resident badass.

Yeah!

First things first, though, I gave a heave and shoved the reptilian beast off me. That done, I stood and dusted myself off a bit – delighted to find I was still in fighting shape.

Next, I cupped my hands to my mouth and began calling for my friends. Sadly, I received no answer save the distorted echo of my own voice.

I took a moment to try and orient myself in the oddly persistent gloom. There were no longer any vibrations under my feet. As for the sounds of battle, they were still there but distant – as if the Druaga thing had carried me for miles in the opposite direction.

If that were the case, though, then why hadn't this fucking dust settled yet? If anything, it seemed to be growing thicker by the minute. It had been a perfectly sunny day when I'd been blasted off my perch, but now you'd have thought it was three in the morning in the middle of London.

That wouldn't normally be a problem for me, but my vampiric vision was far more adept at cutting through standard darkness than walls of dust.

Stranger still, I began to notice the particles in the air

around me had taken on a greenish tint – hopefully just a trick of the light.

Yeah, this was getting stranger by the...

Despite the dusty gloom, now sticking to my clothes and probably making me look like some sort of half-assed ghost, I spied a dim reddish light at the very edge of what I could see.

What the...?

I inched forward, trying to be more cautious of my surroundings since I didn't want to get steamrolled by another Godzooky. Finally, I was able to make it out – a sliver of crimson red running along the ground, disappearing into the gloom in both directions.

Sheila's tether! It had to be.

Sure enough, it looked just like the one she'd shown us. Guess Christy's spell was still in effect.

But wait. That meant she was at one end of it, but waiting at the other...

Fuck! One way would lead to a friend, the other to a fiend.

Decisions, decisions.

I probably should've just waited where I was until the others found me, but screw it. At least now I had a path to follow.

Player logic dictated right-hand rule, but that had fucked me over more than once. Besides which, Dave was gone. There would be no more games under his vengeful eye. It was time to be my own DM for a change.

Left it is. Try to anticipate that, motherfuckers.

I turned that way, but then considered what I was about to do. It was more than likely my companions were still together. But in case they weren't, it might not be a bad idea to take a page out of Sheila's book.

Come on, tether!

I willed my own tether to appear and sure enough it did – a gleaming silver shit running from the bottom of my pant leg off into the distance.

If any of the others had gotten separated along the way, maybe it would lead them to me.

There was also the distinct possibility it could also lead untold horrors my way, too, but if the Sasquatch force was half as large as it had sounded then I had a feeling the Great Beast's army would be kept preoccupied for some time.

I set off to my left, following Sheila's tether into the greenish bleakness while mine trailed off behind me – leading the way back home, however distant that might be.

Whatever the case, I doubted I had too far to go either way. That thing had only carried me for maybe a minute or so before dropping my ass like a moldy cum sock.

That meant Sheila had to be close by.

Of course, she'd kinda implied the other end had been near as well.

Not a pleasant thought. I didn't relish running into the Great Beast on my own. Although I had no idea what it even looked like, I had a feeling it wasn't pleasant. I mean, this was the fucking alien queen that signed Leviathan's paycheck. What the hell could boss around a whale-sized water dinosaur? I didn't know, but whatever it was had to be big and terrifying as fuck.

Christy had mentioned H.P. Lovecraft earlier, a subject I knew a bit about. So naturally what came to mind was how the presence of the Old Ones was supposedly so horrifying as to drive one instantly and irrevocably insane.

I had to admit, the thought of my eyeballs melting from my head as I shit myself to death wasn't super appealing. However, I also tried to remind myself that those stories had been written during simpler times, long before people regularly binge-watched things like splatterpunk and hentai.

The men of Lovecraft's day might've been driven mad at the sight of a tentacled monstrosity, but this modern age found us more likely to question the number of Japanese school girls it was currently fucking.

Nutty as it was, I tried to hold onto that thought as I continued forward – the greenish tint in the air growing stronger until Sheila's tether more closely resembled the world's longest Christmas tree light.

"Freewill..."

I spun at the sound, only to see nothing there.

"*Come...*"

Yep, definitely a disembodied voice.

"*To me...*"

Forget towering tentacle beasts, I was going to be driven nuts by paranoia alone. Some fucking vampire I was, about to piss myself because I thought I heard...

Goddamn, I was an idiot.

The dust must've been playing tricks, not only with sight but sound as well. What I'd heard was probably my friends calling out to me, the sound waves distorted by the fucked up pea soup I was trudging through.

"I'm here!"

"*Here...*"

"Yeah, that's what I said."

That time the voice had been much clearer. Better yet, my ears seemed to pinpoint it as coming from directly ahead.

Squinting my eyes, I began to make out a form in the gloom. Better yet, Sheila's tether led right to it, snaking up what I assumed to be the person's legs. *Yes!*

I took it slow because, hopeful or not, I wasn't a complete idiot – making out more of the shapely form as I walked. No doubt about it, definitely female.

Moving closer, I made out legs leading up to a ... *whoa* ... a cute as fuck ass, then a slender back beneath shoulder length hair.

Why the hell is she naked?

Wait, something wasn't right here, and it wasn't just the complete lack of clothing.

Whoever this person was, she was shorter than Sheila. In fact, if I had to guess, she topped out at barely five-foot, the same height as...

The figure turned partially toward me, her bright green eyes locking onto mine.

"Sally?"

47

THE DEVILS IN THE DUST

The perfect roundness of Sally's ass was ever so slightly distracting, to the point that it took a moment for me to realize her hair was bright green again.

Come to think of it, her skin was too.

Uh oh.

Either she'd recently decided on a career move to nude She-Hulk cosplay – not the worst idea I'd ever heard – or, much as had happened to me and the Wanderer, I'd just found her missing other half.

"You're not Sally, are you?"

Not-Sally narrowed her eyes but in a semi-seductive way – more than enough to send my crotch mixed signals. "I am so much more than your friend. I am *her* harbinger."

Her voice was just like Sally's, after an overdose of horny goat weed – dripping enough sex that I almost had to slap myself.

Down boy! I tried to focus on something decisively non-sexy – Tom naked in his old body. Yeah, that worked. "You ... you can't have her."

"That is not for you to decide, Freewill." She inclined her head, still half turned my way – enough for me to get some

408

side-boob to go with all the ass on display. "You are revered among your species, yes?"

"Revered is maybe a strong word."

"So small ... yet resilient nevertheless," she continued.

"Wait, I didn't say small."

"It is an admirable trait."

At this point I wasn't quite sure whether we were talking about dicks or not. "What is?"

"The resiliency of your species. You are ... survivors."

"So are cockroaches. What's your point?"

She flashed me a predatory grin, reminding me that a significant chunk of the Beast's invading force had been basically that – giant mutant roaches. "Very well. You may serve."

"Excuse me?"

"I offer you the chance to serve the Great Beast, to serve *her*. Pledge your kind to the service of she who is above all others."

"Not really sure I can speak on behalf of every other vamp, especially since a good chunk of them are assholes."

"You are their Freewill," she replied, as if that explained anything.

I opened my mouth, not entirely sure what was about to escape my lips, when I noticed something odd about Sheila's tether. It snaked up evil Sally's shapely calf muscle and thigh before disappearing around her waist to the side still facing away from me.

"Um ... do you mind turning around?"

Harbinger Sally's eyes looked down at herself then up at me again, once more forcing me to think of the least enticing things possible.

Turd's gaping asshole! Yep, that'd certainly do it. "I didn't mean it like that. I just wanted to..."

"You wish to lay your unworthy eyes upon she who is above all others, so that you might pledge yourself?"

I let out a sigh. "Okay, let's cut the shit. Sally's tits are nice, no question about it, but I'm not sure I'd say they're above all others." Mostly a lie, but still... "And no, I'm not pledging shit to anyone."

"You will."

She began to turn before I could tell her off properly, maddeningly slow as if this were some kind of peep show – which, in all fairness, it might've been.

Maybe humanity had simply interpreted Lovecraft's stories wrong all this time. Perhaps it wasn't Cthulhu's horrific appearance that had driven people mad at first glance. Maybe it just had such an epic set of boobs that men immediately lost their minds.

At my first glimpse of nipple, I began to wonder if perhaps there wasn't something to that theory, but then she continued turning and I caught sight of a patch of bright green fur.

Fur?

I was about to question whether Harbinger Sally was in need of an epic chest waxing when I realized it wasn't hers. She was holding something in her arms, cradling it like a small child.

Whatever it was, one thing was clear – Sheila's tether was attached to it.

The fuck?!

I glanced at the thing in Harbinger Sally's arms, then at her, then back at the thing, wondering if the dust in the air was more toxic than I realized.

"So ... is there a reason you're carrying a radioactive koala?"

That was the best way I could describe it. Either that, or I was watching a live-action *Lilo and Stitch* – if Lilo was a hot stripper and Stitch had color contrast issues.

The thing in her arms was small, furry, and bright green, with big ears and equally large eyes that kind of gave it a dorky perplexed appearance.

Had Tina been there, she would've squealed with delight before snatching it out of Harbinger Sally's hands and giving it all the love a five year old girl was capable of, which was no small amount.

Hold on.

I did a double take, noting Sheila's tether again. No doubt about it. It was attached to one of the tiny critter's adorable paws.

That meant this thing was...

No way!

I tried to rationalize this. Maybe I'd followed the wrong tether, or perhaps Sheila's death had caused her some sort of traumatic brain injury.

My mind had been prepared for nearly anything – Godzilla in an octopus hat, the Kraken from *Clash of the Titans*, a gibbering horror made of teeth and leprous dicks, anything but what I was looking at.

I mean, shit, watching Harbinger Sally cradle the stupid thing, I was reminded more of a bad *PETA* ad than an Armageddon level threat.

Fuck it.

"I'm just gonna come right out and ask, so there's no misunderstandings later. Is that fat little ferret you're holding supposed to be the Great Beast everyone is losing their fucking minds over?"

Not the most diplomatic way I could've put it, but whatever. I'm sure it got my point across. Now to see what happened next, not that I was all too worried. I mean, what was going to happen? Was this Sally clone going to fly at me in a rage, intent on smothering me to death with her C cups?

Rather than answer, though, she looked down at the critter in her arms as if seeking permission.

It, in turn, opened its mouth and screeched unintelligibly, sounding like a parrot with a broomstick shoved up its ass.

"Um, sorry. I didn't bring any koala treats with me. Must've left them in my other outfit."

No doubt about it. I was seriously weirded out, but I couldn't quite bring myself to feel all that threatened. It was like being cornered by the school bully, but instead of beating you up he merely shit his own pants before winking at you and walking away.

The creature inclined its head against Harbinger Sally's ample cleavage, snorted once, then opened its mouth again.

"C ... uh... Can ... you ... understand me now?" it asked slowly, as if speaking to a moron – its voice high pitched and reedy, sounding like your typical anime high school girl.

I blinked a few times before nodding.

"Good. Always takes me a moment or two to remember how to communicate with lower life forms. The language of sub-creatures is just so gosh-darned crude."

"Did you actually say gosh-darned?"

"Is that the wrong phrasing?"

"No, not really, I guess."

"Great," it, or *she*, replied in its disturbingly innocuous tone, more suited to teaching three-year-olds the ABCs than ... whatever the fuck we were doing. "Come closer, I want to get a better look at you."

I raised an eyebrow but held my ground. The fact that this thing was being held by Sally's exceptionally naked body double was almost the least strange part of this whole exchange.

"So, you're the Freewill?" it continued, seemingly unperturbed by my obstinance. Its eyes opened wide as it looked me over, making it appear more like a Disney animatronic than a living creature. "Aren't you the cutest thing?"

"Excuse me?"

"I just want to cuddle you in my arms and hug you to death."

"Wait, what?"

"Ooh, I know." It craned its head up at Harbinger Sally. "Rip one of your fingers off, I want to see if he'll accept a treat from me."

The fuck is wrong with this thing?

Make that *both* of them, as Harbinger Sally lifted the hand not currently holding the psycho puppy, stuck her index finger into her mouth, and proceeded to bite down.

Blood started pouring down her arm as she worked her teeth against the digit.

Holy shit.

She spat the severed finger out, just in time for the Beast to nimbly catch it in its paw. Gotta say, I hadn't been expecting that.

"Here you go, Freewill. Go on, try to catch it." It tossed the bloodied finger at me, watching it bounce off my shirt before falling to the dusty ground. "Aw, so close. Let's try one more time."

"Are you crazy? Is that your problem, you psycho fucking Ewok?"

It again inclined its head. "Hmm, tell me something. Are you what your species might call a fertile male?"

"Let me just stop you right there. No, I am not fucking you."

"Me?" it asked, sounding way too amused. "Oh no, you misunderstand. You see, I'm currently fostering a rather fascinating specimen." It held up Sheila's tether. "I think they used to call her the Icon. Anyway, I have this crazy idea, but hear me out. How cute do you think your pups would be?"

"Our pups?"

"I know, some will argue that purebreds are the way to go, but I personally disagree. In fact, I'd say the most fascinating offspring occur when you mix and match species, even if it sometimes requires a bit of meddling to make it work."

"Um yeah. Fascinating I'm sure, but we're the same species..."

"Are you now? Personally, I'm not entirely convinced, but I'm more curious as to what I should call your litter. I-wills ... or maybe Freecons? Either way, I bet they'd make the most adorable additions to my menagerie."

"Yeah, well, I've seen the things you work with and..."

The Beast made a tsk-tsk motion with its paws. "As I'm well aware. You killed poor Grelcrx, not his real name mind you, but the closest your primitive tongue can come to it without shredding your vocal cords. Oh well. Don't worry, I'm not mad. These things happen."

I was starting to get the impression that this asshole was fucking with me. I was willing to take a lot of crap when it was doled out by monsters big enough to stomp me into paste, but this little pile of shit was barely big enough to make a pair of gloves out of. Hell, I could've punted it halfway to the horizon at my current power level, something that was starting to sound better by the moment.

Still, I preferred to wage my battles with words, at least for now. I could always play soccer with its face later.

"Why don't we cut the shit and get down to things? I'm not joining your kennel club, and you can go fuck yourself before I agree to be your breeding bitch."

"Huh," it replied, sounding not put out in the least. "I thought you'd be up for that. I mean, from listening to her chirping about it, I was under the assumption you and the Icon were rather fond of each other."

"Wait, she said that?" I shook my head. No, that was a distraction I didn't need. "Never mind that. Still not happening."

"Very well. If you're that dead set against it, I'm sure I can find some other species to breed her with."

"That's not what I meant."

"Then what did you mean?" it asked, sounding genuinely curious.

"Well, it's just ... you can't do that."

"Why not? She's my property to do with as I please."

"No, she isn't."

"I'm fairly sure your people are evolved enough to understand the concept of trade, but let me keep it simple for you anyway. Her essence was bartered to me in exchange for my services. I not only provided your world with the help that was requested, but I also empowered one of your kind to act as my Harbinger. If we're being fair, your realm made out pretty good in the deal. I have to say, the skin slug that reached out to me was one shrewd negotiator. Of course, I'd just woken from a long slumber, so perhaps I was a bit out of sorts, but far be it from me to renege on a deal struck in blood."

Amusing as it might be to see Gan's reaction at being referred to as a skin slug, I didn't allow myself to be distracted. "That's not a binding contract. We're talking one person out of billions. She doesn't speak for the rest of us."

"Maybe you should have considered that before allowing her to act as your delegate."

"We didn't delegate shit. She just did it."

"Then you should be proud. She showed real initiative. Would have made a humdinger of a harbinger, but maybe it's for the best she didn't get the role. I could sense the rebellious streak in that one a mile away. Besides, I like the one I have. She gives the absolute *best* belly scritches."

Almost as if on command, Harbinger Sally started giving the Beast a belly rub with her mutilated hand, smearing her blood across its fur.

"Oh yeah. Right there."

For fuck's sake. I was way too sober to be dealing with this shit.

"Sally doesn't want to be your harbinger." I pointed at her evil naked clone. "And no, this thing isn't her."

"Not yet, but soon," Harbinger Sally replied, as if remembering she had a voice. "With every day that passes her will becomes mine and mine becomes hers."

Oh, that didn't bode well. "Yeah, well, you're here and she's ... somewhere else. So maybe you two won't..."

"Won't matter," the Beast replied with a shrug. "Once you go back home they'll be together again – my sweet Harbinger, she who will welcome me with open arms so that I might get tummy rubs while making your world into the paradise it deserves to be."

I could barely comprehend the idiocy that was being spouted, but it did confirm my fears. Sally definitely had the same deal as me and the Wanderer. Here, we were separate beings, but when it came time to return we'd be put back together.

"Oh, and while we're at it," the Beast continued, "you can tell your friend that her plan won't work."

"Sally?"

It let out a chuckle. "That's what I like about you, Freewill. You're the cutest thing, even if you aren't that bright. Some are obsessed with intelligence in their pets, but not me. As I always say, dumb and loyal beats..."

"Get to the point, Gizmo."

"Fine. I was talking about the witch, the extra annoying one."

It must've meant Christy. "You mean the one who's been thwarting your every move?"

"Wow, did you actually use thwart in a sentence? Look at you using your words."

"I swear, I'm gonna..."

"Anyway, I'd call it more a temporary inconvenience than anything else, including the little distraction she has going right now. You can tell her I figured out her plan easily enough and that it won't work. Even if she manages to pull it off, I still have friends already in your world. And let me tell you, they were so happy to hear from me. I can't wait to catch up with them in person."

I held up a hand. "Won't happen, because we're going to stop you here."

It chuckled, the sound disturbingly high, almost like a mule braying. "I will admit that being banished prematurely would be a bit annoying, especially with the job only half done, but no. I wasn't talking about *that* plan. I meant her plan for your friend – my Harbinger."

Sally? "Uh huh. And what plan is that exactly?" I asked, wondering what other whackadoo conspiracy theories it believed in. Maybe I could look forward to a sermon about how the flat Earth made perfect sense.

"Didn't she tell you? It's her real plan to keep me from entering your world. You see, the witch doesn't believe her other idea will work, the one she told you about. But that doesn't matter, because she intends to sever your friend's connection back home, stranding her – my Harbinger – here for all eternity."

What?!

48

TERRAFORMING AN OPINION

I opened my mouth, fully prepared to tell this nutty little mogwai it was full of shit.

Except that wasn't necessarily true.

Christy herself had told me that killing Sally might very well still be on the table. I knew her well enough to know that hadn't been idle chitchat.

From the moment we'd met, it was obvious that Christy wasn't just some blowhard when it came to getting shit done. She could throw down as well as anyone. And when push came to shove she was more than capable of ending a fight – especially if her loved ones were threatened.

She and Sally were friends, no doubt about that. But we weren't just talking about Sally here. This was about everyone on Earth – and maybe even beyond. More importantly, it was about Tina. Hell, this crap had already touched her life. It was part of the reason we'd been forced to retreat to a fucking campsite in upstate New York.

Christy wasn't a means to an end sort of person, but I knew there came a point when practicality won out over constantly searching for another way. Much as I loved her, I didn't try to fool myself. If there was ever a choice between saving Tina's life and blasting me to hell, I knew to watch my ass.

417

That's why I found myself hesitating. What this little freak was claiming was actually far less than the nuclear option. Stranding Sally in another realm was, for all intents and purposes, both merciful and practical – especially compared to the alternative.

I had no idea what kind of fallout that might cause to this world, but that was a secondary concern. The bottom line was, it made sense. I had no logical reason to think this fucker was bullshitting me, especially since any such lie would be easy to uncover with a single question.

Fuck me!

"So what do you say?" the Beast asked, sounding way too upbeat for my liking. "Ready to join the winning team and help me finish my job here? As a bonus, I'll let you breed with whoever or whatever you please. Heck, I might even let my Harbinger give you some belly scritches too."

I glanced at Harbinger Sally's shapely form. In truth that wasn't the worst deal I'd ever been offered. Even so, I hadn't gone through all this shit just to end up as Kwicky Koala's lapdog. "Here's a counteroffer. Why not just stop and go back to wherever you came from?"

"Stop?"

"Yeah. From what I hear, you already have your own hellscape. Why fuck around with other worlds? They have enough problems of their own. Just go home, relax, and rule with an iron fist ... or paw."

It tilted its head as if actually considering this, although I knew that was too good to be true. "Well, for starters, my realm isn't a hellscape. That's just propaganda and I'd thank you not to judge my home without first seeing it for yourself. Secondly, I don't rule with an iron fist. I am the most benevolent of deities."

"I'm thinking survey says bullshit on that one."

"Oh? Tell me, Freewill, how many gods have you actually met?"

"Well ... um ... just one, at least so far."

"And what were they like?"

"Pretty awful actually."

"Exactly," it cried.

"Hold on. It was one of your..."

"That's the problem with gods, demigods, and other eldritch beings. They're all so gosh darned terrible. You're just made to think they're not because they're the ones handing down the rules. I mean, seriously, who's going to make themselves out to be the bad guy in their own scripture?"

"Point taken, but I'm not sure that proves anything."

"Think about how I must feel then. I finished up creation at home and then decided to rest, only to wake up to a multiverse full of nastiness. Petty gods, all happily abusing those beneath their heel. So all I'm doing is stepping in and making things right, just like any good neighbor would."

"Tell that to Sheila."

"Who?"

"The Icon."

"Ah, sorry. Too many pets, you see. Hard to remember all their names sometimes. But what of her? I take her with me to every single world I visit and let her run free. She's allowed to explore, make new friends, even breed with whoever she pleases. I'm simply expanding her horizons by showing her the multiverse."

"Oh really?" I bounced up and down a few times, feeling the disturbingly spongey ground beneath my feet. "And what about the pile of fucking corpses we're literally standing atop right now?"

"That's exactly my point. You saw the being these creatures worship, yes?"

I nodded.

"Was it preaching equality and happiness for all, or was it sitting around barking orders as if it was above the rest?"

"Well..." Okay, maybe the little shithead had a point there.

"That's the problem. Those you call gods have you brainwashed. They make you think you're standing up for your own cause, when in reality you're simply dying for theirs. I've seen your world, Freewill, both through the eyes of my Harbinger and the others I've sent ahead. It's an ugly place.

Wars, hatred, pettiness. It's enough to make me blush with shame. And worse, your gods have mostly abandoned you to continue the cycle."

"Yeah, well, I've met some of your friends. Hell, I can't even go down into the goddamned sewer anymore out of fear that they'll eat me."

"And do you enjoy being in the sewer?"

"No, not really."

"Then what's the problem?"

"I ... well..." Goddamn, I hated when they used logic.

"Just messing with you." The Beast let out another high-pitched chuckle. "I suppose I should apologize for that. Some of my friends can be a little excitable in their zeal to prepare the way."

"Your buddy Leviathan enslaved half the people I know!"

"And did I mention a wee bit over-enthusiastic at times?"

Fuck it. I tried.

This was going nowhere fast. I'd tried debating ethics with the Furby that time forgot, only to have it justify genocide by way of a Mister Rogers speech.

Now it was time to be more *proactive*.

Don't get me wrong, I most certainly planned to ask Christy if it was true that she'd been plotting against Sally behind my back, but the time had come to put these juiced up powers of mine to use.

As it once more launched into a speech extolling the virtues of joining Team Beast, I stepped in and took a swing – trying to be as quick and deliberate about it as I could.

Sadly, this thing must've rolled a twenty on its perception check, as it leapt from Harbinger Sally's arms in the instant before my fist connected.

Too bad for Evil Sally that she wasn't nearly as quick when it came to surprise rounds.

Crack!

Oops. I caught her in the sternum with my blow, sending her flying from the sheer force of the hit. On the upside, it's not like she was the real Sally. If that were the case, I might've been worried.

"Really, Freewill?" the Beast asked, staring up at me from where it stood. "Don't you think you're overreacting just a little?"

"The only thing little here is going to be the smear you make when I bust your head open."

I threw a kick, almost knocking myself off my feet as it nimbly sidestepped.

Goddamn, for something that looked like it had all the mobility of a stuffed animal, it sure as hell could be fast when it wanted to be.

Screw it. No more Mr. Nice Vamp. I unsheathed my claws, reminding myself that strength was only part of the equation. If I was amplified in one way then I was probably amped all over.

Sure, I wasn't exactly an expert at hand-to-hand combat, but I didn't need to be. Super powers were the great equalizer in all things. So, with that in mind, I launched into a frenzy of clawing, slashing, kicking, and anything else I could do to nail this little bugbear.

Pushing myself far beyond my normal limits, I found myself moving at a pace that was best described as ludicrous speed. Yet I might as well have been standing still for all the good it did.

Holy shit! It was like fighting Yoda, and I don't mean the doddering puppet from *The Empire Strikes Back*. No, this was the CGI micro-ninja from the prequels – dodging, weaving, and effortlessly leaping past every single attack I made.

All the little bastard was missing was a lightsaber.

It was almost inconceivable how fast the damned thing could move, like fighting a miniature troglodyte version of the Flash.

For every move I made, it had a counter – reminding me of Gan in her younger days. Equally maddening, was that it kept talking as I tried my damnedest to carve its fucking face off.

"You really need to watch your temper, you know that?"

Slash.

"All you're doing is embarrassing yourself."

Punch.

"Oh come now, Freewill. That one wasn't even close."

Grr!

As crazy powerful as I was in this world, it wasn't nearly enough. What I wouldn't have given to have a few vampires around to bite. There was no way of telling how much of a boost I'd have needed to match Speed Racer here, but any little bit would've helped. Sadly, the only one around was this creepy little Beanie Baby and...

Harbinger Sally!

Movement caught my periphery and I turned, seeing her form rise silhouetted by the dust cloud. My punch had sent her flying a good thirty feet, hard enough to have killed a normal person several times over.

She was far from normal, though. Harbinger Sally staggered once or twice before turning my way, the look on her face anything but happy as the air around her began to shimmer.

Oh crap.

I knew what came next, but maybe I could use that to my advantage.

"Now let's all calm down here," the Beast said, although whether it was to me or her I wasn't certain.

In truth, I didn't really care.

Instead, I hit the ground, throwing myself into the dirt while at the same time kicking out at the Beast. *Come on, dodge it...*

Yes!

The little gremlin leapt high over my attack in the same instant a shockwave of power exploded from Harbinger Sally's body.

The dust around me whipped into a maelstrom as the massive energy wave passed above my head. That was all well and good, but even better was when it slammed into the Beast, nailing it like a runaway truck and sending the little Garbage Pail Kid careening away into the gloom.

Oh yeah! Spider-man could dodge shit all he wanted, but occasionally Doc Ock got lucky and tagged his ass.

Hmm, maybe it was best not to identify with the bad guy in that analogy, but fuck it. This was no time to debate morality, not when evil Sally was likely reloading for another shot.

Fuck it. I doubted it would work, after all she wasn't a vampire, but nothing ventured... Besides, even if it failed, it's not like ripping her throat out would be any big loss.

I pushed off and raced her way, trying to ignore the give of the ground and how many dead Sasquatches I was kicking in the face.

This was no time for quips or other dumb fuckery, not with her powers. Hesitating for even a second too long could mean being diced like an onion. So instead, I grabbed her and pinned her arms as I willed my fangs to descend.

Then I dove at her neck, biting down hard and letting the blood flow free.

Two things happened simultaneously.

I felt something in my mind, that semi-familiar sensation of a door opening. Then Sally spoke up – except her voice was coming from somewhere *behind* me.

"Mind telling me what the fuck you're doing, Bill?"

49

FLIGHT MAKES RIGHT

It was about fucking time the others caught up.

I'd just kind of hoped Sally wouldn't be at their forefront, at least not while I was busy assaulting her naked body double. No way was this going to not look weird.

Speaking of weird, her blood tasted anything but normal. The best way to describe it was *old*. Not like curdled milk, but there was an odd aftertaste to it that somehow spoke of long years. I don't know how else to describe it other than it was like biting down on my grandparents' old plastic covered couch.

To say it didn't sit well in my stomach was an understatement.

Ugh!

"Bill?" This time it was Christy's voice calling to me.

I backed away from Harbinger Sally, my stomach churning as I vaguely registered the change in the light around us. Thankfully, the Harbinger didn't seem in much shape to retaliate, dropping to her knees and clutching at her ruined neck.

Whatever caused her to heal crazy fast back in our world seemed to be stunted here for whatever reason, not that I was complaining.

Either way, it seemed like we had a few seconds to spare.

I turned on unsteady feet, looking around. The dust was finally settling, revealing the sky above and leaving a clear space around us about fifty feet in diameter.

Either that shockwave had caused the change, or blasting the Beast had. Whatever the case, it was enough to let me see that I was no longer alone in this fight. All of my friends were there, ready to join the battle. Hell, even Turd had joined us.

"We interrupting something?" Sally, the real one, asked, one eyebrow raised.

"It's her," Sheila said. "That's the Harbinger."

"Kinda figured," my partner in crime replied, appearing way less freaked out than I probably would've. "Looks like she's the main course as well."

I grinned, happy to see them. "Just ... for ... the record. You taste terrible."

"Bite me."

"Already did."

Christy, fortunately, was far more intent on keeping us on track. "The Beast? Did you...?"

"I couldn't even ... touch the fucking thing." I pointed in the direction it had flown, the air there still too thick to see much. "It's over that way somewhere."

"Are you okay?"

"I'm fine. Just ate ... someone that disagreed with me."

Sally let out a laugh. "Serves you right, going for the cheap imitation instead of the name brand."

"As amusing as this all is," the Wanderer said, "might I suggest we do what we can to finish this post haste."

I nodded. "Like I said, it's over there. Keep your eyes peeled ... for a nuclear green koala. You can't miss it."

"A koala?" Sally asked.

"Trust me, I said the same thing."

"Whatever. Let's go kick this puppy."

"Not yet." Christy held up a hand. "V, if you would."

Before I could ask what she was talking about, I felt the

thrum of power inside my mind. They were about to cast a spell.

Both witches raised their hands, simultaneously screaming out an incantation – the words ringing in my ears. My lips began to move seemingly of their own accord, trying to repeat the spell echoing inside my brain. I actually had to bite my lip to stop it. Not knowing what might...

It was as if the heavens themselves opened up, serving an extra helping of wrath of God. Despite the sky being clear, an earthshaking barrage of lightning suddenly rained down where I'd pointed – a hundred yards wide and nearly as deep.

Holy fuckaroni!

My hair stood on end from both the proximity and sheer ferocity of the attack, kicking up even more dust and leaving the ground a charred ruin as the scent of burnt flesh rose into the air.

I'd seen whole covens of Magi in action before, but never anything like this – and all from just two witches.

Hell, a spell like that could've ended the war between the vamps and Sasquatches in a hot second, so maybe it was a good thing this was merely a fluke of being alive in the land of the dead. I, for one, didn't relish the thought of going up against a Magi with the power to drop a fucking nuclear strike on my head.

No. Not just them. I had this power now too.

Hell, I could feel it inside me, practically begging to be let loose. If anything, it's like my tongue wanted to repeat the words they'd just said – the magic calling to me, telling me to use it, to...

No!

Tempting as it was to bring the pain, I forced myself to remember what had happened when I tried to conjure a little bit of fire. Thankfully that had been before Christy's little speech about pushing beyond our limits. Who knew what could happen now?

Best to save it for home. At least then the damage would be limited.

Finally the barrage ended, leaving a wall of smoke

behind. Not for long, though, as Veronica whipped up a breeze to clear it.

"Holy shit," Sally cried, as dumbfounded as me by what we'd seen. "I think you got her."

"Don't be so sure," Christy said, pointing.

Sure enough, Veronica's wind spell cleared the path ahead of us, revealing countless burnt Sasquatch corpses – the dust atop them having been blown away by the assault.

"Oh my God."

I wasn't sure if V was talking about the field of screams we were looking at or the diminutive creature standing in the middle of it, its bright green fur barely singed.

"Well, that was rude," it opined, raising one paw to pick at its teeth.

Sally stepped to my side. "Please tell me that's not the Great Beast."

"'Fraid it is."

"Our life has gotta be some sort of bad comedy, right?"

"Not gonna argue."

"It ends here," Christy cried, ignoring our banter.

"Does it?" the Beast replied. "Not exactly the first time you've said that if I recall correctly."

"No, but it'll be the last," Sheila said, sheathed sword still in hand.

She and Christy shared a not insignificant glance, reminding me of what I'd been told.

Please don't let it be true. Before I could say anything, though, Turd let out a roar of rage from behind me.

I turned his way, fearing this was the moment he was gonna pull a fast one, but his ire appeared to be fully directed toward the Beast.

"Let's end this," Christy cried out. "For both our worlds!"

◆———✦———▶

"Be careful! It's..."

Really fast. I trailed off as everyone ignored me, racing into the fray while I stood there like a doofus.

Well, maybe not everyone. In the next instant I found myself eating dirt as Turd shoulder-checked me out of the way – letting out a chuckle as he joined the others in playing whack-a-beast.

Fucking asshole.

I tried to push myself back to my feet, but one extra-large stomach gurgle found me upchucking all over the ground ... and the dead Sasquatches entombed within.

Blecch!

Oh yeah, Evil Sally was definitely off the menu. Either she had some serious funk in her blood, or this place had fucked with my digestive tract more than I realized.

Considering the sizzle coming from the ground beneath me, I had a feeling which it was. Thank goodness for vampire healing, because otherwise I'd probably be wishing for a truckload of antacids right about then.

At least she was as much out of the fight as me, still on her knees with her hands pressed to her ruined throat. The only question was which of us would get back into the fray first.

For now, I couldn't do much more than wait for my stomach to stop doing flipflops. At least the last of the unnatural dust cloud had finally cleared – allowing me to see again in all directions.

That wasn't necessarily a good thing, as off in the distance large swaths of the forest were clearly ablaze – telling me the battle there had most certainly been joined. Alas, the Sasquatches would have to make do without any assistance, because shit was getting real on our end of things.

I spied the Wanderer, moving almost faster than my eyes could track as he attempted to tag the Beast. Too bad he wasn't having much more luck against the ridiculously nimble trash panda. However, unlike me, I saw he wasn't trying to beat it on his own.

In the next instant, he raced in and took another swing, only for the Beast to once more dodge it. This time, though, a stun blast was waiting where it landed – courtesy of Christy

– missing by millimeters as the Beast sidestepped at the last moment.

The strategy was obvious – a coordinated effort to attack it physically, forcing it to either eat the damage or move, while our ranged attackers waited to nail it whenever it dodged.

The only ones not engaged in this were Sally and Sheila. That kinda made sense. For all intents and purposes, juiced or not, Sally was human here. That put her at a significant disadvantage compared to the rest of us.

Sheila was the one I was more interested in, though, standing in front of Sally with sheathed sword still in hand. Her eyes were on the battle, hopefully looking for an opening to join in – as opposed to waiting for a signal to betray...

No!

I needed to push that shit out of my brain. I was probably doing exactly what the Beast had been hoping for – fucking me up with some psychological warfare 101 shit.

Beating it was our first and best option, and in order to do that we needed all hands on deck.

Fortunately, my stomach finally seemed to be calming down – meaning my rest break was over. *Thank you, vampire healing!*

Rising to my feet, I took a few experimental steps. Then, finding no urge to puke my guts out, I considered my options. Yeah, I could try to finish off Harbinger Sally, but there were two problems with that. The first was I had no idea what that might do to the real one. Equally as important, I wasn't even sure I *could* kill her. Ripping into her throat should've been fatal but obviously wasn't, so who was to say anything else I might do would be?

There was also the fact that I'd be abandoning my friends, letting them risk life and limb against the real big bad while I ignored them to play minion tag.

That settled it. I turned toward the battle with the Beast, trying to gauge where next our quarry might land as the Wanderer once again closed in.

Maybe there wasn't any need, though.

The Beast leapt high, flipping over my friend's attack. This time Veronica was on hand, readying a spell while the little gremlin was still in the air.

Yes! This was it. There was no way she was going to miss while it...

"*Turd crush you!*"

Gah! The stupid fuckhead leapt for the Beast, either too dumb to realize the strategy at play here or simply not caring.

Shit!

It was an instant for me to realize he was going to screw it all up. *Not on my watch.* There was barely any time to react but I didn't need much, not at the level I was currently operating at.

I kicked off, accelerating far past my normal limit, making it almost seem like the rest of the world was moving in slow motion. There came a crackle of power, telling me V had loosed her spell, but that was okay. In the next instant I slammed into Turd, tackling him out of the way so that...

"I appreciate the assist, Freewill!"

So that the Beast could use one paw to kick off my back, redirecting itself so that Veronica's spell hit nothing but empty space.

Shit!

Unfortunately, there wasn't much I could do about that as my momentum continued carrying me forward until I landed atop Turd, faceplanting in his midsection and getting a good long sniff of his rancid crotch.

Yeah, that was about par for the course.

"*Get off Turd!*"

His meaty hands grabbed me by the neck and yanked me up until I was staring the angry ape in the face.

"Knock ... it ... off," I gasped. "I'm ... trying ... to help."

"*Turd not want stupid Freewill's help.*"

Oh enough of this shit.

It was painfully obvious that Turd's version of helping would only do the opposite. With him moving at a fraction of the speed the Wanderer and I were capable of, the chances of him doing anything other than getting in the way were slim to none.

So, I slapped his hands off me, allowing myself a moment of satisfaction at how easy it was. Ah, if only every meeting with this asshole had been like this.

Oh well. I gave Turd just enough time for his dull-witted eyes to register surprise, then I hauled off and decked him in the jaw – dropping the stupid ape as brutally as Cathy Hoffman had dumped my ass during sophomore year of high school.

If only he'd been the main target of this fight.

"If you're quite through manhandling our allies," the Wanderer called, "I could use some assistance with ... oof!"

I turned at the sound of his voice, only to see him go flying past me to land in a heap on the ground.

Oh fuck.

I guess it was only a matter of time before ninja Teddy Ruxpin got tired of the razzle dazzle and decided to go on the offense.

Sure enough, the Beast stood there dusting its paws off – looking disturbingly non-threatening despite having just coldcocked my friend, a vampire with probably ten times my fighting skills.

It let out a huff of annoyance. "I have to say, I'm starting to get a tiny bit miffed here."

Before I could contemplate what we could possibly do to this thing, other than get our blocks knocked off, Christy and Veronica began to glow an angry red.

"Now!" the former shouted.

The Beast turned to face them – no doubt ready to dodge whatever they threw at him.

Except it wasn't an attack.

The air around them shimmered – a glamour! Then it dropped, revealing the ruse had been a color coded one. The power they'd been gathering hadn't been offensive.

The Beast inclined its head, looking adorably confused as a purple force dome at least fifty feet wide appeared around it.

"I see," it said, sounding less than impressed. "And your plan is what – to hold me here indefinitely?"

"No," Christy replied. "Just long enough." She inclined her head, causing the force bubble to shrink to a third its original size before turning my way. "Come on, Bill, it's almost time to go."

"It is?" It was a stupid question. Hell, I'd wanted nothing more than to leave since the second I'd found her.

"Just as soon as we finish this."

She didn't need to tell me twice.

I began to understand her strategy. The force bubble limited the space in which the Beast could move – space that was now entirely controlled by Christy.

It was, in essence, like shooting fish in a barrel.

Not particularly sporting, but fuck it. Anything to take this fun-sized grizzly bear down.

Speaking of which, it struck the side of the bubble with one paw, a love tap at best, but I could feel the vibrations from where I stood. Whatever they were planning, we didn't have long.

With that in mind, I double-timed it back to where she waited. All I had to do was focus on my tether and give it a couple tugs with my mind, then it would snap the two of us back home. That was it. The extra ethereal weight of bringing a passenger along would be Liz and Tina's signal to start reeling everyone else in.

As I made it to where Christy waited, she turned to Veronica. "You first. Go!"

"No! Not without..."

"I can handle this next part," she told the younger witch, "but it'll take everything I have, which means I need to close myself off. So go."

"But..."

"I'm serious, V."

Christy's coven-mentor voice wasn't much different from her mom voice. I could see Veronica's resolve start to crumble. She turned to me as if seeking confirmation.

I had maybe a moment to consider this at most, but the

choice was obvious. I chose to believe in Christy, so I gave our friend a single nod.

That was it. In the next instant, Veronica's body grossly extended – almost as if she were going to warp speed. Then she disappeared in a quick flash of light.

"Well, that was certainly wild," Sally said, wide-eyed.

"I'll say," I replied, just as the beast leapt at us.

It struck the side of the force dome like some sort of fuzzy cruise missile, causing the very ground beneath our feet to rumble.

Holy fuck!

"That won't hold it for long," Christy said.

"You don't say." Fuck it. We could quip later. "Whatever you're going to do, now would be a good time."

"Not me ... *her.*"

I followed her gaze back toward where Sheila stood.

Shit! I'd almost forgotten about her in the confusion. If we left now, she'd be stuck as the Beast's slave. "Wait! We need to figure out a way to bring her with us. We need to..."

I trailed off, however, as she finally drew the sword from its sheath.

Blazing white light ignited at the very tip of the weapon, traveling down the blade and enveloping Sheila's body with an aura of pure faith magic – lighting her up like an avenging angel.

All at once it was clear why Christy had wanted me to bring the sword.

The Icon was back, and she did not look happy.

50

BEASTLY BURDENS

"My God!" Sheila cried. "I'd ... I'd forgotten how it felt."

"Now!" Christy shouted from alongside me. "We need to finish this."

I expected Sheila to turn on her master, using her rediscovered powers to slice it up like a Thanksgiving turkey.

Instead, she glanced my way for a single second, no more, enough time for me to register the regret in her eyes.

What the?

Christy once more gestured with her hands. However, instead of something horrific happening to the beast, the shine of silverish light caught my attention – causing me to turn my head and realize Sally's tether had suddenly become visible. But why?

Sadly, the answer was obvious.

Oh no. Please not that. Don't...

"I hate to say I told you so, Freewill," the Beast said from within its prison. "But I definitely told you so."

I ignored it, turning to face Christy. "Don't do this. You don't have to..."

"I'm sorry, Bill," she said, tears in her eyes as she grabbed hold of my arm. "This is the only way to be certain."

Realization hit. Christy hadn't wanted the sword because

it was capable of killing the Beast. Hell, that should've been obvious, since Sally's power cancelled out Tom's back in our world. But the blade, infused with the power of faith itself, was still formidable. It might not have been able to kill a god, but that didn't mean it wasn't capable of severing someone's tether.

"There has to be another way!"

"Even if there is, we can't afford to let this opportunity pass."

"The hell we can't!"

I tried to pull away, but she was ready for that. I didn't even make it a single step before a jolt of energy passed from her hand into me – knocking me to the ground as blue electricity arced across my body.

Fuuuuck!

None of those still standing were stupid in the least. Even as Sheila turned, sword raised, Sally was on the move – obviously realizing what was happening.

She took a swing, going for a cheap shot, not that I could blame her in the least.

Regrettably, Sheila's newly reactivated faith aura, though harmless to humans, was enough to blunt the blow. And with Sally's evil other half separated from her, she lacked the power to slice through it.

Didn't mean she couldn't use it to her advantage, though.

Christy turned her way and loosed another stun spell, but Sally had stepped in close to Sheila – the faith aura enveloping her enough to negate the spell.

Smart.

"Just ... for the record," Sally gasped, trying to grapple with my ex, "I don't blame you for this, but ... oof ... that doesn't mean I have to like it."

Sadly, scrappy as Sally was in a fight, she wasn't a match for her opponent's martial prowess. Sheila spun, dropping low as she swept Sally's legs out from beneath her.

Then, before my partner in crime could even hit the ground, Sheila continued the attack – turning and bringing down her blade.

She wasn't aiming at my friend, though.

There came a spark of bright light as the sword connected, and then the tether connecting Sally back to our world abruptly vanished.

No!

Throwing all sense of rationality to the wind, I reached deep inside myself looking for that spark of magic, not sure how I was going to use it, only that I needed to do something to...

Except the door connecting my mind to Christy's was now closed.

That was why she'd sent Veronica back before the rest of us.

Christy was a full witch. She didn't need to receive help from another Magi, nor did she have to share it. With Veronica gone, there was no one else for me to *sync up* with.

Unless...

I tried to reach for the vape pipe with my quivering arms, knowing it could make up for my magical shortcomings and then some, but then stark realization hit. It was pointless to even try. I'd chosen to ignore the warning that had been given to me, and now it was too late. The deed was done.

Sheila lowered the sword and stepped away as Christy released me from her spell – leaving me to glare at her from the ground.

She wiped her eyes and met my gaze, refusing to look away. In her face I saw regret, yes, but also resolution hard as steel. "I'm sorry. I really am, but I can't let what happened here happen to our world. I just can't. You can both hate me if you want. It doesn't matter so long as my baby girl is safe."

Goddamn. This would've been so much easier had it been Gan or any of a hundred other assholes. But it wasn't. This was Christy. She was everything to me. How could I possibly hate her knowing her motives?

This was her Kobayashi Maru and, much like Spock, she'd simply determined that the needs of the many outweighed the needs of the few. Sheila too.

Neither of them were wrong, but that didn't mean I would cheer their decision either.

Instead, I stood and made my way over to Sally – offering her a hand to help her up. "You okay?"

"Yeah. Nothing bruised but my pride."

"Well now, that was certainly something," the Beast remarked from still inside the force bubble. "But hey, what's a little betrayal among friends?"

"Oh shut up," Sally snapped, turning Christy's way.

I readied myself for whatever happened next, knowing Sally didn't exactly have a reputation based on forgiving and forgetting. However, she surprised me.

"Do me a favor, will you? Raise Tina well and don't let her take shit from anyone."

"I promise," Christy replied, the tears now freely falling.

"And be sure to let her know her Aunt Sally loves her."

"Always."

"All right, well, I'm not one for long goodbyes, so why don't you guys get the fuck out of here while the going is good."

"Wait..."

"It's fine, Bill," she replied. "I think we all knew it would come down to this. And let's face facts, this is a much better option than some of the others on the table."

Silence descended for several long seconds, at least until Christy said, "No. We can't go. Not yet."

"Listen," Sally replied. "I get it. There's no hard feelings. So please..."

"Saving our world was my first priority. It always was, but that doesn't mean I won't at least try to save this one." She turned to face the Beast, compressing her hand into a fist and causing the force dome to shrink again. "Don't think I've forgotten about you."

"I'd be insulted if you had," it replied, staring at her with its big eyes.

The force dome shrank in on itself until it was barely twice the size of the Beast, robbing the little mogwai of its speed. Nevertheless, it was stupid to think it was helpless, not with its power. Yet, despite everything, it merely stood there, as if curious to see what would happen next.

Christy gestured again, much as she'd done to Sally when she'd exposed her tether. What appeared around the Beast, though, was like nothing I'd seen before. Instead of a single strand, its tether was more like a massive interwoven chain made of crimson fire – with hundreds, perhaps thousands of tiny tendrils leading away from it in every direction.

I remembered what Christy had said. Our tethers acted as a way home for us, but for a creature of the Beast's power, they were more like an anchor – keeping this small portion of their essence connected to this place.

"Ah, I see," the Beast said, glancing at it curiously. "So that's your plan? You want to deny this world everything I'm offering it."

"Everything and more. Because once you're gone I'm going to make sure every other world you've invaded learns how to fight back."

"Invaded is such a messy term. I prefer liberated."

"And I prefer you never again dirty those I love with your foul influence."

It folded its ears back and blinked at her. "Words hurt, you know."

"I only wish I could make them hurt more." She turned toward Sheila. "If you'd kindly do the honors."

"It would be my pleasure." Sheila stepped forward, eyes blazing and sword at the ready. Despite the sheer thickness of the Beast's tether, I had a feeling she was determined to saw through it with everything she had. But first she turned and met my eyes. "I'm sorry, Bill, for so many things. I know I can't ask your forgiveness, but please ... try not to think too badly of me."

Before I could say anything, she raised the sword high above her head – preparing to sever the Beast's connection here once and for...

"That won't work," it said, idly picking its teeth.

"Oh, I think it will," Christy replied.

"Then you'd be wrong. Hate to say it, but you forgot one small ingredient in this recipe."

"Really? You'll be banished from this world while the Earth Harbinger is left stranded here, where she has no power to call you forth."

"Maybe true on the first," it said with a shrug, "but a bit less so on the second."

"And how is that?"

The Beast pointed one of its tiny claws Sally's way. "Because that skin-slug over there, charming as she might be, isn't my Harbinger."

"What?"

"Yeah, you might want to get your eyes checked. I hear myopia is a common ailment with sub-creatures your age."

Oh shit! In all the confusion we'd completely forgotten about Harbinger Sally.

I glanced over my shoulder only to find her back on her feet, looking ready to stir shit up again. *Fuck!*

"Everyone down, now!" I dove at Christy, tackling her to the ground.

Thankfully, our Sally knew the drill. She hit the dirt a split second after we did.

That left only two others standing – Sheila and the Great Beast – as the air around Harbinger Sally once more began to ripple.

No!

Sheila raised her sword defiantly, her aura flaring around her as if this were a regular attack – apparently not realizing that Sally's power could cut through faith magic like a hot knife through butter.

Sadly, I was a second too late in crying out a warning.

The shockwave forced my head down for a moment as I tried to protect Christy from its fury. Then there came a brilliant flash of light from my periphery, nearly blinding me.

When the spots finally cleared from my eyes, Sheila was nowhere to be seen. *Oh no!*

Sadly, the force bubble around the Beast was likewise

gone – shredded by the Harbinger's power, while passing harmlessly over her master's diminutive frame.

"Ah, so much better," the Beast said, dusting off its paws and stretching.

Double crap!

"What did you do to her?" I snapped, pushing myself to my feet.

"*Me*? I was just standing here minding my own business."

I was about to fire back at the little weasel when Christy stood up next to me. "Thanks for the save," she said sheepishly.

I threw her some side-eye, albeit not entirely unkindly. "Just because I'm not happy with you right now doesn't mean I love you any less."

She opened her eyes wide, but the Beast was faster on the draw.

"Aww," it replied. "That is so sweet."

"Nobody asked your opinion."

"Oh very well, I suppose you're right. Back to business then." It looked past me. "If you'd be so kind, my Harbinger, it's time to return and prepare for my arrival. On the upside, I think you'll find your body a bit less crowded when you get back."

Wait ... return? *Fuck!*

And just like that it all became clear. I'd already deduced that Sally and the Harbinger were no different than me and the Wanderer. We'd both been separated upon our arrival. But, if the Wanderer had his own tether back, then that meant so did...

"She has a tether too!" I cried, turning. "We need to stop her before she... Argh!"

Something small and furry slammed into my back with roughly the force of a fucking freight train, driving me into the ground.

My spine shattered – sending bone shards slicing into my favorite organs in the second before I lost all sensation below the waist.

"Sorry about that, Freewill," the beast whispered from

atop me. "I really am, but I can't have you interfering in this part."

"Bill!"

"Her either."

I heard the hesitation in Christy's voice. She couldn't blast the Beast, not without hitting me, too, which would almost certainly happen thanks to this thing's speed and agility.

In that same instant, however, I felt the door within my mind open a crack, telling me I had access to Christy's power again – as well as her blessing to finally use it.

Maybe all wasn't as lost as I'd thought.

51

SCRATCHING THAT LICH

I tried not to overthink it – instead focusing on that lightning spell from earlier, the one my lips had tried to repeat all on their own.

Earlier, when I'd synced with Veronica, I'd inadvertently gotten some of her memories and vice versa. Hopefully, the same could be said of more practical stuff than who was whacking it to who.

Come on ... bring the lightning.

Yes! Though the words were a garble inside my memories, I sensed they were still there regardless. I didn't question how or why. I simply latched onto them – silently mouthing the spell as quickly as I could, until I felt the power collecting inside of me and then...

ZAP!!!

Red hot electricity coursed through my body, causing me to flop around like a fish out of water – my nerves on fire as surely as if I'd bitten down on a power line.

Needless to say, it hurt – *a lot.*

"As fascinating as that was to watch," the Beast said, now alongside me, "might I recommend working on your aim a bit."

"T-thanks for the tip."

"Anytime, buddy."

Oh yeah, I definitely needed to remember this moment when I got back – especially if I got the itch to try out magic again without proper instruction first.

On the upside, at least my broken back ensured I only felt half my body burning with electrical fire. Unfortunately, none of it was going to help me stop the Harbinger from returning to our world, where she could take over Sally's body completely.

"Oops, sorry, gotta run," the Beast said.

What?

I spied a blur of movement from my left, something headed at high speed toward where Harbinger Sally stood.

The Wanderer! He was back in the fight.

For about a second anyway.

He made it close enough to take a swing, knocking the Harbinger off balance in the moment before a flash of green fur intercepted him. The Beast slammed into the Wanderer like a bus, sending them both tumbling in the dirt.

"Christy," I cried. "Now! While it's.."

"Don't worry. I've got this."

I felt more than saw the buildup of energy as she stood over me, preparing to do whatever she could to take the Harbinger out before she could escape.

"Not so fast. Catch!"

Shit! As fast as the Wanderer was, he might as well have been a Cheeto-fingered couch potato compared to the Beast. It grabbed him by the leg, spun, and flung him like a Tomahawk missile. I craned my neck to watch as he sailed over my head, helpless to do anything as Christy was forced to go on the defensive or risk having every bone in her body shattered.

She managed to partially erect a force dome, but there hadn't been time to brace it. The Wanderer bounced off the construct with the sharp *crack* of multiple bones breaking. Sadly, the impact was enough to overload the spell – driving Christy to the ground and leaving her dazed.

That left me to do something. Sensation began to return to my legs as my spine knitted itself back together – an unpleasant sensation at best – but I had a feeling I was still better suited to flopping on the ground than launching myself into the fray.

Didn't mean I wasn't going to try, though.

I extended my claws and used them to pull myself forward, my strength enough to allow a reasonable pace, at least until I looked up and found the Beast staring down at me – or more like eye to eye. The fucker really was small.

"I gotta hand it to you, Freewill. You don't give up easily."

"Yeah, I'm annoying like that."

"Not to me. Personally, I like gumption. Still, I can't have you mucking with my plans. Harbinger, if you would..."

"It would be my pleasure..."

"Oh no you don't!"

What the?

The ground at the Harbinger's feet seemed to come to life, making me wonder if Humbaba had invoked some sort of curse ensuring that this realm's dead didn't rest easily.

A moment later, though, I caught a flash of yellow and saw multiple eyeballs open up.

Glen!

Holy crap, I'd totally forgotten about the little blob during the course of the battle, assuming he'd either gotten distracted by a shiny rock or had maybe headed back home early to retrieve his camera – neither of which would've surprised me in the least.

I realized now the others had been saving him as our secret weapon – leaving him to slither up close for an ambush, while the rest of us were jumping around like methed-up jackrabbits.

He once again assumed a disturbingly humanoid shape as he proceeded to wrap his *arms* around Harbinger Sally's naked form – probably giving himself a thrill in the process. Oh well, who was I to begrudge him copping a feel against an evil interstellar entity?

"Go, Glen!"

Human-shaped or not, I doubted he was much of a

threat. But hopefully he could at least prove to be distraction enough to keep her from concentrating on her tether.

"Oh, I don't think so," the Beast said with a disapproving tone. "This won't do at all."

It turned and launched itself at my friend – looking almost comical with its still visible massive tether in tow, even if there was nothing remotely funny about this.

Much to my surprise, though, Glen was ready for it.

His body lost its humanoid form, quickly stretching into a disgusting blanket of snot in the instant before the Beast collided with him – engulfing it in goo and eyeballs as they landed upon the ashen ground.

"You might want to hurry," he cried. "I don't think I can hold it for long." Sure enough, one of the beast's tiny claws ripped through Glen's slime. "Ooh, that was certainly unpleasant."

It was now or never. Hopefully my stupid legs were ready to start taking commands again, whether they wanted to or not.

I pushed myself to my feet, my legs shaky but holding. Thank goodness for vamp healing. Now to hope they gave me enough speed to make it there before...

"Ladies first!"

Sally stepped past me, running toward the Harbinger – even though I had no idea what she could do in this situation.

The Harbinger turned and grinned as she saw her body double approach, no doubt thinking the same thing. She was battered and bloody, but unbowed as my friend stopped directly in front of her.

"You're too late," the Harbinger said. "I will return to your world so that I might offer it up to our master."

She was right. I could see the optical illusion of her body starting to elongate, the light around her beginning to distort. She'd activated her tether. It was only a matter of moments before she was snapped back to...

"Your master, not mine," Sally said. "And the only offer you're getting is a coupon ... for a free lobotomy!"

What?

Sally pulled something from the belt of her pants – a crude stone knife. Wait! It was the one from the hut. She must've taken it with her when we...

None of that mattered, however, as she stepped in and slammed the blade into the side of the Harbinger's skull, driving it in deep.

Holy fuck!

Sally tried to step back, but the Harbinger's hands spasmed, clutching hold of her.

"Stop her!" she cried. "Cut the tether beforrrrre weeeeeeeeee..."

Her words hung in the air as they both disappeared – their bodies stretching out and intertwining before vanishing completely in a flash of light.

What the...?

It was an instant for me to realize what had happened. Sally's way back home may have been cut, but in wrestling with her evil doppelganger while her tether had activated, she'd been dragged back as well.

Oh no!

Two souls carried back home via one tether. That was our signal to start bringing everyone back, our safe word if you will. Once those on the other end sensed them, that was it. We had minutes left at most, maybe less.

"Everyone get ready! It's time to go!"

I turned toward where Christy was just now pulling herself from the ground, only to hear a squelching noise from the direction where both Sallys had vanished.

Knowing I shouldn't, but unable to stop myself, I looked to see the Beast tear its way out of Glen.

"Ouch!" my roommate complained as the Beast brushed an eyeball off its shoulder.

It turned my way, snorting in annoyance. Then, in the next second, I was pinned down beneath it – its speed and strength simply incredible to behold.

God, what a joke. I'd thought we'd stood a chance against

it, amped as we were, but in reality it had just been playing with us.

Case in point as I tried to shove it off. It turned its head and neatly sheared the fingers from my right hand with its teeth – the action so quick and clean that it took a good second or two for my nerve endings to register it.

Fuuuuuck!

"I tried to be nice, Freewill," it said, spitting my digits from its mouth. "But even I have to admit that really chuffed my fur."

"If that chuffs your fur, just wait until you see this!"

Both of us turned at the sound of the familiar voice.

No way!

Sheila stood about twenty feet away, looking bruised and battered, but somehow still alive – or dead-alive anyway. Regardless, she was still with us, sword in hand ... mostly. Half the blade had been cleaved off. Broken or not, though, it still glowed with the white hot fire of faith.

Better yet, she was looking down at the massive red chain that served as the Beast's tether to this world.

"No!" it cried as she raised the weapon.

Too bad I wasn't letting it go without a fight, meager as that threat might be. Even as it spun, no doubt readying to launch itself at her, I slapped out with my ruined hand – knocking its stubby legs out from under it.

It landed atop me, not much heavier than a children's toy, in the same instant she brought down the broken blade.

Despite the seemingly impossible girth of its tether, the sword cut through it like it was made of paper – sparking red and white fire as it severed the Beast's toehold to this world.

Whoa!

The ground began to rumble as the Beast clambered to its feet on top of me.

"Darn it all," it said, sounding only moderately put out as it looked down at me. "Don't be looking all smug, Mister. You and I are going to have a long chat about this. I can assure you of thaaaaaatttttttttt."

Its last word continued to echo as the Beast simply imploded atop me – its body folding in on itself, collapsing until it was a marble sized dot hanging in the air right above me.

Well, okay then.

Unfortunately, it was still too early to call this a victory, as there came a hiss of air, and then the *marble* began sucking things into it like some sort of miniature black hole.

So much for this being a mark in the win column.

52

BACK TO WHERE IT ALL BEGAN

I won't lie. I may have come perilously close to shitting my pants as the tiny singularity floating above me started sucking shit in.

First was the massive tether where Sheila had split it – somehow sucked into that tiny opening back to wherever the fuck the Beast called home.

I immediately began to claw at the ground for purchase – being only partially successful as I was missing half my fingers.

Fortunately, rational thought took hold as I realized I wasn't being dragged to my demise – something that would've been pretty inescapable considering my proximity to the miniature vortex of doom.

The only thing being sucked in was its tether ... or make that *tethers*.

All those mini-tethers that had been connected to the main chain began to pull taut as they were likewise dragged in – like strands of impossibly long spaghetti.

On and on it went, almost making me forget I was on a timetable myself, at least until an eight foot long cockroach monster sailed over my head, again making me almost soil myself, only to be instantly compressed and sucked into the black hole.

Holy shit!

I could only stare wide-eyed as the same happened to more monstrosities, then even more – a seemingly endless parade of freaks being dragged in over my head.

"You need to move!"

"Huh?" I replied, still awe-stricken as two pairs of hands hooked beneath my arms and started to drag me away.

I looked up to find both Christy and the Wanderer had come to my aid.

"Are you okay, Freewill?"

I held up my injured appendage. "Let's just say I could use a hand."

"I take it you'll live."

"Is this what I think it is?" I asked, watching as more and more creatures were dragged away.

"The Great Beast has been banished from this realm," Christy confirmed, stepping to my side. "Everything it brought here, those still attached to it, they're all being pulled back as well."

"Alas, it would appear they're not the only ones facing eviction."

I looked up to find the light around the Wanderer had started to distort.

"Oh crap!" I scrambled to my feet and turned toward Christy. "I need you to get over here now! There's no time to explain. Our failsafe. Sally inadvertently triggered it. It's time to go."

Rather than step into my arms, though, she asked, "Are you sure?"

"What? Why the fuck wouldn't I be sure?"

"What I did... What I tried to do to Sally. It's..."

"It's fine. Even if it's not, we'll deal with it after we're back home. Hell, you can buy the first round if it'll make you feel better."

"I..."

"Good luck, Freewill," the Wanderer said. "See you back in our bodddddyyyyy."

Then he was sucked away, back to where we'd come from. Now for...

When I turned back, though, I found Christy had actually taken a step away. "Don't wander off. It's almost time to..."

"Time," she replied, watching as the Beast's horde continued to be sucked away. "That's the problem. So much has passed. I feel almost like ... I'm a different person now. The woman I used to be, the one you remember, she wouldn't have done what I did. She..."

"Sure she ... *you* would. You've always been willing to make the hard choices. The only thing that's different is you've been stuck in this shit hole, which has probably skewed your perception a bit."

"That's putting it mildly."

"My point is, before you left you told me that a hard choice might need to be made. Yes, I would've preferred if you'd been upfront about it and..."

I paused as the legion of monsters continued flying past us, realizing some of the faces I saw were far less freakish than others.

The vampires Gan sacrificed. And among them – Komak.

Holy shit!

And then they were gone, sucked through the portal where their master had disappeared.

I couldn't help but feel pity for the poor bastards. They hadn't signed up for this. None of them had foreseen the cruel fate waiting for them, including...

Sheila!

The flow into the micro-portal was starting to slake, telling me it was almost over. Beyond it, I saw her – still standing there watching it happen, her expression unreadable, as if she was ... waiting her turn.

No!

Sure enough, her tether was still visible, attached to her while the other end...

"What an intriguing sensation."

What the? I turned toward the voice, spying Glen. He'd

pulled himself back together, just as his body began to elongate in an entirely different way.

"See you back home, Freeeeewwwwwwiiiiiiilllllll."

And then he was gone, too, leaving only me. There was no time to be nice about things. "Get your ass over here now!"

"I don't know, Bill..."

"I *do*! There's a little girl out there who just wants her mother back. That's all that matters. We can sort out the rest in good time."

She hesitated for a second as if unsure. Then she took hold of my hand and stepped in, wrapping her arms around my neck and looking me in the eye. "All right. Let's go home."

"That's what I wanted to hear."

"One last thing. Before we go, I want you to see the truth."

"The truth?"

"About..."

"Bill!" Sheila cried out, catching my attention just as the parade of monsters began to die down. "Catch!"

Huh?

"It may be scuffed, but I think its new owner still needs it." With that, she threw the sword my way, sending it tumbling through the air to land in the ground at my feet.

I stared at it for a moment, then back at her, realizing that the slack of her tether was starting to be sucked into the portal as well. *Shit!*

"It was so good to see you," she said, wiping her eyes. "All of you. I – I won't forget your faces this time. I promise. I..."

Fuck it!

"Don't ask any questions. Just follow me." I let go of Christy and grabbed the sword – ignoring the burning pain in my hand as I raced forward, watching as Sheila's tether began to grow taut.

In that same instant, the light around me began to distort.

Not yet!

Either way, this was gonna be close.

I ducked beneath the last of the cockroach monsters just as Sheila was pulled off her feet, unsure if the weapon would work in my hands but determined to try anyway.

I swung the sword. *Come on!*

Somehow I managed to miss her legs – slicing through the tether at the very last second. She dropped to the ground just as the Beast's portal closed up with a *schlup* of hissing air.

"What?" she cried, looking down at herself as if unsure what had happened. "H-how am I still here? What does it...?"

"It means you're free," I replied, grinning. "As for this place, it's the land of the honored dead. It's about damned time there was a resident who lived up to that title, one who... *ugh*."

My body suddenly felt all weird, almost like it was made of water.

"Go!" she said. "Before it's too late."

"I..."

"I know, Bill. I've always known. Thank you! You saved me back when I was alive, and now again when..." She wiped her eyes, looking like she wanted to say more, but we were out of time. "Just go!"

I threw her one last smile before turning back. Fortunately, Christy was hot on my heels.

I held out my arms as I stepped toward her. This was it. It was finally time to go home, where we could take some time to heal and make sense of all of this shit.

Sheila called out from behind me again, but this time her voice was distorted – as if I was hearing her from far away.

"Biiiiillll!"

Probably one last goodbye before...

"Loooooook Ouuuuuutttttt!"

Look out? For what?

Christy's fingers touched my outstretched hands as my eyes met hers – noting the light must've been playing tricks again, as she once more seemed to have a streak of white through her hair over worry lines that stretched across her...

Then she was pulled from my grasp – knocked aside as something massive and hairy stepped in front of me and wrapped its meaty hands around my throat.

"Great Beast is gone. Turd has done his duty, which means now Turd can finally kill you!"

"W-uh?! N - no!"

Sadly, that was all I was able to say before I found myself being whisked away. Despite the speed at which I flew, it felt like slow motion, giving me an agonizingly long view of Christy as she reached out for me – her hand just outside my grasp no matter how hard I tried.

I'D EPILOGUE THAT FOR A DOLLAR

I screamed without a voice for what seemed like an eternity, reaching out my non-corporeal hands for the woman I'd utterly failed to save.

Then my head clonked down against something and I found myself lying upon the rocky ground with the remains of Sheila's sword next to me.

"I think we got him! He's back."

"B-back?" I sputtered, the room around me still spinning.

"What the fuck did you do to my sword?"

"S-Sheila?" I replied, still trying to get my bearings.

"You high or something, asshole? Hey, wait a second. Where's Christy?"

Christy?!

I sat up, trying to push the dizziness away, but was only partly successful.

Easy, Freewill, a familiar voice said from inside my head. *Take a moment to acclimate.*

W-Wanderer?

Indeed. And, though I must admit it was nice to have my own body for a time, it's good to be back.

He ... was inside my mind again? That meant...

I shook my head and looked around. From what I could

tell, everyone was present and accounted for – including Petunia, curled up on the ground unconscious and shaking. Poor cat probably had PTSD thanks to us. Still, that was of minor concern as I laid my eyes on Sally, noting her hair was back to being nuclear green. "Are you...?"

"I'm fine, or at least I think I am," she replied, looking over my injuries, "which is more than I can say for you."

"Huh?"

"Here," Zoe said, leaning down and holding out a canteen. "Take this. You probably need it more than I do."

My nose immediately identified the contents as blood, causing my stomach to gurgle. Trying to resist the urge to bite into the side, I graciously accepted it and took a long swig. That did the trick. Within seconds, my thoughts began to clear.

"Okay, so where's Christy?" Sheila ... err ... Tom demanded once again. "Is there some kind of, I dunno, delayed reaction we're waiting for?"

"I ... don't think so," Liz said. "It ... doesn't work ... that way."

I turned to find her leaning against the wall of the cave. She looked utterly haggard, as if she'd given everything she had to give and more. "How long were we gone?"

"An hour maybe," she replied. "Felt a lot longer, though."

Sally shook her head. "You have no idea."

Only an hour? Then I remembered the time difference Humbaba had told us about. That must've been it. Still, neither he nor his errand boy Turd were important right then, not compared to... *Turd!*

Shit!

I looked around again, half expecting to see a half-ton of angry ape skulking in the corner. "D ... did anyone else come back with me?"

"Obviously not, asshole," Tom snapped. "Why do you think I keep asking?"

Oh God!

That's when it truly hit me – the full weight of my failure.

I turned my eyes toward the Source – where Tina still stood, staring into it as if waiting for her mother to return from the abyss. "I'm so sorry. I tried, but ... I-I couldn't... I..."

"Seriously? That's your excuse? You had one job. One fucking job!"

"It's all right, father," Tina interrupted, turning to face us. "Everything is as it's supposed to be."

"What the hell does that even mean?"

She ignored him, meeting my eyes instead. Guess her older self was still there calling the shots. "You didn't fail, Uncle Bill. I need you to understand that. All is as it should be. As it was *meant* to be."

"But..."

"She's not alone anymore. You saw to that. Mom's where she needs to be, and she has help now ... more than she realizes."

Help? Does she mean Sheila? "How do you...?"

"I ... spoke to her, just now."

"You did?" Tom and I both asked.

"Yes, and she's sorry for what happened."

"Sorry?" Tom replied. "It's not her fault this asshole fucked up."

Tina continued to ignore him, her oddly mature gaze still locked on me. "She doesn't want you to feel guilty or think you did anything wrong. She needs you to be strong now. We all do."

Tears began to fall from my eyes. "I ... I don't know if I can be."

Rather than turn away in disgust at my weakness, though, Tina smiled. "*I* know. They do too. That's why they asked me to give you something that'll help."

They?

Before I could say anything, Tina stepped forward and placed a finger to my forehead. There came a flash of yellow light before my eyes and then ... that was it. I didn't feel any different. If anything, I...

In the next moment, however, Tina's eyes rolled back into her head and she collapsed.

"Shit!"

Fortunately, both Veronica and I were there to catch the tyke before she could hit the ground.

She helped me lay her down and then checked her over. "It's okay. She's just overexerted herself, that's all."

"Guess even a miracle child can have limits," Liz remarked before shaking her head. "Okay, that's enough. We should probably get going..."

"Wake her up," I interrupted, finding my voice stronger than I'd expected it to be.

"What?"

"I said wake her up. We need to go back."

"Bill...," Sally started.

"No! We can't stop now. We need to go back and do this right. I need to get her."

"I'm with him," Tom said.

"Me too," Glen added. "It was a most exciting adventure."

"Are you all nuts?" Zoe snapped. "The kid's out cold and Liz isn't too far behind. You're not going anywhere right now."

Crap! She was right. There had to be a ... wait! The vape pen! "Hold that thought. I have something that'll get them both back on their feet."

"Bill..."

"Just give me a second." I reached into my pocket, finding nothing there. Then I checked my other pocket. It too was empty. *What the fuck?!*

"Bill..."

"Where the hell is it?" I checked my pockets again. "Shit! I had it with me just a little while ago. Where did it...?"

"What are you looking for?" Liz asked.

"Obviously the rest of my sword," Tom continued to whine.

"The vape pen," I said. "It was right here. It..."

"What vape pen?"

Sally stepped in front of me and looked me in the eye. "That's enough."

"No! You don't understand. We can use it to..."

Crack! The words died in my mouth as Sally hauled off and slapped me across the face. "I *said* that's enough."

"What's he talking about?" Liz asked.

"Nothing. He's still messed up from the trip back. Things got a bit screwy over there near the end." Sally once again looked me in the eye, as if daring me to contradict her.

"Whatever," Zoe said. "Even if we could try again, there's no time left."

I cradled my cheek as I turned toward her. "What are you talking about?"

"Fuck that noise," Tom said. "We can take those assholes if they come back."

Zoe shook her head, though. "No, we can't."

"Wait." I held up my uninjured hand. "What assholes?"

"We had some uninvited company not too long after you left," she explained. "Just a couple maintenance guys, but they had an armed guard. Guess they were here checking on those cameras we took out."

"What happened?"

"We did." She threw Tom some side eye. "Mostly me. But anyway, we took out one of them but the guard turned out to be a vamp – one like you with yellow eyes. Took a bit longer to deal with him. By the time we did the other worker had gotten away."

"Gan's people," I surmised.

Zoe shrugged. "They weren't wearing nametags, but seems a safe bet."

"That probably means they'll be back in force."

"Probably?" Sally replied, one eyebrow raised.

"Fine, *definitely*. And if they find you here..." I trailed off, the meaning hopefully clear.

"We'd still have a shot," Tom groused, "if *someone* hadn't broken my fucking sword."

Zoe shook her head. "Get real. Everyone here is either injured, exhausted, or both. Two kids and a dog could take us out."

"She's right," Liz said. "I'd be lucky to light a match right now. V?"

"I'm okay, but I'm not sure one catalyst witch will make a difference if they throw an army at us."

"Two," I added.

Tom inclined his head. "Two what?"

"Two mages. Her and me. Not that it would matter much either way."

"Dude, did you hit your head while you were busy failing over there?"

Veronica ignored him, turning to face Liz instead. "You can feel it, right?"

Liz glanced from her to me and then back. "I feel *something*. Doesn't make any sense, though." She narrowed her eyes for a moment before shaking her head. "You know what, save it. Show and tell will have to wait for later."

"Seconded," Zoe said. "We have maybe an hour left before the sun rises, and I'd prefer to be gone before we end up trapped in here."

Goddamn it!

I turned and looked back at the Source, knowing that somewhere beyond its orange glow Christy was waiting. It made me want to do nothing less than dive headfirst into it.

But what would that accomplish? Without Tina to guide me, I could end up anywhere. That assumed I wasn't outright vaporized or turned into a freakish rock monster – both big ifs.

That was the true problem. Much as I wanted to, I couldn't do this without help or putting others at risk.

It's funny. Seeing it right there while knowing we had to leave, I thought I'd be utterly crushed by guilt. But instead, I was surprised to find myself thinking rationally.

And that rational thought was telling me there'd be another chance – that I could take comfort in knowing we'd saved the world she was trapped in. She was safe for now, or as safe as anyone could be around the Feet.

Besides, Tina was right. Her mom wasn't alone anymore. I hadn't brought Christy home, but that didn't mean we hadn't done some good. Sheila's soul was free now. I doubted Sasquatch Heaven was the afterlife she'd hoped for, but it was a fuckload better than being the Great Beast's lapdog.

What we'd done hadn't exactly been a win, but it wasn't a total loss either. That was the important thing. Christy was safe. I knew that for a fact now.

There was no doubt we'd try again, but for now we needed to retreat, regroup, and make sense of all that had happened.

But there was no fucking way we'd be doing any of that if we were still here once Gan's goon squad showed up.

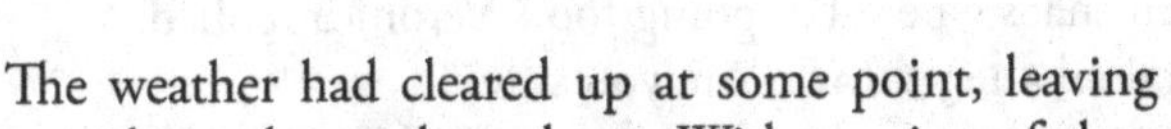

The weather had cleared up at some point, leaving it quiet outside in the predawn hour. With no sign of the police or Gan's reinforcements, we took advantage of the lull to beat feet.

It wasn't long before we found ourselves in the forest again, having made it out unseen and minus any explosive episodes of note – no doubt in part due to Tina being totally zonked out. It was a small victory, but one I was happy to accept.

"So what now?"

Liz let out a sigh, telling me she was about to say something we probably wouldn't like. "I need to find Ux and the others, learn who made it out and who didn't. After that, we'll have to see, but I have a feeling there's going to be a lot of work trying to rebuild."

"I'm going too," Zoe said to the surprise of absolutely no one, even if she didn't sound particularly hopeful.

"Not to read between the lines," Sally replied, "but I'm sorta getting the impression the rest of us should pick another direction."

Liz shook her head. "Purgatory's doors were always open. I don't want that to change."

"You can still hold the doors open while heavily hinting some folks would be better off elsewhere."

"None of you were responsible for what happened."

I wasn't so sure of that. "And yet the shit didn't hit the fan until we arrived. Seems to be a common theme with us."

Sally chuckled. "Go figure, Bill. After all these years, you still have a knack for fucking up the unfuckable."

"I prefer to play to my strengths."

"Fine," Liz said at last. "How about this? For now it might be best if we each focused on where we're needed most. For Zoe and me, that's catching up to the survivors and making sure they're okay."

"Fair enough," I replied. "As for us, we still have friends trapped in an economy-sized fish fry back at the Hudson."

"Then that's where I'm going too," Veronica replied.

Liz raised an eyebrow. "Are you sure?"

"If it means rescuing Kelly then yeah." She hooked a thumb at me. "Besides, there's a certain someone who could use a bit of wizard training."

"Care to enlighten us on that one before we part ways?" Liz asked, eying me.

"Ed's bite," I explained. "That upgrade I was telling you about. It worked ... differently on me, because I'm a Freewill. I know it's hard to believe but..."

"It's not." She tapped her forehead. "I can feel it up here. I'm not sure what it means, but I believe you."

"Wait, you weren't shitting us?" Tom asked. "You're a fucking wizard now?"

I nodded. "Yep, and I can prove it."

Almost instantly, I felt the door inside my head slam shut – from more than one direction as both Liz and V cried, "No!"

Huh. Talk about giving a guy a complex. "Fine."

"Aw come on! I want to see some hocus pocus," Tom said.

"No," Veronica replied. "And that's final."

I sighed before turning to face my best friend. "She's right. It's not a good idea."

"For plenty of reasons," Liz added.

"But, the bottom line is it's true. I'm a vamp wizard now."

"Fuck that noise," Tom said. "You're a goddamned lich is what you are."

"Huh?"

"What the fuck are you babbling about?" Sally asked.

"I'm talking about this dumbass. He's saying he's an undead magic user now. Isn't that the very definition of lich?"

I blinked as I considered this. "You might actually have a point."

"And you call yourself a gamer."

"Yeah, except that my soul isn't stuck in a phylactery somewhere."

He shrugged. "Fuck the details."

I couldn't help but laugh. "Bill the lich. I kinda like that."

Sally, of course, rolled her eyes. "You would."

"Call yourself whatever you like," Liz said. "Just don't be stupid about it. Do me a favor, V. Take it slow with him. Make sure he learns the beginner stuff first."

"You don't have to rub it in," I replied.

"Yes, I do. I want to hear that you're conjuring flower petals, not fireballs." She pulled Falcon's phone from her pocket. "And just to be safe, I'm holding onto this for now."

"Are you sure?"

She shook her head. "Not in the slightest. Truth be told, I don't want it. Hell, I'm tempted to chuck it into the nearest stream. But I have a feeling we're going to need it, especially when it's finally time to try again."

"When do we think that will...?" Tom started.

"I don't know."

"That's not good enough."

"Do I look like a fucking calendar to you?"

"No, you look like a..."

"Shush, Daddy," Tina muttered in his arms, still mostly asleep. "You're being loud."

And that was the end of that argument.

Sadly, Liz had a point. Gan was almost certainly going to up the security on the remaining Sources. Knowing this one was here was useful, but getting to it again would almost certainly require a lot more effort next time.

Although, maybe by then we'd have Bill the lich backing us up with some magic.

Fuck that. No maybe about it.

It was time to get serious about this shit, and if that meant conjuring daisies first, then I'd best pick up a hoe and a gardening hat.

Purgatory may have been an open community, but it had also been a slightly paranoid one. When not in use, they'd made it a point to keep the encampment's vehicles well hidden, using both magic as well as practical camouflage.

And with at least a small portion of its population having consisted of vampires, most of them came equipped with tinted windows. We bid goodbye to Liz and Zoe before splitting our remaining group among two of them, for both comfort and safety purposes. Veronica and Tom took a Ford Explorer, leaving Tina to sleep in the back.

That left Sally, Glen, and I to grab an old Subaru Outback. We had Petunia, too, snuggled in the backseat as Sally drove while I took shotgun – still being short a few fingers.

We didn't have a lot of time to discuss destinations before heading out, especially with the sun about to rise. With nowhere better to go, Veronica suggested we regroup at Christy's apartment for now.

Upon pointing out the current lack of wards, she was quick to remind me that we now had three mages to rebuild the apartment's defenses with, at least one of whom needed all the practice he could get.

With no better options on hand, we hopped in our respective vehicles and set out back toward the city.

"So how are you doing?" Sally asked, once we were well underway. "I mean really."

"Honestly? I don't know. I'm still processing it all. I

mean, I know I should feel like absolute shit for leaving her behind..."

"But you don't?"

I shrugged. "It's the weirdest thing, I tell you. It's like I want to wallow in misery, but my brain keeps pointing out the positive shit instead and ... well, it's kind of winning."

"That's because you're awesome, Freewill," Glen replied from the backseat.

"Thanks, man, but I can't help but feel it shouldn't be this easy."

"Maybe that's because leaving her behind wasn't your fault," Sally offered.

"I suppose. God, I really hope she gave Turd a piece of her mind – preferably by setting his ass on fire."

"Can't say that would bother me much."

"Still, I won't lie. It's hard to be mad even at that asshole, knowing she's okay."

She glanced at me then back at the road. "Yeah ... okay is one word for it."

"What do you mean?"

"Nothing. Go on."

"Anyway, I keep thinking about it. It sucks that she's stuck there, I mean really sucks, but at least we know she's safe now. Oh, and she's not alone either, and I don't mean Humbaba's smelly ass. We just can't take forever getting back there. I don't want her to be stuck sitting around in Turdland for a whole other year."

Again she looked at me.

"What?"

"It's nothing."

"Obviously it's something."

She lapsed into silence, letting a mile or two pass before saying, "Please tell me you were kidding back there."

"About what?"

"About Matt's pen, idiot!"

"What kind of pen?" Glen asked. "Are we talking ballpoint or fountain or maybe..."

"The kind you smoke out of," I said. "And no. It must've

fallen out of my pocket while we were getting bounced around by Murder Me Elmo over there."

"Are you fucking serious?" she replied. "Kelly threw it to you as her last act before being mind-fucked by Leviathan, her final act of defiance against a freaking demigod. And you fucking lost it?"

"When you put it that way..."

"For fuck's sake, Bill. You and magic really do not mix."

"The smoking pen was magic?" Glen asked.

"Yeah, long story." She let out a sigh. "I don't know. Maybe it's for the best. Probably not, but maybe."

"How do you figure that?" I asked, curious since she'd just chewed me a new asshole over it.

"There's no doubt in my mind we could've used it. But it could just as easily fuck us as well."

"How so?"

"Because someone in this car is a brand new Magi, and that certain someone doesn't always make the best decisions when their back's against the wall."

I glanced her way. "I guess."

"Especially when that certain someone's idiot friend is whispering in his ear, egging him on to try something he knows he shouldn't."

"Okay, I get it!" I considered this, remembering the unpleasant sensation of being hit with my own lightning. She probably had a point.

"Remember what the kiddo said, about everything being the way it's supposed to be? Who knows? Maybe she meant that in more ways than one."

"I suppose. Although, just for the record, I hope she's done with the fortune telling."

"Me too," Glen replied, raising one eyeball stalk between us. "Hearing Miss Tina talk that way sent chills through my nuclei."

"Same here, buddy. I've never liked the creepy kid trope. Leave that shit to the horror movies."

Sally nodded. "At least she sounded like herself again back there when she woke up."

"True," I replied, sensing an opportunity to change the subject. "Speaking of which, how are you doing?"

"I'm good, although I have to admit it was nice to be alone in my own body back in that other world, Feet or not. Don't get me wrong, I really didn't want to end up stuck there, but that almost made the tradeoff worth it. But now..."

"We're right back where we started."

"Maybe, maybe not," she said, glancing at me with her strange green eyes. "But I get what you mean. I'm here, so the Beast is still a threat."

"Not to mention you're still a target."

"Trust me, I know."

"What Christy tried to do..."

"Was the right call," she interrupted. "And no, I don't blame her one bit. Hell, if push came to shove, I might even admit that Gan has a point in wanting me dead."

"Hold on. You're not saying..."

"Relax. I'm not ready to give up yet. Even if I was, I'd sooner step in front of a train than let that bitch take the credit. There's also the little problem of not even knowing if it would work. Hell, I could try to eat a bullet, only to spit it out."

"Okay, Dr. Banner."

"Excuse me?"

"Never mind. Anyway, it sounds like Christy managed to take down Bigfoot World's version of you. So it is possible."

"Did she say how?"

"No."

"Then my point stands."

I gestured toward the top of her head. "How's it looking up there?"

"Quiet as a mouse so far. I'm hoping my little bit of unnecessary brain surgery made her realize I'm not about to go quietly into the night. Guess we'll have to see."

An uncomfortable silence settled in the car, so I decided to lighten the mood by turning on the radio.

Needless to say, that proved to be a mistake.

"*Werewolves and witches in New York. Debate is raging*

online between those who say what happened in Bay Ridge, Brooklyn was real versus those who think otherwise – claiming the incident was, among other things, a publicity stunt gone wrong.”

“A publicity stunt? Are they fucking for real?”

“Yeah,” Sally scoffed. “Performance art is so last year. Everyone knows unleashing werewolves on a major city is the in thing to do these days.”

“Expert opinion has been mixed, with some outright dismissing the footage as fake while others have gone so far as to admit, off the record of course, they can find no evidence of digital enhancement. We polled our listeners and found senti-ment is at an all-time high that monsters not only exist, but they walk among us. Many believe the Strange Days have returned and they point to recent events as evidence for...”

“Enough of that shit.” Sally reached over and turned it off.

“Ooh, does this mean I can stop wearing a disguise now?” Glen asked.

“No!” we both replied.

“Think it’ll blow over?” I asked after a moment or two. “Or is this the one that’s gonna bite us in the ass?”

“Hard to say, but it’s not looking good. Go figure. Every freak of nature out there has managed to stay hidden in the shadows for god-knows how long. Yet all it takes is one merry band of inbred hicks to fuck it up for everyone.”

“Can’t say that’s entirely surprising.”

“Me neither.”

“Freewill...”

“Yeah, Glen?” I replied.

“Freewill.”

“I heard you the first time. You got something in your throat? You sound a bit scratchy.”

“Um, that wasn’t me,” he said.

I turned in the passenger seat. “What do you mean that wasn’t you?”

“Freewill!”

“I think it was ... her,” the little blob replied, his eyeballs turned toward the kitten lying next to him, the one whose eyes were now open and staring directly at me.

She opened her mouth, but instead of a tired meow, what came out instead was, "*Stupid t'lunta!*"

What the fuck?

"*Turd will kill you!*"

And then Petunia, all two and a half pounds of her, launched herself at my face – claws and all.

"*Let Turd out! Turd wants to kill you!*"

We stepped into the apartment, the first to arrive, both of us holding carry-on bags. Glen was inside mine. From Sally's, however, came a nonstop barrage of death threats, the kitten's voice fortunately low enough that I doubted anyone without vampire ears could hear it.

Fucking A.

The little furball had almost caused us to crash as it attacked me. Fortunately, Sally managed to pull over, allowing us to pry the fur-covered Cuisinart from my face and secure her before continuing onward.

Needless to say, that had added an extra layer of weird to our journey back.

Aside from my initial paranoia, I hadn't seriously considered that Turd would've been able to follow us back home. I mean, unlike Christy, he was actually dead. So much for assumptions. I had no fucking clue how he'd managed it. The nearest I could figure, his spirit had hitched a ride back to the land of the living, but with no body of his own he'd somehow co-opted the near-comatose kitten's instead.

I couldn't even begin to understand how that made sense.

"*Why is Turd small?!*"

"So," Sally asked glancing down as I let Glen out of my bag, "when are we returning Petunia here to your parents? Because I really want to be there for that reunion."

"*Turd will kill you too, stupid female t'lunta!*"

"Oh shut up," she snapped, smacking the side of the bag.

"Are you fucking insane?" I replied. "My mother still blames me for what happened six years ago."

She laughed. "Isn't that when you...?"

"Got high and bit her cat? Don't remind me."

"Man, your parents really need to just pay for a damned pet sitter."

"Tell me about it."

"So, anyway, what do we do with her?"

I shrugged. "I'm open to suggestions."

"Well, we're pretty high up and there's plenty of windows to choose from."

I stared at her horrified. "She's a kitten!"

"That's currently possessed by one of our mortal enemies."

"I... Let's table that one for now, until I've had a chance to think."

"Fine. You do that. I'm gonna go next door and let her out in the bathroom before she shits in my suitcase. Maybe that'll give the stupid thing a chance to calm down."

"Yeah, sounds good."

"Ooh, I'm coming too," Glen said. "Maybe you can give us both a bath."

Sally chuckled as she opened the door connecting Christy's place with the apartment next to it. "Y'know, that doesn't sound like a half bad idea. What do you say we go polish this Turd?"

"It would be my pleasure!"

I shook my head as she pulled the door shut behind them.

Just what I fucking needed. Atop everything else going on in my life, now Turd was back. And knowing my luck, he wasn't litterbox trained.

Great! How the fuck was I going to explain this to my parents?

Maybe Sally was right and we needed to take a little *ride* to the vet, which was a far less gruesome fate than what she'd suggested – while still being in the same ballpark.

Either that or maybe we could find Eric and see if he was

looking to adopt. There was some irony to Grulg keeping Turd as a pet.

Yeah, I kind of liked that. It made sense in a sick sort of...

I looked up as there came a tapping sound from the front door.

Thinking it was Tom, I headed that way. Hopefully the distance between Tina's room and the next door apartment was far enough, otherwise we'd need to figure something else out for Sally. If that was the case then maybe we could...

That train of thought derailed as I opened the door and realized it wasn't our friends after all. A familiar pair of assholes was waiting there instead.

"Mighty one," Be'af greeted, stepping past me unbidden. "I sensed your return, so I thought we might stop by and show you some of our new wares."

"Yeah," his partner Kwe'af added. "We've got some new stuff you're gonna love."

"Is that a fact?"

"I trust all is well and your secret has been kept," Be'af said, pulling off his pack and beginning to unload it.

"Yeah, about that. I've been meaning to *thank you* guys for selling me Thundersmite."

Be'af looked up, a note of worry in his eyes. "Did you perchance have reason to use it? Because if so I can assure you..."

"Nah. It's been a slow week. Not much going on."

"Excellent to hear, Freewill. Now, if you'll gather round, we have some newly procured enchantments that are practically a steal."

Fuck it. The day was young. I could deal with everything else later. For now, I was feeling almost disturbingly confident, despite all the craziness going on in my life. "That's all fine and well, but first I have something to show you guys if you're interested."

"Oh? You have something to trade?" Be'af asked, sounding curious.

"You could say that."

"Well, then I suppose it would be rude of us to say no."

I smiled as I closed the front door, my mood surprisingly upbeat despite everything. There was so much to do – rescuing Christy and our kidnapped friends, stopping the Great Beast, training to be a wizard and more. But I figured the universe could allow me a moment for some payback.

Are you sure about this? the Wanderer asked, speaking up and sounding somewhat surprised. *No offense, but it's a rather bold move for you.*

Maybe, but I figured I could use a little more bold in my life. It sure as hell beats feeling sorry for myself.

Indeed it does, but confidence has only been one of your issues as of late. The other is needing to listen to advice when it's offered. You're not alone in this. You never have been.

He was right, as usual. *Does that mean you're advising me to let them go?*

These two charlatans? he replied. *Quite the contrary. No. I'm advising you to lead with your left. I think you'll find that works best.*

"You got it, buddy," I said with a grin, cracking the freshly regrown knuckles of my right hand as I turned my attention back to our uninvited guests.

I'd suffered more losses as of late than I knew what to do with, but despairing over them wasn't going to solve anything.

If I was going to make a difference, I needed to rack up a few points in the win column.

And there was no better time to get started than the present.

THE END

◆———━———◆

Bill Ryder will return in
BYTE FORCE (The Tome of Bill – 13)

If you enjoyed this book, want to stay up to date on new releases, and would enjoy receiving freebies from all of my main series, then please consider joining my newsletter at:

https://rickgualtieri.com/newsletter/

AUTHOR'S NOTE

Well, that was certainly a roller coaster ride, one I hope you thoroughly enjoyed.

Looking back on it, I felt it was time to let Bill evolve a bit. One thing I've tried to avoid over the course of his many books is power-creep – in which the hero keeps growing ever stronger, to the point where they're punching out deities before stopping to break for lunch.

Much as I enjoy *Dragonball Super*, there have been more than a few times when I've found myself chuckling about how Goku could destroy the Earth with an ill-timed fart.

Obviously, Bill has gotten some buffs over the years, but I've always preferred him as the underdog, surviving despite being in way over his head. But even an underdog needs a boost every now and then.

That said, I wouldn't be too worried about this being his Super Saiyan Ultra Instinct moment. If I know anything about Bill, it's that he can be a slow learner for anything he doesn't take as seriously as he should.

We'll see, though.

I'm still working out the various ways this'll no doubt hinder as much as help him.

For now, I'll just say this book was a lot of fun to write –

both the big moments as well as the small. And likewise the old faces as well as the new.

All that out of the way, I'll admit I let myself go a bit nuts with the Beast and I absolutely love how it turned out. The original idea in my head being essentially, "What if the progenitor of all monsters was this harmless looking teddy bear thing?"

So yeah, if it felt like I was cackling out loud while I wrote those scenes, you can be almost certain I was.

Regardless, we're now four books deep into Bill of the Dead and the stage is set for lots of mayhem to come – some of it world-ending, and some of it just a pain in the ass for our cast of characters.

I hope you're as excited for what's to come as I am.

Until next time...

Rick G

ABOUT THE AUTHOR

Rick Gualtieri lives alone in central New Jersey with only his wife, three kids, and countless pets to both keep him company and constantly plot against him. When he's not busy monkey-clicking words, he can typically be found jealously guarding his collection of vintage Transformers from all who would seek to defile them.

Defilers beware!

Also by Rick Gualtieri
THE TOME OF BILL
Bill the Vampire
Scary Dead Things
The Mourning Woods
Holier Than Thou
Sunset Strip
Goddamned Freaky Monsters
Half A Prayer
The Wicked Dead
Shining Fury
The Last Coven
BILL OF THE DEAD SAGA
Strange Days
Everyday Horrors
Carnage À Trois
The Liching Hour

FALSE ICONS
Second String Savior
Wannabe Wizard

Halfhearted Hunter
Deviant Dark Dryads

HIGH MOON
The Girl Who Punches Werewolves
The Girl Who Fights Witches
The Girl Who Hunts Fairies
The Girl Who Defies Fate